A W APART

IRINA SHAPIRO

Storm

Previously published in 2013 as *A World Apart* by Merlin Press LLC.

Ebook ISBN: 978-1-80508-651-2
Paperback ISBN: 978-1-80508-652-9

Cover design: Debbie Clement
Cover images: Shutterstock

Published by Storm Publishing.
For further information, visit:
www.stormpublishing.co

ALSO BY IRINA SHAPIRO

A Tate and Bell Mystery

The Highgate Cemetery Murder

Murder at Traitors' Gate

Wonderland Series

The Passage

Wonderland

Sins of Omission

The Queen's Gambit

Comes the Dawn

The Hands of Time Series

The Hands of Time

A Leap of Faith

A Game of Shadows

Shattered Moments

The Ties that Bind

PROLOGUE
OCTOBER 2012

Weak rays of autumn sunshine filtered through the shop windows, dust motes twirling lazily in the shafts of light, settling onto the scuffed floor. The wooden counter, the only object left in the empty room, reflected the sun. Just yesterday, Hugh Sanders had his men crate up the inventory and remove it to his own shop in Plymouth. Hugh rubbed his hands with pleasure, congratulating himself on the low price he'd paid for the lot. Only patches of unfaded wallpaper remained where paintings had hung for years, and scratches on the floor bore testament to pieces of antique furniture that crowded the small showroom.

Frederick Taylor looked around the empty room before closing the door behind him for the last time. By next week, this place would be an internet café, or yet another gift shop. He'd stop by the estate agent's and drop off the keys before taking himself out for a leisurely breakfast. After that, he'd be on his way. He'd spend a few days in London, as planned, then catch a flight to the States. He had some unfinished business in colonial Virginia; business that he'd put off for far too long.

ONE

VIRGINIA OCTOBER 1622

Valerie bolted out of bed at the sound of the closing door. Finn's footsteps creeping down the hall toward the stairs a few moments ago chased away the last remnants of sleep, so she threw on her dressing gown, pulled aside the curtain, and opened the window. She knew she should just let him go, but as a mother, she simply couldn't. The sun was just rising above the treetops, long shafts of weak light dispelling the gloom of the bedroom. Valerie hoped that Finn wouldn't turn around and catch her watching him. He wouldn't like that. At sixteen, he fancied himself a grown man, and having his mother fuss over him was cause for an argument — one they'd had many times.

Finn looked around stealthily before disappearing into the shed and re-emerging a few minutes later with a bulging sack. He locked the shed behind him, slung the sack over his shoulder, and strode purposefully away from the house, melting into the still-dark woods. Valerie watched him until he disappeared from view, sighed, and turned from the window to find Alec watching her, his hands behind his head, hair fanned on the pillow.

"What's troubling you, sweetheart? Why don't you come

back to bed and tell me about it?" Alec pulled the coverlet aside in invitation, but Valerie crossed her arms and began pacing the room. "Is it Finn?" Alec sat up in bed, his amorous ideas forgotten for the moment.

"I'm worried about him, Alec. He's off again, and he took a large sack with him. I can only guess what's in it — skins and tobacco. I think he's trading with the Indians. I saw him hiding a tomahawk in his room the other day. There is only one place he could've gotten that." Valerie continued to pace in her agitation, oblivious to the haze of morning sunshine creeping into the shadowy recesses of the room. She briefly noticed that Alec's eyes looked golden in the light, and that his hair had copper highlights from spending so much time outdoors, but she ignored her husband's charms and continued with her tirade.

"I cannot believe that he would trade with them after what happened barely six months ago. So many people massacred; crops burned. Just because we were spared doesn't mean we're safe. How can he be so naive? What's to keep them from killing him as well? He thinks that just because they share an interest in hunting that makes them friends.

He's sixteen, Alec. He should be interested in something other than hunting. If he were living in the twenty-first century, he'd be looking at colleges, choosing a career, and making plans for a life filled with choices and opportunities. What opportunities does he have here? What will he do with his life?" Valerie turned to Alec, daring him to answer her.

"Valerie, I realize you can't help comparing this life to the life you've known, but Finn doesn't miss something he's not aware of. This is the only reality he understands. Besides, he's not trading with the Indians. He would have told me. Stop worrying. In time, he'll marry and inherit the estate, become a landowner. The tobacco business is very lucrative, so I have every confidence that he will prosper and be able to provide for the family."

Alec tried to sound reasonable, but Valerie wasn't ready to capitulate. She was too agitated. The March massacre was still fresh in everyone's mind. Hundreds of people were butchered by the Indians; homes burned, crops destroyed. Many people would be struggling this winter, with not enough supplies to carry them through to spring. King James had promised help and extra supplies, but would they get to the colonists in time? Valerie had been terrified when she heard of the slaughter. Many of the nearby settlements had been attacked, leaving Rosewood Manor miraculously untouched. The Indians never troubled them, since they were somewhat remote and kept to themselves, but other plantations had not been so lucky. People they knew had been killed, including two of the three Catholic families in the area.

"And who will he marry exactly? There is only one Catholic family that we know of within miles of here, and Finn would rather marry a goat than Susan Selby." She watched Alec, her foot tapping anxiously on the wooden floor.

"I can't say I blame him. Given the choice, I'd probably opt for the goat myself, although a sheep might be more practical for intimate purposes." Alec tried to stifle a grin, infuriating Valerie further.

"This is no laughing matter. We are talking about our son's future."

"I realize that, darling. Your stories of the future have captured my heart and fired my imagination, but despite all that, our life is here and now. I know it must be difficult for you to accept the limitations our children will be faced with, but there's no other choice. There are many people who would give their eye teeth to be in the position we're in. We must be grateful for what the good Lord has seen fit to bestow on us. Now, come here and let me kiss that frown away. Being angry with me won't help Finn avoid copulating with livestock."

Valerie finally exhausted herself and climbed into bed next

to Alec, allowing him to pull her into his embrace, his intentions clear. A wail pierced the silence, eliciting another sigh from Valerie.

"I think that baby has only two sound settings — loud, and louder." She snuggled next to Alec, grateful not to have a hungry newborn.

"You're worried they'll leave, aren't you?" Alec asked, kissing her brow. He knew his wife well enough to sense her fear.

Valerie nodded miserably. "They won't go anywhere now, but come spring, I think Kit will want to go home. He's restless, Alec. I can see it in his eyes. By springtime, they would have been here nearly three years, and he misses home." Valerie angrily wiped away the stray tear gliding down her cheek. The idea of losing Louisa again caused her indescribable pain.

"Valerie, Kit has estates in England, and responsibilities. His nephew can't be expected to see to Kit's interests forever. Robin's got his own life to lead. Isn't he getting married soon?"

"Yes, and Caroline has been unwell. I know Kit worries that she might take a turn for the worse. She is his only sibling, and he misses her." Valerie didn't protest as Alec's hand slid into her nightdress, cupping her breast. She was still upset, but he always knew how to make her feel better.

"Sweetheart, forget all that for now. No one is going anywhere for the time being, and it's only England, not the moon. Ships sail back and forth all the time. Now come here."

Alec flipped Valerie onto her stomach, pushing up her nightdress and spreading her legs as he pinned her down with his own body. He held down her wrists as he entered her, moving slowly and deliberately, until she forgot her worries and began to move her hips in time with his. Sometimes she liked the feeling of being taken, rather than made love to. There was something deliciously primal about surrendering herself to a man and letting him have his way with her. Alec knew her well enough to recognize that by relinquishing control of her body, she was also relinquishing control of the situation that had been tormenting her. Sometimes life had its own plan, and it was wise to remember that, rather than attempting to fight the unstoppable march of destiny. Valerie shuddered beneath Alec as her body reached its climax. She sighed with pleasure as Alec rolled off her, satisfied. He kissed her shoulder and closed his eyes, signaling his refusal to get up and start the day.

Valerie pushed down her nightgown and rolled over onto her back, her mind returning to the problems at hand. Alec was right. She was just winding herself up. Finn was very lucky for a boy of this time. He would inherit a profitable estate, which would ensure a comfortable life for himself and his family. And if Kit decided to return to England, Valerie would just have to go for an extended visit and enjoy all that England had to offer.

Another wail filled the house as Lady Evangeline Sheridan protested getting her clout changed, no doubt. For a one-month-old, she certainly had very definite ideas of what she didn't like.

TWO

Finn glanced at the cloudless aquamarine sky, judging the position of the sun. It was probably around 8 a.m., and he was getting hungry. He had plenty of time before he was due to meet his friends, despite the three-hour walk ahead of him, so he chose a dry, fallen log, and hung up his sack off a branch to prevent the tobacco from getting damp. He'd made himself breakfast before leaving the house this morning and sat down to enjoy his meal. The cider in the stone bottle was cool and refreshing as it slid down his throat. Finn closed his eyes for a moment, enjoying the peace of the forest. A thrush was singing somewhere in the distance, mingling with the ever-present rustling of leaves and breaking of dry twigs as small animals darted to and fro beneath the undergrowth. The rays of the sun piercing the canopy of the forest were getting warmer, and quickly evaporating the dew on the leaves and grass.

Finn had always loved the woods. It wasn't just the game that attracted him, but the peaceful balance of nature, so lacking in their overcrowded house. These days he needed the escape more than ever. Baby Evangeline was always howling, and little Louisa had gone from being a sweet little girl to a moody, brooding witch. His mother said it was normal at this age, and would eventually pass, but Finn had his doubts. Louisa was growing into a woman, after all, and women were quite beyond his understanding.

Thinking of women reminded Finn of the Indian girl he'd seen the last time he met his friends by the waterfall. He promised his father he'd never go back there after breaking his leg two years ago, but he was drawn there, nonetheless. The spot was beautiful, and Finn was intrigued by the Indians he'd heard while hiding in the cave. It didn't take long for him to make contact, and now they met routinely to trade, smoke a pipe, and tell stories. Many people feared the Indians, especially after what happened in March, but Finn wasn't afraid. His family had never interfered with the natives, and the local Indians felt no resentment toward the Whitfields.

Finn only knew a few words of their language, and they knew even less English, but they managed to communicate using hands, and even drawing pictures in the dirt to illustrate their point. The Indians were as curious about him as he was about them. Finn didn't really need the things he traded for, but he craved the companionship of boys his own age. He enjoyed the company of his father and uncles, but it wasn't the same as having friends. Finn met some other young men his age at church, but they came mostly from Jamestown and didn't share his interests. They would follow in their fathers' footsteps, becoming tradesmen and landowners. Tobacco was the currency of the colony and the quickest path to comfort and prosperity. Finn would become a landowner as well, but for the time being, he could indulge his other interests and let his father deal with the daily responsibilities of running a tobacco plantation. It would be years until his father passed on the reins, and Finn was in no hurry.

Finn's Indian friends were of the Algonquian tribe; one of the many tribes making up the powerful Powhatan Chiefdom.

Each tribe still had its own lands and chief, but there was also a head chief of whom Finn thought as the king. His friends told him that the Powhatan had lived in Virginia for thousands of years before white man came and numbered in the thousands. Finn never dared to go to their village despite overwhelming curiosity to see how they lived. The villagers would scalp him first and ask questions later.

Finn was happy to meet by the waterfall once a month and hear his friends' stories. The three braves that always came were Achak, whose name meant Spirit in Algonquian, Keme—Thunder, and Mingan—Gray Wolf, for the wolf he killed when he was seven. From time to time, one or two other young men showed up, but Finn didn't consider them to be friends. The braves wore clothes made of deerskin to protect them from scratches and bites, and moccasins on their feet. The right side of their head was shaved while the hair on the left side was left long, and frequently braided and decorated with trophies of the kill, such as feathers and fangs. Finn thought that was terribly strange until he understood the reason for the odd hairstyle. Indian men shaved the right side of their head to avoid having arrows getting caught in their hair while hunting.

The last time they met, Keme's sister, Sokanon, tagged along. Keme joked that her name meant "rain" because of all the crying she did when she was a baby. Finn thought that would be a suitable name for Evangeline. Sokanon was the first Indian girl Finn had ever met. He'd seen some Indian women in Jamestown, their baskets full of corn and cradleboards strapped to their backs; the infants gazing at the world around them from their upright position on the mother's back, but he'd never seen a girl his own age. He tried not to stare at the brown skin of her arms and bare legs, but his eyes kept straying of their own accord. She wore a leather dress and some sort of beaded neck-lace, her hair hanging halfway down her back, black and shiny as a raven's wing, with a single thin braid on the left side, decorated with a few feathers. She hid behind the men, taking discreet peeks at Finn and giggling behind her hand. He must have looked strange to her as well.

Later that night in his bed, Finn tried to imagine what Sokanon looked like under her leather attire, but his mind drew a blank. He'd never seen an unclothed woman and had only a vague idea of what to do with one. His father had tried to talk to him when he was fourteen, but Finn hadn't been ready to listen. He'd been terribly embarrassed, especially when he woke up in the mornings with his nightshirt soiled. He tried to wash the telltale stains away, but then the shirt was wet, and the maid assumed that he'd wet himself, which was even worse.

Eventually, he asked Uncle Charles. Being only eleven years older than Finn, Charles was more like an older brother than an uncle, and only too happy to oblige. Charles explained the basic facts of female anatomy and advised Finn to pleasure the woman first, but only if he cared for her. If not, it was fine to pleasure himself. Finn wasn't really sure what he meant by that but felt too foolish to ask.

Charles suggested that Finn might start paying attention to Minnie, who took over as maid of all work after Agnes left to marry Richard last month. Minnie was slight and pretty, with a shy smile and beautiful dark eyes. She was quick to blush every time Finn looked at her, and Charles thought she might be a willing participant in Finn's education, but Finn had his doubts. Minnie and her father had come over from England a few weeks ago; leaving their fishing village behind in search of a new start after a tragedy had torn their family apart. Minnie's mother died of childbed fever — her newborn twins with her. Minnie never spoke of her loss, but a terrible sadness lurked just beneath the surface, always there in her eyes. Finn secretly wished that he could do something to ease her pain. He couldn't imagine what it must have been like for her to be torn away from everything and everyone and brought across the ocean to a dangerous and untamed land by a father who was mad with grief. He might have wanted to get away from the place where he'd known so much pain, but he obviously hadn't given much thought to his fifteen-year-old daughter, selling her into indentured labor for seven years and leaving her to live among strangers.

Finn had to admit that he found Minnie very attractive, but he didn't want to hurt her in any way or ruin her chances of a good marriage. He'd be more than happy to take a walk together or steal a kiss, but he thought himself too much a gentleman to take her maidenhead. She'd been through enough and deserved better than to be used and callously discarded.

Finn finished his roll and cider and rose from the log, ready to continue his walk.

THREE

The house was strangely silent as Valerie came down the stairs. Normally at this time, everyone was coming down for breakfast and discussing their plans for the day, but today there was hardly anyone about. Alec was still shaving upstairs; Finn had gone, and little Louisa had asked to spend a few days with Charles and Annabel in Jamestown. She enjoyed playing with their son Harry, who was just starting to walk, and toddled everywhere on his chubby legs, grabbing anything he could reach. Valerie peeked into the dining room but found it empty and went down the hall toward the kitchen. She found Mrs. Dolly kneading dough while making silly faces at baby Evie, who was lying happily in the crook of Kit's arm as he tried to eat breakfast single-handedly.

"Good morning, Valerie," Kit said through a mouthful of bread, taking a gulp of ale to wash it down. "Louisa was up half the night with Evie, so I thought I'd let her sleep awhile. She seems to like the kitchen." He looked proudly at his daughter, whose coal-black eyes were taking in her surroundings with considerable interest.

"Let me take her, so you can breakfast in peace." Valerie

scooped up her niece, planting a kiss on the tip of her nose. The baby resembled Kit so much that it was impossible to find any traces of Louisa in her little face. Kit looked up with gratitude, resuming his breakfast with both hands.

"I have some business at the docks this morning. Will Alec be joining me? I would be happy to fetch little Louisa home from Charles' house. The house seems awfully quiet without her."

"No one is throwing a temper tantrum if that's what you mean." Valerie had found Louisa incredibly difficult to deal with these past few months. She was sullen one minute, giddy the next, but tears never seemed to be too far away. Valerie couldn't recall being so volatile at fourteen, but her sister assured her that she was an absolute monster and should have patience with her temperamental daughter, who didn't have the outlets Valerie and Louisa had during their own teenage years. It had to be difficult for her to be stuck at home most of the time with no girls her own age for company. Thank God there was Minnie. Valerie liked the girl immensely and hoped that she would be a good influence on Louisa. They came from different backgrounds and social classes, but they were teenage girls, and Valerie often caught them giggling together or taking a walk around the lake after Minnie had finished her chores for the day.

"Where's Finn?" Kit interrupted Valerie's thoughts as he rose from the table, kissing the top of Evie's head. She was wearing a bonnet that had belonged to little Louisa when she was a baby, but strands of jet-black hair escaped, framing her face in angelic curls.

"Finn left early this morning, no doubt to avoid another lecture from me. Any idea where he went?" Valerie didn't actually expect an answer. Even if Kit knew anything of Finn's activities, he'd never snitch on him. Kit had genuinely taken to Finn when he came to live at Rosewood Manor and would never betray him willingly. She supposed that was admirable but wished that the men would stop treating her like a worrywart.

"Don't fret, Valerie. I know he tries your patience sorely, but he is safe. That's all that matters." Kit took a last sip of his ale just as Alec came down the stairs. "Are you coming to the docks with me, Alec?"

"Why don't you saddle the horses while I break my fast? I will be out shortly." Alec was already reaching for a roll and pouring himself a cup of ale. Valerie hoisted the baby on her shoulder, wishing she had a modern carriage.

"Let's go for a walk Evie and let your mom sleep. She's earned it, poor thing. Now, what were you fussing about last night, you naughty girl?" Valerie asked affectionately as she headed out the door into the glorious October morning.

It was so pleasant out that Evie didn't even need a blanket to keep her warm. They would take a walk by the lake, and then Valerie would join Lou for breakfast once she was up, and Evie was fed yet again. Valerie had forgotten how much work a newborn was. Come to think of it, where was Bridget this morning? Normally, she was up at dawn, but she hadn't come down yet. She was probably enjoying the peace and quiet and getting some much-needed rest.

Valerie was just coming back to the house, having worked up an appetite, when she spotted something in the distance. Alec and Kit had left not half an hour ago, so it couldn't be them, unless they'd forgotten something. Valerie shielded her eyes from the sun and focused on the road. It was a solitary rider, his mule ambling down the road at glacial speed. The road led directly to Rosewood Manor, so the visitor must be for them, which was unusual. Valerie went into the house and handed over Evie to

Louisa, who was in the dining room, looking tired and worn from her sleepless night.

"Someone is coming, and it looks like a stranger," Valerie announced. "I'll go see who it is. Where is Bridget this morning?"

"I don't know. I haven't seen her, and even if I had, I probably wouldn't have noticed. I'm still half asleep. The little princess kept me up half the night and look at her now—sleeping like she doesn't have a care in the world."

"She doesn't," laughed Valerie. "Mom always said you were a cranky baby. Payback is a bitch." She giggled at the sour expression on her sister's face and went back outside to greet their visitor, who was now within a short distance from the house.

Valerie watched as the old man got closer, his mule in no rush to reach its destination. The man's breeches and coat were dusty from the ride, his curly wig making his head look disproportionally large under his wide-brimmed hat. There was something vaguely familiar about him, but Valerie couldn't place him. Maybe she'd seen him with Alec or Kit. At any rate, he seemed harmless enough. The man got off the mule with some difficulty and bowed to Valerie, lifting his hat off his dusty curls.

"Mrs. Whitfield, I presume. May I come in?" The man clutched a leather satchel in his right hand, but he didn't seem to be armed or dangerous. He looked around, uncertain of what to do with his mule before tying him to a nearby post and turning his attention back to Valerie.

"Who do I have the honor of addressing, sir?" Valerie asked, stepping aside to allow the man to walk up the steps. There were only four, but his breathing was labored by the time he reached the top, and he needed a moment to catch his breath before replying.

"Frederick Taylor at your service." The man searched her face for signs of recognition as Valerie felt her extremities grow cold. She wouldn't have recognized him on her own since she'd seen him for only a few moments years ago, but she knew the name well. What was he doing here now, after all these years?

"Come in, Mr. Taylor. I must say, this is an unexpected pleasure," added Valerie with a hint of sarcasm. "My sister will be happy to see you."

"Ah, so she is here. I am glad. She was so determined to find you. I tried to talk her out of it for fear that she would be stranded in the past, but she wouldn't be deterred." Mr. Taylor stopped next to Valerie, searching her face for signs of hostility, but Valerie kept her expression bland.

"Yes. She told me all about it. Do come in. You must be parched from your long ride. A cup of ale?" Valerie tried to focus on the mundane to slow her racing heart. Why was he here and what would induce him to come at this stage? She led the old man into the dining room, watching Louisa's mouth open and close in shock as she recognized the man under the wig. Louisa tried to say something, but only a croak came out, prompting her to grab her cup of cider and drain it before attempting again.

"Mr. Taylor, what are you doing here?" Louisa whispered as she took it his satchel. "Did you bring the clock with you?"

Frederick Taylor set down the satchel next to a chair and sat down. Close up, he looked exhausted and old; his face lined with wrinkles, his eyes squinting at the sleeping baby. Valerie remembered that the man wore glasses, but he didn't have them on now. She poured him a cup of ale and moved the plate of rolls toward him, inviting him to help himself. She'd been angry with him for a long time right after she found herself in the past, but all she felt now was pity. She glanced over at Louisa who was white as a sheet, clutching Evie to her breast.

The old man took a long pull of ale, savoring its cool bitterness, before setting the cup down and turning to the sisters. "As one gets older, one takes inventory of one's life, searching for answers and trying to rationalize one's mistakes. I've been doing that for a few years now, but the mistakes I couldn't rationalize had to do with you two.

I must admit that I didn't feel as guilty about Erzsebet as I did about you, Valerie. I'd warned Erzsebet before she turned the hands of the clock. She knew what would happen but chose not to believe me. You were just an innocent victim of my carelessness. I knew at the time I should have gone after you, but I'd been a coward. I was afraid of what you'd tell the police, so I left you to fend for yourself, hoping that you'd survive."

Mr. Taylor looked at Valerie for a response, but she just watched him in silence, eyes narrowed. Her heartbeat was beginning to return to normal, and she was curious to hear what the man had to say. He obviously had a reason for coming all that way, and it couldn't be just to apologize.

"I did try to talk Louisa out of going back in time, but she was adamant, and in some small way I felt as if I were atoning for what I'd done. If you two were reunited, then I had done you a kindness. But then, I saw the clock. Louisa's hand had shaken so badly that she turned the clock to the wrong time. I had no idea if she would find you, Valerie, and I couldn't rest not knowing what happened to you both." The old man took another sip of ale, his eyes never leaving Valerie's face. She knew he wanted her forgiveness, but she wasn't ready to give it.

"So, why now, Mr. Taylor? Louisa had been here for over two years. Surely, if you were so worried, you would have come sooner."

"You're right. I should have, but I knew that Louisa would have to make the journey to America to search for you, and I thought I'd give her time before following. I see that she overcame the odds and that you are both well and happy."

"So, this journey was just to put your mind at rest that you're not responsible for ruining our lives? If that's the case, then thanks for stopping by." Valerie turned to Louisa, waiting for her to say something, but Louisa remained silent, watching the old man.

"Actually, there was something else, Valerie. I have a digital device that I've used to come here. It's not as cumbersome as the old clock, and much more precise." Mr. Taylor pulled up his sleeve, exposing the digital watch on his left wrist. It looked like any modern watch, with a small screen and numbered buttons. "I wanted to offer you the opportunity to return to the future, should you wish to. I know that you've built a life for yourself here, but maybe you still long for the twenty-first century."

Valerie gaped at the man in disbelief. Was he serious? He was watching her with an expression of undisguised expectation, as if she should fall at his feet overcome with gratitude.

"Mr. Taylor, had you come after me the day I wound up in the past, I would have happily returned with you, and thanked you for the rest of my life, but it's too little too late now. I've been here for seventeen years. I have a husband and children. Do you propose that I simply inform them that we're going to be transported nearly four hundred years into the future? My husband knows the truth, but he's the only one. Even Louisa's husband doesn't know where she came from. We thought it wise to keep that to ourselves. I'm sorry your journey was in vain." Valerie sank into a chair, suddenly feeling worn out despite the early hour. That was certainly one decision she hadn't expected to be making today.

"Valerie, may I have a word in private?" Louisa rose from her seat, baby Evie asleep on her shoulder, and walked out of the room, expecting Valerie to follow. She didn't stop until she was outside on the porch, away from anyone who might overhear. Valerie reluctantly followed, terrified of what Louisa might say. Maybe she wanted to go back, and Valerie was presuming too much by rejecting Mr. Taylor's offer.

"Val, I understand your anger, and you have every right to feel as you do. I would be furious with the man in your place, but don't throw him out just yet. I'm not saying I want to go back to the future, but this is our only chance to make that decision. Once he's gone, we are here for the rest of our lives. Maybe we should discuss it with the men. I know Alec longs for the future, and maybe it's time I told Kit," Louisa whispered. "What do you say we let him spend the night?"

Valerie wiped beads of perspiration off her forehead, suddenly feeling an overwhelming need to pull off her cap. She ran her hands through her hair, turning her face to catch the gentle breeze before feeling composed enough to answer her sister.

"Lou, would you seriously consider it after all this time? Say Alec and Kit were willing to leave, what would they do in the future? Can you honestly imagine them sitting in front of the TV, drinking beer and watching sports? They swordfight for fun, for God's sake. Here they know exactly who they are and where they stand. They are men of property and wealth, as well as high social standing. Who would they be in the twenty-first century? And what about everyone else? What would we tell Charles and Kit's sister, and all the people who depend on us for their livelihood, like the household staff and the indentured field workers? And what about the children?"

Valerie pressed her point as she saw Louisa waver in her resolve to let Mr. Taylor stay. The more she thought about the possibility of going back to the future, the more impossible it seemed. There would be countless obstacles to overcome, if they even managed to get that far.

"Lou, how would we establish identities for people for whom there's no record of being born? You need social security numbers and picture ID's to get a job or a driver's license. How would we be able to ease Alec and Kit into modern society at their age without any kind of proof of existence?" Valerie twisted her hands in agitation. Was it possible? Would the men even consider it?

Louisa sat down slowly, transferring Evie from her shoulder onto her lap as she considered Valerie's argument. She closed her eyes for a moment, her expression one of fatigue and uncertainty. Not even the gentle sunshine could erase the deep shadows under her eyes. Valerie knew that Louisa dreaded telling Kit the truth. At first, she'd been afraid of his reaction, but as time went by, she feared that he would feel betrayed by her lack of faith in him. It was wiser not to bring it up. After all, there'd been no point until today. Louisa finally opened her eyes and met Valerie's searching gaze.

"I haven't actually thought about any of that. There's so much to consider. I can't even begin to imagine how Kit would react to the truth. He's never asked me too many questions. I think he's afraid of the answers. Would you want to go back if Alec agreed?"

"Honestly, I haven't thought of going back since I married Finlay. I knew it was impossible, so I put it out of my mind. I'd kill for a pair of jeans and some Chinese food, but that's not reason enough to uproot everyone. We have a good life here, despite some issues. Every age has its problems though. Alec's place is here. Finding himself in a world he doesn't understand might crush his spirit. Of course, it would open up a world of opportunity for the children. Oh, Lou, this is such a difficult thing to contemplate. I didn't think I'd ever have to make this choice." Valerie paced the porch in her agitation. Her earlier concerns about Finn seemed almost trivial compared to the question at hand.

"Val, let's not say anything to the men yet. Let's think about it. We can just tell them that Mr. Taylor is someone I knew in the past, which is true. He can stay for a day or two while we consider all the angles. Surely, there's no harm in that?"

Valerie gazed at her sister, unable to refuse. She could understand Louisa's feelings. Lou had only been in the past for two years, so her memories of modern life were still vivid. She seemed genuinely happy with Kit and besotted with her new baby, but the memories of modern conveniences and especially medicine were often on her mind. Now that she had a baby, she fretted about the lack of vaccinations and antibiotics, and had a panic attack every time Evie so much as sneezed. Valerie remembered only too well how she felt for the first few years, comparing everything to the life she left behind and making a conscious choice every day to accept her situation and move forward. There had been no choice. It was either sink or swim, and she'd never been one to give up without a fight. Now, suddenly, there was a choice, and she had no right to take it away from Louisa without giving her ample time to consider and consult her husband. Valerie couldn't begin to imagine Kit's reaction to the news, but if Louisa were willing to take the chance, Valerie had to stand by her.

"All right. We'll let him stay, but let's not say anything to Alec and Kit until we figure out how we feel. I'm too over-whelmed right now to make any decision, one way or the other. Come back inside with me." Valerie walked back into the house, conscious of Louisa trailing behind her.

Frederick Taylor sat staring at the doorway, no doubt waiting for them to return. His face was a mask of misery; his rheumy eyes filled with sadness. "Valerie, Louisa, I am so sorry for the trouble I've caused. Once again, I seem to have blun-dered. I thought I would be doing something good and kind by giving you the chance to return, but I seem to have caused you grief. I'll take my leave now." He reached for the satchel at his feet and made to rise, but Valerie stopped him, gesturing for him to sit back down.

"Mr. Taylor, you haven't blundered. Your intentions were obviously good, but you must realize that a decision like this is not made on a whim. We have to discuss it among ourselves and then present it to the men. Anything we decide would affect a number of people, not just the two of us. We have family to consider and the people who work in the house and on the land. Why don't you stay with us for a few days while we think about it? We have a spare room in the attic. Unless you have other commitments someplace else."

"That's good of you, Valerie. My sole purpose in coming here was to see you both, so I'm entirely at your disposal for as long as you like. I would be happy to stay in the spare room until you come to a decision. Just tell me what you want me to tell your husbands, and I will comply. Thank you for not turning me away."

The relief in the old man's face was so obvious that Valerie felt a bit guilty for being so harsh with him earlier. He only wanted to atone for his mistakes. It took courage for him to come here, so she had to give him credit for it. Deep down, she knew what her decision would be, but what could it hurt to let the man stay for a few days?

FOUR

Finn had lost track of the time. He usually left in time to get home for supper, but this time the braves brought another friend with them, making the afternoon more enjoyable. The new friend was called something completely unpronounceable, but he spoke more English than the others and told Finn his name meant Moose. He was a few years older than the others and more familiar with the ways of whites. Moose was able to translate what the others were saying, allowing Finn to converse more freely. He discovered that the Indians had a sense of humor and liked to tease each other good-naturedly about their shortcomings. Moose informed Finn that Thunder got his name from farting so loudly, which left the others choking and snorting with laughter.

"What does your name mean, Pale Face?" Moose asked, passing Finn the pipe.

"It doesn't really mean anything. I was named after my father," Finn answered, inhaling the fragrant smoke and attempting to blow smoke rings like the Indians.

"We should give you an Indian name. What are your talents?" Moose studied him intently. "Maybe we should name you "Chaste One". You've obviously never had a woman." The boys began to giggle again, making Finn blush furiously.

"And how would you know? Are you so experienced?" Finn retorted, trying to hide his embarrassment.

"I don't know what "experienced" means, but if you're asking me if I've been with girls, the answer is yes. Besides, I believe you've met my wife, Sokanon. You, my friend, still have mother's milk on your lips." He patted Finn affectionately. "Do not worry. We will fix that problem. I know just the girl for you. You come to our village, and I will personally make the introduction." Moose winked at the others, who nodded in unison, grinning and making noises of approval.

Finn wasn't sure if Moose was joking or not, so he decided to change the subject. "I am a proficient hunter. Give me a name to do with that. I'd like an Indian name."

"Pale Face, I name you Megedaqik. It means "Kills many" in our tongue. Here, take this as a symbol of our friendship." Moose took off his amulet and put it around Finn's neck. It was some kind of bluish stone, surrounded by feathers on a leather thong. Finn felt his chest swell with pride at such an honor. He'd never take it off.

"Thank you. I will be proud to wear it." The braves clapped Finn on the back in approval, calling him by his new name and giving him a turn at the pipe. "Kills many" might sound unflattering in English, but in the language of the braves it was synonymous with bravery and great skill at tracking and hunting.

"Oh, God. I have to go." Finn jumped to his feet and walked off after saying his goodbyes. It wouldn't do to tell the Indians that his mother would be upset with him if he was late for supper. Their mothers treated them like men, not little boys to be scolded and lectured. As a matter of fact, most of the braves were already married, and not living with their mothers at all.

Finn had a long walk ahead of him, but he hardly noticed the miles. He was still basking in his friends' approval, fingering the amulet around his neck. He wished he could visit their village and see things for himself. Would they really find him a girl? Finn tried to envision himself in the embrace of some beautiful, dark-skinned girl, naked on a pile of skins. Her silky hair would brush his chest as she kissed him, her eyes reflecting the flames of the fire burning in the longhouse. In his mind, the girl was Sokanon, despite being married to Moose, only this time, she wasn't giggling. She was moaning with pleasure, her body warm and willing under his. Finn tried to imagine what it would be like to actually make love to her, but there his imagination failed him. He groaned with frustration at his limited knowledge.

* * *

Finn tiptoed up the steps and turned the handle as quietly as possible. He could hear the hum of conversation coming from the dining room, including a voice he didn't recognize. To walk in right now would only annoy his parents, so the best thing to do would be to make himself scarce and then raid the kitchen for leftovers later. Mrs. Dolly usually made enough food to have some left over for the midday meal of the following day, so there would be plenty. He'd stop by Minnie's room in the meantime and leave her the bracelet he traded from the Indians. It was made of some kind of smooth beads in different colors. Maybe she'd like it so much that she'd be willing to give him a kiss of thanks.

Finn fingered the bracelet in his pocket, enjoying the smoothness of the stones. He'd brought something similar back for his sister once, and she wore it all the time, hiding it under her cuff. He'd show Louisa his amulet once she got back from Charlie's house. She might not appreciate its significance, but she'd think it pretty and admire it. Maybe he'd show it to Minnie as well in the hopes of impressing her.

Finn crept up the stairs to the attic, careful not to make too much noise. Minnie would still be in the kitchen helping Mrs. Dolly, but he would just leave the bracelet on her pillow. She would be pleasantly surprised when she finally came up later, tired and ready for her bed. The landing was normally dark, but tonight a single candle burned on a small table between the two bedrooms. That was unusual. Minnie brought up a candle when she came up. To leave a candle burning for hours was wasteful and unnecessary, according to Mrs. Dolly, who kept a tight rein on the household supplies.

The door to Minnie's room was closed, but the one to Amelia's old room was slightly ajar. No one had occupied that room since Amelia hanged herself two years ago, fearing her ghost still walked at night, unable to rest after killing her lover. But now there was a leather satchel by the foot of the bed, a curly wig on the nightstand, and some odd object next to the pitcher and ewer. Finn inched into the room, looking around. He didn't believe in ghosts, but this room still made him shiver with apprehension. He hoped their guest didn't believe in rest-less spirits. He must be staying the night. Finn smirked at the wig, pushing it aside with one finger. He thought wigs were the height of stupidity, making middle-aged men look foolish beyond words. He was glad his father and Kit never bothered with wigs. They simply tied their hair back, which was a lot manlier in his opinion.

Finn picked up the object from the nightstand and turned it over in his hands. He'd never seen anything like it before. It was made of a strange material, not wood and not leather. The piece in the center was hard, but the two straps on the side were firm, yet flexible. Finn stepped onto the landing to get better light from the candle. *What is this thing?* he wondered as he held the object to his face. The square part in the middle had a clear strip of some sort with little numbers below it. Was it a new kind of abacus? The only reason to have numbers was to add them, but how did this work? Finn noticed "On" inscribed on one of the tiny squares and pressed it. The strip at the top lit up with a greenish light, as if several light bugs were trapped inside. This was curious indeed. He'd try to press the little squares and see what happened. This week Finn had caught seventeen rabbits, seven possums, and five foxes. He punched in 1775 and stared at the object. The number showed in the green strip, but nothing seemed to happen.

Suddenly, Finn felt a wave of dizziness as the hallway around him tilted, then went dark. He had just enough time to drop the object on the table next to the candle before slumping to the floor. *Serves you right for interfering with things you don't understand*, thought Finn as he got to his feet a moment later, rubbing his head. He looked for the object, but he couldn't see it in the darkness. The candle must have gone out, although he hadn't noticed it guttering. Finn felt a sudden thirst. He'd just go to the kitchen and have a cup of water. If Minnie was there, he'd give her the bracelet in person, which was even better since he'd be able to see her reaction. Finn skipped down the stairs, happy with this new idea. Why creep about in the dark when he could just present Minnie with her present? She'd be pleased as punch.

The door to the dining room was now closed, but there were voices coming from the parlor. Had they finished supper so quickly? He must have come in later than he thought. Finn hoped Mrs. Dolly saved him some food. He hadn't eaten since he met the Indians by the waterfall, sharing some flat bread and smoked meat that his friends brought for their midday meal. But that was hours ago, and Finn's stomach was beginning to growl in anticipation of food.

Finn peeked into the room and felt the blood grow cold in his veins. The parlor looked completely different than it had that morning. Nothing was the same. Even his mother's portrait over the hearth was gone. A man sat on the settee facing away from Finn, but he wasn't his father or Kit. Was that the guest? Finn looked deeper into the room. A young woman sat reading by candelabra. Her auburn curls were covered by a lacy cap; her hand held protectively over her bulging belly as candlelight reflected off her gold wedding ring. Who was she and where was everyone? Had his father and Kit brought new furnishings from the docks? This was terribly odd. Finn turned and walked toward the kitchen. He'd ask Mrs. Dolly what was what.

The woman who turned from the oven was short and squat, but most of all, she was black. A red kerchief was wrapped around her kinky black hair, tied at the top with points sticking out. Her eyes grew huge in her glistening face as she spotted Finn in the doorway.

"Who are you?" Finn asked confused. "Where's Mrs. Dolly?"

"I be Bertha the cook, young master, and who you be?" The woman looked taken aback, her hand reaching for the rolling pin in alarm as if she were planning to strike him with it.

"I'm Finn. Where are my parents?" Finn looked around, suddenly noticing that things didn't look quite the same. What was going on? Another black woman walked into the kitchen, carrying a tea tray. She was younger and prettier than the cook, but there was a marked resemblance between the two women. Maybe they were mother and daughter. *Kit must have bought slaves in the West Indies*, Finn thought. That was the only explanation. But why would he acquire Negro slaves? That just wasn't the thing. And where were Mrs. Dolly and Minnie?

Finn never got a chance to pursue that thought because the woman from the parlor walked into the kitchen. She looked around in confusion before her eyes lit on Finn, and she let out a horrible shriek. "Intruder!!!" she yelled as the man came charging into the kitchen, his eyes wild and fists clenched. He pushed his wife behind him for protection as if Finn would attack the woman.

"Who are you, boy?" he roared, "and what are you doing in my house?" The man was advancing on him, backing him into a corner. "What's your business here?"

"I'm ssorry," Finn stammered as he tried to back away. His mind was reeling. Where were his parents and Louisa and Kit? Where was baby Evie?

"Get out before I have you whipped," the man bellowed, grabbing Finn by the arm and dragging him to the back door. He pushed him savagely into the night, slamming the door behind him, and leaving Finn on the ground, shocked and confused. Finn rose to his feet and walked a short distance away from the house. This was just some kind of hallucination. The Indians occasionally took something that caused such things. Had they slipped him something as a joke? Everything would be back to normal in the morning. Finn turned toward the barn. He'd just sleep there tonight and let this strange feeling pass.

* * *

Finn looked around. The barn should be to his left, and still was, but the structure he saw was much larger than their barn. He heard the soft bleating of sheep and the lowing of cows but dared not enter. This wasn't their barn. Finn turned toward the shed where he kept his loot. There was nothing there, but there was another outbuilding further away from the house that hadn't been there that morning. Finn began to shake, sweat breaking out on his forehead. He turned toward the house and promptly vomited into the grass. The house looked utterly different. It had been made entirely of wood with black shutters, but now the façade was made of red brick, the shutters a ghostly white in the moonlight. Finn turned and ran into the woods, panting, and clutching his heaving stomach. He was shaking all over, praying to God that he was just having some strange reaction to something he ate or smoked. Everything would be all right in the morning. Everything would be fine. He would just sleep it off. Everything would be back to normal. He kept repeating it like a mantra as he fell into a dreamless sleep under a tree, curled into a fetal position, his hatchet in hand.

FIVE

Valerie trudged up the stairs after Louisa. The day hadn't started out well, and the arrival of Mr. Taylor had completely unnerved her. She'd just go to bed early and deal with everything in the morning. She hoped Evie would sleep through the night and give them all a bit of peace, especially Bridget, who was still unwell. She hadn't left the room she shared with Mrs. Dolly the whole day. Minnie had brought her some beef tea to settle her stomach, but Bridget hardly touched it. Bridget hadn't been sick a day since Valerie met her all those years ago, so Valerie hoped that she would recover quickly. She had a robust constitution and a remedy for nearly every ailment known to man.

"Goodnight, Lou. I'll just check on Finn before I go to bed. I thought I heard him sneaking in earlier. He probably didn't want to hear a lecture."

"Goodnight, Val. Tomorrow will be a better day. You'll see." Louisa disappeared into her bedroom as Valerie walked toward Finn's room. All was quiet and dark. Maybe he tired himself out and went to sleep, but that wasn't likely. Valerie opened the door quietly and peered into the room. Empty. Where was he? She could have sworn she heard him go up the stairs. Maybe he went out to the privy. She was too tired to go searching for him. She'd speak with him in the morning. She had to admit that she wasn't angry with him anymore. He was a sixteen-year-old boy. He was practically required to cause some mischief.

Valerie shut the door to her bedroom and sat down on the bed, pulling off her mobcap and releasing her hair from its pins. She was just about to untie the laces of her bodice when there was an urgent knock on the door. Alec knocked sometimes, but this wasn't his soft knock. Valerie jerked the door open to find Mr. Taylor outside, pale and sweating, his eyes full of panic.

"Valerie, something's happened. You must come with me at once. Please!"

Valerie forgot all about her fatigue and ran up the stairs to the attic after Mr. Taylor. "What is it? What's happened?" Her heart was hammering in her chest, her breath ragged. Mr. Taylor stopped on the landing by the little table and turned to Valerie. Louisa came running up the stairs, her hair tumbling around her shoulders.

"I left the watch by my bed when I went down to supper. I didn't want your husbands to see it and question its purpose. I'd locked the door behind me. I am fairly sure of that. When I came back up just now, I saw the watch on this table on the landing. It was on. The time was set to 1775. Someone is gone."

Valerie slid down along the wall, little bursts of color exploding in front of her eyes. Louisa was saying something, her mouth opening and closing, but Valerie couldn't hear. Her ears were ringing, her hands cold as ice. She knew exactly who was gone. It was Finn. Everyone else had been downstairs except for Bridget, and she was in her bed, most likely asleep. Her son was gone. Valerie looked up as Alec lifted her off the floor, his face full of concern.

"Alec, he's gone. Finn is gone," she whimpered.

"He'll be back, sweetheart. He'll be back. Now, let's get you to bed." Alec looked into her face, trying to determine if she felt ill.

"You don't understand," she screamed. "He is GONE! He went to 1775. This man is Mr. Taylor. MR. TAYLOR, Alec! The one whose clock sent me to the past."

"Oh, dear Lord," Alec groaned, letting go of Valerie and grabbing onto the table. "What's to be done?"

"What's amiss?" Kit appeared at the top of the stairs, taking in the scene. "Is someone ill? Valerie, are you all right?" He held out a hand to Valerie but became distracted by his wife's wail.

"It's all my fault!" Louisa sank to the floor, her hands covering her face. "It's all my fault. I asked you to let him stay. Oh, Valerie. I had no idea this would happen. What have I done?"

"Alec, we must go after him. I won't lose him. I won't!" Valerie screamed. "We must go now. He can't be far. He's probably lost and confused. He'll be somewhere close to the house. We must go NOW!"

"Will someone tell me what's happening?" roared Kit over the din. "Who's gone where?" He pulled Louisa to her feet, searching her face for answers. "Louisa, what is it? Who is gone?"

"Kit, Finn has gone to the year 1775. Please, don't ask me to explain now. I just can't put it into words. Just believe me." Louisa averted her eyes from Kit's, unable to face his disbelief.

"Darling, allow me to escort you to bed. You are obviously unwell, and you must feed Evie. She's crying. Can't you hear her? We'll sort everything out in the morning. Finn will be back from 1775 or from wherever he is. Come, dearest." Kit was trying to maneuver Louisa toward the stairs, but she wasn't budging.

"Don't speak to me as if I'm insane. I am telling you the truth. Just ask Alec and Valerie. They know." Louisa pushed Kit aside and ran down the stairs to fetch Evie, whose hungry howls were growing louder by the minute. She welcomed the distraction. Anything to get away from the horror of what was happening. Anything to get away from the look in Kit's eyes.

"Alec, please explain. I'm afraid I'm at a loss." Kit looked to Alec, who was running his hands through his hair, his eyes far away. "Alec!"

"Kit, step outside with me. I can't explain here. Valerie, go lie down for a bit. I'll be back shortly. We need a plan." Alec was about to go down, but Valerie grabbed his arm, hissing urgently.

"We need to go NOW! He's getting away. Alec, please!"

"Sweetheart, we can't just leave. I must prepare. I don't know how long I'll be gone or what I'll encounter. I must give instructions to Kit. Please pack me a change of clothes." Alec tried to sound reasonable, but Valerie wasn't having it. She grabbed him by the arm, forcing him to turn back and look at her.

"You? How long you'll be gone? Do you really think you are going alone? I'm coming with you. I won't lose both of you and just sit here waiting, going crazy. You are not going without me."

"Valerie, we have our daughter to think of. We can't both disappear."

"Louisa will stay here with Lou and Kit. She'll be fine. With any luck, we'll be back very soon. We'll just get him and come back. He won't have gone far."

"Bloody hell. Will someone explain?" Kit was quickly losing his patience. He looked from Alec to Valerie, then to Mr. Taylor who appeared in the door of the attic bedroom, a strange object in hand.

"Kit, we don't have time for a detailed explanation. Louisa

will tell you the rest. Both Louisa and Valerie came from the future, as did Mr. Taylor. The object in his hand is a time-travel device which Finn used to transport himself. I must prepare. I trust you will take care of everything until my return. Please, say nothing to Charles. He doesn't need to know." Alec gave Kit a searching look, imploring him to understand and comply with his request, but Kit was looking at Alec the same way he'd looked at his wife a few moments earlier.

"You expect me to believe that three people have dropped in from the future? You actually believe this?" Kit looked at Alec bewildered. He always found Alec to be a man of sound judgment, so this revelation was about as plausible as Alec suddenly announcing that he came from the moon.

"Kit, my grandmother came from the twentieth century. I knew of time-travel long before Valerie showed up. Mr. Taylor is a man of science who was able to build a time-travel device. I don't know why he's here now, but I don't have the time to find out. I must prepare and go after my son. Kit, please believe me. You've known me long enough to know that I'm as sane as you. Just ask Louisa. I must be going." With that Alec sprinted down the stairs, followed by Valerie, leaving Kit open-mouthed and stunned.

"Christopher, they are telling you the truth. I came here to offer them a chance to go back. I felt it was my duty to give them that opportunity before it was too late. You see, it's because of me that they're here." Mr. Taylor looked up at Kit, who was much taller than him, craning his neck, looking for understanding.

"Too late for what?" asked Kit bemused. "You knew my wife in the future?"

"I did. Louisa came to me, asking me to help her find her sister. I transported her to the seventeenth century. That's why I'm here now. I thought she might like to go back."

"But she has me and Evie. How can she go back? What are you saying, old man? Are you suggesting that she leave us?" Kit leaned against the wall for support. He was finding all this too much to take in. The strange old man was peering up at him, imploring him to listen.

"I wasn't suggesting that she leave you. I was merely offering Louisa and Valerie a chance to return to the future if they wish it." Mr. Taylor took a step back, watching Kit. "Maybe you should sit down. You don't look well."

"I don't wish to sit down. I might never get up. So, what happened tonight? Maybe you can explain it before I go question my wife."

"It appears that young Finn found the time-travel device and activated it. I don't know what made him choose that particular year, but he seems to have transported himself. Thankfully, he had the presence of mind to leave the device behind; otherwise, he'd be stranded there, and I would be stranded here. I will give the watch to Valerie and Alec to go in pursuit of their son. They can't return without it." Mr. Taylor continued to watch Kit. He thought the man might just hit him and took another step back just to be on the safe side.

"And what will you do if they take the device?" asked Kit, his eyes narrowed.

"I must stay here until they return. There's no way for me to get back to my time without it. I'll stay with you, if I may."

Kit just glared at the old man. At the moment, he wasn't feeling very hospitable. He wanted to grab him by his shabby coat and shake him until his anger had abated or the old man's head flew off, whichever came first. Kit ran down the stairs, suddenly feeling as if he couldn't breathe. He needed to get outside where things were still as they had been a few hours ago and the world made sense. Kit strode toward the lake, his long legs covering the lawn in record time. He felt as if someone had punched him in the stomach and kept punching him until he couldn't take the pain. His brain was on fire, unable to accept what he'd just found out. He wasn't sure what to address first, so he stomped around the lake, trying to get his thoughts into some kind of order, but the facts just kept coming at him mercilessly, leaving him helpless and devastated.

Kit felt an actual pain in his heart that squeezed the life out of him with its intensity. His wife had come from the future and withheld the truth from him all this time. He'd trusted her with his heart and soul, but she didn't trust him enough to be honest with him. All of them had known and treated him like a fool, keeping him in ignorance while they all talked about their past life behind his back. Alec, whom he trusted and loved like a brother, had not seen fit to tell him anything, leaving him to believe that all was as it should be.

Kit took a deep breath, but the ache in his heart only grew worse. He and Louisa had had plenty of arguments in the past, but he'd never doubted her love for him. They were just minor disagreements that were usually resolved with a few sweet words and a kiss, but not this time. She'd lied to him for years, played him for a fool. They all had. And now she was thinking of going back. Had she even considered him?

Kit stopped walking and turned to the lake. The pale orb of the moon was reflected in the glassy black surface of the lake, its perfection occasionally marred by floating leaves. Frogs croaked loudly, creating a cacophony of sound that blended seamlessly with the sounds of nature. The muddy smell of the bank was strangely comforting, as was the rustling of leaves in the gentle evening breeze. Kit sat down on the bench, staring at the still water, his mind focused on the day Evangeline was born. The baby had been past term, according to Bridget, and Louisa was cranky and tired, anxious about the wellbeing of the infant. She paced the house like a wild beast in captivity, wearing out the floorboards and herself. Kit tried to calm her, but nothing worked. Bridget had suggested taking long walks to bring on the labor pains, but the walking didn't seem to help. Louisa was getting more frustrated by the moment, her agitation spreading through the rest of the house like an illness.

Kit had been in Alec's study composing a letter to his sister when Louisa came in. She was so large that she barely fit through the narrow door; her belly arriving a few seconds before she actually entered the room. She had a smile on her face and a look of determination that Kit knew only too well. He laid down his quill, all his attention on his wife.

"Have the pains started?" Kit asked, rising to his feet. "Is it finally time?" He'd been as eager as Louisa to welcome this baby into the world, but he tried to contain his enthusiasm in order not to upset her further. He hoped it was a son, but a daughter would be just as wonderful. He'd longed to be a father for so long that the anticipation was killing him. Over the past few weeks, he'd had dreams of holding a newborn babe in his arms, waking with a feeling of euphoria until he realized that his arms were still empty.

"Not yet, but I know something that will help. Will you join me?" She gave him a cryptic smile and left the room, heading for their bedroom. Kit followed obediently, happy to do whatever it took to help. Louisa shut the door behind them, turning to him with a seductive smile.

"Make love to me—hard." She was already unlacing her bodice, her eyes never leaving his.

"Are you mad? It will harm the baby. What kind of man would lie with his wife when she's about to give birth?" He was stunned, but Louisa seemed to be serious.

"The kind of man who wants to help her go into labor. Now, will you unlace those breeches, or do you require help?" She'd already pulled off her bodice and skirt, remaining in her chemise and cotton stockings. Louisa reclined on the bed, pulling the chemise up to her waist. Kit's breath caught in his throat. She was like a ripe fruit, ready to burst with its sweetness. His traitorous body responded immediately, his cock straining against the fabric of his breeches.

"Please, Kit. It won't hurt the baby, and it won't hurt me. It's perfectly safe. I need you." She spread her legs further, the smile never leaving her face. "You know you want to."

Kit finally gave in, going to her. It had been a while since they'd made love, and he was as desperate for her as she was obviously for him. He tried to hold back, but Louisa wasn't having it.

"Give it to me hard, Kit. Harder." She was grinding her hips against his, driving him mad with need.

"Woman, have you gone daft?" he asked, panting as he thrust harder per her request.

"Stop talking and fuck me, husband," she answered. That was all it took to break through his reserve. Kit gave her what she wanted, conscious only of the hunger between them, and the feeling of completion when he finally rolled off her, sweating and sated.

"Was that to your liking, madam?" he asked, looking over at her. Louisa didn't answer. She was looking down at the wet spot between her legs.

"My water broke," she announced gleefully, sliding off the bed. "It won't be long now."

She'd been right. Evie arrived a few hours later, screaming and red, black fuzz covering her little head. Kit's breath caught in his throat as Bridget placed the swaddled baby in his arms, smiling at his wonder and joy. He'd forgotten all about wanting a son. His daughter was perfect, as was his life.

Kit rose from the bench and threw a stone into the lake, watching the distorted reflection of the moon as the still surface rippled and rolled. How naïve he'd been. His life wasn't perfect now. His wife had deceived him, and now she might leave and take his daughter with her. He knew he had rights as a father, but all she had to do was activate the device and just disappear, and all his rights would disappear with her. She'd be gone forever, to a place where he couldn't follow. Would Alec and Valerie go too, leaving him alone and heartbroken? Kit felt a sudden rage tear his soul as his hurt turned into terrible anger. He spun around and marched back to the house. He wouldn't be a pawn in this game.

SIX

A bitter moon shone down from the heavens, bathing the house in a silvery glow. Finn wasn't sure what woke him, but he couldn't go back to sleep even if he tried. He felt his guts twisting with anxiety as he walked to the edge of the wood and stood there, looking at the dark, eerie building. This wasn't his home, and his family wasn't inside. He wasn't hallucinating or imagining things. This was frighteningly real. Finn leaned against a tree, gazing at the silent house. He'd complained about being treated like a child, and now he felt like one. He was scared, confused, and desperate for his parents to make everything all right, but that wasn't going to happen. He had to think like a man and act like a man. What would his father do in this situation?

Finn did the only thing he could think of; he began walking toward Jamestown. His only hope was to find Charles, if he was still there in his house. What if Charles and his family were gone as well? He'd go to Agnes and Richard if he failed to find Charles, but that would probably be futile. If Charles was no longer there, chances were that Agnes and Richard wouldn't be either. Richard had set up as a carpenter in Jamestown, using an outbuilding behind the house as a workroom. Finn had visited them once since they got married, but he remembered exactly where their house was. As of now, that was the plan.

Finn fought waves of nausea, punctuated by pangs of hunger as he stumbled down the road in the direction of the town. The moon periodically hid behind clouds, leaving the world dark and cold. The October night was chilly, so Finn walked faster, trying to warm up, praying all the while that Charles would be there. He would help him make sense of things. Charles would know what to do. He always did. *Oh, please be there, Charlie*, Finn thought as he saw the dark outline of buildings in the distance. *Be there.*

Finn's hopes were dashed as soon as he got closer. The houses began much sooner than he anticipated, many of them made of brick and mortar rather than wood. The street was paved with cobbles, and not the mud that was usually churned by passing wagons and sometimes ankle-deep after rain. Finn stared at the houses that had appeared like mushrooms after rain since the last time he'd been to town. Finn passed shops shuttered for the night, and several pubs, disgorging their last customers into the cool air of the night. He heard laughter from an open door as light spilled into the street, two gentlemen stumbling onto the pavement, reeling drunk. Finn desperately wished he was drunk because that was the only thing that could explain what he was experiencing.

His attention was distracted by loud screams coming from what he thought would be the center of town. The two drunks suddenly perked up, nearly running toward the noise. Finn decided to follow. Charlie's house was in that direction anyway. More and more people appeared as he drew closer, the light of torches illuminating the odd scene. Several men were dragging something from the house in the square, their faces covered with a sheen of perspiration in the light of the torches. The onlookers roared in approval, yelling something Finn couldn't understand. He inched closer, trying to get a better look. The thing dragged from the house appeared to be a middle-aged man. His nightshirt billowed in the wind, exposing pudgy white legs as his wife hovered in the doorway, her fist pressed to her mouth as if to suppress a scream. The man was obviously terrified, begging his attackers to let him go. His nightcap fell off his head, instantly trampled by the mob as they followed the procession, still chanting.

"Go back where you belong, English scum. We have no room for Royalists here." The men dragged their victim along toward the docks, bystanders trying to kick him as he passed by.

"You'll be on the next ship to England come dawn, and don't try to return. We'll lynch you if we catch you back here. Give our warmest regards to King Georgie."

Finn pressed himself against the wall as the mob passed him, intent on the pursuit of the hapless man. King Georgie? What happened to King James? Finn turned a corner to put distance between himself and the mob and trudged along to Charlie's house. He knew it wouldn't be there before he even reached the correct address, but he dutifully walked up and down the street, looking at the darkened windows of the houses that hadn't been there last week.

Finn began to walk. He had no idea where he was going. Nothing looked familiar. Going to Richard and Agnes was pointless now, so he needed a new plan. Maybe he would go to the docks and see if one of their ships was in the harbor. He knew it was an exercise in futility, but he had to do something, anything. A broadsheet fluttered in the wind, twirling like an autumn leaf, about to land on the ground. Finn snatched it up before it landed in a pile of muck and held it up, trying to read it by moonlight. It said something about Royalists and revolutionaries, but he wasn't sure what it meant. A date at the top of the sheet caught Finn's attention. October 2, 1775. Finn stared at the black ink, trying to comprehend what he was seeing. How could it be 1775, and why did that number look familiar?

Suddenly, Finn felt as if someone punched him in the stomach. The number looked familiar because he'd entered it into the odd object he found. Seventeen rabbits, seven possums, and five foxes. 1775. Finn started to run. He had no idea where he was going, but he couldn't stop. His heart was hammering in his chest, and hot tears ran down his face, obscuring his vision. He got a stitch in his side, but he continued to run as if a pack of wolves was after him and would tear him to bits if he stopped. He had to keep moving, because if he stopped, he would go mad. Maybe he was mad already. Finn hadn't even noticed when the town fell behind and the cobblestone street turned into a dirt road, dark and silent. The tree line was barely distinguishable from the inky sky, and there wasn't a glimmer of light or sign of life anywhere in the distance. Finn lost his footing a few times as he slid on some mud or stepped into a depression in the earth, but he kept running, for stopping would mean having to face the reality of his situation.

SEVEN

Louisa watched from the window as Alec and Valerie left the house and headed toward the woods. She couldn't bear to say goodbye, so she waved as Valerie turned to take one last look at the house. Alec had strapped on his sword, taken his pistol, and hidden a dagger in his boot. He took anything small of value he could find to be used for trading, since the coins might be useless. He carried a small valise containing a change of clothes for him and Valerie and some food. Mr. Taylor had given them the device, showing them both how to use it, and strapping it on to Alec's wrist, so he wouldn't drop it. If he did, they'd never get back.

Louisa stifled a sob as they disappeared into the woods. It was the safest place to go according to the old man. They wouldn't want to find themselves in someone's living room if they tried to go directly from the house. Louisa turned from the window as Kit strode into the room. She hadn't seen him since the scene on the landing. Kit locked the door behind him but didn't come further into the room. His eyes were blazing, his voice strangely quiet and controlled when he finally spoke.

"All this time and you never told me. I feel such a fool."

"Kit, I didn't want to burden you with the knowledge. There was no point. To be honest, I didn't want to talk about that life. It would keep me from accepting this one wholeheartedly. Forgive me, Kit. I didn't mean to deceive you." Louisa took a step toward him, but he stepped back, cold and angry.

"You and Valerie must have spoken of the old life, and Alec knew," added Kit bitterly. "How you must have laughed behind my back." Kit turned away from her, looking down at his sleeping daughter. Louisa couldn't see his face, but she could see the rigid stance and the clenched fists. She'd expected disbelief, but she didn't expect such anger.

"Kit, we never laughed at you. We actually didn't speak of it too often. It all seems so long ago. Our life is here, with you. Kit, please don't be angry. I can't bear it right now. I need you." Louisa came up behind him, putting her arms around him, refusing to let go.

"But you were thinking of going back. You and Valerie were considering it." Kit didn't push her away, but he didn't turn around either. He didn't want to look at her.

"Kit, we weren't really considering it. Neither one of us wanted to go, but we needed to be sure. We never expected this to happen. I'm so scared of losing Valerie again, but even more than that, I am scared of losing you. Kit, please, look at me."

Kit turned around then, his eyes unreadable as he looked at her in the darkness. The moonlight drained all color from his face, making him look slightly demonic, his black eyes lost in shadow. Kit suddenly lifted her up, tossing her onto the bed like a sack of turnips. Louisa scrambled out of his reach, but he grabbed her by the ankles and pulled her to the end of the bed, undoing his laces. She didn't protest as he pushed up her skirts, ramming himself inside her. Kit had never touched her in anger, but she could understand his rage and confusion. Louisa bit her lip to keep from crying out. This was the first time since she had given birth to Evie, her body not as responsive as before. Kit's thrusts grew less frenzied as he collapsed on top of her, his cheek wet against her face.

"I won't lose you, Louisa. I won't. You are mine, now and forever. Don't ever forget that. I'll never let you go. If you go, you might as well kill me, for I'm nothing without you and Evangeline."

Louisa wrapped her arms around Kit, drawing him closer and kissing his face. He began to move again, gentler this time, kissing her lips, his eyes never leaving hers.

"I'll never leave you, Kit. You are mine as much as I'm yours. Nothing will come between us. I promise."

EIGHT

Finn couldn't remember when he stopped running, or when he left the road. All he could remember was finding the farmhouse and crawling into the hay in one of the empty stalls of the barn. He was exhausted, hungry, and scared. His body shook uncontrollably, making his teeth chatter loudly in the silence of the stall. Finn's thoughts raced like rats in a maze, scurrying and colliding, but not making any sense. He would give anything in the world to see his mother's face or to feel his father's strong arms around him. He'd often longed for his biological father, imagining him as a romantic, heroic figure. His father died for his beliefs, unapologetic and unafraid. He was a hero. Alec wasn't like his real father. He was safe and solid, never wavering from his course, and Finn wanted him at that moment like he never wanted anyone before.

"I'm sorry, Daddy," he whispered into the darkness. "I'm sorry for not appreciating you as I should have. Please come and find me. Please. Find me like you found me that time in the cave." Finn began sobbing as he remembered that day; the relief he felt when his father climbed into the cave and pulled him out. He also thought of the baby his mother lost that day. All because of him. Finn cried harder, shoving his fist in his mouth to stifle the sobs. He'd never been so scared in his whole life, or so alone. Eventually, he exhausted himself and fell asleep, dreaming dreams of home and family.

* * *

"Raise your hands above your head and get to your feet." The command came from somewhere to the right, but Finn couldn't see who was speaking from his position in the corner of the stall. He did as he was told, getting up and inching out slowly with his hands on his head. A feeble light from the open door illuminated a boy of about fourteen, holding a pitchfork aimed directly at Finn's stomach. The boy looked as scared as Finn felt, but he held his ground and gestured toward the door with the pitchfork.

"Walk." The boy allowed Finn to pass in front of him, prodding him gently as he passed to demonstrate the seriousness of his intentions. Finn had no choice but to obey. *Could things get any worse?* he wondered as he was marched to the farmhouse by his captor.

The appetizing smell of frying bacon and freshly baked bread assailed Finn's senses as he entered the farmhouse. The family was obviously at breakfast; several children of various ages seated on benches around a wooden table. An older woman was in the act of setting a pot of porridge on the table but stopped with the pot in midair when Finn walked in, turning to her husband for an explanation. The man sat at the head of the table, pewter tankard in hand, ready to take a sip of whatever he was drinking.

"I found him sleeping in the barn, Pa," the boy announced, his chest swelling with pride. "I took him prisoner. He's most likely a Royalist spy." The boy prodded Finn again, forcing him to advance further into the room. Finn hoped no one heard his stomach growl as he inhaled the comforting smell of hot porridge.

The older man put down his tankard, his gray eyes never leaving Finn's face. "Put down the pitchfork Jonah before you hurt someone. Well done," he added hastily, noting the look of hurt on his son's face.

"Now, who might you be?" He looked more curious than angry, giving Finn hope that he might escape unscathed.

"My name is Finlay Whitfield. I didn't mean any harm, sir. I was lost and needed a warm place to sleep. I'm deeply sorry for any offense I have caused. May I be on my way?" Finn tried to ignore the curious glances of the other children, their food forgotten for the moment.

"Where are you headed, Finlay Whitfield?" The man sounded serious, but his eyes twinkled with good humor as he studied the young man in front of him.

"I don't know, sir. I have no place to go." Finn averted his eyes as hot tears sprang into them unbidden, making him feel like a little boy. He wouldn't give these people the satisfaction of crying.

"You must be hungry, son," the woman said. "Why don't you join us for breakfast? There's plenty for everyone." She was already setting a place at the table, but Finn looked at her husband before answering. The man nodded in agreement, gesturing toward the empty place at the table. "Sit down and have some food. You look the worse for wear. We'll talk more after you eat."

Finn stole a glance at Jonah, who looked abashed by his father's reaction to the stranger. He slammed the pitchfork against the wall before taking his place at the table, his face red with anger.

"Who do I have the honor of addressing, sir?" Finn asked, taking a seat. "I've given you my name, but I have yet to learn yours."

The man smiled warmly, clapping Finn on the back, his gray eyes dancing with amusement at Finn's forced formality. "You are right, of course. I failed to introduce myself. I'm John Mallory, and that's my wife, Hannah. You've already met Jonah." He pointed to the eldest girl at the table. "That there is Martha, followed by Abigail, Sarah, and Annie. Where is your family?"

"I don't know, sir. We've become separated recently." Finn gratefully spooned porridge into his mouth, the warm mush soothing his aching belly. He'd leave the bacon and bread for last since it was the tastiest. God only knew when he'd get to eat again.

"Are your parents Royalists or do they support the cause of freedom?" Mr. Mallory asked, taking a large bite of bread and chewing thoughtfully. Finn was about to blurt out that his family was loyal to the king, when he recalled the man being dragged from his house by the mob the night before. They'd called him a "Royalist". Maybe boasting of his loyalty to the king wasn't such a smart idea.

"We are not Royalists, sir."

"Hmm," the man said, shaking his head. "I see." Finn wasn't really sure what he saw, but thought it was better to say as little as possible until he figured out what was happening. Everyone ate in silence for a little while, spoons scraping plates, the only sound aside from the fire crackling in the hearth.

Finn was fairly sure that the Mallorys would let him leave after breakfast, although he had no idea where to go. He wondered if he should hide a piece of bread in his doublet for later, since he had no money for food. Going to Jamestown to look for Charles had been the extent of his plan, and now he was at a loss, which obviously showed in his face. Mr. Mallory wiped up some bacon grease with the heel of his bread, his eyes still on Finn, before speaking.

"It seems to me, you're in a bit of a predicament, young

Finlay," Mr. Mallory said at last. "You see, son, I'm in a predicament as well. My eldest, Samuel, is a corporal with the Continental Army. Enlisted in the spring. Jonah here is burning to enlist as well, but he's only fifteen and too young to fight, thankfully. With all these women, I find myself short of help on the farm, and seeing as you have nowhere to go, maybe you'd be willing to stay for a while. I can't afford to pay you, but I can provide you with a warm, dry place to sleep and three meals a day. There is no contract so you would be free to leave any time you chose to. Now, does that sound like something that might appeal to you?"

Finn looked up from his bacon, surprised by the offer. They seemed like a nice family, and if he could stay for a while with no obligation, that would give him a chance to get his bearings. It's not like he had anywhere else to go, and at least he'd have food to eat and a roof over his head. Finn sighed at the thought of his parents. They must be sick with worry, not knowing what happened to him. He needed time to figure out what to do.

"Thank you, sir. I'm most grateful for your offer, and I gladly accept. You won't be sorry, sir. I'm a hard worker," he added for good measure, although his father always said he was lazy and spoiled.

"Very well then. You can sleep in the loft with Jonah." Mr. Mallory popped the heel of bread into his mouth and took a last sip of ale before making to rise from the table.

"That's Sam's bed," piped in Jonah, obviously outraged. He'd remained silent throughout the meal, but couldn't hold in his frustration any longer.

"Well, Sam's not using it at the moment, is he? I might have some of Sam's old clothes as well," suggested Mrs. Mallory. "Your garments seem somewhat out of date, if you don't mind me saying so." She looked at Finn's leather doublet and breeches as if trying to put a date to them.

"That would be most kind of you, Madam. Anything you

can spare." The idea of wearing someone's clothes wasn't appealing, but he had no wish to stand out.

"Now, Jonah can show you around the farm after breakfast. We have a field to clear today, so your help will be most welcome, Finlay." Mr. Mallory rose from the table, ready to start his day.

"Please, call me Finn. Everyone else does." Finn smiled in gratitude as Mrs. Mallory added more bacon to his plate. She seemed like a kind woman - like his mother.

NINE

Louisa bolted out of bed just as the first rays of the rising sun began to caress her face. She hadn't meant to fall asleep, but she was tired and must have dozed off. Thankfully, Evie was still out, content after her 3 a.m. feed, and Kit was sleeping soundly, his face serene. He had no trouble sleeping through stressful situations, but Louisa usually tossed and turned, unable to find oblivion. She must have been more overwrought than she realized.

Louisa slipped on her dressing gown and crept from the room, crossing the hall to Valerie's bedroom. Her heart hammered in her chest as she turned the handle and looked inside. The bed was neatly made, the Whitfields still gone. *There's still hope*, she told herself as she made her way downstairs. Mrs. Dolly was alone in the kitchen, teasing the smoored fire back to life, so Louisa changed track and peeked into the parlor. Empty. Her stomach did a somersault as she stepped out onto the porch. The morning was fresh and cool, making her shiver in her thin dressing gown. There was no sign of anyone. Louisa trudged back upstairs with a heavy heart. She'd fervently hoped that Alec and Valerie would find Finn quickly and return before anyone was even up, but that obviously wasn't the case.

"They're not back," Kit said quietly. It wasn't a question; it was a statement of fact. He was sitting up in bed, gently rocking the baby. Her tiny mouth was already opening and closing, searching for a nipple. Louisa just shook her head and took the baby, sitting down in her nursing chair and putting the baby to her breast.

"They're not back," she repeated, almost to herself. "You know what this means, Kit. If Finn had stayed close to the house, they would have found him quickly. If they're still not back, it means he's left the area and he could be anywhere by now. And there's a war on." Louisa sniffled, using the sleeve of her gown to dab at her wet eyes.

"What war?" Kit was alert now, his interest piqued. "You hadn't mentioned anything about a war last night."

"I never got the chance. Finn's landed in the middle of the Revolutionary War. I wonder what made him pick that year," Louisa added absentmindedly as she switched Evie from one breast to another.

"Revolutionary War? Who revolted?" Kit asked with undisguised interest. Louisa had forgotten that Kit had no idea about what happened in the future. Alec had gotten an education from Valerie, but Kit had known about things for less than twenty-four hours.

"The colonists rebelled against England. They wanted to break with England and govern themselves." Louisa watched as Kit's eyes widened in shock.

"Really? What an extraordinary notion. That must have been a short conflict. Did England beat them back into submission?" Kit was warming up to the subject, his face aglow with boyish curiosity.

"Actually, no. It lasted for years, and the American Colonies won their independence. They became the United States of

America and eventually grew from thirteen to fifty states. England never did get over the shock."

"Fascinating," Kit said. "Who would have thought it was possible to defeat England? Were they very well-armed and trained?"

"Not as well as the British. The Continental Army was better armed and trained, but the Militia was mostly farmers and tradesmen, armed with pitchforks and hunting rifles. The British didn't take them seriously enough until it was too late."

"Fascinating," Kit said again, his eyes shining with wonder. "Who became their king? Was the rebellion led by someone of royal blood?"

"Kit, I'll tell you more later, but right now, we have more pressing issues. Since they're not back, we have to figure out what to tell everyone. We need a plausible explanation for Mrs. Dolly and Minnie, and the field workers. Charles will have to be told something as well, and what about little Louisa? How do we explain the disappearance of her brother and parents and the appearance of Mr. Taylor? He'll have to stay here until they return since he's got nowhere to go. Oh, Kit, what if they can't find Finn?"

"They'll find him, Louisa. They must. Think good thoughts. There's nothing more we can do now, except make sure that everyone is calm and ignorant of the truth. Let's tell them that they went to North Carolina."

"Why would they suddenly go to North Carolina?" Louisa asked.

"Everyone is worried about the lack of supplies for the coming winter. We'll just tell them that they wanted to barter for some additional items, not available here. Finn would have gone with them. I don't think anyone will question it. As far as Mr. Taylor goes, just say that he's a relation come from England to visit."

"All right. I suppose that'll do since I can't think of anything better at the moment." Louisa sighed. "I'm so frightened, Kit. What if they don't come back?"

"Sweetheart, you managed to find Valerie after going back in time, crossing an ocean, and surviving a pirate attack. Alec and Valerie have much better chances since they know where Finn went, and have some useful knowledge of the future. Even if Finn left the area, he must be somewhere close by. They will find him. You'll see. Now, get dressed and come downstairs. We must act normally."

"You're right, of course. I'll just change Evie's clout and check on Bridget before I come down. She's been unwell. I hope she's feeling better today. I wish I could tell her the truth, Kit. She's always so practical and resourceful; she'd know how to make me feel better." Louisa unwrapped Evie's blanket to a howl of protest. She hated getting her clout changed.

"Louisa, you must say nothing to Bridget. I know she can be a source of comfort to you, but the fewer people know, the better. I'll go have a word with Mr. Taylor and advise him of the plan."

TEN

Wispy ribbons of mist wrapped themselves around tree trunks and pooled in the hollows still shrouded in darkness as the sky began to lighten in anticipation of sunrise. The air was cold, turning their breath to white puffs as they walked in silence down the road to Jamestown. Alec desperately wanted to say something to comfort Valerie, but no words sprang to mind. She walked beside him, silent and distant, lost in her own thoughts. They'd spent the whole night searching the area, but found no signs of Finn, and they both knew what this meant. He could have gone anywhere. Going to town seemed like the most logical idea, since Finn would likely try to find Charlie before realizing that he was in a different time. How long would it take him to grasp the reality of the situation? What would he do then? With no one to turn to, Finn might take to the woods, making him impossible to find.

They left the woods before the current inhabitants of the house began to rise and go about their business. Alec didn't really have a plan, but it was vital to make Valerie believe that he had an idea. Her eyes looked haunted in the gray light of the early morning, her face pale and drawn. He hated to admit it, but she had been right last night. They should have gone immediately. The hour it took them to prepare probably made all the difference, although Finn might have already gone by the time Mr. Taylor raised the alarm. They had no way of knowing at exactly what time Finn transported himself. Valerie thought she heard him on the stairs, but it could just as easily have been Minnie. Finn obviously came home sometime after they sat down to supper, which had been a lengthy affair. He might have been gone for as much as two hours by the time they discovered him missing. Alec turned to Valerie, trying to appear much calmer than he felt.

"Sweetheart, here's what we'll do. Once we get to town, I'll find us an inn where you can freshen up and rest. You need to sleep. I'll search the town. Someone must have seen him. Are you hungry?"

Valerie just shook her head. She was exhausted and terrified, her stomach revolting against even the sip of cider she took a few moments ago. She'd like to have argued with Alec, but at the moment, sleep was the only thing she craved, aside from the sight of Finn. She needed to lie down, if only for a short while. Alec must be exhausted too but arguing with him would be futile. He wouldn't stop to rest for fear of allowing Finn to get even further away.

"Why don't we go over everything you remember about 1775?" Alec suggested. "I know they are in the middle of the Revolutionary War, but what else can you tell me? I must know as much as possible."

Alec would never admit it to Valerie, but he was excited about finding himself in the future. This wasn't the future he'd dreamed of, but it was still one hundred and fifty years past his own time, and he was more than curious to see how life had changed. The idea that the colonists could take on the might of

Britain and win boggled his mind, making him strangely proud of the future citizens of the United States. He only hoped that Finn would stay clear of the conflict, and not set himself up as a target for the revolutionaries.

Valerie suddenly stopped walking and turned to face Alec. Her eyes looked even more panicked than they had a few moments ago, although as far as Alec could tell nothing had changed.

"Something's been niggling at me all night, and I finally remembered what it is. It's been a very long time since I've studied American history, but I seem to remember that at some point during the seventeenth century the capitol was moved from Jamestown to Williamsburg. Jamestown eventually fell into decline and ceased to exist altogether, but I can't remember exactly when that happened. There might not even be a Jamestown any longer, Alec. What do we do then?" Valerie looked at Alec, her expression forlorn. If Finn wasn't in Jamestown, they would have no clue where to look for him.

"Let us wait and see, shall we? It can't be as bad as all that." Alec fervently hoped that he was right. What if there was no longer a Jamestown?

Jamestown eventually came into view, bringing relief and despair. The town had grown since their own time, but it had the distinct air of decline, especially at the outskirts. Alec and Valerie passed several abandoned houses and the ruins of a church on their way to the center. The buildings in the heart of the town were much grander than they were in the seventeenth century, but some of the windows were still shuttered, giving the square a melancholy air. The sun was fully up by this time, and the place should have been a beehive of activity, but it was strangely quiet. A few masts could be seen rising above the roofs of houses facing the docks, but there wasn't the usual flurry of activity. Several women, some of them colored, passed by, baskets slung over their arms, obviously en route to a shop or a market.

A wagon rattled past, loaded with barrels of something; the driver wearing a beat-up tricorn, which obscured the upper half of his face.

"What manner of hat is that?" asked Alec, looking after the wagon.

"That's a tricorn. They were very popular during the eighteenth century." Valerie barely paid attention to their surroundings, tired as she was. Her feet were swollen in her shoes from hours of walking, and she grew more anxious by the moment, seeing the sad state of the town. How would Finn react to seeing this? Where would he go next?

The bed was lumpy and hard, but Valerie didn't care. They were lucky to have found this much. There were only two inns, and one of them had been full. The Crowing Rooster was a bit run down and in need of a good clean, but at least they had rooms available. Their room was on the uppermost floor, small, with a sloped ceiling and a tiny window which refused to open. Valerie poured some water from the pitcher, splashing her dusty face and washing her hands, before sitting down on the bed and kicking off her shoes.

Alec washed his face and hands, wolfed down a sausage roll and drank the last of the cider, before heading into town to look for Finn. He assured her that it was all right for her to stay at the inn and get some rest. Alec would also find someplace to trade his gold ring for currency. They'd need to buy food and pay for the room.

Valerie peeled off her gown, used the chipped chamber pot under the bed, and climbed under the covers in her shift. She felt guilty for resting while Finn was out there somewhere, scared and confused, but her body refused to obey any of her commands, forcing her to seek oblivion. She'd been up all night, but it was the anxiety that really wore her out. Her eyes felt heavy, and her mind shut down, refusing to dwell on any more fearful thoughts until it got some rest.

It was nearly dark by the time Valerie finally woke up, hungry, but rested. There was no sign of Alec, so she stood on tippy toes to try to see out of the window. She couldn't see much from her vantage point since a ledge from the floor below blocked the view of the street. For a moment, Valerie considered going outside, but quickly changed her mind. Alec would worry if he came back and found her gone. She'd just stay and wait for him to return.

A half hour turned into an hour before Valerie finally heard the sound of footsteps on the creaky staircase outside. She made for the door, yanking it open just as Alec reached the top of the stairs. He looked exhausted, his clothes soiled and smelly. He carried a pot and a loaf of bread under his arm.

"Alec, where have you been all this time?" Valerie asked, taking in his disheveled appearance.

Alec sank onto a wooden chair and handed the pot and bread to Valerie as he removed his boots. "I spent the first few hours walking around asking anyone I could find if they'd seen Finn, but no one could remember anyone like him. I decided to go to the docks to ask there. Same result. A vessel was being unloaded, and extra men were needed to help the sailors. I thought it a good opportunity to earn a little money since there was nowhere to trade the ring. I stayed until the work was finished, earning enough to pay for the room and some supper. The proprietress promised to send up some ale to go with our meal."

Valerie's hunger vanished after hearing Alec's account, but she forced herself to eat the oyster stew, and drink the ale, which had been brought up by a scrawny girl in a stained frock. Alec ate slowly, his eyes heavy with fatigue. Valerie wanted to ask him what they would do next but decided to wait till morning. In the meantime, she'd wash his shirt and stockings. They would be dry by morning, in case they needed to leave.

ELEVEN

"Kit, look—it's Alec," exclaimed Louisa as she looked out of the window. The rider was still far away, but she was sure it was him. "They must have found Finn in Jamestown. I wonder where Valerie and Finn are." She was already on her way down when Kit called after her.

"Louisa, it's not Alec. It's Charles." Louisa slowed her pace, disappointment filling her heart. Of course. Charles looked a lot like Alec from a distance. What did he want anyway? Louisa would have trusted Alec with her life, but her trust did not extend to the brother. Charles was always charming and polite, but there was something in his jade-green eyes that was sly and self-serving. There was a cool formality between the brothers that had been caused by Cora's death two years before, when Charles accused Alec of murder. He'd apologized once it came out that Amelia had bashed Cora's head in, but the relationship remained fractured, Alec unable to forget his brother's betrayal. One thing that Louisa could say in Charles' defense was that he wasn't giving up on mending his bond with Alec. He came as often as he could, offering help around the estate and trying to be as agreeable as possible in the hopes that Alec would eventually forgive him.

Charles jumped off his horse and tied the reins to a post before jogging up the steps and coming into the house. Up close, he looked tired and pale, his hair coming out of its tie, his mouth a grim line. Charles yanked the tie out, letting his dark, wavy hair cascade onto his shoulders.

"Good morning, Charles. Would you care for some refreshment?" Louisa asked as she invited him to come into the parlor. She'd never seen him look so agitated.

"Some ale wouldn't come amiss," Charles replied, settling on a wooden settee. "Is Alec here? I'd like a word."

"Alec and Valerie aren't here at the present," answered Kit as he joined them in the parlor. "Can I help?"

Charles accepted a cup of ale from Minnie and drained it in one gulp, holding out the cup for a refill. "Perhaps I should wait for Alec to come back. I must speak with him. Where has he gone?"

"Alec and Valerie went to North Carolina," Louisa and Kit answered in unison.

"What on earth for?" Charles drained another cup and handed it back to Minnie without looking at her, his eyes on Kit.

"They thought they might trade some tobacco for foodstuffs," explained Kit. "What was it you wanted, Charles?"

Charles looked at his hands for a moment, as if buying some time before speaking. He tied his hair back and finally looked up at Kit. "I wanted to ask Alec if Annabel and I can move to Rosewood. Winter is around the corner and the situation in town is not a good one. With so much of the crop destroyed during the Indian attack, there are shortages of food. I can't see how we can make it through the winter without reinforcements. The king is said to have sent supply ships, but there is no sign of them, and if the supplies don't come, we are likely to starve.

There's plenty of game in the woods, and fish in the stream. We'll not go hungry here."

"I can't imagine that Alec would refuse," said Kit thoughtfully. "Would you be bringing Annabel's father and brother with you?"

"The old man wants to stay in town. He thinks the supplies will arrive any day now, and we'll all be saved. Thomas would most likely stay with his father, which is for the best, considering."

"Considering what?" asked Louisa, noticing something in Charles' face.

"Considering that little Louisa seems to have developed an attachment to him. I told Annabel not to leave them alone at any time. Thomas is eighteen and not to be trusted alone with a young woman." Charles looked absurdly uptight, his mouth pressed into a tight line.

"Does Thomas share her feelings?" Louisa had only seen him once or twice, but she could understand her niece's infatuation. He was a good-looking boy, charming and well-mannered.

"I think he might, which is why it's for the better if he remains in town with his father," Charles replied.

"When will you come? We need to make room." Louisa was already mentally rearranging the inhabitants of the house.

"I thought we might come by the end of the month. Would that suit? Alec and Valerie will likely be back by then. Little Louisa offered us her room. She said she could share with Minnie. You know how close those two are," said Charles, rising to his feet. "I think that would be ideal."

"Yes, that would help with the sleeping arrangements," mused Louisa. "I'm sure Minnie wouldn't mind sharing with Louisa for a few months. Mrs. Dolly and Bridget are sharing a room, and we have a guest at the moment who might be staying with us for a while. He's in Amelia's old room."

Charles merely shrugged his shoulders at the mention of a

guest. He was obviously preoccupied with the situation at home. With every day that passed without supply ships arriving from England, the fear of famine loomed ever larger.

"Annabel will be so relieved. She's terrified for Harry. He's still so little. She thinks there might be looting once the supplies start to run low. People will have to trade with the Indians again, despite their feelings. There's no other choice. Well, I better go home and give Annabel the good news. Charles kissed Louisa's hand and said goodbye to Kit before leaving them.

"What if Alec and Valerie aren't back by the end of the month?" Louisa asked, turning to Kit. It was only the first week of October, but Louisa was scared. Every day that they stayed away meant they hadn't found Finn and that their chances grew slimmer. Would they come back without him or stay and continue searching?

"Only time will tell, darling. In the meantime, we have to store provisions for the coming winter. It's all hands on deck, I'm afraid. Those ships are not coming, and we need to prepare for the worst."

TWELVE

Finn leaned on the spade and wiped his face with the sleeve of his shirt. It was unusually warm for October, and he was sweating profusely. He was accustomed to walking for hours and tracking game, but he wasn't used to this kind of work. He and Jonah spent several days clearing the field, which was tedious, backbreaking work. Thankfully, they finally finished that morning, and had been sent by Mr. Mallory to fill in the old privy and dig a new one. The smell of the privy still lingered in his nose as he sucked in fresh air.

Finn was grateful not to be wearing his leather doublet. Mrs. Mallory had given him two shirts and a pair of brown breeches, as well as a coat and a tricorn that had belonged to Sam. Jonah kept his silence out of respect for his parents, but Finn could feel his resentment. A stranger was sleeping in his brother's bed and wearing his clothes. Finn didn't blame him. He would have felt the same. Thankfully, Jonah's silence didn't last long, since he was naturally a chatty lad. Finn encouraged him to talk by asking numerous questions about the conflict between England and the Colonies, and making all the appropriate noises, praising Jonah's knowledge and patriotism. Questioning Jonah was the best way to find things out and get his bearings in this inexplicable situation.

"I can't wait until I turn seventeen," Jonah announced. "I hope the war won't be over by then. I'll join the Continental Army on my birthday, despite what Pa says. He didn't want to admit it, but he was proud when Sam joined up. Sam is serving with the 8th Virginia Regiment under General Peter Muhlenberg. Even Martha said he looked dashing in his uniform. I wonder if he's ever seen His Excellency, General Washington. What I wouldn't give to catch a glimpse of him." Jonah stopped digging, sidetracked by his fantasy.

"We will win this war. You'll see Finlay. We'll send those Lobsterbacks crawling back to their king with their tails between their legs." Jonah began to dig with renewed vigor as if he could dig his way to victory.

Finn found it difficult to believe that a bunch of colonials could defeat the king's army, but he kept that opinion to himself. He didn't feel the need to take sides. His mind often wandered off while Jonah was prattling on, agonizing over his dilemma. Was there any way he could get back home? It was obvious to him that it was the strange object that had sent him into the future. If only he'd managed to hang on to it. He would have been at home with his family by now, but without it, his chances of getting back were nonexistent. Finn sighed and began digging again. This couldn't be it. It simply couldn't. He couldn't be trapped here forever, surrounded by strangers, never seeing his parents again.

THIRTEEN

Firelight flickered on the whitewashed walls of the farmhouse, making it appear snug and cozy. It had been warm during the day, but the temperature began to drop as soon as the sun went down. The evening was cold and crisp, the smell of hay and pine in the air. The women had just finished clearing up after supper, eager to spend some time relaxing by the fire before turning in for the night.

Finn sat in the corner, wishing he was invisible as he observed the Mallory family. Mrs. Mallory and Martha were talking quietly as they sewed something called a "trousseau" for Martha's upcoming wedding. That's all she talked about, blushing every time the name of her intended came up. Finn was curious to see this fine specimen of manhood since Martha made him sound practically god-like. Six-year-old Sarah was showing her cloth dolly to baby Annie, and Abigail sat at the table, reading a well-worn book. She glanced up from time to time, looking away embarrassed when she noticed Finn watching her from his perch in the corner.

Mr. Mallory sat on a low stool by the hearth, using a special spoon to hold pieces of lead over the fire, and then pouring the molten metal into a bullet mold. He already had a sizeable pile of bullets next to him, cooling, before he put them into a leather pouch. Mr. Mallory sang under his breath, content to be in the bosom of his family.

> Yankee Doodle went to town
> A-riding on a pony,
> Stuck a feather in his cap
> And called it macaroni.
>
> Yankee Doodle keep it up,
> Yankee Doodle dandy,
> Mind the music and the step,
> And with the girls be handy.

Finn liked the melody of the song, but he couldn't understand the words. They didn't make any sense to him, but the rest of the family seemed to know exactly what Mr. Mallory was singing about, especially the younger children who gleefully joined in the chorus.

Finn suddenly felt tears sting his eyes, and ran from the house, clutching his stomach. Let them think he went to the privy. He was too embarrassed to allow anyone to see his misery. Finn climbed onto a stile, facing away from the house, and gazed up at the stars. The night sky was clear, with thousands of distant stars twinkling in the velvety heavens. He tried to focus his attention on finding familiar constellations to distract himself from his morbid thoughts, but it wasn't working.

Were his parents looking up at the same stars right now, or were even the stars different? Hot tears ran down his cheeks, drying quickly in the cool evening breeze. What did his parents think happened to him? Did they believe he was dead? The thought of his parents mourning him nearly broke his heart. They wouldn't even have a body to bury or a grave to visit. Was there no way to get home and let them know that he was alive? Finn wrapped his arms around himself as his chest constricted with terrible longing.

He didn't hear Abigail come up behind him until she leaned against the stile, silently taking his hand. She handed him a handkerchief without looking at him; her face turned up to the moonlit sky. They remained that way for a while, lost in silent camaraderie. Finn suddenly realized that this was the first time he was holding a girl's hand. Abigail was almost sixteen, with wide brown eyes and blond curls that escaped from her cap, framing her heart-shaped face. They hadn't really spoken, but Finn caught her watching him a few times, a look of intense sympathy in her dark eyes.

"They are dead, aren't they?" she asked quietly. "Sometimes it helps to speak of it."

Finn supposed that even if they weren't dead, by 1775 they certainly would be, so he wasn't lying when he nodded. By now, all traces of his family would be long gone.

"I know how it feels to lose someone. I had a twin. His name was Luke, and he died of a fever when he was ten. He was my best friend. When I was little, I thought I could marry him when I grew up, before I knew that brothers and sisters couldn't marry. I thought that nothing could be more perfect than being married to your best friend, one you've known since before you were even born. I still think of him every day. He pops into my head at the oddest moments, like when I'm really happy or really sad. I suppose those are the moments that I wish I could share with him. Knowing that I will never see him again still breaks my heart. Ma and Pa don't speak of him often, but I know he is always there, in their thoughts." Abigail leaned closer to Finn, finally looking at his face.

"I'm sorry about your brother. I had a sister—Louisa. She was always following me about when she was small; wanting to me to play with her. I had no patience. I wanted to do grown-up things, manly things. Now, I wish I would have been kinder to her. I miss my parents. I should have been kinder to them as well, especially my father." Finn wiped away another tear, thankful that Abigail couldn't see it in the darkness.

"Why weren't you kind to your father?" she asked, looking up at him.

"My real father died before I was born. He was a hero. He died fighting for what he believed in. His brother married my mother and raised me as his own. I always thought that my real father would have been better somehow, braver and stronger." Finn felt a terrible guilt even uttering the words.

"Wasn't he a good father to you? Was he cruel?" Abbie was watching him, her face illuminated by the light of the moon. Her eyes looked bottomless in her face, giving her a solemn expression.

"No, he was a wonderful father. I was just too stupid to realize it. I wish I had the chance to tell him that, just once. I wouldn't feel so terrible if he knew that I loved him." Finn felt his heart squeeze with regret. What a fool he'd been.

"I think he knew you loved him. Parents have the ability to see past the silly things we say and do and see what's in our hearts. Well, I'd better go in. I'm cold."

Finn drew Abigail to him without thinking, sharing his warmth with her, grateful for the warmth she'd shared with him. "Thank you, Abigail. You made me feel better."

"You can call me Abbie, if you like. Abigail is so formal. I'll see you inside, Finn. Maybe we can take a walk after church on Sunday," she suggested shyly just before she ran back to the house, her skirts fluttering in the wind.

"I would like that very much," whispered Finn to her retreating back, feeling marginally better.

FOURTEEN

Abbie climbed into bed next to Martha and turned toward the wall, pretending to be asleep. She wasn't in the mood to talk about Martha's wedding tonight. She had her own thoughts to contend with. Abbie had surprised herself when she offered to walk home with Finn after church. She hadn't meant to do it, but it just slipped out. Normally, Matthew Granville walked her home after church, as had been their pattern for the past few months.

Matthew had been the first boy to show any interest in Abbie, and she had been surprised and flattered by his attention. He was a nice-looking boy with flaxen hair and light eyes that were the color of the sky on a cloudless summer day. Abbie had been terribly nervous the first time Matthew had asked to walk her home, but she tried to retain her composure, letting him do most of the talking. They'd never had a proper conversation before, so Abbie was curious as to what Matthew's personality was like. She had to admit that although she found him to be handsome; he was a bit of a braggart, always going on about his accomplishments and dreams. She had dreams too, but he never really asked her about them. Still, being courted by a boy was exciting and new. Martha said that Abbie had to be nice to him and try to be coy to pique his interest. After all, there were lots of girls he could have invited to walk with him, but he'd chosen Abbie.

By the time Matthew had walked Abbie home for the third time, she felt more comfortable with him. All she had to do was ask him a few questions, and he was off talking. She didn't have to work very hard to keep him interested. Abbie wondered if Matthew would eventually say something about the future or try to kiss her. She didn't have long to wait. Just two weeks ago, Matthew had let it slip that his parents approved of Abbie highly and would like nothing more than to have someone like her for a daughter-in-law. They thought her to be hardworking and obedient; two extremely desirable qualities in a wife for their son. Abbie didn't think of herself as being particularly obedient, but there was no need to disillusion Matthew. He'd find out for himself soon enough.

All that talk of possible marriage brought Matthew to his real purpose. He asked permission to give Abbie a kiss. Her heart pounded in her chest as she nodded mutely, closing her eyes and raising her face to receive the kiss. She'd fantasized about being kissed often, since seeing Gil kiss Martha. She wasn't sure what a proper reaction for a woman was supposed to be, but she hoped to find out. Matthew's lips came down on hers, kissing her softly, then retreating again. Abbie opened her eyes, to find Matthew watching her, a smug look on his face. She had to admit that she was somewhat confused. He'd done exactly what he was supposed to do, but she felt nothing. His lips had been warm and soft, but it didn't feel any different than kissing Annie or Sarah. It just felt, for lack of a better word, nice.

Abbie slid her arm through Matthew's as they continued their walk. She felt as if she'd sealed a bargain with that kiss, but her soul was in turmoil. Was that all? Is that what it felt like to

kiss a husband? What about the other stuff? She'd begged
Martha to tell her what happened in a marriage bed, and
Martha reluctantly explained; her cheeks blazing as she avoided
meeting Abbie's eyes. She didn't go into any details, but she said
it was much like the animals, except that people usually faced
each other during the act. Martha said that it was supposed to
feel nice after the first time, and that according to her sources,
which were a few of her now married friends, the wives didn't
really mind.

Abbie tried to imagine having Matthew do that to her, and
if she would mind, but she simply couldn't picture it. The idea
of having Matthew stick his prick into her just seemed ludi-
crous. He'd probably just keep talking as he did it, expecting her
to ask questions and fan his ego all the while.

Abbie thought of what happened after their last kiss. She'd
turned to Matthew, interrupting the flow of his monologue.
"Kiss me again," she'd demanded, raising her face to his. There
had to be something more. She was sure of it. Maybe if they
kissed often enough the feelings would come.

"Oh, liked it, did you? I've been told that I'm a good kisser."
With that Matthew bent down to kiss her, but Abbie turned
away, shocked.

"Oh, and who told you that, Matthew Granville?" She was
glaring up at him, all thoughts of kissing forgotten. Matthew
obviously realized that he'd said the wrong thing, backtracking
immediately.

"Oh, it was no one. I'd only kissed my cousin once, and she
said it was nice. We were just playing, mind. It meant nothing.
It's you I want to be kissing. Please, Abbie. Let me kiss you
again. "

Abbie relented, allowing Matthew to kiss her again. The
kiss was much like the first — soft, warm, and completely devoid
of anything she thought it was supposed to be. Abbie sighed and
continued to walk, oblivious to Matthew's confused gaze. She

supposed that's how it was, and her imagination had gotten the better of her. Abbie sighed, smiling up at Matthew as he started chattering again. He fancied himself a great wit and tried to impress her with his observations of their neighbors.

But now there was Finn. At first, Abbie felt sorry for him. He seemed awfully sad and lost, even bewildered, when Jonah first brought him to the house. Abbie felt a strange urge to comfort him and make him feel as if he had at least one friend, but she had to admit that her motives weren't completely pure. She couldn't help noticing his lovely eyes. They were the color of summer leaves, fringed with thick dark lashes. He had the body of a hunter, lithe and lean, his movements economical and precise. Abbie could see the muscles in his forearms stretch the fabric of his shirt when he moved. He was strong, but graceful. As Abbie looked at him, she couldn't help noticing his lips. They were full and looked so soft, especially when he smiled. She had no problem imagining Finn sticking his prick in her. The unbidden thought made Abbie blush crimson, but once she imagined it, the picture kept coming back. Would his kiss be the same as Matthew's? Would it be wrong to find out?

Abbie closed her eyes, willing herself to go to sleep. Finn would walk her from church on Sunday. That was all. There was nothing between them other than friendship. Matthew might be upset, but Martha had told her to be coy. Let him think that Finn was sweet on her as well. Maybe that would make him take more of an interest in her as a person, not just a potential wife.

FIFTEEN

Finn tried to ignore his aching bladder and go back to sleep, but the tactic wasn't working. He'd had too much ale at supper, and now he'd have to drag himself outside to the privy. Despite the warmth of the day, the temperature dropped rapidly after sunset, frost glittering on the grass at dawn. A chamber pot would have come in handy, but the Mallorys only used chamber pots for the two youngest children. Mrs. Mallory couldn't abide the reek come morning with so many people living in such close proximity.

Finn suddenly had a wicked thought. He'd get up quietly, so as not to wake Jonah, and piss out of the window. No one would be the wiser, and he wouldn't have to leave the warm loft and freeze his bollocks outside. There'd be enough of that come winter. He froze at the thought of still being here in the winter but put it out of his mind and crept to the window, opening the shutter just enough to do his business. Finn was just untying his flies when a voice from outside stilled his hand.

"How is it with you, John?" the voice asked. It was gravelly and low but audible enough.

"All's well. We're all hoping that Sam will be able to come

home for Martha's wedding. It might serve a dual purpose, come to that. What's the news?" answered John Mallory. The sweet smell of his pipe drifted up to the window, so he couldn't be too far.

"The news could be better. Seems Governor Dunmore has been busy since he fled Williamsburg. He's aboard a Royal Navy vessel in Norfolk with his family."

"Yes, I know. He's been there since June," John Mallory replied. "What's he done?"

"He's been begging for reinforcements, so General Gage has ordered several detachments of 14th Foot Regiment to Virginia. Seems they've been raiding the countryside for military supplies in order to undermine the rebellion."

"Where are they taking these supplies?" asked Mr. Mallory.

"They've hastily constructed a few forts, using them as their base."

"I think the Militia needs to focus on protecting what's ours and retrieving what's been taken, Alfred. We can't fight a war without ammunition."

"Right you are, John. Right you are. We'll have to watch and wait, choosing an unguarded moment to seize back what's been taken. Now, tell me about this boy that you've taken in. Do you reckon that's wise in these turbulent times?" Finn decided that whoever Alfred was, he liked to stir things up.

"He's a good lad, Alfred. Seems that he's lost his parents but hasn't come to accept it yet. I need help on the farm with Sam gone, and the boy needs a place to live. Seems like a fine arrangement to me." John Mallory sucked on his pipe, letting out a wheezy cough.

"And what of his family? Where did their loyalties lie?" Alfred asked, obviously not ready to let the matter drop.

"I can't rightly say, Alf, but the boy is no Loyalist. I think he grew up in the backwoods somewhere. Doesn't seem to know much about the political situation. I saw him gaping at Jonah when he mentioned Lobsterbacks. Didn't even know he was referring to British soldiers. He's no threat, Alfred. I think I'm a good enough judge of character to know that; otherwise, I wouldn't be fit to be doing the work I'm doing for the Committee."

"As you say, John. I've never had cause to question your judgment. I'll be taking myself off now. I still have to visit the Crosby farm before returning to Williamsburg. Will I be seeing you there next week?" Alfred asked, already mounting his horse by the sound of it.

"Yes, at the usual place."

"Until then, and give my regards to my sister and the children."

"That I will, Alf. Don't forget the pie. Hannah would be put out if you didn't take it. She made it just for you."

The sound of hoof beats faded into the night as the stranger left. Finn waited until he heard Mr. Mallory go into the house and close the door behind him, before emptying his bladder into the night, climbing back into bed and falling into a deep sleep.

SIXTEEN

The sound of the rain lashing against the wooden shutters and the roof was somewhat soothing, but the damp chill of the room kept Valerie from sleeping well, not to mention her constant state of worry. She finally gave up, sitting up in bed just in time to see Alec's shadowy form slipping through the door.

"Did I wake you?" he asked, tossing his hat onto the table and sinking into a chair to pull off his boots.

"No, where have you been?" Valerie could smell the liquor on his breath all the way from the bed.

"I just had a tankard of ale with a merchant I met at the tavern. We got to talking about the Revolution, and I lost track of time. Did you know that the colonists threw chests of tea into the Boston Harbor?" Alec asked, grinning in the dark.

"Yes, I've heard something about that about a hundred years ago, or was that a hundred years from now? What else did he tell you?" Valerie was wide-awake now, eager to hear what Alec had learned.

"Oh, we just talked about the grievances of the colonists against the king, and England's response to their complaints. Very interesting. I've spent my life being a loyal subject of the king, even in times when I didn't agree with what he stood for. It takes great courage to rebel against the might of England," Alec sounded strangely impressed, making Valerie smile.

"Are you turning into a Revolutionary, Alec Whitfield?"

"No, I'm just in awe of what these people are trying to accomplish at such great risk to themselves and their families. We know that they'll win this conflict, but they don't. They're risking everything."

"Yes, they are. That's what makes them so brave. Are you coming to bed?" Valerie scooted over to make room for Alec, but he continued to sit in the shadows.

"Val, there's something I want to talk to you about, but please hear me out before you get upset." His face was lost in the shadows, but Valerie could hear the urgency in his voice.

"What is it? Is it Finn?" Her heart was pounding, fear pooling in her stomach and spreading to her limbs.

"We've been here for a week now, and it's clear that Finn isn't here. I've walked back to Rosewood several times, and there's no sign of him there either. We need to make a decision, Val."

"I'm not going back without my son," Valerie retorted, sounding harsher than she meant to.

"I wasn't suggesting going back, although maybe we should use the device to go back and check on the family. I think we need to widen the search. The merchant I was speaking with is going to Williamsburg tomorrow. He's offered to take us along. I feel we should go." Alec came closer and sat on the side of the bed, taking Valerie's hand in his.

"Alec, why would Finn go to Williamsburg? For what purpose? It would make sense for him to come to Jamestown, but Williamsburg?" Valerie looked into Alec's face, trying to understand the reasoning behind the suggestion.

"Sweetheart, nothing makes sense. I keep going over it in my mind, trying to figure out what would make Finn choose

1775. I don't expect that he knew what the device was for, but why that number? What is the significance of 1775? Maybe if we could understand his logic, we might figure out where he went. I keep trying to put myself in his place and think of what I would do if I found myself in such a predicament, and I think I would go to Williamsburg."

"Alec, I don't know what the significance of 1775 is. I've certainly never mentioned it to Finn. He might have just been pressing random numbers to see what the thing was for. I don't think there's any special clue, but why do you think he'd go to Williamsburg?" Valerie was surprised by Alec's suggestion. She wasn't sure if Finn was even aware of Williamsburg's existence.

"If he came to Jamestown as we suspect, he would quickly see that there's nothing for him here. He'd take some time to figure things out, but eventually his survival instinct would take over. Finn is a tracker, a hunter. He knows how to follow clues. Jamestown seems to be in a decline, but Williamsburg is the capital of Virginia. The place must be teeming with life and opportunities. If Finn has to find a way to survive in his new surroundings, he would go to a place where he has the best chances, and it wouldn't be here." Alec searched Valerie's face to see if his explanation made sense but saw only confusion.

"Alec, you said it yourself. Finn is a hunter. What if he is living rough somewhere in the woods? His natural instinct would be to escape from the life he doesn't understand and go to what he knows. I'm sure he has his hunting knife and his tomahawk with him. That's all he needs to survive." If Finn was indeed living in the woods, they'd have no chance of finding him. He could be anywhere.

"No. Finn's not in the woods. He loves the hunt, but he doesn't like living rough. He never stayed in the woods overnight if he didn't have to. He always came home. Even if he ran scared and spent a few nights in the woods, he would eventually seek people. It's his nature. Anyhow, what choice is there? We either go back home or widen the search. Which will it be?"

"We can't go home, and I don't want to just pop in. It would only confuse everyone, especially little Louisa. We continue to look for Finn. If you think we should go to Williamsburg, then that's where we'll go. I'm not giving up." Valerie wrapped her arms around Alec as he pulled her close, kissing her forehead.

"That's my girl. No giving up." With that, he finally climbed into bed and was asleep within minutes, leaving Valerie to ponder the wisdom of going to the capital.

SEVENTEEN

Louisa Whitfield continued to work on a chemise, looking serene in the morning light streaming through the window. She glanced at Annabel from time to time, waiting patiently for her to leave the room and go put Harry down for his afternoon nap, but her insides were jumping. She cast her eyes down to her work, pulling the needle through the fabric with quiet precision. He would be waiting for her in the garden. The garden was small and unkempt, but there was a tall hedge at the back that hid them from view of the house. Louisa put the needle down momentarily, unable to make even stitches as she recalled their last kiss. It had been so sweet, so tender. She'd asked Annabel if she could stay a few more days, using her love of Harry as an excuse, but it wasn't Harry she was in love with, although she had to admit, he was as cherubic as they came. It was Tom she wanted to be close to.

At eighteen, Tom was her ideal of the perfect male. He was tall, handsome, and charming. His sky-blue eyes haunted her teenage dreams, and his soft lips turned her legs to jelly. Tom's hair was a shade darker than his sister's, a lovely honey-blond that looked like spun gold in the sun. Louisa was positive that this was love. She'd had a momentary passion for Kit when he first came to Rosewood, but that was just a childish fancy. What girl wouldn't be mesmerized by those black eyes and roguish smile? After Aunt Louisa had told them how Kit saved her from the pirates, she was even more impressed. Louisa watched him from afar, imagining that someday she would meet a man just like Kit, who would marry her and sweep her off on romantic adventures. Louisa often became shy and tongue-tied around him, but Kit teased her, eventually making her giggle and forget her shyness.

Tom was different. Louisa tried to picture herself married to him. She sighed, thinking of how romantic it was to be married. Her mother had explained to her where children came from when she reached womanhood two years ago, leaving Louisa shocked and disgusted. She watched her father out of the corner of her eye, wondering if he did those things to her mother, but he must have, since they conceived her. Louisa eventually came to terms with the facts, watching the adults around her for signs of affection. Her parents kissed often, and once she saw Kit push her aunt up against a tree, kissing her roughly in the woods. It didn't seem so bad. Aunt Louisa certainly didn't seem too put out.

Louisa hadn't entertained the notion of kissing anyone herself until she saw Tom. She'd seen him from time to time since Charles and Annabel had married, but he'd been a gangly youth, never paying her more attention than propriety demanded. This time was different. He seemed to notice her as if for the first time as soon as she came to visit. Tom's eyes followed her around the room, and a few days ago, he joined her for a walk in the garden, skillfully maneuvering her behind the hedge, where he took her in his arms and kissed her. Louisa thought her heart would explode with joy. His kiss left her in no doubt that he was the one. They'd met behind the hedge every day since, making the most of a few stolen moments of privacy.

Louisa's lips felt tender and tingly as she demurely walked around the garden afterward, needing a few moments to recover. She was sure he loved her. Now all she had to do was convince him to speak to her father.

Annabel finally set aside her sewing and went to fetch Harry from the nurse, leaving Louisa on her own. She continued to stitch for a few more minutes, before stowing her unfinished chemise in her work basket and heading outside. She purposely passed a mirror on the way to the door, checking her appearance and pinching her cheeks a few times to give them some color. Louisa pulled out a few strands of hair from underneath her cap, allowing them to curl freely, framing her lovely face, and smoothed down her skirt before walking into the garden.

The air smelled of damp leaves, late-blooming roses, and herbs from the herb garden by the kitchen. She inhaled deeply, enjoying the aroma. It was quiet in the garden, until one stopped to listen. Insects buzzed over the late blooms, birds sang their hearts out, enjoying the last sunny days before the coming winter, and the wind whispered in the trees, the leaves rustling as if having a secret conversation. Everything seemed more vibrant and colorful somehow since she discovered that Tom loved her. Louisa sashayed toward the hedge, stopping along the way to admire some golden mums. Their shaggy heads swayed in the autumn breeze, bringing a burst of color to the dying garden.

Tom was already there, his hat in his hands, pacing back and forth. He smiled broadly as he saw her, holding out a hand, which she took with no reservations.

"You look lovely, Louisa. I thought you might have changed your mind about coming." He gave her a searching look.

"I had to wait for Annabel to leave the room. She wouldn't approve of us meeting this way. I was counting the moments until we could be together," she said breathlessly, raising her face for his kiss. Tom pulled her closer, kissing her sweet lips. His kiss was tender at first, but became more demanding as his tongue slid into her mouth, leaving Louisa momentarily shocked. He hadn't done that before.

"I'm sorry. Did I frighten you?" Tom pulled back, his arms still protectively around her.

"I'm not certain. Why don't you try it again, and I'll let you know," Louisa answered coyly. Tom kissed her again. This time she opened her mouth, imitating what he was doing with his tongue. She liked the sensation. Her heart was beating wildly, her body leaning into him in an effort to get closer.

Tom finally broke the kiss, holding her away from him. "You're a surprise, Mistress Louisa." His eyes were full of something she didn't quite understand, but he was panting, his lips parted.

"A good surprise, I hope," Louisa said, hoping he wouldn't disagree.

"The best kind." Tom cupped her cheek, smiling into her eyes. "Who knew you'd grow into such a beauty?" He kissed her again, his warm hand cupping her breast through the fabric of her gown. Louisa felt weak in the knees as he ran his thumb over her nipple, massaging it in a circular motion. Strange feelings were coursing through her, completely new and indescribable.

"Don't stop," she breathed as he took his hand away, but Tom had no intention of stopping. He carefully pulled down her bodice on one side, bending his head to draw her nipple into his mouth. Louisa nearly swooned with the sensation of his warm lips sucking, then biting her nipple gently. She leaned into him, afraid her legs would betray her.

"Do you like that, my little dove?" he asked, momentarily stopping what he was doing.

Louisa just nodded mutely. She wanted him to go on. She'd never known this yearning before. Tom kissed her neck, then moved on to the tops of her breasts, running his tongue over the creamy skin. She barely noticed as he lifted the hem of her gown, sliding his hand up her leg until his fingers reached the bare skin above the stocking. Louisa sucked in her breath, terrified of what he might do, but didn't ask him to stop. Tom's finger slid into her moist cleft, stroking and probing until she thought she would die of pleasure. It seemed only logical that she should touch him as well, so she reached out shyly and put her hand on his breeches, rubbing her hand against him.

Suddenly, Tom stopped his exploration, pulling away from her. His face was flushed, his breath coming hard and fast as he looked down at her. "Louisa, you are irresistible, but I must stop. I never meant for it to go this far. Charles would skin me alive, then pass me on to your father who would finish the job if he ever found out. I would never dishonor you in any way. You are a lovely girl and should be a maid when you go to your husband's bed."

Louisa looked at him in confusion. Didn't he want to be her husband? Why would he kiss her and touch her this way if he didn't? Did he not find her pleasing? What had she done wrong?

"Did I displease you?" she asked, tears glittering in her eyes.

"Oh, no, you didn't. I wouldn't be able to stop myself if this went any further. I'm doing this out of my regard for you. You're not some trollop to be used and discarded. You are to be loved and cherished, Louisa. Don't ever forget that. I must go, little dove, before I do something I might regret."

"Why would you regret it?" she asked petulantly.

"Because I'm not ready to marry. I'm due to sail to England at the end of the month. My father has arranged a position for me as secretary to one of his friends, who is a favorite at court. I long to see something of the world, Louisa, and what better way to start than with spending time in London at the court of King James? I was born in England, but I don't remember anything.

All I've known is this God-forsaken colony. I long to see new places and meet new people, and a wife is not in my plans just now. Forgive me, little dove. I hope I didn't raise your hopes." Tom gave her a courtly bow and walked away, leaving her angry and confused.

What did he mean? He said he had regard for her, and she was to be loved and cherished, yet he didn't want to be the one to love her? He'd enjoyed touching her. She was sure of that. Wasn't that evidence of his love? Did he think that he would meet someone better in England? He probably would. The ladies of the court were legendary for their wit and beauty. He would forget her as soon as he set foot on that ship, and all would be lost.

Louisa wandered through the garden, thoughts racing through her head. She had to make Tom love her. She just had to show him her devotion, then he would understand. If only she could do something to make him postpone his journey until spring. All she needed was a little more time. He was already smitten with her; she was sure of that. He just needed to realize that she was the perfect bride for him. Louisa smiled serenely as she bent down to smell a yellow rose. All the other blooms on the bush had already wilted, but not this one. It was resilient and persistent, as Louisa would be. A plan was already forming in her mind.

EIGHTEEN

The white spire of the church pierced the cloudless blue sky, the metal cross glinting in the sun. This church was different from the church the Whitfields and Sheridans attended in Jamestown. It was spacious and full of light, with arched windows lining the walls, shafts of light streaming through the glass onto the congregation. The church he'd gone to with his parents had been a low wooden building, with a dirt floor and rough benches for the parishioners. Here, the pews shone with polish, as did the floorboards and the pulpit, a smell of beeswax permeating the air.

Finn looked at the people filing into the church with undisguised interest. This was his first outing since he fled Jamestown nearly a week ago. He'd achieved some sense of balance at the farm, but going to church reminded him once again that this was a different world than the one he was used to. He wondered if the service would be familiar. Finn took a seat next to Jonah and glanced over at Abigail, who just entered. She walked next to her mother, her lace-edged tucker demurely covering her bosom above the bodice of her gown, her wide-brimmed hat shading her face. She caught his gaze and smiled, before responding to someone's greeting. Mrs. Mallory shepherded the younger girls inside, followed by Martha. Mr. Mallory brought up the rear, having stopped to speak with an acquaintance.

Finn allowed his mind to wander as the minister plunged with unconcealed zeal into the second hour of the sermon. He'd always hated going to church, but he'd give anything at this moment to be sitting next to Louisa and his parents in their parish church, his aunt and uncle behind them, Mrs. Dolly, Bridget and Minnie in the third pew. Were they thinking of him today as they went to church? Were they praying for him? The thought nearly made Finn cry, so he snuck a peek at Abbie to distract himself. It was only Jonah's jab in the ribs that reminded him to stand up and sing the hymn with the rest of the congregation.

Finn mouthed the familiar words, wishing the service would end. He looked forward to his walk with Abbie and tried to hide his smile as he noticed her looking at him from under her lashes. She blushed prettily, looking away in embarrassment. Finn suddenly wondered if Mr. Mallory would allow him to walk Abbie home. He didn't want to upset the man who'd been so kind to him. He resolved to ask his permission after the service. Yes, that would be the proper thing to do, but would that mean he was officially courting Abbie? Finn sat back down, agitated and confused. If he escorted a young woman home from church back home, everyone would assume that they were betrothed. Was that the case now as well? He didn't think so since Abbie wouldn't have been so quick to ask him to walk with her. He might not know the ways of this time, but she did. Finn resolved to stop worrying and just enjoy the rest of the day.

* * *

It turned out easier than expected. Abbie simply called out to her parents that she was walking home with Finn and led him away from the church before he had a chance to approach Mr. Mallory. The older man was engaged in a conversation with the minister and just waved at them absentmindedly, sending them on their way. Mrs. Mallory was chatting and laughing with a few other women while Sarah and Annie ran around the churchyard with other children, happy to play unsupervised for a few minutes before their parents shepherded them to the waiting wagons and took them home for Sunday dinner. Finn noticed Martha speaking to an older couple, who were her fiancé's parents, according to Abbie. They were smiling and nodding at her, obviously pleased with their son's choice. A young man approached them just as they started to walk away. Finn was surprised by the look of belligerence on his face. He sneered at Finn before removing his hat and giving Abbie a stiff bow.

"Shall I walk you home, Mistress Abigail? I'm sorry to have kept you waiting, but I had to assist my mother into the wagon." The young man gave her a searching look, obviously expecting her to leave Finn and walk off with him.

"Matthew Granville, this is Finlay Whitfield. I've invited him to walk me home today. I hope you don't object. He's new to the area and would like to see something of the countryside," she answered coyly, her arm still linked with Finn's. "I wish you a good day. Shall we go, Finn?"

As Abbie began to walk away, Finn glanced back just in time to see a look of naked fury on Matthew Granville's face. He wouldn't forget this insult in a hurry. Was he Abbie's beau, and if he were, what was she playing at? Finn gave Matthew a beatific smile and walked off with Abbie, hoping the walk home would be a very long one.

* * *

"What did you think of our church?" Abbie asked, walking close to Finn, but not touching. They were alone on the narrow road, ancient trees forming a green canopy over their heads; shafts of light piercing the foliage and dappling their faces with sunlight. The day was warm, but several trees were already beginning to change color, going from a lush green to vibrant red and orange. These woods would be ablaze with color within a few weeks, a chill creeping into the air to remind them that winter was just around the corner.

"It's nice, I suppose. Fancier than the church I went to with my family. The sermon was just as dull though," he chuckled, trying to get a little closer to Abbie.

"I like the minister," answered Abbie. "He's a Revolutionary. He even rides with the Militia from time to time. I admire that in a man of God."

"Really? Are you a Revolutionary, Abbie?" Finn was joking, but he was curious to hear her answer.

"Of course I am, as is anyone in their right mind." She gave Finn a look, daring him to challenge her sanity.

"Why is all this so important to you? That's all Jonah talks about when we're working. I'm not one for politics." Finn shrugged his shoulders, indicating his indifference.

"Then you are a fool, Finlay Whitfield. Freedom means everything. I was born here, as were my parents. Why should we be ruled by someone who's thousands of miles away? We are Americans and should be governed by Americans, chosen by the people. We should be free to rule ourselves."

This was a radically new idea to Finn, who'd only known the concept of monarchy up until last week. No king — what a thought. A government chosen by the people? These rebels were radicals. Finn wondered what his father would make of all this. Would he consider the Mallorys to be traitors or visionaries? It was an intriguing question. Amazing how differently people thought in this century.

Finn thought of something to say to change the subject. He didn't want to speak of the Revolution. He felt out of his depth since he was still trying to figure out all the aspects of this conflict between England and the American Colonies. Most of his information had come from Jonah, and he wasn't sure how much a fifteen-year-old boy really understood of what was happening.

"So, when is Martha's wedding?" he asked. Girls loved talking of weddings, so that should distract Abbie from her rebellious thoughts.

"Thanksgiving. We're hoping Sam will come home for the wedding." Finn was about to ask what Thanksgiving was but didn't want to make a fool of himself. It was probably some religious feast day.

"Is Martha's fiancé in the army as well? I was introduced to Gil's parents, but he wasn't there, was he?"

"Gil is with the Militia. Martha worries about him all the time. She'll have to stay with Gil's parents after the wedding until he comes back. It's not the best way to start married life, but some things are more important." Abbie looked up at Finn from under the brim of her hat. "I'm thirsty. There's a brook just over there. Let's go get a drink." She took Finn by the arm, leading him off the road into the woods.

The water in the brook was cold and sweet, a welcome respite for Finn's dry throat. He took a few large gulps, then joined Abbie on a fallen log. She turned her face up to the sun, enjoying the warmth of the October afternoon.

"I don't think Martha loves Gil. She's known him all her life, but I don't think she loves him. When I get married, I want to be in love," Abbie announced, watching Finn's face for a reaction.

"How do you know when you're in love?" asked Finn. Abbie seemed awfully knowledgeable about these things.

"You just do," she answered cryptically. "You can start out by kissing and see if that works."

"What do you mean?" Finn had never actually kissed anyone, so had no idea what she was talking about, but didn't want to seem ignorant.

"It feels different when you're in love, or so people say. It feels magical. That's why I don't think Martha loves Gil. I saw them kissing, and she didn't look as if she was enjoying it at all. She kept pulling back as Gil kept leaning forward until she nearly fell off the bench." Abbie giggled at the memory.

"Have you ever kissed anyone?" asked Finn, intrigued.

"Yes, once, but I didn't feel any magic. It felt like any old kiss. I want to know what it feels like, Finn."

She was looking at him with those lovely brown eyes, flecked with gold in the gentle sun. Finn leaned in for the kiss, praying that she wouldn't lean back like Martha. Abbie's lips were like velvet beneath his, soft and pliant. He drew her to him without thinking, kissing her with all his youthful enthusiasm. Abbie didn't lean back. She drew closer to Finn, wrapping her arms around his neck and pulling him to her. Finn wasn't sure if this was magical, but it sure was wonderful. He hoped she wouldn't notice his erection. He didn't want to offend her.

Abbie finally drew back, looking at Finn with wonder. Her lips were parted, her breath shallow and fast. Finn didn't dare say anything for fear of ruining the moment. Her tucker moved while they were kissing, exposing an extra inch of creamy skin. Finn tried not to stare but was desperate for a glimpse of her breast.

"So, what's the verdict?" he asked, trying to sound cavalier. "Any sparks?"

"Definitely," she breathed, leaning in for another kiss.

NINETEEN

Louisa Whitfield bit her lip in concentration as she composed the note. It had to be just right; not pleading and not overly demanding. She just wanted to meet Tom one more time before Charles took her home the following day. Just one more kiss was all she wanted. She smiled to herself, hoping it would be more than a kiss. Her whole body quivered every time she remembered Tom's fingers probing her so skillfully. She folded the note and slipped it under her pillow before saying her prayers and climbing into bed. She would pass the note to Tom at breakfast.

Louisa closed her eyes, replaying that afternoon's encounter. She shyly slid her hand into her nightdress, cupping her breast and running a thumb over her nipple. It didn't feel the same, but it was nice, so she closed her eyes, picturing Tom's face. She felt a strange sensation between her legs as she continued caressing her breast. What would it feel like to do what he had done? Would God punish her for being so wicked? He probably would, but Louisa was too curious to stop now. She slowly moved her hand down, sliding it between her legs. She tried to imitate what Tom had done. It felt new and exciting, and oh so good. She heard a noise outside and abruptly yanked her hand back, afraid of being caught. What she was doing had to be wrong. Men and women copulated to produce babies, so their union was blessed, but what she was doing was surely a sin. Besides, she wanted Tom to do it. She patted the note under her pillow and tried to sleep. Tomorrow was another day.

* * *

Louisa purposely chose a seat facing the window as she entered the parlor with her work basket. Annabel was already there, surrounded by a pile of garments that needed mending. Louisa couldn't concentrate on embroidering her chemise, so she offered to help Annabel with her sewing, choosing one of Harry's gowns. He still wore a long frock since he just turned one and wouldn't be allowed to wear breeches until he was fully toilet-trained and able to tie and untie the laces on his own. He was so sweet with his golden curls and blue eyes. Did Tom look like that when he was a child? Louisa allowed her mind to drift while she carefully mended the torn hem, looking up at the window periodically. What if he read the note but decided not to come?

Louisa finally spotted Tom in the garden and laid down her sewing, craning her neck to get a better look. She smiled sweetly at Annabel's look of surprise as she rose from her seat and nearly ran into the garden, going straight for the hedge. Tom came at just the right time, well before Annabel left to put Harry down for his nap. Louisa rounded the hedge, her heart beating wildly with anticipation. Tom stopped his pacing and smiled at her, pulling her into his embrace.

"I couldn't resist your summons. I was tormented by dreams of you last night," he whispered into her ear as he kissed her urgently, his hands cupping her buttocks. Louisa leaned into him, moving her hips against his, enjoying the sensation of his manhood hard against her pelvis. She pulled down her bodice slightly, pushing his head down to her breasts.

"Good God in Heaven! What's all this?" Annabel appeared behind the hedge, her face frozen in a mask of horror. "Louisa, cover yourself this instant, and you..." She was shaking with anger, her normally pale cheeks blazing with color. "How dare you touch her, you scoundrel? She's naught but a girl. Louisa, go in the house this minute. I would have a word with my brother in private."

Annabel scarcely looked at Louisa as the girl ran past her, so she didn't see the satisfied smile that lit up her face. Her plan had worked perfectly. Now all she had to do was wait for Annabel to tell Uncle Charles. She ran to her room and fell onto her bed, gleeful as only a fourteen-year-old girl could be.

TWENTY

Kit led the horses out of the stable, letting them graze at will. In the past, he would have given them some oats, but oats were in short supply and were to be saved for people. He'd muck out the stalls, then see to the rest of the livestock. Help was scarce these days. With Alec and Valerie gone, and Louisa caring for the baby, only Minnie and Bridget were on hand to help. Minnie had already milked the cows and taken the milk to the spring-house, and Bridget was last seen collecting eggs. She looked pale in the early light of the morning, circles under her eyes. Louisa had mentioned that Bridget had been unwell, but this was the first time Kit had noticed for himself. He offered to collect the eggs, urging Bridget to go get some breakfast and a hot drink. She argued for a while, but eventually relented, thanking him profusely. Kit didn't mind the work. It gave him something to do, especially since his mind was in a whirl.

He was still coming to terms with Louisa's revelations, trying to reconcile himself to the idea that his wife had lived four hundred years in the future. How was such a thing even possible? He asked her endless questions about life in the twenty-first century, grappling with the pictures her words painted. The things she described just seemed like fantastical fairy stories, products of a fertile imagination. He was mesmerized by descriptions of mechanical contraptions used to transport people at incredible speeds, and the notion of being able to use something called a "telephone" to speak to someone miles away. It was like magic.

However, what Kit found less than magical was the morality of the twenty-first century. Louisa informed him that young men and women began dating once they reached their teenage years and were frequently intimate with each other without the benefit of marriage. Women had children out of wedlock and were still respected and accepted by society, while men openly lived with numerous women without offering them their name or protection, not even if the women became pregnant with their offspring. The concepts of honor and duty had been entirely done away with, replaced with selfishness and indifference. Kit didn't think he'd like to live in such a world, no matter how technologically advanced it was.

Kit was polite to Frederick Taylor, but secretly wanted to strangle the man. Why did he have to drop into their lives, bringing such unexpected troubles? He wished he would just go away, but of course, he couldn't go back without his time-travel device. At least he made himself scarce, exploring the estate and chatting to Cook while she worked. He seemed to feel more comfortable in the kitchen, not that Kit blamed him. He was the source of all this trouble, and he knew it.

Kit's thoughts were constantly on Alec and Valerie, and especially Finn. Where was the boy? They hadn't come back in a week, so things weren't looking good. The longer they were gone, the less chance of finding Finn. Kit sighed, attacking the stall with renewed vigor. He was sweating profusely, his boots covered with muck, and his hair falling into his face. He'd need to clean up before he went back into the house. Louisa was fanatical about hygiene, especially since Evie was born. He smiled thinking of his daughter. She'd smiled at him when he held her that morning, something she'd never done before. He couldn't wait for her to start walking and talking. They would have many adventures together, just father and daughter.

The sound of hooves pounding dry earth distracted Kit from his thoughts, as he left the pitchfork leaning against the wall of the stable and came out into the chilly morning air. His heart leaped with joy at the thought of it being Alec and Valerie, but his hopes were quickly dashed when he made out the figure of Charles driving the trap with little Louisa seated beside him, holding on for dear life. Charles was driving like a madman; his hat jammed onto his head, his hair flying in the wind. The grim set of his mouth only confirmed Kit's suspicions that something was terribly wrong.

The trap came to an abrupt halt in front of the house as Charles jumped down, dragging Louisa with him. He'd never known Charles to be angry with his niece. He doted on her, teasing her and making her smile as he called her "petal".

"Where is my brother?" Charles snarled at Kit, pulling Louisa into the house. Kit forgot all about his dirty boots and followed them inside, anxious to see what all the fuss was about.

Mrs. Dolly and Bridget were already in the hall, gaping at Charles as he pushed Louisa into the parlor, motioning for Kit to follow. Charles slammed the door shut, turning to Kit. "Where is my brother? I urgently need to speak to him."

"Charles, you know Alec is not here. Can I help?" Kit looked over at Louisa, who sat demurely in a chair, her eyes downcast, a small smile playing on her lips. She didn't seem overly upset or worried. What had gotten Charles so worked up?

"You can tell me what to do with his daughter, who has dishonored herself with my brother-in-law. I'd like to have the foolish pup whipped for what he's done, but I wanted to consult Alec first. She's his daughter, so he should mete out the punishment." Charles was pacing the room, covering the space between the unlit hearth and the door in a few strides, then retracing his steps.

"Can you tell me what happened?" Kit turned in relief as his wife entered the room, her eyes full of anxiety. She'd handed over the baby to Bridget, who could be seen in the doorway, peering into the room, her eyes round with curiosity.

"Charles, what's happening? Louisa, are you all right?" The girl just nodded, refusing to meet her aunt's eyes.

"It seems my sweet little niece has been playing the whore to Tom. She's been meeting him behind a hedge in the garden, permitting him unspeakable freedoms. Annabel caught them at it yesterday afternoon but didn't tell me until this morning. I think she was afraid of my reaction. Well, she had every right to be. Tom denies any wrongdoing, but I think the evidence speaks for itself. She's been despoiled, and something must be done."

Kit never imagined Charles being this upset about anyone being deflowered, but he supposed this was different. Louisa was just a child, not yet fifteen. Her chances of a good marriage would be forever ruined if anyone found out about this transgression. There could be consequences. Maybe she was already with child.

"Wait a minute," his wife stepped in. "I would like to speak with my niece. In private," she spat out. "Please leave us. Charles, go to the kitchen and have a cup of ale. You seem in need of it. Kit, make sure he doesn't kill anyone." With that, Louisa pushed them out the door, turning to her niece.

"Sweetheart, are you hurt?" The girl shook her head, still not looking at her aunt. Her hands were demurely folded in her lap, but she didn't seem hurt or scared.

"Did he seduce you? I'll personally rip his bollocks off if he did anything to hurt you." Louisa now took over Charles' pacing route. "The cad. The absolute cad."

"Aunt Lou, Tom didn't do anything to hurt me," she said miserably.

"What exactly did Annabel see?"

"She saw him kissing me behind the hedge. My bodice was not exactly covering my bosom," replied Louisa.

"Exactly how much of it was actually covered?" asked her aunt, already guessing at the truth.

"Not very much."

"Did he touch you anywhere else, Louisa?" Having a teenage daughter was apparently difficult in any age, not just in the modern world.

"Just a little, but only with his hand. Aunt Lou, Charles fell in love with Annabel when she was fifteen, so I thought we could be betrothed for a while before we married. I know father would never allow me to be wed at fourteen, but maybe by sixteen. Where is father, anyway?"

"Your parents are not here at the moment. Uncle Kit and I will have to sort this out."

"What will happen, Aunt Lou? Charles wouldn't let me speak to Tom before he dragged me off this morning. I don't know how he feels. He hates me, most like." The girl began to cry, wiping her eyes with a hanky that she pulled out of her sleeve.

"What reason would he have to hate you? He's the one to blame for this mess. He's eighteen. He should have known better." Louisa realized just how ridiculous that sounded. What eighteen-year-old boy said no to some kissing and groping behind a hedge? Her niece was beautiful. With her dark curls, amber-colored eyes, and pouty lips, she would be desired by any young man, especially in a place where there weren't many young women to choose from.

"Sweetheart, why don't you go up to your room while I deal with Uncle Charles? He seems more distraught than you are," added Louisa with a chuckle, going across the hall to the kitchen, where Charles was nursing a cup of ale, glaring at Kit balefully.

"Charles, it seems nothing happened. Louisa is young and foolish, but she's still a maid. I think poor Tom deserves an apology." Louisa accepted a cup of ale as she sat down across from Charles.

"It's too late for that," said Charles quietly.

"What do you mean?" Kit and Louisa stared at Charles.

"I mean that I lost my temper. Several neighbors heard me shouting at Tom and saw me dragging Louisa from the house. The only thing that can save her from ruin is a betrothal. Otherwise, her reputation will be in shreds. Alec wouldn't forgive me that. With him not here, I'm her closest male relative. She will have to marry Tom, which is what she wanted in the first place, I think. I had no idea she'd grown into such a sneaky little minx." Charles drained his cup and slammed it onto the table. "I must go face my wife, her father, and the reluctant bridegroom."

"Charles, surely that isn't the only option. They both swear nothing happened." Louisa looked from Charles to Kit, who was rubbing his stubbly jaw.

"Louisa, I'm afraid Charles is right. The truth doesn't really matter. What matters is what people believe the truth to be. If people believe that something untoward occurred between Tom and Louisa, her reputation will be ruined. In a community as small and tight as Jamestown, everyone will know within the hour. Louisa will be shunned and ridiculed, her chances of a good marriage forever destroyed. Alec and Valerie wouldn't want that. We must have them betrothed as soon as possible." Kit put his hand on Louisa's arm, but she yanked it away.

"You must be joking. She is fourteen. This could only lead to disaster. I can't believe you're in favor of this, Kit." Louisa stormed out of the kitchen. This was ridiculous. Valerie would crucify them all when she got back for allowing this to happen. Damn Frederick Taylor for showing up on their doorstep. None of this would have happened had Finn not disappeared.

* * *

Louisa was still raging when Kit came into the room a half-hour later, cleaned up and carrying Evie. He handed the baby to Louisa, then sat down on the bed, watching as she unlaced her bodice, putting the baby to her breast.

"You look murderous," he said softly. "I was only stating the obvious."

"And what if this was Evie? Would you be so calm and rational?" Louisa demanded, still angry.

"Evie is an infant. I can't even conceive of her lying with someone, but I suppose I'd want to do whatever it took to protect her future and reputation. Louisa made her bed, my sweet. At least if she is truly still a maid, there's no need to rush to the altar. They can announce their betrothal and wait for Alec and Valerie to come back."

Louisa wasn't even sure why she was so angry. She knew that what Kit was saying was right. Kissing and touching might be perfectly acceptable for teens in the modern world, but here it was as good as actually having intercourse. It didn't matter that her niece was still a virgin. She was now tainted, and the only thing that could save her was a marriage to the man who despoiled her. Louisa had made her bed, and now she would have to lie in it with an unwilling husband, who might be full of resentment and anger. She didn't envy the girl. On the other hand, Tom should have known better, so he had no right to blame anyone.

Louisa sighed. She was thinking with her twenty-first

century brain, but Charles and Kit weren't. They knew the reality. Louisa only wished they could wait for Alec and Valerie to return. It didn't seem right to make a decision of such magnitude without them.

TWENTY-ONE

Charles felt slightly calmer by the time he stabled his horse and walked into the house. At least Kit had agreed with him, which took some of the responsibility off his shoulders. He only wanted to do what was right by his niece and, in turn, his brother. With Louisa staying at his house, it had been his responsibility to make sure that everything was above board, and he had failed miserably. He'd never expected sweet little Louisa to be so wanton. She'd always been such a beautiful child, loving and obedient. Charles momentarily thanked his lucky stars for having a son. Girls were too much trouble. He recalled his own courtship. True, he'd started courting Annabel when she was fifteen, but they didn't marry until she turned sixteen, and Charles had never laid a finger on her until their wedding night. He'd laid his fingers elsewhere, but not on his future bride.

Annabel was sitting in her favorite chair, viciously stabbing a needle through some needlework, her mouth compressed into a thin line. She hardly ever questioned his judgment outright, but the look on her face was enough to alert Charles to the fact that she was displeased and would not let matters rest until he set things to rights.

"Belle, are you angry with me?" Charles asked, coming to sit next to his wife, but not daring to touch her.

"Angry does not begin to describe it," she spat out. "What you did this morning was unforgivable. Simply unforgivable. Instead of handling the situation quietly and discreetly, you practically shouted from the castle walls that your niece and brother-in-law have been caught in a compromising position, ruining both their lives in the process. Louisa's reputation is now tainted, and Father has forbidden Tom to travel to England. Tom is devastated. Had you handled this with discretion, we might have avoided a scandal, sparing everyone involved. As it stands, we have no choice but to force a marriage." Annabel never looked at Charles during her monologue, continuing with her sewing as if her very life depended on it.

"Belle, you are right. I acted intemperately, but Louisa is my niece. I've known her since the day she was born, and I have a duty to her and my brother. If Tom wanted a bit of fun, he should have bedded a maid."

"Is that what you did?" Annabel was staring at him, her eyes narrowed in speculation. Charles had never told his wife of his youthful indiscretions, and now didn't seem like a good time to start.

"No, my sweet. You were my first love." Well, technically that was true, in the spiritual sense.

"Of course," Annabel said, rolling her eyes. "It's all right, Charlie. You don't have to lie to me. I know you've had other women, and I don't mind as long as it was before we were married. I suppose you are right. Tom should have picked someone else, but that doesn't excuse what you've done."

"No, it doesn't. Is Tom very angry with me? Louisa will make him a wonderful wife. She is beautiful, clever, and wealthy. What more can a young man want?" Charles got his answer directly from Tom, who walked into the room, a murderous look on his face.

"A young man might want the freedom to make his own choice. I'm not going to marry her, Charles," Tom said. "She's still a maid, and if she isn't, it certainly isn't my doing. I won't be forced into marriage over a few stolen kisses. Thanks to you, Father has forbidden me to go to England."

Charles rose to his feet, towering over his brother-in-law. Sometimes it was nice to be the tallest man in the room. "You will marry her, and you will consummate the marriage if I have to stand there holding a candle and giving instructions. A few kisses might have been overlooked, but from what I understand it was considerably more than that. She is naught but a naïve girl, but at eighteen, you should have known better. There are other ways to satisfy your needs without compromising my niece. And God help you if you try to run out on her, I will personally come to England and drag you back home. Is that understood?"

"I'm afraid he's right, son." Mr. Gaines entered the room, the sound of his walking stick punctuating his words. He looked stern as he spoke the words, but there was a twinkle in his eye that was hard to miss. "You must marry the girl. I'd marry her myself if I were fifty years younger. What a beauty she is. I can't blame you for losing your head."

Tom took a deep breath, trying to control his exasperation. "I'm not denying her beauty or charm. I just don't want to marry her right now. I want to go to England and see something of the world before I settle down and start a family."

"I'm afraid that ship sailed when you decided to slide your hand under her skirt," his father said with a smirk. "We'll have the banns read in church on Sunday, and you will be married in thirty days' time. And say thank you to Charles for not horse-whipping you. I would have whipped any man who dared to touch my darling Annabel. Charles knew that, didn't you, Charlie?" The old man chuckled, winking at Charles before turning back to his son. "With any luck, you'll give me a grandchild to dawdle on my knee before God sees fit to take me. I'd like a granddaughter as pretty as Louisa. Do you think you can manage that?"

Tom just looked at all of them with disgust before striding out of the room. Charles had to admit that he felt sorry for him.

TWENTY-TWO

The morning was dreary and cool, a steady mist coating everything with a patina of moisture. Drops of dew rolled off the leaves, falling like tears onto the dirt of the street and mixing with mud already churned by hooves and wheels of passing carts. A huge pile of fresh manure lay in the middle of the road, steaming in the chilly air. Valerie shivered, pulling the hood of her cloak over her head as she stepped from the inn. She had to admit that she was glad to leave the place. She'd have nothing but sad memories of the week they'd spent in eighteenth-century Jamestown.

Mr. Carson was already waiting downstairs, his horses stomping their hooves restlessly and tossing their heads to avoid the drizzle falling into their eyes. The back of the wagon was loaded with barrels, leaving just enough room for Alec to sit. The man gave Valerie a friendly smile as Alec helped her up onto the bench. She was grateful not to have to sit on the dirty straw of the wagon, but quickly realized that Alec might have gotten the better part of the deal. Mr. Carson was inclined to talk, and talk he did, without pausing to hear the answers. Judging by his attire and general lack of grooming, Valerie assumed that the man was either a bachelor or a widower. His coat was torn in several places; his boots were filthy, and his hat was bent out of shape in several places, making him look quite disreputable. He could, however, be a source of information, so Valerie settled in to listen patiently.

"Good morning, Mrs. Whitfield. A pleasure to make your acquaintance," Mr. Carson said, tipping his hat to Valerie before taking up the reins. "I think you will find Williamsburg to your liking, ma'am. Your husband tells me that you're searching for your son. Well, let me tell you, if I were a young man looking for adventure that's where I would go. Of course, I would probably join the Continental Army, but if I couldn't, Williamsburg would be my choice. Teeming with life, it is.

"There's lots of entertainment to be found. Not of the disrespectable kind, my dear lady. There are run-ins between the Lobsterbacks and the inhabitants of the town, not to mention the attacks on the Royalists. Those are always good for a bit of fun. Nothing like watching some poor sod dragged from his house in the middle of the night and humiliated in front of the crowd. Most of the time they get off with just bruised pride, but sometimes things do turn ugly. Goes further than a bit of a lark, it does. Some people are just baying for blood. Leave the poor merchants alone, I say. Direct your energies toward the military. What good is attacking a banker or a butcher, I ask you?"

Mr. Carson scratched his head, either confused by lack of common sense shown by the Tories in attacking the merchants or plagued by lice. He jammed his hat back on his head and continued, giving Valerie a nearly toothless smile.

"On the whole, Williamsburg is a rebel town in my opinion. His Excellency, General Washington himself, got his surveyor's license from the College of William and Mary, did you know that? It's one of the finest institutions of learning in these here Colonies. Has a Royal Charter and all. General Washington was just a young lad at the time, but we are proud of the association all the same. Some of the best legal minds of the colony have been educated there." Mr. Carson seemed to be warming to this theme, so Valerie decided to cut in.

"Tell me Mr. Carson, would there be a place in Williamsburg where we can trade some valuables for money? We haven't been in Virginia long, so I would appreciate any insight you could give me on the currency of the colony."

"Ah, there you might have a problem, my dear Mrs. Whitfield. You are better off holding on to your valuables. The paper currency is only worth as much as the people's trust in the government, and that changes from day to day. Mr. Randolph himself had signed all the new notes to authenticate them, with 'Death to Counterfeit' printed on the back, but that doesn't stop the forgers, no ma'am. There are many counterfeit notes circulating throughout the colony, so most people still prefer to get paid in coin. Silver is silver, but paper is only good for wiping your arse with, if you'll pardon my saying so, if it's not backed by anything. Lots of people still prefer the barter system. At least you get something of value for your pains, not just a worthless piece of paper with a signature. Do you know of a place to stay?"

"No, we would be most grateful if you could recommend a respectable inn." Valerie wiped the moisture off her face, wishing it would stop drizzling. It was such a miserable morning, much like her mood. Alec sat quietly in the back of the wagon, his eyes closed. He wasn't sleeping, but fatigue was etched into the lines of his face, suddenly making him look older.

"There are several inns on Duke of Gloucester Street. There's the White Hart, and the King's Arms, and Shield's Tavern. That's where I'm headed, as a matter of fact. The proprietors are good friends of mine, and will give you a clean room and meals, should you desire it. The taproom tends to get somewhat rowdy in the evenings, but not a British soldier in sight. They don't frequent the place. And they do have the best beer, if I might be permitted to say so. After all, it's provided by yours truly." Mr. Carson's laugh sounded like the opening and closing of a creaky door. So that's what was in the barrels.

Thankfully, the ride to Williamsburg wasn't a long one, and the outskirts of the town began to appear on the horizon. Valerie turned slightly, watching Alec as they drove into the town. Mr. Carson was still blathering on about something, but she was curious to see her husband's reaction. Despite his anxiety about Finn, Alec was excited to be in the future. He was drinking everything in, analyzing the changes and familiarizing himself with the politics of the time. Alec looked around with great interest as the wagon rumbled down the street.

Duke of Gloucester Street was the main street of the town and was lined on both sides with a variety of buildings. Some of them were built of wood, but others were built of brick, looking solid and prosperous compared to the primitive structures of seventeenth-century Jamestown. Most of the buildings had shops on the ground floor, boasting everything from a wig maker to a jeweler. The impressive façade of the Capitol building could be seen at the end of the street, with it being the tallest structure in the town. The street was teeming with wagons and carriages, and people darted between the contraptions to cross the street. Many well-dressed ladies and gentlemen walked on the sidewalk, giving the town an air of prosperity. Shops were everywhere, selling foodstuffs, bolts of fabric, hats, and even books. They passed a printer's storefront, followed by a chemist. Valerie wondered what eighteenth-century medicine was like compared to their own time. Surely, it wasn't as primitive. It might be a good idea to stop in at the chemist to see if she could find something useful to take home.

Shield's Tavern was everything Mr. Carson said it would be. The taproom was crowded with patrons, but the rooms upstairs were clean and bright, with canopied beds and gaily painted ceramic pitchers and ewers on the nightstand. There were even clean towels, and a copper bathtub could be made available upon request, for an extra consideration. The meals were served in the downstairs dining room, which was thankfully quieter than the taproom. They would make the inn their home while searching for Finn. The location was ideal, being at the very center of town.

Alec helped Mr. Carson unload his shipment to thank him for the lift to Williamsburg while Valerie went up to their room. She felt a nagging misery as she took off her damp cloak and sat down, hands in her lap. Compared to Jamestown, Williamsburg was booming. According to Mr. Carson, there were several thousand inhabitants, half of whom were Negro slaves, plus the people coming and going to and from the surrounding areas. How would they find Finn? It was like looking for a needle in a haystack, assuming the needle was even there. Maybe Finn had come by here, but who is to say he remained? He might have been intimidated by the place and moved on. *Oh Finn, where are you?*

Valerie closed her eyes, trying to feel something, some gut feeling telling her whether Finn was close, but all she felt was a vast emptiness, yawning like a chasm inside her soul. She'd lost her son, was separated from her daughter, missing her sister, and completely at a loss as to what to do. Alec seemed optimistic about coming here, but Valerie didn't share his enthusiasm. She had no idea what to do if they failed to find Finn.

TWENTY-THREE

Finn suffered through the church service, buoyed by the promise of another walk with Abbie. He'd relived their kiss all week, hoping that there would be more where that came from. All his attempts to catch Abbie alone during the week failed as he was working in the field, while Abbie was at home helping her mother with household chores. Finn went back to the stile several evenings in a row, hoping that Abbie would join him, but Mrs. Mallory had been under the weather and needed help washing the dishes after supper and putting the younger children to bed. Abbie threw Finn an apologetic look as she cleared the table and swept the floor, as the little ones begged for a story before bedtime.

Today was his chance. Mrs. Mallory was feeling better, and even promised them some apple pie for dessert after Sunday dinner. Finn had never had apple pie, but anything combining pie and apples couldn't be half bad, so he was looking forward to sampling this new dish. Mrs. Mallory sat next to Martha, listening to the service with rapt attention, and nodding in agreement with the minister. Abbie sat between Annie and Sarah, looking pious and demure. The girls were getting fidgety, tired of the long sermon. Finn did catch Abbie glancing at him a few times, but she quickly looked away after giving him a little smile. Finn assumed that Abbie would allow him to walk her home again after the service, but he was in for a surprise when Matthew Granville stepped in to escort Abbie home.

Abbie looked flustered as Finn approached, giving her a questioning look. Did she want him to walk away or was she in need of rescue? Finn nodded to Matthew Granville in greeting, unsure of how to proceed.

"Well, if it isn't Finlay Whitfield, the hired help," sneered Matthew at the sight of Finn, sarcasm dripping like venom from his lips. "Hope the work is not too much for you, Whitfield." There was something smug and arrogant about Matthew Granville, and the look he was giving Finn was decidedly belligerent.

"I think I'm up to the task but thank you for your concern all the same. Are you ready to go, Abbie?" Finn asked, knowing full well he was provoking a scene. He'd be damned if he allowed this insufferable prig to walk Abbie home.

"The young lady will walk with me, sir," Granville said stiffly, his cheeks growing red with indignation.

"Why don't we let the young lady decide for herself, *sir?*" replied Finn with mock politeness. "I think Abbie knows her own mind." He gave Abbie what he thought was a winning smile. If there's anything he'd learned about Abbie was that she had her own opinions and needed them to be heard and respected. Abbie had just opened her mouth to reply when Granville cut her off.

"A respectable young lady is always happy to defer to the judgment of a man, sir, and in this case, she will agree with my opinion that she's better off escorted by someone who has serious intentions toward her rather than a day laborer who has nothing to offer her but grievous insult."

Finn didn't bother to reply. His fist met Granville's nose

with a satisfying crunch, as the boy fell on his arse into the mud with a yowl of pain. A thin trickle of blood flowed from his injured nose into his mouth, staining his teeth red. Some blood dripped onto his snowy stock, infuriating Granville further. He wiped his nose with the back of his hand, staring at the blood in disbelief.

"You scoundrel!" Matthew Granville roared his face puce with rage. "Abbie, come here this instant. I forbid you to associate with this vile ruffian."

Finn nearly laughed at the expression on Granville's face. What an arrogant prick. He'd just hammered a nail into his own coffin by trying to tell Abbie what to do. Finn averted his eyes from Matthew's face, watching Abbie's reaction from under his lashes. Her cheeks turned a lovely shade of pink as she took in what Matthew had just said. She looked as if she was about to say something she would regret later, but changed her mind, turning up her nose at Granville instead.

"I'm terribly sorry, Matthew, but as Finn pointed out, I think I can decide for myself, and I've just decided to allow him to walk me home. Good day to you, Mr. Granville." With that, Abbie slid her arm through Finn's, turning to him with a charming smile. "I'm ready now, Mr. Whitfield."

Finn turned away for a second to hide his twitching lips from Abbie, suddenly catching the eye of Mr. Mallory, who had been watching the argument along with every other member of the congregation still in the churchyard. The older man gave Finn a mischievous wink before handing his wife into the wagon. Finn smiled happily. He'd won this round against Granville, and the approval of Mr. Mallory. This was turning out to be a very good day indeed.

TWENTY-FOUR

The sweetness of Abbie's lips on his was still fresh in Finn's mind as he mucked out the stable on Monday morning. He'd been right to appeal to Abbie's independence of spirit. She was no meek girl who needed to be told what to do. She was feisty and smart, and wanted a man who appreciated that in her. Finn had plenty of experience of feisty women, so he recognized the signs. Neither his mother nor Aunt Louisa liked being bossed around, and they spoke their mind completely unafraid of their husbands. Sometimes Finn had been surprised by the men's patience. Finn knew plenty of men in Jamestown who would not have hesitated to punish their wives for such impertinence, but his father usually just smiled and heard his mother out with consideration and respect, as did Uncle Kit. Charles' wife never spoke out against him, but Finn had seen her give Charles a look that stopped him in mid-sentence, so she had the power to influence him as well.

As Finn got older, he realized that dealing with women was not as straightforward as he expected. They were much more complicated than most men gave them credit for, as Abbie had demonstrated yesterday. Knocking the irritating Matthew

Granville onto his arse had certainly fanned the flames of Abbie's ardor, with Finn reaping the benefits. She let him kiss her until she was breathless. Her cheeks were pink, and her eyes shone with affection as they finally drew apart, reluctantly heading home. They would be missed if they didn't return soon. Mr. Mallory was no fool. He'd been a young man himself once, and Finn didn't want to cause offense.

"Ooooowww," Jonah yelled as he crumpled onto the barn floor in a heap after jumping off the ladder leading up to the hayloft. "I've broken my leg." He was rolling on the ground clutching his ankle, and whimpering like a little girl.

"Let me see," said Finn, prying Jonah's hands away from his injured leg. Finn gently examined Jonah's ankle, ignoring his pitiful cries. "You didn't break it. You just sprained it. Here, let me help you up. That happened to me before. You just need to stay off it for a few days."

Jonah gave him a suspicious look. "Are you certain it's not broken? A broken ankle could take months to heal." He put a little weight on his leg experimentally, yowling in pain again.

"I'm certain. Let's get you back to the house. Your mother will just tell you to lie down and give you something good to eat. That's what my mother used to do when I hurt myself." Finn felt his chest constrict at the thought of his mother, so he turned to Jonah, needing something else to focus on. "Lean on me and walk slowly."

It took them nearly a half-hour to walk back to the farmhouse. Jonah was walking so slowly, Finn almost wished he could carry him. *So, you'll be joining the Continental Army, you big chicken*, Finn thought as he dragged Jonah toward the house. *I only hope your brother and his compatriots are more courageous than you, or your whole enterprise is doomed.* He was glad to be relieved of his burden, sitting Jonah on a bench as the women gathered around him, clucking like hens. Jonah was given a piece of freshly baked bread, spread with butter and honey, and some chicory coffee to wash it down with. He looked much happier, munching on his breakfast, and enjoying the ministrations of his mother and sisters.

"Looks like you won't be coming with me, Jonah," Mr. Mallory said, walking into the house. He was dressed for traveling, in his best coat and hat, the wagon already outside. "Have you ever been to Williamsburg, Finn?"

"No, sir. I'd be happy to accompany you if you're in need of help." Finn suddenly wanted nothing more than to go to Williamsburg. He longed to see something of this new world he'd landed in, and both Jonah and Abbie had mentioned the town several times. The only town Finn had ever seen was Jamestown, and that had been more of a small settlement, built entirely of wood and punctuated by narrow, muddy streets. Seeing this town they kept talking about would be very interesting.

"Have you had your breakfast yet?" Finn hadn't eaten, but he was afraid Mr. Mallory would leave without him. The older man saw his hesitation and laughed. "Eat your fill, son. Williamsburg will still be there two hours from now. I wouldn't say no to some coffee and porridge myself. It's getting colder out there, and there's nothing like warm porridge in your belly on a cold morning."

Mr. Mallory took off his coat and hat, sitting down at the table next to Jonah and reaching for the honey as his wife put a bowl of porridge in front of him. Finn was grateful for the chance to eat. He was always hungry, no matter how much he ate. Thankfully, the Mallorys all had good appetites and his gluttony didn't draw much attention. For a skinny lad, Jonah could put away an incredible amount of food, especially after working all day. Poor Mrs. Mallory seemed to spend most of her time either cooking or doing the washing. Finn had always taken it for granted that his parents had servants, but in the Mallory house, everything was done by Mrs. Mallory and the girls. They worked from dawn till dusk, cooking, washing, baking, mending, and doing some farm chores. Their only free time was the hour or so after supper when they sat companionably by the fire, reading, sewing, or simply talking.

Finn had noticed a few Negro slaves. Some of them had driven their masters to church, but hadn't come in. Jonah said they had their own services separate from the white folk. Finn tried not to stare, but he'd never seen Negros, and was fascinated by them. He wondered if they were happy to be rescued from the wilds of Africa and brought here to serve white men, or if they were resentful like the Indians, hating the whites who oppressed them. Would there be any Negros in Williamsburg? Did they just walk around the town the way Indians used to stroll through the settlements before the March attack? He wanted to ask Mr. Mallory but changed his mind. The less ignorance he showed, the better. The man already thought that he came from some backwoods; there was no need to confirm his suspicions. Finn had been educated well and chafed at the notion of being thought ignorant. Either way, the trip to Williamsburg would be an education.

TWENTY-FIVE

Alec opened his eyes to find the room already bright with morning light. Valerie always insisted on leaving the shutters open, claiming that she felt entombed by the impenetrable darkness. She liked to see moonlight streaming through the window as she fell asleep, and to wake up to a room bathed in sunshine. Alec didn't mind. He'd gotten used to her eccentricities over the years.

They'd slept a little later today, probably due to the good food and the comfortable bed. Their inquiries didn't lead anywhere the day before, but today was another day, and they'd start fresh. Alec had an idea that he wanted to discuss with Valerie, but it could keep until later. He looked over at his sleeping wife. Valerie looked slightly more relaxed after a good night of sleep. She'd been so agitated that he was worried for her. Alec knew she blamed herself. She should have listened to her gut instinct and sent the old man away, but she allowed him to stay, setting off this chain of events. Poor Louisa probably felt even worse, knowing she'd talked Valerie into letting the man stay. Alec could understand her motivation. Had he been in her place, he would have needed time to think things over as well.

Valerie stirred, opening her eyes and gazing at Alec. She actually smiled, so Alec decided to try his luck and reached for her, pulling her close. They hadn't made love since the day Finn vanished, and he was hungry for her and the release only her body could provide. He slid his hand up her thigh, but Valerie pushed his hand away. "I'm sorry, Alec. I just can't. I can't make love while our son is missing. I hope you understand." She jumped out of bed, looking for her clothes.

"Valerie, please come back. This has nothing to do with Finn, and everything to do with us. Making love doesn't mean that we love him any less. I miss you." Alec hoped his plea would change Valerie's mind, but he seemed to aggravate her further. Her movements were jerky as she grabbed her stockings off the chair where they'd been drying by the fire.

"I just can't, okay? Rolling around in bed while Finn is God knows where just feels like a betrayal. I know it doesn't make sense, but that's how I feel right now. I simply can't relax. I feel like a wound-up spring." She turned her back to him, pulling on stockings and stepping into shoes. Alec didn't know what a wound-up spring felt like, but he knew that talking to Valerie while she was in this kind of mood was pointless. It wouldn't get him anywhere.

Alec had to admit that he felt frustrated with Valerie's lack of affection. She wasn't the only one suffering, but sometimes she made him feel as if he didn't care as much about Finn as she did. As a man, he'd been taught to keep a tight rein on his feelings, and he was doing so now for his wife's benefit. He didn't want her to see his panic or helplessness. It would only upset her further. He needed to be strong for her and make her believe that he had some kind of plan, or at least an idea for finding their son. With every day that passed without finding Finn their chances grew slimmer, making Alec feel sick with dread.

"I'll see you downstairs," he said, pulling on his own clothes and walking out the door. He needed a drink.

The taproom was nearly empty at this time of the morning, so Alec took a seat, meaning to order a tankard of ale, but realized just in time that he had no money. That made him even angrier. He felt dejected and miserable, angry at himself, at Valerie, and most of all at Finn for getting himself into this situation. He thought of going for a walk to release some of his frustration, but he didn't want to worry Valerie by disappearing without a word. He'd just have to wait for her to come downstairs.

"May I join you?" the other man at the bar asked, waiting patiently for Alec to reply. Alec didn't want company at the moment, but it seemed churlish to turn the man down, so he nodded curtly. The man took a seat, signaling the barkeep for drinks. Alec began to protest, but the main raised his hand to silence him. "Allow me to buy you a drink. You seem in need of one."

"I suppose I am," replied Alec. "I'm Alexander Whitfield."

"Alfred Hewitt. I was meant to meet someone, but they seem to be running rather late. I thought it would be nicer to have a drink with someone rather than by myself. You're not from around here, Mr. Whitfield?"

"Strictly speaking, no," Alec replied cautiously. He didn't care to be questioned by the stranger.

"Have you recently arrived from England, perhaps?" the man asked. Alec had a sudden urge to tell him that he'd lived in Virginia for the past one hundred and fifty years but fought the impulse. The man would simply think him mad.

"No, Mr. Hewitt. I live some miles from Jamestown. And what about you? Do you live here in Williamsburg?" He didn't care where the man lived but wanted to deflect the man's interest in his past.

"No, I come here from time to time to meet with my

associates. I don't spend much time at home since my wife passed, and both my sons are in the Continental Army. Do you have children, Mr. Whitfield?"

"Yes. As a matter of fact, my wife and I are here looking for our son." Alec felt strangely reluctant to tell the stranger that Finn was missing, despite the fact that he might know something of his whereabouts.

"Ran away and joined the army, did he? That's what half the young men in Virginia are doing these days." The man finished his ale and set his empty tankard on the table, wiping his mouth delicately with a handkerchief.

"My son didn't join the army. He's too young. Please excuse me, Mr. Hewitt. I must return to my wife, and thank you for the drink."

"Good luck finding your boy," the man called after Alec as he walked out of the taproom.

* * *

Alec and Valerie left the inn shortly after. Neither one mentioned anything about their tiff in the morning, preferring to focus on finding Finn. Valerie liked Alec's idea, but she needed supplies. Alec suggested that Valerie, who was a proficient artist, draw a likeness of Finn and take it to the printing shop they saw on their way to the inn. They could print some broadsheets and hang them up all over town. Maybe someone, or even Finn himself, would see them and come forward. The idea made Valerie strangely sad, reminding her of the pictures of missing children on milk cartons. Were any of those children ever found? Most likely not.

Valerie suddenly stopped, catching sight of her reflection in a shop window. She hardly recognized herself. The woman who stared back was rigid with tension, her mouth compressed into a thin line and a deep furrow between her brows. She looked like someone who'd recently suffered a bereavement and was just putting one foot in front of the other in the hope that eventually she would relearn how to walk.

Valerie was momentarily shocked. This would never do. She was not some weakling who gave up at the first sign of trouble. They hadn't found Finn yet, but they would. Alec's idea was a great one. Pictures on milk cartons might not have always worked in a country of millions, but Williamsburg was a town of several thousand inhabitants, so the haystack was considerably smaller, making that needle just a little bit easier to find.

Valerie straightened her shoulders, forced her face to relax and smiled at her reflection. There, that was better. She looked up at Alec, who was watching her with concern. She'd been selfish and self-absorbed, taking her frustrations out on him when he was trying his best to find Finn while dealing with her grief. She'd make it up to him, just as soon as she got some paper and ink and drew a portrait of their son.

"How will we pay for the printing, Alec?" Valerie looked over at him, already concentrating on the details of the plan. They still hadn't managed to convert their valuables into money. Alec had brought some silver coins, but living in seventeenth-century Virginia, they hadn't used any currency other than tobacco in years. Anything could be bought or traded for bags of tobacco, so no other money was necessary.

"I'll try using some of the coins I have from the past. You heard what Carson said. People prefer silver to paper money, so they might be eager to take the silver coins, even if they are out of date. It's worth a try. If that doesn't work, there's a jeweler's shop just down the street. I'll see what the proprietor is willing to pay for my ring. Don't worry, Valerie. I'll see to it."

"I know you will." She was already looking for a place to buy some paper and ink. She supposed they should try the Post Office since they were sure to find some paper there. They would also need some quills. A quill wasn't ideal for drawing a portrait, but it would have to do. At least it would provide clean lines, which would show up well on the printed copies. Valerie slid her arm through Alec's as they walked down the Duke of Gloucester Street. She had to admit that she felt better. Taking action was always the best antidote to helplessness.

TWENTY-SIX

Finn looked around with undisguised curiosity as the wagon rumbled into Williamsburg. He's never seen a city this size before. Some of the buildings were made of wood, but were built in a different style than the ones in seventeenth-century Jamestown. Several others were tall and imposing, made of red brick and punctuated by large windows, now blazing in the brilliant morning sun. They passed the church and the Court House as they made their way down the Duke of Gloucester Street. Finn gaped at the glass storefronts as the wagon made slow progress down the congested street. He'd never seen so many shops. They sold all kinds of wonderful things; things that he would have loved to explore at length.

"What's that building over there, Mr. Mallory?" Finn asked, pointing across a stretch of grass.

"Why, that's the Governor's Palace, son. Impressive, isn't it?" Mr. Mallory smiled at Finn's enthusiasm, slowing down the wagon to let him have a better look.

"Is the governor there now?" Finn asked, trying to imagine what it must be like to live in such splendor. The palace was large enough to accommodate a hundred people, if not more.

"He's not been there for some time," answered Mr. Mallory cryptically. Now that he mentioned it, the palace did seem somewhat quiet. The building looked more like a mausoleum than a residence that must house dozens of people. There didn't seem to be sentries at the gates and the large yard in front of the palace was deserted. Finn shrugged his shoulders, turning his attention back to the busy street.

Looking at the passersby, Finn was once again grateful to Mrs. Mallory for giving him some clothes. He would have looked decidedly out of place in his leather doublet and knee breeches with garters. Thankfully, he hadn't been wearing a ruff when he activated the device. No one wore those anymore. Finn liked the style of dress popular during this time. The triangular hats were kind of ridiculous, but the narrower breeches worn with waistcoats and coats looked manlier in his opinion. He spotted a few men wearing wigs. These wigs weren't like the ones he saw back home. They weren't long and curly, but rather more coifed and usually white; the hair tied back with a ribbon. Why would anyone want to wear a wig when they had perfectly good hair of their own? Mr. Mallory didn't wear one, but then he was a farmer and not a gentleman.

Finn transferred his attention to the ladies. The modern gowns weren't as radically different as the men's attire, but he did notice that most women wore a tucker like the Mallory women, using it to cover the flesh above the bodice. The wealthier women had ones made of lace, but the poorer ones wore simple cotton. They also wore wide-brimmed hats with shallow crowns, sometimes right over their mob caps, which looked kind of odd in his opinion. Most of the white women were followed by Negro slaves as they did their marketing. The slaves walked respectfully behind their mistresses, carrying the shopping baskets and keeping their eyes fixed on the ground. The ladies barely paid attention to the slaves, going about their business as if they were alone.

Mr. Mallory reined in the horses in front of an inn, a wooden sign depicting a fat man flanked by a ham and a chicken and reading Shield's Tavern, creaking in the wind. He threw the reins to a young boy and bid Finn to follow him inside. It was close to noon, so the taproom was swarming with patrons, drinking large tankards of ale, and sharing news and gossip with relish. A thin man of middle years sat in the corner, surveying the scene with interest. His graying hair was tied back with a ribbon, his clothes austere, but clean and well-made. He had a plate of something in front of him, dipping pieces of bread into the gravy and slowly putting them in his mouth, his dark eyes never leaving the door. John Mallory slid onto a bench across from the man, smiling in greeting.

"Sorry we're late, Alf. Jonah took a bit of a spill, so Finn came with me instead. Finlay, this is my brother-in-law, Mr. Alfred Hewitt." Finn bowed to the man, instantly recognizing his voice. He was the man with John Mallory the other night. Now that he saw his face, he could detect a slight resemblance to Mrs. Mallory, but her face was much kinder, her dark eyes full of warmth and humor. Alfred Hewitt made him feel as if he were looking straight into his soul, trying to extract every wicked thought and possible sin. The man should have been a minister.

"Finlay, Mr. Mallory and I have some urgent business to discuss. Would you do me a kindness and run to the print shop down the street? Just tell the printer to include the following announcement in next week's Gazette." Alfred Hewitt spoke with quiet authority, obviously used to being obeyed. He handed Finn a folded sheet of paper before he even agreed to go, already turning his attention back to his brother-in-law.

"Shall I tell him it came from you, sir?" Finn asked, glancing at Mr. Mallory. He didn't like this man treating him like a servant.

"No names are necessary. He'll know what to do. Just tell

him it's for the Committee, and to put it on our account." There it was again—the mention of the committee. He'd have to find out more, but he couldn't ask outright. He'd have to steer Jonah in that direction and see if the lad would divulge something useful.

"Finn, we don't have to leave for some time yet, so you can visit some of the shops if you like," suggested Mr. Mallory kindly, obviously aware of Finn's displeasure at being treated like an errand boy. "Just don't take too long about it. Now, off with you."

Finn quickly left the inn, glad to have a little time on his own. He'd drop off the notice, then take a quick walk around, taking in the sights. The print shop was just down the street next to the Post Office, as Mr. Hewitt said. A bell tinkled somewhere above the door as Finn entered the premises, announcing his arrival. Finn gave the note to the man behind the counter, waiting patiently while the printer read it, and enjoying the smell of paper and ink. He wondered what kinds of things were printed in the back room of the shop. All the pamphlets and tracts on the counter looked highly respectable, but they must be printing seditious articles as well, judging by Mr. Hewitt's patronage and association with the mysterious Committee. Finn expected some questions, but the man just pushed his spectacles to the top of his bald head after he finished reading the notice and nodded in under-standing.

"Very good, young man. It will be in the next edition." The man gave him a curt nod and retreated into the back room, their business obviously concluded.

Finn left the shop and turned right, eager to see what inter-esting shops the street might have. He didn't have any money, but that didn't matter. He just wanted to see what new and wonderful things this century had to offer. He wished he could find some books on astronomy. It had always been a favorite subject of his. He couldn't pay for a book, but maybe they'd let him look.

Finn walked the length of the street, stopping into a few places. He didn't find a book shop, but there were plenty of other things to see. He eventually turned back, walking briskly back to the tavern. The smell of freshly baked bread and brewing coffee from Carlton's Coffeehouse reminded him that he hadn't eaten since breakfast, and he hoped that Mr. Mallory would offer him something to eat before they left for the farm. It was hours till supper, and he was already hungry.

"There you are," exclaimed Mr. Mallory as he spotted Finn entering the tavern. "Come and have some dinner. This beef is rather good, but don't tell Mrs. Mallory. She likes to think no one can make boiled beef as good as hers." Mr. Mallory winked at Finn as he pushed a plate of beef and half a loaf of bread toward him. The beef was good, and he enjoyed his meal as John Mallory talked of the family and Martha's upcoming wedding. Whatever private business they had was obviously concluded. Mr. Hewitt appeared somewhat less frosty than before, thanking Finn for delivering the notice and asking him a few questions about himself. He told Finn about his own sons, clearly proud of them for joining the army.

"We'd best be off now. Good to see you Alfred. Keep me informed and thank you for the meal." John Mallory put on his hat and made for the door. The place was getting more crowded by the minute, patrons coming in for their dinner and a drink. "I just have to fetch a few things for Mrs. Mallory, and then we'll be on our way. I'd like to get back before nightfall. With both of us gone all day and Jonah laid up with his ankle, I'm sure there's lots to do before supper."

"Yes, sir," Finn mumbled as he followed Mr. Mallory out of the tavern. He had to admit that he was glad Jonah twisted his ankle. Coming to Williamsburg had been an education, and Finn hoped that maybe Mr. Mallory would bring him again. He only wished he had some money so that he could get something for Abbie; just a little trinket or a ribbon to show his affection. Then he suddenly remembered the bracelet he brought for Minnie. He still had it, wrapped in his old shirt and hidden under the bed with his tomahawk. He'd give it to Abbie next time he got her alone.

Thinking of Abbie made him smile. She was the only bright spot in this incomprehensible adventure that had befallen him. Without her, he would be totally desolate, despite the kindness of the Mallorys. He glanced down the street, noting a tall man stepping out of the Post Office. He was too far away to see his face clearly, but something about his posture, coloring, and profile reminded Finn of his father. If only. He sighed and looked away, suddenly miserable.

TWENTY-SEVEN

Satisfied with her drawing at last, Valerie handed it to Alec for his opinion. They'd retreated to the coffeehouse after purchasing the supplies, assuming it wouldn't be too busy at midday. Valerie chose a table by the window, which gave her a flat surface to draw on and plenty of light. Alec had used one of his silver coins to pay for the paper and ink, and the clerk at the Post Office actually gave him change in the form of paper notes. Alec examined them carefully before stuffing them into his purse, having never used paper money before. All the same, it gave them a little cash and Valerie eagerly ordered some coffee to sip as she worked on her drawing. She hadn't had proper coffee since she left the twenty-first century, and although this coffee wasn't nearly as strong or flavorful, it still tasted like the elixir of the gods to her. She asked for a second cup as Alec studied the drawing carefully.

"It's a good likeness. I think it will help. Let's take it to the print shop now. Maybe they can even print it today if they're not too busy. How many copies do you think we might need?" Alec rolled up the drawing into a tube and tied it with a piece of string to prevent it from getting creased.

Valerie hadn't thought of that. How many copies did they need? Should they start small or plaster the whole town with broadsheets? "Why don't we ask for fifty and then see if we need more later?" she suggested. Alec nodded, already rising from the bench, the rolled-up drawing under his arm. Valerie took a last gulp of her coffee before following Alec outside. The print shop was right next to the Post Office and when they passed by earlier, it had seemed to be empty. Hopefully, it wasn't closed.

They walked to the print shop, feeling marginally more hopeful than they had in the past few days. Valerie couldn't help noticing how many boys Finn's age passed her in the street. From a distance, so many of them could have been her son. How many people actually paid enough attention to their facial features to recognize them from a broadsheet? Her spirits sank somewhat, but she refused to allow herself to pursue such thoughts. All it took was one person to recognize Finn.

A bell tinkled as they walked into the shop. The scarred wooden counter was cluttered with tracts and pamphlets scattered randomly, their topics varying greatly. A strong smell of ink wafted from the back and the steady thump of the printing press could be heard coming from the back room. Several faded broadsheets hung on the wall, more to illustrate the different types of print rather than to actually announce something. A heavyset, balding man came out in response to the bell. His glasses were sliding down his nose, his forehead glistening with perspiration. He wiped his hands on the leather apron tied around his rotund belly, smiling at them pleasantly.

"Good afternoon, sir, ma'am. How can I be of service?" The man pushed up his glasses, leaving an inky smudge on his nose.

"We were interested in printing some broadsheets." Valerie handed the drawing to the man, who examined it closely.

"You're trying to find this lad?" the man asked, peering at them over his spectacles.

"Yes, he's our son," Valerie said, confused by the man's astonishment.

"I hope I'm not mistaken since I wouldn't want to mislead you, my dear lady, but this lad was here not an hour ago," he stammered, lowering the drawing to the counter. "I'm certain it was him."

"Where did he go?" asked Alec. "What was his business here?"

"He brought me a notice for the Gazette, then left. He didn't give his name or address, and I didn't ask. There was no need." The man looked genuinely upset at his inability to help them.

"Who wrote the notice for the newspaper? Was there a name? Someone we could contact?" Valerie fired off the questions, desperately hoping the man could answer at least one of them. Only moments before, she wanted one person, just one, to recognize Finn, and now someone had; only he seemed unable to help them.

"I'm terribly sorry, but the notices are usually submitted anonymously." The man was rubbing his forehead, thinking.

"Come now, man. There must be something you can tell us. Someone pays for them to be printed, do they not?" Alec's voice was becoming agitated, forcing the man to step back from the counter in sudden apprehension.

"Look, Mister, there's only one thing I can tell you, at a great risk to my own person, you understand. These notices are billed to the Committee." The man looked scared, his voice almost a whisper when he mentioned the Committee.

"What committee?" Valerie and Alec asked in unison.

"The Committee. Where have you two been?" he asked, taking in their outdated attire. "The Committee of Secret Correspondence."

"How does one get in contact with this committee?" Alec asked, gentling his voice.

"You don't get in touch with them; they get in touch with you. The names of the members are kept secret to protect them and their families. Your best course would be to join the Militia. There's always someone who is in contact with the members, or so I would presume." The printer looked as if he would like nothing more than for them to leave. "Do you still want the broadsheets then?"

"Yes," Valerie said, putting a silver coin on the counter. "Will this cover it?"

The printer looked at the coin, then at the two of them, shrugging his shoulders. "Come back tomorrow. I'll have your order by noon," he said, palming the coin.

* * *

"Shall we go back to the inn?" Valerie asked, taking Alec's arm as they left the shop.

"Let's take a walk. I'm too agitated to sit right now." He pulled Valerie along, his stride chewing up the pavement. Alec was muttering something to himself, making Valerie nervous. In her opinion, this was good news. The printer had seen Finn, so at least their search wasn't in vain.

"Alec, slow down. Why are you so upset?"

Alec stopped abruptly, facing Valerie, his face a mask of confusion. "I don't understand it, Valerie. I don't understand any of it. Just over a week ago, Finn was at home, hunting, fishing, doing his best to avoid learning Latin and Greek, and pilfering tobacco from the storehouse to trade with the Indians."

"So, you knew about that?" asked Valerie, offended that he'd lied to her.

"I didn't know, but I suspected. Anyhow, he was just his usual self. If the boy the printer saw had indeed been Finn, then nothing makes sense. Why did he choose 1775? Why did he come to Williamsburg? Who is he with? What is his connection to this Committee? What does he think happened to him? I don't understand any of it. Do you?" He obviously expected Valerie to shed some light on all this, but she was just as lost. Alec was right — nothing made sense. If Finn was delivering notices for the Committee, he had to be working with someone. How could he have gotten his bearings so quickly and managed to affiliate himself with a committee that was probably the first known agency of espionage in America? How did he explain being transported to the eighteenth century, and was he looking for a way to get back? Of course, there was no way to get back, but did he realize that?

"I don't know, but we're going to find out," Valerie answered with considerably more optimism than she felt. She followed Alec as he started walking again, turning off the main street into a quieter lane.

"The only explanation I can think of is that the printer saw the wrong boy," said Alec quietly. "He might not have had his glasses on or was distracted by something or someone. He might think it was Finn, but it might have been some other tall, dark-haired boy. We mustn't get our hopes up, Valerie."

"That's right. Ye mustn't get yer 'opes up," a gruff voice came from the mouth of the alley. "My, isn't that a nice, posh British accent I 'ear? Do ye know what we do to Royalists in these parts?"

Two men were advancing on them slowly, cudgels in hand. The one who'd spoken was in front, his ruddy face split into a vicious grin. He was short and barrel-chested, with thick arms that strained the fabric of his dirty shirt. His sleeveless coat was covered with dust, and his beat-up hat was low over his face, obscuring his features. He was slapping his club menacingly against his palm in an effort to intimidate his prey. He was obviously enjoying himself very much, having found an opportunity not to be missed. The second man was taller and thinner. He was hanging back slightly in anticipation of what was to come, evidently more of a sidekick than a leader. Valerie noticed that he had only a few teeth left in his mouth as he grinned at her, sliding his tongue over his thick lips.

"Get behind me, Valerie, and stay there no matter what," Alec said quietly.

"What is it you want with us?" he asked, his voice clear and calm.

"Hmm, let's see. 'E wants to know what we want, Bobby. Should I tell 'im?" The man was slowly advancing on Alec, his dark eyes full of intent. "We want yer kind to go back where ye came from. Go back to yer king with yer tails between yer legs and leave us to rule ourselves as we please. That's what we want. Any more questions?"

"You are not revolutionaries—you're just thugs," Valerie said, stepping forward. "If you are so worried about your independence, join the army and fight like real men."

"Thank you, Valerie. That was very helpful," whispered Alec.

"Real men, eh? We'll show ye what real men are made of as soon as we've finished with yer lily-livered 'usband. I reckon ye'll 'ave trouble walking for a few days after we're done with ye, yer ladyship," he grinned at her, his smile full of lewd intent.

Alec was seething, but he said nothing, his body tense and ready for a fight. The two men exchanged a look before charging Alec, their clubs raised about their heads, ready to strike. Valerie landed painfully on her behind as Alec shoved her out of the way in an effort to put some space between her and the men. She sat up, trying to get her bearings as the fight broke out. It was hard to tell exactly what was happening. Valerie looked around in panic, searching for anything that she could use as a weapon to help Alec. He was outnumbered and completely unarmed. She heard a thud as the club found its mark. Alec doubled over in pain as a terrible cry pierced the momentary silence.

Valerie watched in helpless horror as events seemed to unfold in slow motion. The man who'd been taunting Alec had a look of sudden surprise on his face as he dropped his cudgel and sank to his knees. His mouth opened, a grimace of pain distorting his features. Blood spurted from his thigh as he pressed both hands to it, trying to staunch the bleeding. His face was a mask of incredulity as he looked at the bloody knife in Alec's hand. Alec held a hand to his own middle, but his eyes were on Bobby, who was advancing on him, club raised. Bobby swung, nearly losing his balance as Alec ducked out of the way, slashing Bobby's arm with the knife. Valerie watched, mesmerized as the man's sleeve turned almost black with blood, soaking the fabric quickly. Bobby was about to swing again, but seemed to change his mind, backing out of the alley; his club no longer raised. He took one last look at Alec and took off at a run, leaving his injured friend behind. Alec was doubled over now, his coat covered in blood.

The man who attacked him keeled over in slow motion, his eyes rolling into the back of his head. Valerie didn't care if he died. She needed to get Alec out of there before Bobby came back with reinforcements to finish what they'd started. She pried the bloody knife from Alec's hand, grabbing him by the elbow and dragging him out of the alley. His breathing was shallow as if he couldn't draw a deep breath, but he was walking on his own.

"Alec, are you badly hurt? I'm so sorry. I should have kept my mouth shut," she pleaded, guiding him in the direction of the inn.

"And why would today be different from any other day?" asked Alec, trying to smile. "I'll be all right. Help me get my coat off. I don't want to walk into the inn covered in blood."

Valerie helped him remove his coat, immensely relieved to see no blood on his shirt. The blood wasn't his. She folded the coat to hide the blood and followed Alec into the inn, walking rapidly to the stairs.

TWENTY-EIGHT

Valerie threw the coat on the floor, bending down to help Alec with his boots. He carefully leaned back until his back was against the propped-up pillows, breathing out a sigh of relief.

"Alec, let me see." He didn't protest as Valerie pushed up his shirt to expose his stomach. Alec's ribs were covered with a livid bruise, which was tinged with blood and starting to swell. It would be terribly painful and tender tomorrow. Valerie carefully felt his ribs.

"Nothing is broken, just badly bruised," Alec said, trying to get more comfortable. "It'll be better in a few days. It just hurts to breathe deeply." He might have been in pain, but he had a look of satisfaction on his face that made Valerie smile.

"How did you manage to stab him?" Her insides were still quivering, relieved that Alec hadn't been hurt worse. Those men could have killed him, and probably would have, had Alec not managed to snatch the knife from his attacker and stab him first.

"I noticed the dagger at his belt while he was talking, so I waited for my chance to grab it. Unfortunately, I had to let him get close enough to club me. He swung at my head, but I shifted to the side, his club coming down on my ribs instead. I managed to grab the dagger as his friend clubbed me from the other side. I can't believe his friend just left him there to bleed," he mused, not sounding particularly concerned.

"I hope he's not dead," said Valerie, imagining what the repercussions of that could be. Alec wouldn't be very difficult to find should someone come looking, and if the man was dead, he'd be accused of murder, despite the fact that he'd been attacked.

"I didn't aim to kill, just deter. If I wanted to kill him, I would have stuck that knife between his ribs. There are no major organs in the thigh. Most likely, he just fainted from shock."

Valerie sighed, unlacing Alec's breeches and pulling them off carefully. He was staying in bed for the rest of the afternoon, so he might as well be comfortable. Alec smiled at her guiltily as she took in his arousal, looking up at him in shock.

"A good fight always gives you a cockstand," he said with a grin. "'Tis a natural reaction to bloodlust."

"Men!" Valerie muttered, turning away from him, but Alec caught her by the wrist. "Don't go."

"Give me a second," Valerie said, turning away and untying the laces of her gown. She slipped out of the dress, letting it slide to the floor as she pulled off her chemise and unpinned her hair. She savored Alec's look of appreciation for a few moments, before getting on the bed and positioning herself between Alec's legs, her bare breasts brushing against his cock as her hair trailed over his stomach. She gently kissed his bruises, watching his stomach muscles tense as her lips touched the sore spots. She looked up at him, smiling, as her lips made a trail of kisses down his flat stomach until she found what she was looking for.

Valerie licked the length of Alec's cock with the tip of her tongue before taking him all in, sucking slowly and rhythmically. Alec closed his eyes, his breath ragged as Valerie continued her task with single-minded determination. She used her tongue to tease him, swirling it around the tip and making him gasp with pleasure, then sucked again, faster and harder. It didn't take him long to spill himself into her mouth, shuddering with release.

Valerie wiped her mouth with the back of her hand, gazing at him innocently. "All better?"

"Mmm," was all he could manage. "I'd like to return the favor, but I'm hurting too much," he said apologetically.

"Not to worry. You'll just have to owe me one. I intend to collect the debt as soon as you feel better. Now just get some rest while I go get us something to eat. I seem to have worked up an appetite."

Valerie bent over Alec, kissing his forehead. "Thank God you're all right, Alec. I was so scared." Alec just grabbed her and kissed her, tasting himself on her lips.

TWENTY-NINE

Louisa gently laid Evie in her cot, watching her face relax in sleep. Her tiny mouth was open just a little; the sooty lashes fanned against her cheek. Louisa tucked a dark strand of hair into the baby's bonnet and turned to Bridget.

"She should sleep for a while, I think. She is full to bursting. I think I'll go into Jamestown, Bridget. I need to speak to Annabel. I know they'll be moving here by next week, but I don't think this can wait."

"Is it about little Louisa?" asked Bridget, following Louisa from the room. She seemed to be feeling better but was still pale with purple smudges under her normally bright eyes. Bridget assured Louisa that she was well enough to resume her tasks, but Louisa had her doubts.

"Yes. She asked Kit to deliver a note to Tom when he went into town, but Tom didn't answer. According to Kit, he didn't even read the note, just threw it on the fire. She spends all her time brooding over what will happen once they're wed. I'll ask Cook to prepare a basket of goodies. A peace offering can't hurt." Louisa was already reaching for her cloak, eager to get out of the house for a few hours.

"What do ye think Annabel can do?" Bridget asked, practical as ever. She followed Louisa down the stairs toward the kitchen, interested to hear the answer.

"Maybe she can speak to Tom. I have a feeling that Louisa isn't as innocent in all this as she pretends to be, but he can hardly blame her. She's fourteen, whereas he's a grown man. He knew good and well what he was doing. No one forced his hand. He must accept responsibility for his behavior and make the best of the situation. I know he has his heart set on going to England, but that's out of the question now. Although, maybe he can go and marry her after he gets back in the spring. She's too young to marry, and I would hate to see her get with child. She's nothing but a child herself."

Bridget looked thoughtful for a moment, obviously remembering something from long ago. Her expression turned serious for a brief moment before she answered Louisa.

"She is strong enough to bear a child. I was her age when I married and had my first baby. 'Tis better younger than older, if ye ask me. Girls are resilient at this age. Consummating the marriage would only bring them closer. No young man can remain angry when ruled by his prick. He's a stubborn one, Tom is. I know he lusts after her; he just won't let himself admit it. His pride has been hurt, and that will take some mending."

"But what can she do to mend it if he won't let her?" Louisa was at a loss. It'd been a long time since she was a teenager, and the teenagers of her day didn't get married at fourteen.

"'Twould be helpful if there was some other young man with his eye on Louisa. Would mayhap stir up some jealousy, but there's no one hereabouts who'd fit the bill. Shame, that is. A bit of jealousy can go a long way." Bridget seemed a little out of breath as she said this, putting her hand to the wall for support.

"Bridget, are you all right? You haven't been yourself lately.

Would you like to go lie down? I can get Minnie to watch the baby for an hour or two."

"Nay, I'm well. 'Tis that time of the month, that's all. I get a bit dizzy sometimes. Don't trouble yerself, Lady Sheridan. I'll be right as rain by the time ye get back. I enjoy Lady Evie anyhow. She's such an angel."

"When she's sleeping, you mean?" Louisa smiled. Her daughter was becoming more demanding with every passing day.

"Nay, she's always an angel. I like feisty ones. Who wants a baby who lays there like a lump of clay?"

"Sometimes I wouldn't mind, especially in the middle of the night. How long do you think until she starts sleeping through the night?" Louisa couldn't wait to get a full night's sleep. She was always exhausted these days, not to mention anxious. Between the night feedings and the terrible dreams in which she was constantly searching for Valerie, Louisa was lucky if she got four hours of sleep a night. She sometimes managed a quick nap while Evie was sleeping, but that wasn't enough. She was dizzy with fatigue, her reflexes not as sharp as before.

"Oh, mayhap another month or so. She'll give ye a little a bit of peace afore she starts teething, poor mite. That will not be easy for ye or her. Ye best be going now afore she wakes wanting another feeding," Bridget added with a chuckle. Evie's demand for food was legendary.

* * *

The ride into Jamestown was uneventful. The day was cool and crisp, splashes of glorious color contrasting vividly with the unbroken expanse of blue sky. Louisa loved this time of year. The yellow, reds and oranges of the changing leaves reminded her of Central Park in the fall. She used to leave the museum at lunchtime, walking through the park, inhaling the pungent smell of decaying leaves and the smoky aroma of warm pretzels and hot dogs sold by the numerous vendors. That life seemed so far removed from reality. She still thought of her parents often, but being with Valerie soothed some of the pain of losing them.

Louisa had to admit that she was enjoying the solitude as she drove the trap toward Jamestown, the basket of food on the seat beside her. She rarely got to be alone these days, as she was always surrounded by family or servants. It seemed strange that before she came to find Valerie she lived alone, the mistress of all that space. Louisa couldn't imagine living alone again after being a part of a large family. It was challenging at times but rewarding as well. Having Valerie there, especially since the birth of Evie, was invaluable. It was hard enough to have a baby in the twenty-first century, but to have one in colonial Virginia without the benefit of an obstetrician, pediatrician, or any of the modern conveniences, was an act of heroism in Louisa's opinion. Every time she felt a bout of fear, she reminded herself that her sister managed to raise two children in these primitive conditions, and that with the help of Valerie and Bridget, she would do the same. Evie seemed to be thriving, so all she had to do was take motherhood one day at a time and stop worrying all the time. Valerie would help her.

As Louisa's thoughts turned to Valerie, she felt the familiar grip of anxiety squeeze her chest. Where were they? What were they doing? Louisa's stress increased by the day that Valerie and Alec were gone. Little Louisa crying her heart out, and Charles and Annabel about to move into Rosewood Manor, added to her worry about the crowding and the discord brewing in the house. With winter coming, they would all be cooped up inside, stepping on each other's toes and possibly struggling to make the food last through the winter. Winter was hard enough without a shortage of food.

Louisa glanced over at the basket she was bringing for

Annabel. It contained a pot of jam that Valerie had made during the summer, a jar of honey, and freshly baked oatcakes, provided by Mrs. Dolly. Annabel was famous for her sweet tooth, so Louisa hoped to soften her demeanor by bribing her with sweets. She hoped that Annabel would invite her to stay and share some of the goodies. Louisa had eaten breakfast, but her stomach was already growling. Breastfeeding left her permanently hungry as her body worked overtime to produce milk for her ravenous daughter. An oatcake with some jam would be most welcome, thought Louisa as she drove into town, her peaceful ride at an end.

Louisa pulled up in front of the house and reined in the horse. A boy of about twelve ran out to help Louisa with the trap and see to the horse while she was inside. He was the son of the cook employed by Charles, and Louisa briefly wondered what would happen to him and his mother once Charles and Annabel came to live at the plantation. She climbed down carefully from the trap. It had rained the day before, so the road was still muddy in places. As Louisa reached for the basket, she swayed dangerously as she lost her footing, her feet sliding under the trap. She tried to grab onto it while fighting to regain her balance, but the mud was slippery, and she slid right under the wheels landing in a pool of mud.

"Oh, damn it all to hell," Louisa shrieked as cloak and gown became instantly soaked with muddy water, seeping into her undergarments. The boy grabbed her under the arms, pulling her from under the trap with all his might. Louisa tried to push off with her feet, but her boots kept sliding in the mud, making it even more difficult for her to get to her feet. She finally managed to find her footing, looking at the damage to her clothes and the scattered contents of the basket. Annabel was in the doorway, her hand pressed to her mouth in shock. Louisa turned to see what she was looking at. A crowd had gathered behind her, the minister pushing his way to the front. He grabbed Louisa by the arm, looking at her sternly.

"Lady Sheridan, you stand accused of profanity, which is a very serious crime indeed, according to the laws of the Virginia Colony. You are to be taken to the prison where you will await trial and punishment." Louisa just gaped in shock as several men stepped from the crowd, seizing her by the arms and dragging her toward the building that housed the so-called prison. It wasn't used as it was in the modern day as a form of punishment, but more of a holding cell for miscreants awaiting trial. What had she said? She'd been so upset she hadn't been paying attention. Louisa normally held her tongue, but being upset about all the things going on and deprived of sleep, she'd let herself slip.

"I'm sorry. It just slipped out," Louisa pleaded with the minister, who walked ahead of the men, leading the way. "I didn't mean it."

The men pushed her into the tiny cell, shutting the door behind her. The sound of a key turning in the padlock made Louisa shake with fright. These men were serious and had no intentions of letting her off with a slap on the wrist. She looked around the cell in an effort to calm herself. The only light in the tiny room came from a small window cut into the wooden logs. The window wasn't large enough to climb through, but just enough to give some light and much-needed air. The cell reeked of excrement, sweat, and fear. Anyone who'd been here knew that they wouldn't escape without punishment. In colonial Virginia, there was no such thing as being found innocent, especially since eager citizens were always willing to testify on behalf of the colony. Several people had heard Louisa's outburst, so she was doomed.

Louisa sank down on the hard bench, ignoring her wet garments and muddy shoes. They were the least of her concerns now. The punishment for profanity could be severe. Thank

God she hadn't blasphemed. She'd heard that the last person to do so had a hole bored into their tongue with a hot poker. Louisa began to shake as she thought of Evie. She'd need to be fed in less than two hours. Her baby would go hungry without her milk. Louisa slumped on the bench, crying her heart out. She hadn't been this scared since the pirates attacked the *Gloriana*.

THIRTY

The feeble light coming through the window began to change from the golden haze of midday to the purple shadows of early evening. No one had come to talk to Louisa or bring her any food or water. She wasn't even hungry, just terrified. Large, ugly circles appeared on the front of her gown, reminding her once again that her daughter needed to be fed. Louisa pulled down her chemise, expressing the milk into the corner of the cell. She'd be soaked and in pain by morning if she didn't empty her breasts. Where was Kit? Did he even know what happened to her? He had to. Annabel had watched Louisa frog-marched to the jail, her mouth open in astonishment, and her eyes as wide as saucers. She had to have told Charles. Annabel was still upset about the situation with Tom, but she was a kind soul, always eager to help anyone in need. She wouldn't leave Louisa to languish in prison simply out of spite.

Louisa leaned her head against the rough wooden logs of the cell, a hysterical giggle escaping as she continued to squirt milk into the corner. How did she get into this mess? She tried not to think of what they would do to her come morning. She prayed they would just put her in stocks for a few hours, but she knew that was unlikely. Colonial authorities meted out cruel punishments in order to set an example to others. She might be tied to a post and whipped, or even branded with a hot iron. This was no *Scarlet Letter* where Hester Prynne got off by having the letter "A" stitched to her bodice. This was the real world, and if she was sentenced to display a letter, she'd be displaying it on her flesh.

Louisa started crying again, her tears mingling with milk on her bosom. Her gown was wet from the mud and the leaking milk. She was cold, hungry, and terrified. Louisa pulled up her bodice and huddled in the corner, hugging her knees to her chest. She closed her eyes, trying to conjure up a happy memory to soothe her frayed nerves. There was nothing to be gained by wearing herself out with worry. She would try to get some rest and pray that whatever awaited her in the morning would not be as terrible as the fearful images her imagination kept imprinting on her brain.

Louisa woke up with a start, shivering in her damp gown. The cell was dark as a grave, no light coming in at all. Someone must have covered the window while she slept, depriving her of moonlight and fresh air. The cell stunk of human waste and sour milk, nearly making her gag. Louisa held up her hand to her face but couldn't make it out. It had to be the middle of the night, but for all she knew it could still be evening. Something had woken her, so she sat up, listening carefully, but all she heard was the silence of a sleeping town. A dog barked somewhere in the distance, and she thought she heard the creaking of a shutter closing against the chill of the autumn night. Otherwise, all was quiet. Everyone was safely in their homes, warm, fed, and surrounded by family. The reality of her predicament crashed over her once again, making her shake even harder, her teeth rattling in her jaw. They would probably sentence her in the morning, and morning wasn't that far away.

The sound of something heavy being dragged caught her attention, but she dismissed it. It had nothing to do with her. Someone was probably dragging a sack of corn or a barrel of ale. People were hiding things for the coming winter, preferring to transfer their goods under the cover of the night, so as not to alert their neighbors. Looting would be inevitable come winter. A noise came from the direction of the door, but Louisa couldn't see anything in the darkness. She backed into the corner, standing still and holding her breath. Maybe it was a rat. The thought nearly made her cry out, so she clamped a hand over her mouth, willing herself to be silent.

Louisa nearly screamed as strong arms took hold of her, pulling her out of her corner. "Not a sound, you understand?" She nearly fainted with relief at the sound of Kit's voice. She was about to throw her arms around him, but he sounded gruff and impatient, eager to leave the cell. Kit guided her through the dark anteroom and into the cold air of the night. Louisa took a few deep breaths, savoring the cool freshness filling her lungs. Thick black clouds blanketed the sky, lighting up with a sinister glow as they floated over the face of the moon. The street was deserted, not a single light visible in any of the windows. Even the dog had stopped barking, probably fast asleep in front of a cozy fire.

"Let's go. Keep silent." Kit wrapped a cloak around her shoulders before taking her by the hand and guiding her toward the docks. Where was he going? Neither one of their ships was in port, so what could they do at the docks? She needed to go home and feed her baby, not to mention change out of her damp, reeking clothes. Louisa suddenly stopped, realizing that this rescue was pointless. They would come for her anyway.

Everyone knew exactly who she was and where she came from. The minister and his minions would be at Rosewood Manor first thing in the morning, demanding that she be turned over to the authorities to face her punishment. Louisa stifled a sob of fear as Kit pulled her along faster.

A rowboat was waiting for them at the docks, bobbing on the black water, a solitary figure sitting at the oars. Kit helped Louisa into the boat, then motioned for the man to start rowing. Normally, there was a lantern to light the way, but tonight the lantern hadn't been lit, the night black and full of unexpected terrors all around them.

"Kit, where are we going? What about Evie?" Louisa felt slightly hysterical as the boat glided away from the dock. There wasn't anyone there, but Kit didn't answer her right away. He waited until they were safely away from the shore before finally turning his attention to her.

"Louisa, are you all right?" he asked, studying her face in the darkness. His voice sounded tense, making Louisa wish she could see his face clearly. Was he angry or just afraid?

"Yes. I'm all right. Where are we going?" she asked again. Louisa would have given anything for a hot bath and a dry gown, but she kept her mouth shut, wondering where Kit was taking her. They weren't going back home, so he must have a plan of some sort, one that involved going out to sea.

"We're going to England."

"What?" she nearly screamed. "We can't go to England. We have no idea where Valerie and Alec are, and Louisa is on the verge of a breakdown. We can't leave. We are needed here."

"Keep your voice down. You should have thought of that before you decided to use profane language in front of the minister. Half the town heard you. I thought you only save profanity for me," he said with a chuckle, sounding more like his normal self.

"Kit, this is no laughing matter. Where is Evie? Are we

rowing to England?" She peered into the darkness, searching for the outline of a ship. She finally saw it as the clouds parted momentarily to allow a ray of moonlight to illuminate the black waters all around them. The ship lay at anchor only a few feet away, its sails still furled; its rigging piercing the dark sky. This vessel was smaller than the *Misty Dawn* or the *Morning Star*, probably a galleon.

"Evie is already aboard the *Sea Maiden* waiting for you. Don't worry. Annabel fed her. Thank God she'd still nursing Harry, or Evie would go hungry unless some kindly soul offered to nurse her in your absence. Bridget is with her on the ship. The *Sea Maiden* is due to sail with the tide just before sunrise, so we'll be out to sea by the time they find you gone."

"How did you get me out? Wasn't there a guard?" Louisa could have sworn they'd posted a guard outside the door, not that she was likely to escape even if there wasn't one. The door was made of solid wood, padlocked from the outside.

"The guard will be nursing a terrible headache come morning, but he'll live. Charles hit him unnecessarily hard." Louisa could hear the smile in Kit's voice. He wouldn't admit it, but he probably enjoyed breaking her out of prison.

"Charles was with you?" she asked in surprise.

"Charles and Annabel left for Rosewood as soon as the minister had you taken away. Charles and I devised a plan while Annabel fed Evie and helped Bridget pack the necessities for you and the baby. I took Bridget and Evie to the docks as soon as it got dark and sent them to the ship with a message for the captain. I know him well. He's a good man, who would never refuse to help. Charles returned to town to keep an eye on the prison. Charles and Annabel will return to the plantation and run things in our absence. They will see to little Louisa. Don't worry." Kit was already rising to his feet as the rowboat came alongside the hull rising above them in the darkness. He called out a greeting just as someone held an oil lamp over the side of the deck. Louisa watched as a rope ladder was tossed over the side, unrolling as it fell down toward the rowboat.

"But what about Alec and Valerie? Now we'll have no news of them until spring," Louisa protested as Kit helped her grab the ladder. She sucked in her breath as her feet left the safety of the rowboat. The rope ladder twisted and turned in her hands, making her feel as if she would plunge into the icy water at any moment. Louisa tried not to look down as she climbed the ladder, gripping the rope with all her might.

"Just be thankful that this didn't happen a month later, or there'd be no more ships sailing the Atlantic until spring. We must leave before they discover you gone," Kit hissed as he held the ladder tighter, making it easier to climb.

A burly sailor helped Louisa onto the deck, steadying her as she nearly lost her footing. The deck was rolling beneath her feet, the tide already going out. Kit jumped onto the deck a few minutes later, thanking the sailor and taking Louisa by the hand.

"Let's get you cleaned up and changed into dry clothes. You look a fright," he said, giving her a once-over, "then you need a strong brandy and something hot in your belly."

"Kit, thank you for rescuing me. I don't mean to sound ungrateful. I'm just shocked." Louisa reached for him, happy to be pulled into his comforting embrace. His warm lips brushed her forehead as he held her close, making her feel safe at last.

"Did you really think I would let them hurt you, my sweet, even if you did cuss like a sailor? I'd have skewered the minister himself if I had to, and then I'd be damned to hell," he said with a low laugh. "Come. The first mate was kind enough to give up his cabin for us. It's small, but at least it's private."

Louisa followed Kit down to the cabin, eager to see Evie. "Kit, what will happen when our ships come into port?"

"Charles will see to it. He's always wanted to be lord of the manor, so this is his chance. Thank God I wasn't away at sea when this happened." Kit helped her down the narrow stairs that led below. The first mate's cabin was just to the right, already occupied by Bridget and Evie.

"Thank God," Louisa whispered, breathing a sigh of relief at the sight of Evie and Bridget fast asleep on the narrow berth of the cabin.

THIRTY-ONE

The morning was fresh and crisp; the mist still swirling between the trees as Finn left the farmhouse and headed into the shadowy woods. He had work to do before breakfast, but all he needed was a half-hour to check his traps. He set them two days ago and hoped that some unfortunate creatures had stumbled upon them by now. He thought it would be nice to present Mrs. Mallory with a few fat rabbits for the pot and impress Abbie in the process. He still hadn't given her the bracelet but hoped to get her alone tonight.

Finn's stomach growled at the thought of food. He was always hungry in the morning and wished that Mrs. Mallory would serve breakfast before the morning chores and not after. He supposed there was no point in wasting time while she prepared the porridge, but he hated working on an empty belly. Time was valuable and nearly every minute of the day was filled with some sort of task. He didn't really mind the work but wished that he could spend a little more time in the vicinity of Abbie. The only time they were in the same place at the same time aside from breakfast was during supper, when the whole family gathered around the table to enjoy their evening meal.

Finn stayed mostly quiet during those times, feeling somewhat out of place among the boisterous family. He ate his food, answered whatever questions were put to him, and either went outside afterward or straight up to bed, depending on how tired he was. He was more likely to head outside if he noticed Abbie watching him from under her lashes, her eyes sliding toward the door. They couldn't be too obvious in their courtship, since living under the same roof might be a problem for her parents.

Finn had nearly reached the place where he set the first trap when he froze in his tracks. Something wasn't right. First, he'd heard the snap of a twig, and then several birds erupted into the sky as if spooked by something or someone. There, he'd heard it again. It was louder this time, as if something large lumbered through the woods. Finn was glad he'd taken his tomahawk with him in case he needed to kill the rabbits. At least he was armed. As the sounds grew closer, Finn realized that what he was dealing with was not an animal. He recognized the patterns of animals, and these noises were made by humans, and they were getting closer.

Three figures finally materialized out of the mist, their hands balled into fists. They were spread out, so Finn's only avenue of retreat was to turn and run deeper into the woods, but he wouldn't run. He was no coward, and this fight would find him sooner or later.

"Three against one, is it? Is that the way you fight your battles, Granville?" Finn asked, tucking the tomahawk back into his belt. Whatever happened, he wouldn't use it. He didn't want anyone's death on his hands. He'd just take it like a man and hope that they didn't intend to kill him.

"I like to be certain of victory," Matthew Granville spat out as he slowly approached Finn. "You didn't actually think that I would allow you to insult me in front of Abigail and get away with it, did you? Everything comes with a price, Mr. Whitfield, and you will pay dearly." Granville was obviously enjoying himself, sure of getting his revenge. Finn wondered how brave he'd be if it were just the two of them, man to man.

Finn glanced at Granville's companions. He recognized both of them from church. They were large lads, probably a year or two older than Finn. One bore a slight resemblance to Matthew Granville, so was very likely a brother or a cousin. The other boy was German. His blond hair gleamed in the morning light as his slanted eyes studied Finn carefully. Both boys seemed bored by the repartee and eager to get down to business. No doubt they had chores to attend to at home and wanted to get this over with as quickly as possible.

"You won't get her back, you pompous prick," Finn stated, grinning at Matthew Granville. If he was going to get a beating, he might as well enjoy taunting his attacker.

"Oh, I don't want her back. She's shown her true nature, and I have no interest in courting an opinionated hoyden who's no doubt already spread her legs for the likes of you. I hope she was worth it."

Matthew opened his mouth to say something else, but Finn didn't care to hear it. He'd heard enough, and no one was going to impugn Abbie's honor. Finn charged Granville, pounding his face with his fists like a madman. He needed to get in as many punches as he could before he was overpowered by Granville's friends. He'd never known such frenzy.

Finn managed to get his foot behind Granville's ankles and shoved him backward, knocking him to the ground and jumping on top of him. He slammed Granville's head against the hard earth as he punched him in the mouth, knocking out a tooth. His fist was covered with Granville's blood as he raised it to hit him again, but he never got the chance.

Finn barely felt it when the other two boys lifted him off their friend and slammed him against a tree, holding him while Matthew Granville punched him again and again, first in the stomach and then in the face. Finn managed to kick him in the bollocks with his knee as he came closer, for which he got his head knocked into the trunk of the tree before Granville's boot found his own stones. Finn saw stars explode before his eyes as a fist smashed his face, hitting his head against the trunk again. The last thing he saw before passing out was Granville's satisfied smirk.

THIRTY-TWO

A canopy of branches nearly blocked out the sky as golden shafts of morning light pierced the foliage like arrows. The leaves rustled overheard, and the birds fluttered from tree to tree, most likely singing all the while, but Finn couldn't hear any of it. It's as if all his senses had been shut off. He couldn't hear, couldn't see through his swollen eyes, or smell anything, since his nose was full of congealed blood. He could taste though. The metallic taste of blood filled his mouth, making him feel sick to his stomach.

Finn knew he needed to get up, but he simply couldn't. He tried moving his legs experimentally. They jerked, but they weren't broken. That was a start. Hands next. Finn forced himself to open his fist and feel the leaves and pine needles beneath his fingers. His hands felt bruised, but he was able to move his fingers. Finn took a mental inventory of his other organs. His head was pounding as if someone was striking it with a hammer, making his temples throb and his eyes water from the pain. His shoulder was sore, and it hurt to take a deep breath, but everything below the waist seemed fine.

Jonah's worried face suddenly appeared above Finn, his

mouth opening as he called out, but Finn couldn't hear him. Jonah's face appeared blurred and distorted, so Finn closed his eyes to keep the dizziness at bay. At least Jonah wouldn't let him die here.

"Finn! Finn! Wake up, please." Jonah's voice came from somewhere very far away, faint and pleading. "I'll go fetch Pa. He'll help you. Just wait here." As if he could leave.

"No," Finn croaked. "Just help me get up." He tried to sit up with Jonah's assistance. His stomach hurt like hell, but he managed it, eventually getting to his feet. Finn leaned against a tree for a moment, closing his eyes. His head was spinning like a top, and he could barely catch his breath. It was a long way back to the house, and he'd need to lean on Jonah for support. He groped at his belt, searching for his hatchet. It wasn't there. He seemed to recall Granville pulling it out of his belt as his friends held him against the tree. Had he taken it?

"Jonah, can you see my hatchet anywhere?" Finn murmured as he tried to breathe deeply to steady his racing heart.

"I'll look." Jonah walked around slowly, searching.

"Look over by the tree," suggested Finn. His vision was beginning to clear somewhat.

"Which tree? We are in a forest, remember?" Finn heard Jonah's intake of breath.

"What is it?" Finn asked.

"Ah, nothing. I found it. It's a nice tomahawk. Where'd you get it anyway?" Finn could hear the nervousness in Jonah's voice. What had he seen? Finn opened his eyes and peered in the direction of Jonah's voice. The tree trunk was covered in blood just where his head had been. Finn lifted his arm and gingerly touched the back of his head. The pain was excruciating, and his hand was smeared with blood as he held it up to his face.

"Come Finn. I need to get you home," said Jonah as he

tucked the hatchet into Finn's belt. "Lean on me and walk slow-ly." Finn didn't argue.

* * *

"Good God, what happened to you?!" Mrs. Mallory's face froze in shock as Jonah pushed Finn through the door, helping him to a chair. "John, come quick," she called through the open door, summoning her husband.

"Well, well." Mr. Mallory shook his head in dismay as he eyed Finn. "Do you need a doctor, son?"

"I'll be all right," Finn whispered, desperate to lie down. He thought he might faint. His head was spinning, and there was a hollow feeling in his belly that had nothing to do with hunger.

"Your head wound needs to be cleaned and bandaged. Just hold tight for a little while longer. Hannah, get me some warm water and a rag. I'll need a strip of linen to bandage his head." Mr. Mallory carefully examined Finn's ribs while waiting for the water. He'd obviously done this before.

"Does it hurt when I press here?" he asked, putting pressure on Finn's ribs.

"Yes," Finn grunted.

"You don't seem to have any broken bones, but your head has been battered severely. I think you might be concussed. Can you see all right?" Finn tried to nod, but more stars appeared out of nowhere, cascading from the ceiling.

"Who did this, Finn?" Mr. Mallory asked him quietly.

"I don't know."

"I think you do." Finn closed his eyes. He just needed to sleep a little. He was nearly there when Mr. Mallory's voice summoned him back to consciousness.

"You need to lie down as soon as possible," Mr. Mallory said as he began to clean the back of Finn's head. The rag came away all bloody, turning the water a murky red within minutes. Finn closed his eyes, letting Mr. Mallory take care of him. He could barely manage to stay awake. His eyes were closing of their own accord, and his thoughts were all muddled and fragmented.

"There. That should do it. Now, let me help you to bed. Mrs. Mallory will bring you something to eat. You must be hungry."

Finn was just about to answer when Abbie walked into the house, a basket of eggs under her arm. Her mouth opened in shock as she saw Finn sitting at the table, his head wrapped in a linen bandage, his face barely recognizable. She let out a pitiful moan as she shoved the basket into Sarah's hands and went to Finn.

"Who did this to you, Finn? Who?" Abbie was on her knees in front of him, looking up into his face, her eyes full of tears.

"Abbie, Finn needs to be in bed. You can talk to him later. Now, go and turn down his bed, while I help him up the stairs," her father said.

Mr. Mallory helped him up and gently laid him on the bed. Finn was out before his head hit the pillow, his battered body no longer able to take the pain.

THIRTY-THREE

The room was lost in darkness by the time Finn finally woke up. Snippets of conversation and sounds of utensils on crockery reached his ears, but otherwise all was quiet. Finn's tongue felt like flannel in his dry mouth, and his head throbbed painfully. He was just about to try getting up when Abbie appeared carrying a single candle. The flickering light illuminated her worried face as she sat on the edge of the bed, holding a cup to Finn's dry lips.

"How do you feel?"

"Couldn't be better," Finn answered, grateful for the water she gave him.

"The doctor was here. Pa sent Jonah to fetch him after you passed out. You slept right through his visit. He reckons you'll be all right. You're concussed as Pa suspected, and your nose is broken. You must have a devil of a headache. Dr. Hillard just happened to mention that Matthew Granville has a broken jaw. Any idea how he came by that?" Abbie was watching him suspiciously, her eyes pools of chocolaty brown.

"None whatsoever." Finn closed his eyes in an effort to discourage Abbie from asking any more questions. He didn't want to admit that it had been Matthew who beat him to a pulp, partly because of his injured pride and partly to spare Abbie the guilt. She would feel awful if she knew she'd been responsible for the attack, although it really wasn't her fault at all.

"Finn, it was Matthew, wasn't it? And it was all because of me." Abbie took his hand, caressing it gently. "I'm so sorry, Finn. I never meant for this to happen." She looked like she was about to cry, her eyes full of anguish.

"Abbie, it wasn't your fault. I humiliated him, and he paid me back in full. Think nothing of it. Anyhow, I would take a hundred beatings just to walk you home." He tried to smile, but it hurt.

"That's an awfully high price to pay just for the pleasure of my company. Was it worth it?" Funny, Granville had asked him the same thing. Yes, it had been worth it. She was worth it.

"It's not too high of a price if you throw a few kisses into the bargain. I could use one right now." Finn closed his eyes as Abbie's lips brushed his, her breath sweet and warm.

"You're a surprising person, Finlay Whitfield," she whispered into his ear, kissing his temple.

Oh, you have no idea, he thought, enjoying the feel of her skin against his cheek.

THIRTY-FOUR

Valerie ignored Alec's pouting as she got ready to go to the printer's shop. Alec was still in a lot of pain; his ribs were terribly bruised and ached every time he took a deep breath. There wasn't much she could do, short of putting cold compresses on the area, not that they helped much. Alec had barely slept during the night, unable to get comfortable since he preferred sleeping on his stomach.

"I'll be back soon. I promise. Are you sure you're not hungry?" she asked again, glancing at the beer and bread she'd brought him for breakfast.

"No, I don't want to eat. I'll be all right," he said, looking anything but. "Please be careful."

"I will. Try to get some sleep."

Valerie gave him a kiss and left the room. She was eager to pick up the broadsheets and start putting them up. She'd wait for Alec to do most of them, but the least she could do was put a few up within walking distance of the inn. Who knew? Maybe someone had seen Finn. If the printer really had seen Finn, then it was quite possible that other people had seen him as well. Maybe he'd gone into other shops. It was important to ask people while their memory was still fresh.

The printer had her order ready and waiting by the time Valerie walked through the door. "So you haven't found him yet?" he asked conversationally. "He hasn't been back since, that I can tell you for certain. Good luck with your search."

Valerie took her packet of broadsheets and stepped out into the afternoon sun. She'd gotten some glue to put up the sheets but had left it in the room. She'd have to go back. Valerie looked up and down the street. She had to admit that she was a little nervous to be out by herself after what happened yesterday. She hoped someone had helped the man they left bleeding in the alley. She sighed with relief as she reached the inn. It was very quiet as she walked in, being about ten o'clock. The midday crowd would start trickling in closer to noon, ready for a drink and a meal. The publican was washing out tankards and setting them on the draining board in readiness as he hummed a merry tune.

"Good day to you, Mrs. Whitfield. All by yourself this morning? You best wait for that husband of yours to escort you. Heard there was a stabbing yesterday only a few streets over. Terrible business." He sighed dramatically as he continued to clean the tankards.

"Do they know who did it?" Valerie asked carefully.

"They reckon Percival got into a drunken brawl with someone. The man has a reputation for brawling, especially with anyone he suspects of being a Royalist. Finally got his comeuppance, I'd say. His crony Bobby Mann is keeping mum. I suspect they're more interested in robbing their victims than upholding the cause of liberty."

"Is he badly injured?" Valerie asked casually.

"He was stabbed in the thigh and lost some blood, but he will recover. The only thing truly injured is his pride. I hear he's never lost a fight. I don't envy the poor sod who stabbed him."

Valerie felt her stomach clench, terrified that Bobby Mann and his friend would seek retribution against Alec. She decided it was wise to change the subject before the innkeeper deduced that the person who stabbed Percival was none other than her husband. She'd washed out Alec's coat last night and threw the bloody water out the window, but someone might have noticed something when they came in through the taproom. If their attackers found out where they were staying, they would no doubt come after Alec.

"Mr. Clements, I wonder if I might put up a broadsheet here in the taproom. So many people come here; I thought it would be a good place."

"Well, now. That depends on the type of broadsheet you want to put up. Anti-British sentiment runs deep in my inn, so as long as you're not going against that, feel free," he said, trying to get a better look at Valerie's packet. She pulled one out, handing it to the publican.

"It's nothing political. It's a likeness of my son. He's been missing for nearly two weeks. I was hoping someone might have seen him," she said quietly, hating to repeat once again that Finn was missing. Every time she said it, she felt as if she lost him all over again.

"He's a fine-looking boy, your son. Doesn't favor you much, does he?" said the innkeeper, studying the sheet. "I hope you find him. You are welcome to put it up with the others," he said, gesturing to the wall by the door, already plastered with a dozen broadsheets. Most of them were yellowed with age, the ink faded from the sun falling on that side of the wall, but some were still relatively fresh, calling for people of Williamsburg to join the Continental Army and fight for their liberty. Valerie was just about to go upstairs for her pot of glue when Mr. Clements called out to her. "Let me see that sheet again, Mrs. Whitfield."

He set a tankard on the counter and dried his hands on his

apron before taking the sheet from Valerie. Mr. Clements studied the drawing closely, holding it up to the light from the window. "I wouldn't want to mislead you, Mrs. Whitfield, but I'm almost certain he was in here yesterday."

Valerie grabbed on to the counter, feelings slightly faint. "Where did he go? Who was he with?" she asked, praying that the man would have some answers, but the innkeeper shook his head, a look of pity on his homely face. "I'm sorry, Mrs. Whitfield, but I don't know. I have a clear view of the door, so I saw him walking in, but then he got lost in the crowd. It gets busy here at noontime. I couldn't see where he went but let me ask my Bessie. She was serving yesterday on account of my wife being unwell."

Mr. Clements disappeared into the kitchen, returning a moment later with his oldest daughter. The girl was about fifteen, with wide dark eyes and an impish smile. Valerie thought that the customers probably liked Bessie very much. She took the broadsheet from the counter, looking at it intently.

"I seen him. He was at the table in the back with two other gentlemen. One was dressed like a farmer, but the other was one was wearing a good suit, although he had a face on him like sour milk," Bessie announced, handing the sheet back to Valerie.

"Do you know their names?" Valerie asked hopefully. At least she was getting somewhere.

"No, sorry. They're not regulars. I've seen the sour-looking one before, but don't know his name. Sorry I couldn't be more help. He is a handsome boy, your son. I noticed his green eyes. So lovely they were, just like emeralds." She sighed at the memory, oblivious to Valerie's disappointment.

"Thank you, Bessie. If you see him again, will you tell him that his parents are looking for him and that we are staying right upstairs?"

"Oh, I surely will, ma'am. I'll look out for him. You can be sure of that," she dimpled at Valerie, clearly expecting a coin.

"I don't have anything to give you now, but there'll be a reward if he is found," improvised Valerie in order to encourage the girl.

"Is there now?" Bessie asked, well pleased. "I hope to be the one to claim it. Well, I have to go help Ma in the kitchen."

"That's something, isn't it?" Mr. Clements asked, gazing at Valerie. "He'll turn up, your boy. Don't get discouraged. So many young lads are running off to join the Army or the Militia these days. It's bound to be hard on the parents, but it's all in a good cause, I say."

"Thank you, Mr. Clements. You've been most helpful. I'll just go up and tell my husband that you and Bessie recognized him. He'll be glad to hear the news."

Valerie wasn't sure how she felt. On the one hand, she was thrilled that three people in two days had recognized Finn. On the other hand, they must have missed him by minutes both at the print shop and at the inn. What were the chances they would come this close again? What if he left town? If she could only find out where he was staying. Valerie sighed as she went upstairs to share her news with Alec. If only they had something more concrete. Who were these men that Bessie had seen Finn with? How did he come to be with them, and what was their connection to the Committee of Secret Correspondence?

THIRTY-FIVE

Finn looked up from his perch on the stile. The pale orb of the moon was still visible in the cloudless sky as the sun held court on the other side, bringing much-needed warmth to the chilly October morning. The woods visible from the farm were ablaze with color, the leaves ranging from a pale yellow to a blood-red crimson. Another week or two and winter would already be in the air, especially in the early mornings when he reluctantly crawled out of bed, ready to start his chores before breakfast.

This was the first time Finn had been allowed out of bed since the beating four days ago. Mrs. Mallory let him out for some fresh air but forbade him to do any work. Finn was thankful to finally be feeling better. He was still sporting some colorful bruises on his face, but his vision was normal once again and the terrible headache that had plagued him for the first few days finally went away. His ribs were still sore, but not nearly as painful as before, allowing him to fill his lungs with fresh morning air, which smelled of wood smoke, hay, and the tang of manure from the barn.

The Mallorys had been really kind. They all took turns visiting him up in the loft and bringing him food and treats.

Even Martha, who hardly took any notice of him, came up and brought him a cup of cider and a piece of freshly baked tart. Annie offered Finn her dolly so he wouldn't feel sad, and Sarah read him a story. The best visits were, of course, from Abbie. She didn't ply him with food, but she did kiss him when no one was about, and that was the best treat of all.

Finn had finally given her the bracelet, watching her face as she examined it carefully. She caressed the smooth beads with her fingers, marveling at the lovely blue color of the stones. Finn didn't know what they were called, but he'd seen many of his Indian friends wearing them in their amulets and woven into their braids. Abbie put on the bracelet and held out her wrist, admiring the effect before tucking it underneath her sleeve and out of sight. She was pleased, and that made Finn very happy.

Finn slid off the stile, deciding to take a short walk. His legs felt wobbly from days of lying in bed, and he just needed to move around a bit. He'd walk to the woods and back. He never did check his traps, but he wouldn't be going into the woods — not today. Finn looked up at the lovely, nearly transparent moon, trying to recapture the dream that had woken him during the night. He couldn't recall any of the details, but something was nagging at him. He'd resolved to remember that part of the dream during the night, but naturally forgot what it was by the time he woke up in the morning.

Abbie called out to him as he passed the barn, her blond curls framing her flushed face as she carried a pail of milk back to the house. He made a move to come and help her, but she waved him away, telling him that he wasn't allowed to do any lifting yet. Finn felt odd, being on the farm but not doing any work. He had to earn his keep or Mr. Mallory might decide to get rid of him. Of course, at the back of his mind, Finn knew that Mr. Mallory would do no such thing. The older man knew who attacked Finn and why.

Finn reached the tree line and found a stump to sit on. He'd just take a little break before walking back. He hadn't expected to feel so tired. Suddenly, the fragment of the dream came back to him, as if his mind was finally ready to surrender that little piece of lost memory. He'd dreamed of the night he found the time-travel device in Amelia's old bedroom. He'd come home and was sneaking past the dining room, trying to avoid detection as he made for the stairs. He hadn't been paying much attention to the conversation inside, but his mind must have registered it anyhow, snippets replaying in his sleep. Aunt Louisa had just been saying something about knowing their guest from her days in England as Finn tiptoed past the door.

Finn stopped to digest this interesting piece of information. All this time he'd been asking himself how he got transported to the future, but he'd never asked why. And there were so many questions he should have asked. Had the man come to see Aunt Louisa? Why did he have a time-travel device, and had he used it to come to the future, or from the future? Were his parents aware of the fact that such a device existed? Why did Aunt Louisa, whom his mother had hardly spoken of, suddenly arrive in Virginia without any warning, and where had she been before boarding a ship at Plymouth? Why did his mother never speak of her family, or her life before Yealm Castle? Who else had used the time-travel device before him? Was it just their guest, or had there been someone else?

Finn got up and began walking again, his mind abuzz with questions. He didn't want to jump to erroneous conclusions, but since he'd found the device in their home, obviously he wasn't the first person to travel through time. He cast his mind over the entire family. His father, Charles and Kit were so clearly men of their time that he dismissed them very quickly. He'd never noticed anything in their behavior that gave him pause, not that he had been looking for anything. His mother and Aunt Louisa, on the other hand, sometimes surprised him. They said things that seemed a bit odd, especially when they thought no one was listening, and their views on religion and the role of women were radical, although they kept those to themselves most of the time. He'd always thought that they were more outspoken than other women, although he had no idea how other women behaved in their own homes.

Annabel always deferred to Charles in the course of a conversation, but his mother and Aunt Louisa always jumped right in, voicing their opinions and arguing with their husbands. Finn pushed his hat further back on his head, looking up to the heavens in search of answers. Was it possible, or was he just reading into things, desperately looking for something that made any kind of sense? Did it make sense? Could it be that his mother and her sister had come from another time? But if they had, did their own husbands not notice anything? Both his father and Kit had been married before, losing their young wives in their twenties. They'd had experience of other women. Surely, they saw that Valerie and Louisa were somewhat different. Even his sister was different, thanks to their influence. She was more outspoken than most girls her age, and definitely more opinionated. Finn momentarily pitied the poor man who got her for a wife, suddenly wishing desperately to see her again, if only to tell her that he hadn't meant to brush her off all those times, and she was secretly his best friend and closest ally at home.

"Finn, come for breakfast. Ma has it all ready," called Sarah, running toward him from the house. She looked even smaller from a distance, reminding him of his sister when she was that age. She was always trailing after him, starved for attention, and he'd been so mean to her, preoccupied with his own interests and plans. Finn sighed and made for the house, ready to eat.

THIRTY-SIX

Louisa leaned back against the rough wooden wall of the cabin, her eyes closing in exhaustion. The ship was quiet around her, almost everyone asleep at this time of night. She found the creaking of wood and the flapping of sails to be as comforting as a lullaby. The sea was calm tonight, the boat rocking gently from side to side as it slid across the Atlantic, chewing up the miles and taking her further and further away from Valerie.

Kit was sound asleep on the opposite berth, his face peaceful in slumber. He turned over, trying to find a more comfortable position, since his legs were too long for the berth, and had to be bent at all times. He was taller than most men, and even their bed at home had been a few inches too short, forcing Kit to use the trunk at the base as an extension. Louisa wondered how tall Kit actually was. He was at least a head taller than her five foot five, so maybe close to six feet. His height would not have been unusual in the twenty-first century, but people tended to be much shorter and slighter in the seventeenth century due to the lack of good nutrition and medicine.

Louisa looked down at Evie, who was sucking furiously.

Normally, she fell asleep after she was full, but she was still going strong. There was no clock in the cabin, but Louisa was sure it was much longer than usual. She switched breasts, hoping Evie would soon be satisfied and go back to sleep, allowing Louisa to get some rest. They'd been at sea for two weeks now, not even halfway to England, and already Louisa was chafing against life on board, dreaming of land. The ship was large by the standards of the time, but in reality, it was the size of a large sailboat in her own time. The crew and their unexpected passengers were crammed on board with not an inch of unoccupied space.

There was very little to do during the course of the day, other than stay in the tiny cabin or go up on deck for some much-needed air and exercise. Louisa was always trying to find a quiet spot to stand, so as not to be in the way of the sailors. She felt claustrophobic in the cabin and needed to come on deck for several hours a day, regardless of the weather. Kit tried to make himself useful to the captain, and Bridget spent most of her time in the cabin, washing their few items of clothing and watching Evie while she slept.

Evie finally exhausted herself, her eyes closing of their own accord as she released the nipple with a gentle pop, growing heavier in Louisa's arms. She normally slept in a hammock that had been put up just for her, but Louisa was too tired to get up, afraid of waking the sleeping baby. She just laid her down gently, curling around her warm, little body. Louisa closed her eyes, willing sleep to come, but despite her fatigue, she couldn't get back to sleep. Her uterus was contracting painfully, and a wave of nausea washed over her as the rocking of the ship became more pronounced. She hoped the weather wasn't changing. They'd already suffered two storms, but thankfully, they weren't bad enough to cause any damage to the vessel. What she wouldn't give for a seat on a plane. Six hours and she would have been in London, greeted by a surly customs officer while praying that her luggage hadn't been lost. Louisa sighed. The days of airplanes were over for her. This was the most expedient mode of transportation, and with any luck, they would be in England by the beginning of December.

Louisa was awakened by Evie's mewling. The cabin was flooded with bright light coming through the porthole, the sound of feet on deck making a racket overhead. It was time to get up and feed Evie again. Louisa glanced over at Kit's berth, but he was already gone, having left the cabin quietly so as not to wake them up. Louisa forced herself to rise, reaching for a clean clout for Evie. She poured a little water into a basin, wet a rag and cleaned the baby before putting on the clout, rewrapping the blanket and putting her to her breast again. Evie began to suck as if she hadn't been fed in days rather than hours. She was grabbing onto the breast with her hand, gumming Louisa painfully. She seemed starved. For some reason, Evie seemed hungrier in the past few days. Maybe she was going through a growth spurt and needed to increase her intake. Louisa supposed that wasn't unusual, although the only person she could consult on the ship was Bridget, who was a walking encyclopedia.

Louisa fought waves of nausea from the rolling of the ship as Evie continued to nurse, still hungry after having drained both breasts. Her little face became red with effort as she tried to suck the last of the milk before finally giving up.

"I brought you some breakfast," Kit announced as he entered the cabin, carrying a cup of ale and a couple of biscuits. Louisa looked at the food with revulsion. She was hungry, but the thought of ale made her nauseous. She had just enough time to hand the baby to Kit before she was sick into the basin.

"Louisa, are you ill?" Kit put a hand to her forehead, checking for a fever.

"No, I'm just seasick. I think I need some fresh air. Would

you take Evie for a walk?" Louisa rinsed her mouth with some water and forced herself to take a sip of ale. It was warm and bitter, making her feel sick again.

"You weren't sick on the last crossing, and we've been at sea for several weeks. Why now?" Kit was looking at her with concern.

"I think it's because the sea is rougher at this time of year. I just need some air." Louisa bolted for the door, leaving Kit to see to Evie. She was fussing, turning her head, her mouth opening and closing as if still hungry.

Louisa gulped the frigid air until she felt marginally better. She found a quiet spot, sitting down on a barrel, enjoying the wind on her face and the briny smell of the sea. Louisa pulled off her cap, allowing her hair to blow in the brisk wind, whipping into her flushed face to the amazement of the sailors who weren't used to seeing a woman with her head uncovered. She closed her eyes, listening to the cries of hungry seagulls overhead, the sound of water lapping against the hull soothing and hypnotic. The nausea passed as suddenly as it arrived, leaving Louisa hungry. She would have killed for a cup of tea and a boiled egg with some toast. Her stomach was in knots from the rough food and lack of fruits and vegetables.

Kit appeared on deck, carrying Evie wrapped tightly in her blanket to keep out the brisk wind. She was twisting and turning in Kit's arms as he tried to keep a firm grip on her. The first mate said something to him that made Kit scowl, but she couldn't hear the words. These men weren't used to seeing fathers taking care of their children. That was women's work, and seeing a man with a baby was usually cause for a snide comment.

"I think she's hungry," he said as he stopped in front of Louisa. "She keeps fussing and smacking her lips. Didn't you just feed her?"

"Yes, just before you came in. She can't be hungry so soon. I

need to eat something before I feed her again. I'm depleted."
Louisa reluctantly rose to her feet, following Kit back to the
cabin. She forced down the hard biscuit and took a few sips of
ale before putting Evie to her breast again. The baby sucked
ferociously, her eyes closed in concentration.

"Kit, would you fetch Bridget please?" Louisa asked,
suddenly worried. Maybe Kit was right, and she was getting
sick. She felt unusually tired and queasy. Her arms and legs felt
as if they were made of lead, and her eyes felt grainy from lack
of sleep.

"Of course. I trust she's feeling better today. Seems as if
both of you have been afflicted with seasickness. She's been
green around the gills for two weeks now. I thought she came
from a fishing village and grew up around the sea."

"It was a long time ago, and she hasn't been on a ship since
she crossed the Atlantic with Alec and Valerie all those years
ago," answered Louisa, trying to get more comfortable. Bridget
was older now, and everything was more difficult with age. How
old was Bridget anyway? Valerie had mentioned something
about Bridget being a year older than her, so she had to be
around forty-three. Louisa always thought of her as being older,
since she looked at least a decade older than Valerie. Her sister
had the benefit of good nutrition and medicine before she found
herself in the past, and it still showed, even after all this time.
Bridget's frizzy red hair was streaked with gray, and there were
some wrinkles on her round, freckled face, especially around
the eyes. She had the type of skin that didn't age well, even in
the modern times where all kinds of moisturizers and lotions
were available.

There were no beauty products in the seventeenth century.
Women did little more than clean their teeth with a twig and
brush their hair. Valerie had mentioned that some of the ladies
in England used lotions made of hog fat to moisturize their
faces, but she couldn't bring herself to put the rancid fat of a

dead animal on her face. It was too disgusting. Valerie did make a sort of egg shampoo when there were eggs to spare, to add nutrients and luster to her hair, but that didn't stop the hair from going gray. Louisa had noticed a few silver strands when Valerie took her cap off, making her feel somewhat sad. Their mother had colored her hair every two months, making sure that no gray hair was ever visible on her head. She looked fabulous at sixty, not something that her daughters would be able to do.

Louisa ran her fingers through Evie's silky curls, watching her cheeks puff out as she sucked. She was so sweet. Her eyes were closed in concentration; the long black lashes fanned out against her velvety cheek. A sharp cramp tore through Louisa's belly, nearly making her double over. It felt like a contraction. She laid the baby on the berth, wrapping her arms around her middle in an effort to control the pain. Evie let out a terrible wail, obviously still not satisfied.

"What's amiss, yer ladyship?" Bridget asked, walking carefully into the cabin, her feet spread unusually wide to keep her from losing her balance.

"I don't know, Bridget. Evie is eating, but she seems hungry all the time. She's been like this for the past few days. It's like she can't get enough, and I have pains in my stomach and feel seasick. How are you feeling?" Bridget did indeed look greenish. Her whey-colored face looked sweaty despite the cold wind, and Louisa noticed that she'd lost some weight. It wasn't abnormal to lose weight aboard a ship, but Bridget looked downright frail.

"Perhaps ye're producing less milk. It happens sometimes due to change in diet. Ye need to drink more." Bridget gave Louisa a searching look. "Ye don't look well, yer ladyship. Have ye gotten yer menses since Evie's birth?"

"No, not yet. I think they'll come soon. I've been very crampy, especially while I'm feeding the baby. It feels like the beginning of labor." Louisa felt another wave of nausea, her hand going to her mouth automatically. She saw Bridget watching her carefully, her eyes narrowed.

"'Tis not unusual to feel crampy while nursing. 'Tis the womb contracting, but there could be other reasons. Have ye lain with yer husband since the baby's birth, yer ladyship?" Bridget seemed a little embarrassed, averting her eyes from Louisa as she waited for an answer. She was the closest thing to a midwife that Louisa and Valerie had, but she still felt awkward asking certain questions. Women didn't normally talk of such things among themselves.

"Yes, why?" Louisa wasn't sure what that had to do with anything. Making love on a narrow berth was nearly impossible, but they did manage it once or twice, with much difficulty. Louisa didn't really mind that it wasn't more often. Her body still felt sore and foreign; the lovemaking more of a trial than pleasure. Kit sensed her discomfort and didn't persist, realizing that she obviously needed more time to heal.

"May I examine ye?" Bridget came closer, taking Evie from Louisa and laying her in her hammock. "Just lie back if ye will."

Louisa reclined on the berth, allowing Bridget's gentle hands to palpate her stomach. It felt nice, so she closed her eyes, still tired despite having slept for a few hours after Evie's feeding. She would ask Bridget to take Evie for a little while and take a nap; otherwise she wouldn't make it through the rest of the day. Louisa's eyes flew open as she felt Bridget's fingers squeezing her nipples hard.

"Bridget, what are you doing?" she yelped; her nipples were terribly sensitive from all the breastfeeding.

Bridget let go of the nipples and sat down on Kit's berth, suddenly even paler than she was before. Her face was glistening with sweat.

"Bridget, are you ill?" Louisa reached out, taking Bridget's hand.

"I'll be all right. It's ye I'm concerned for. I think ye might be with child, yer ladyship, and ye're not producing enough milk. Only a few drops came out when I squeezed yer breasts. Should have been at least a trickle." Bridget squeezed Louisa's hand in sympathy.

"No, that can't be. You can't conceive while nursing. Isn't that true?" Louisa was sure she'd read that somewhere, and anyway, even if she had, the milk didn't dry up due to another pregnancy. Lots of women fed their babies while pregnant. She'd had a friend in New York who fed her son until he was nearly two while pregnant with her daughter. Bridget shook her head, smiling at Louisa's naiveté.

"Haven't ye ever heard of Irish twins? Some women conceive afore they even get their courses after birth. It's very possible. Normally, they continue to produce milk, but it does make the womb contract, and they're more tired since their body is under such strain. Ye also have the anxiety over yer unexpected departure. 'Tis possible that combined with the pregnancy, yer body is making less milk."

"Oh, Bridget, what if it dries up altogether? How will I feed Evie? She's only two-months-old. She can't survive without me." Louisa felt a terrible panic. It's not as if she could just run to the store and get some formula or even find a wet nurse. They were in the middle of the Atlantic with no other nursing women on board. Tears welled up in Louisa's eyes, spilling onto her cheeks.

"Do not fash yerself, yer ladyship. There are steps we can take. Firstly, ye must drink more, much more. That should help. I know ye don't care for the ale, but it works. If that doesn't do it, we'll need another plan. We won't let this precious baby go hungry. Ye just take care of yerself now. Ye need yer strength. 'Tis hard to tell with any certainty if ye're really with child. 'Tis too soon, but time will tell. It always does. All will be well. Ye'll see."

Bridget sat down next to Louisa, wrapping her arm around

her as she cried. This couldn't be happening. She couldn't be pregnant again so soon. It took them a long time to conceive Evie. How could she get pregnant right away? It must have happened that time when Kit found out the truth of where she came from. Good God, she was probably at least a month along. And Evie — what would happen to Evie?

THIRTY-SEVEN

Valerie pulled down the coverlet to examine Alec's ribs. The bruises were still a rainbow of colors with deep violet in the center, and shades of green and yellow at the edges where the bruising was already beginning to heal. Alec had been resting for two days but was rearing to get out of bed.

"One more day," Valerie pronounced her verdict. "You're not ready to go out yet. For all we know your ribs might have been fractured. Just give it another day. There's no rush. I'll just go out this afternoon and put up a few more broadsheets."

She pulled the coverlet back over Alec, rising from the bed. She had to admit that she was terribly disappointed. Other than the printer, the innkeeper and his daughter no one had come forward. Valerie had put up broadsheets within about a mile radius of the inn, but maybe it was time to go a little further and explore some of the side streets. She kissed a disgruntled Alec, picked up her sheaf of papers and a pot of glue, and left the room.

Valerie was lost in thought as she walked away from the inn, considering where best to put up her remaining leaflets. She had about twenty left and wanted to use them to the best advantage.

She'd assumed that the way to get the most people to see them was to post them at taverns and pubs, but she'd already put up a broadsheet in nearly every pub, as well as by the courthouse, church, and near the Capitol building. Valerie decided to walk in the direction of William and Mary College. She hadn't put any broadsheets there, and maybe some student had seen something.

The afternoon had turned dreary, rain threatening to come down at any minute. Valerie was glad that she'd worn her cloak. The weather had turned over the past week, going from mild, sunny days to frosty mornings and cold nights. She didn't have enough warm clothes. She'd naively imagined that they would find Finn and get back home before they were even missed. Now it was nearly Halloween, and still his trail was as cold as ever.

Valerie briefly wondered if Halloween was celebrated in the eighteenth century. Somehow, she didn't think so. Despite the mixed origins of the holiday, starting out as a pagan ritual and eventually becoming a Catholic prelude to All Saint's Day, the colonies were mostly Protestant. Valerie had always hated Halloween, put off by what it had become over the years. It had been fun when she was a child, dressing up and going trick-or-treating with Louisa and her parents, but she didn't like the scarier element that adults invariably brought to it.

As Valerie walked toward the college, the street began to change from a busy thoroughfare lined with shops, to a more rural road with fewer houses and businesses. She could see the buildings of the college up ahead, but there didn't seem to be much between the center of town and the college. Valerie suddenly stopped and looked around. She could have sworn she heard footsteps just behind her, but there was no one there. She was probably just overreacting since she was thinking of all the creepy Halloween movies she'd seen as a teen. Valerie put Halloween firmly out of her mind and began to walk faster. She

would just put up a few sheets by the college and turn back
before it began to get dark.

Valerie was just about to cross the road when a wagon came
rumbling toward her, the horses slowing down, presumably to
let her pass. She hung back, waiting for the wagon to stop. She
wasn't taking any chances. She'd seen a slave woman get run
over just the other day, the driver not even bothering to check if
she was all right, before leaving the scene of the accident. If
passersby hadn't pulled the woman from under the wheels of
the wagon, it would have rolled right over her, probably killing
her. Valerie had been horrified, but no one seemed to care,
leaving the injured woman on the side of the road as they went
about their business.

As the wagon finally slowed down in front of her, Valerie
glanced at the driver. Her blood ran cold with fear, and her
knees began to buckle as she recognized the man who attacked
Alec the other day. She spun around ready to run, just as Bobby
Mann came up behind her, knocking her to the ground and
pulling a sack over her head. He viciously twisted her arms
behind her back, binding them with a thick rope. Valerie began
to struggle, trying to call for help, but a blow to the side of her
head silenced her, leaving her disoriented and dizzy. She was
dumped into the back of the wagon like a sack of potatoes, as
the contraption lurched under her, the horses picking up speed.
Valerie was dimly aware of motion and the hard boards beneath
her, but her ears were ringing from the blow; her eyes shut tight
against the terrible pain in her head.

Where were they taking her? Her heart was beating wildly
as the full realization of what was happening finally hit her.
Thank God she'd left the time-travel device in the room, so Alec
could get back if he ever found Finn. Tears choked her as she
contemplated her fate. She couldn't imagine that these men
would just let her go, unless they wanted to use her to get to

Alec. She'd never tell them where to find him, for they would kill him for sure if they did.

The terrain beneath the wheels began to change, becoming bumpier, the road obviously more rutted. They were taking her out of Williamsburg. Valerie struggled desperately, calling for help. She screamed as someone kicked her in the ribs, but the pain only lasted until the second blow to the back of her head. This time it knocked her out, leaving her limp on the bed of the wagon.

THIRTY-EIGHT

Finn had to admit that he was glad to be working on his own that day. Jonah was helping Mr. Mallory mend a fence, and Finn was cutting the corn stalks left after the harvest. It was tedious and tiring work since the field was vast, but he was in no rush. The stalks would be used for compost, so there was no great urgency to cut them quickly. He was working his way through his section of the field, steadily and methodically, his mind occupied with questions from his epiphany the other day. He'd been thinking about it for a few days now, but he was no closer to answers.

Speculation was all well and good, but he had no real proof of anything, other than the fact that he wound up one hundred and fifty years in the future. Finn had to admit that other than missing his family, he kind of liked it here. The sense of patriotism and urgency he felt all around him was infectious, making him suddenly wonder about all the things he simply accepted in his old life. Why shouldn't these people govern themselves and make their own laws? It was a radical concept, but an exciting one; one that people of his time would never accept. A government chosen by the people — what a thought. Finn momentarily imagined going back home and describing this Revolution to his father. His father would be incredulous and outraged by the mere notion of a government without a monarch. *Oh, Daddy, how I wish I could talk to you*, he thought.

Finn was distracted from his thoughts by the sight of Abbie, walking happily through the cleared portion of the field. She was swinging a pail in her hand, obviously bringing him his dinner. The midday meal was his favorite. Supper was more of a light meal, but the midday meal was the heartiest. Usually, Mrs. Mallory made some kind of stew with meat and vegetables and even served pickle on the side. Finn felt his spirits rise. He hoped Abbie would stay with him while he ate. She was also one opinionated woman. He wondered what his mother would make of her. She'd probably like her. Abbie had a mind of her own, and there's nothing his mother admired more in a woman. Come to think of it, all the Mallory women had a mind of their own, even little Annie, who could manipulate the entire family with a few tears or a timely kiss. She seemed to have taken a shine to Finn, often climbing in his lap and demanding a story.

"Ma sent you some dinner," Abbie announced as she finally reached him. "There's a nice spot there under that tree, why don't we sit down? I have to get back soon, but I'll stay for a few minutes," she said, smiling into his eyes. Finn thought of their kiss last night, hoping he might persuade her to give him another. He followed her obediently to the spot she chose, sitting down and accepting the still-warm pail. Abbie handed him a stone bottle of cider as she sat down next to him, smoothing out her skirt.

"Ma asked me to walk down to the Fletcher place. Seems Mrs. Fletcher promised her a cut of lace that Ma wants to use to make a wedding present for Martha. It's all a big secret," she said with a grin.

"Isn't it a long walk to the Fletchers?" Finn asked, tucking into his stew. "Would you like to share my meal?"

"Oh, no. I've already had some. It's a two-hour walk, but I don't mind. It's a lovely day and I welcome the break from doing chores. Mrs. Fletcher is a kind soul, who has a fondness for baking," she answered, dimpling at him. "I hear she was all set to make apple fritters this week." Finn laughed. He wouldn't have said no to apple fritters himself. He wished he could accompany Abbie to the Fletcher farm. It was a lovely day as she said, and a walk alone with her would be a treat.

"Ma is hoping Sam will come back in time for the wedding. She's worried about him, being with the Army and all. Isn't that just the fate of women? Pa is proud of his boy, while Ma frets quietly, crying into her pillow," Abbie said sadly. "She'll never recover if something happens to him. I wish the blasted British would just admit defeat and go away, so we could all get on with our lives. They'll lose one way or the other."

"You seem awfully sure. What happens if they don't lose?" Finn was sorry as soon as he asked the question. Abbie's eyes blazed with fervor as she turned on him.

"They will lose. Just you wait and see, Finlay Whitfield. Our cause is just, and we will win, no matter how long it takes. We will have democracy and become the greatest nation in the world."

"I'll drink to that," said Finn, raising the bottle of cider in salute, sorry that he ever brought up the subject.

"Me too." Abbie took the bottle out of his hands and took a sip of the cool cider. Her lips were moist as she handed the bottle back. She gazed at him coyly, suddenly shy. Finn knew his moment when he saw it, so he took her by the shoulders, kissing her parted lips. She kissed him back, leaning closer; her breasts pressed against his chest. Her heart was beating rapidly, echoing his own as their kiss deepened, his hand straying to cup her breast. Abbie gently moved the hand away, but didn't break the kiss, opening her mouth under his, tasting of fermented apples.

"I best be going," she said, jumping up. "Ma will be expecting me back by sunset. I'll take the pail with me and wash it out by the creek. Maybe Mrs. Fletcher will give me an apple fritter or two for my young man," she said with a wicked grin and ran off.

Finn watched her go, his heart still racing from their kiss. All kinds of wicked thoughts ran through his head as he looked after her. What he wouldn't give to have her all to himself for a while. His cock was stiff, throbbing in his pants and aching for what only Abbie could provide. Finn reluctantly went back to work, cutting down the stalks with much less enthusiasm. The sun was riding high in the sky, puffy clouds floating overhead as the leaves rustled all around him, caught up in their private conversation. Finn looked around. Abbie had long since vanished from view, but not from his thoughts. He'd worked every day except Sunday, doing whatever he was told to do without a word of complaint. Today, he was going to do what he wanted.

Finn walked from the field, following in Abbie's footsteps. He momentarily thought of leaving his scythe behind, but then reconsidered. Tools were precious, and if someone decided to help themselves, Mr. Mallory would have his head. He'd just have to take it with him. At least it was a hand scythe, and not one with a long wooden handle. That would have been uncomfortable to carry for a long period of time. Abbie had a head start of about forty minutes, but she was walking at a leisurely pace. If Finn walked quickly, he would catch up with her within a half hour. Finn threw one last look at the field, then raced after Abbie.

* * *

Finn looked around in confusion. Abbie should have been in his sights by now, but there was no sign of her anywhere. She wouldn't have walked through the woods when there was a path running through the meadow. Finn stood still, listening. Usually, if you listened hard enough, you could hear something. He waited a moment. The sounds of nature surrounded him; birds singing, leaves rustling in the breeze, insects buzzing, filling the air with their hum. Then he heard it, the neighing of a horse. Abbie was on foot, and there were no farms between the Mallorys and the Fletchers in this direction. The horse had to be with a person. Finn walked swiftly in the direction of the sound.

As he got closer, he heard laughter coming from a copse to his left. The laughter sounded mean, not like an expression of joy, but rather like someone jeering at another person. Finn walked deeper into the woods, deciding to approach from the other side. Whatever was happening, he didn't want to walk straight into it. He could have sworn he heard Abbie's cry, but it could be his overactive imagination playing tricks on him. On the other hand, it might not be. What if Matthew Granville hadn't been satisfied with getting his revenge on Finn and decided to teach Abbie a lesson as well? He'd as good as called her a "whore", so what if he meant to cause her harm?

Finn walked on silent feet, keeping to the shadow of the larger trees. He could see a glimmer of something red between the trees but needed to get closer. A blur of white caught his attention as he heard Abbie cry out again. Finn positioned himself behind a wide tree trunk as he took in the scene. Two British soldiers were in the small clearing, their unbuttoned coats blending in with the foliage all around them. Their hats were on the ground with their swords and packs, and their horses were hobbled nearby, chewing peacefully. The remnants of a fire sent curling wisps of blue smoke into the chilly air. The soldiers must have either camped there for the night or stopped to have a rest and a meal. The path was clearly visible through the sparse trees, so they must have spotted Abbie walking along, alone and unprotected.

This was the first time Finn had seen British soldiers at close range. He'd expected them to be young and fit, splendid in their crimson tunics and white trousers, but these men were middle-aged, balding and thickset. Their once-white shirts were dirty, and their breeches covered with stains and dust. They looked disheveled and filthy. One of the men held Abbie in front of him; his thick arms wrapped around her like bands of steel. He was grinning lewdly as his friend ran his stubby finger just over her bodice, tracing her breasts. Abbie's tucker had been torn off and lay in the grass nearby. The soldiers were laughing and taunting her, obviously in no rush to get to their real purpose. They didn't expect anyone to interrupt them.

"You're a fine one, aren't you? A tasty morsel for any man. How would you like to have two men at the same time? I bet you'd like that, wouldn't you?"

Abbie struggled valiantly, but the man holding her clamped his hand over her mouth, preventing her from screaming. She must have bitten him, for he yanked away his hand, yelping in pain, and giving her a vicious shake.

"Let's get on with it, Gerald," he said. "We don't have all day and all her squirming is making my stones ache. If you want to go first, then get on with it. I want my turn, and I intend to take my time about it." He pushed Abbie to the ground, forcing her hands over her head and holding them in a tight grip at the wrists. Abbie began to struggle desperately as the man named Gerald lifted her skirt, shoving his hand between her legs. She tried to kick him, but he skillfully pushed her legs apart with his own, pinning them against the ground.

"Don't you like that, sweetheart?" he asked, breathing hoarsely as he forced his fingers into the struggling girl. "Come now, be honest. You like old Gerald, don't you? Now, lookie what I have for you here." Gerald unlaced his breeches, pushing them down far enough to reveal his engorged cock. Abbie's eyes opened wide in horror as her body went rigid with strain. She tried to free her legs, but Gerald was too strong for her. He pushed her skirt to her waist, leering at her bare legs and the triangle of curly golden hair.

"Let me go!" she screamed. "You'll be hanged for this."

"And who will believe you, you filthy little strumpet? Just pray you don't get a swollen belly. That would be hard to explain to your oh-so-patriotic father. You'd have a British bastard, and not even know who the father is. Hold her down, Bert. I won't be long."

Gerald positioned himself above Abbie, driving his knee between her legs to pry them further apart. Finn didn't have a moment to waste. He charged from the trees, shrieking like an Indian as he grabbed Gerald by the hair, pulling his head back and bringing the blade of the scythe down on his Adam's apple with vicious force. The sharp blade sliced right through the skin of the neck, sending a spray of hot blood all over Abbie's legs. Bert fell back in shock, scooting away on his backside as Finn turned his attention away from the dying man. He couldn't let the man go. He would just go back to headquarters, and Finn would be charged with murder. The men seemed to know who Abbie's father was, so they'd have no trouble finding him.

Bert had managed to get to his feet and was running to the trees, his red coat flapping like wings. Finn let out another shriek and came after him, knocking him to the ground and sitting atop his back. It was the first time in his life that Finn had known bloodlust. He'd heard his Indian friends speaking of it, but he'd not experienced it himself. He had no wish to ever kill a man, but he had no choice now. His Indian amulet fell out of his shirt, reminding Finn of his Indian name—"Kills many." He never thought it would apply to people, just animals, but he had no choice. Finn grabbed Bert by the hair and sliced off his scalp in one fluid motion. He was nearly sick as he looked at what remained of the soldier's head, but he turned away quickly, tossing the scalp to the ground. The other man still sat on his haunches, a look of shock on his face; his eyes glazed in death. Abbie sat on the ground, her knees pulled up to her chest, her eyes closed. She was shaking hard, tears rolling down her cheeks and into her mouth, which was open in a silent scream.

Finn went to her, pulling her into his arms and crushing her in his embrace. He held her until the shaking subsided, and she finally began to sob out loud. She needed a good cry. Finn hardly realized that his own tears fell atop her head as his mind finally acknowledged what he'd done. He'd killed two people, which was a mortal sin, but he had no choice. It was either saving Abbie or his soul, and there was no question which came first.

"Abbie, look at me," Finn commanded. "Look at me. It's all right. It will be all right. Come, let me help you up." Abbie clung to him as he helped her off the ground, her eyes not meeting his, but turned away from him as soon as she was on her feet, looking off into the forest. She was probably horrified by what he'd done. Finn tried not to look at the fresh corpses on the ground. He had no idea what to do with them. They were British soldiers, and someone would come looking for them sooner or later. Questions would be asked. But more than the dead soldiers, Finn was worried about Abbie. She had seen him at his worst, and now she would never look at him again without seeing him wielding that scythe as he killed two men. She wouldn't even look at him now.

"Abbie," he called to her wistfully. "Please look at me."

Abbie turned to him then, her eyes still full of tears, and walked into his arms, burying her face in his neck. She wrapped her arms around him, holding him with her all her might. "You saved me Finn. You risked your life to help me. How can I ever thank you for what you've done for me?" She looked up at him, her brown eyes darkened by intensity.

"Abbie, you don't have to thank me. I would do anything for you. Just tell me that you are not horrified by what I've done. I couldn't stand it if you despised me." Finn stroked her hair and face, kissing her forehead.

"Despise you?" she looked up confused. "You were so brave, going up against two armed soldiers. Wait till I tell Pa." She was cupping his cheek, still looking into his eyes as if he were a hero.

"Abbie, we can't tell your father, or anyone else. We must keep this a secret. When they find them, they'll likely think it an Indian attack. If they think they were killed by the rebels, there might be a reprisal against civilians. We couldn't risk that. We must go to the Fletchers as planned and act as if nothing's happened. I'll walk you. I just need to clean my scythe, and you need to wash out your dress. There's a stream a little further into the woods. Just wash out the blood and the dress will dry by the time we get to the farm. Bridget always said that nothing gets out bloodstains quicker than cold water."

"Who's Bridget?" asked Abbie, examining her bloodstained skirt. It wasn't too bad. Most of the blood got on her legs and would be easy enough to wash off. Abbie absentmindedly picked up her tucker, brushing off the leaves and dirt. It wasn't damaged otherwise.

"She was my nurse," answered Finn, picking up the scythe. "Come, we should hurry." Finn couldn't wait to wash his hands. They were covered in blood, making him feel soiled. He'd have to wash out his shirt as well. Most of it was clean since he got both men from behind, but the cuffs were stained with blood, which was turning a rusty brown as it dried. Finn washed his hands thoroughly before taking off his shirt and washing out the cuffs. The blood came out easily, coloring the water for a few seconds before dissolving in the stream and fading from view.

Abbie took off her shoes and walked into the creek, gasping as the cold water swirled around her ankles. She kirtled the skirt above her knees and washed the blood off her legs before untying the skirt and washing out the stains. Finn was surprised that she hadn't been wearing hose, but he supposed she only wore them to church and when it was cold, and the past few days hadn't been so bad. He tried not to stare at her bare legs. They were slim and shapely, but her flesh was covered in goose bumps from the cold water. He tried not to allow his imagination to go further and dwell on what he'd seen earlier. Abbie would be mortified to know that he'd witnessed her nakedness. Let her think she'd been blocked from view by the man's broad back. She deserved to retain some dignity after what happened.

Finn took off his coat, wrapping it around Abbie's shoulders to prevent her from catching a chill. The homespun fabric would dry quickly in the breeze, looking as good as new by the time they got to the Fletcher farm. He adjusted her cap, twirling a curl around his finger until she smiled. Finn took Abbie by the hand and let her back to the path, avoiding the clearing. He had to admit that he didn't feel much remorse. Those animals got what they deserved. He shuddered to think of what would have happened had he decided not to follow Abbie. They would have raped her, probably hurting her very badly. The poor girl would never again feel safe with a man, not even her husband. He was secretly proud to have saved her from such a fate, suddenly wondering what it would feel like to be a husband and have a woman of his own to protect.

* * *

Mrs. Fletcher greeted them happily, instantly inviting them in and offering them a cup of beer and some apple fritters. Finn had never tasted anything so delicious. The fritters were wonderful, bursting with warm chunks of apples and drizzled with honey. Mrs. Fletcher instantly added a few more to the still-hot skillet, knowing they'd want seconds. Abbie told Finn on the way that the Fletchers had an apple orchard on their land, so nearly everything they ate in the fall had some form of apples in it. They also took bushels of apples to Williamsburg and other surrounding villages to sell or barter, obtaining some supplies for the coming winter. Abbie wanted to have a few apple trees when she was married and had a house of her own. She liked the fruit, but what she liked most were the beautiful, white blossoms that covered the trees like huge snowflakes.

Abbie was still in shock, but she drank the beer and ate the fritters, her hands shaking slightly. Mrs. Fletcher prattled on about the lace for Martha and her sons, who were also in the Army with Sam. Her two younger children were playing outside, chasing each other with the maximum amount of laughing and shrieking. Finn tried to answer Mrs. Fletcher politely to distract her from the fact that Abbie was uncommonly quiet. He didn't want her to get suspicious, so he nudged Abbie under the table with his foot, his eyes sliding to Mrs. Fletcher and back. Abbie instantly got the hint and joined the conversation, asking after Mrs. Fletcher's boys and complimenting the lovely lace, which would make an exquisite trim for a tucker or a cap.

"I promised Ma I'd be back before it got dark, Mrs. Fletcher. Thank you again for the fritters. They were divine," she added, glad to see the look of pleasure on the woman's face.

"You're welcome, my dear. Let me give you some apples to take home for the little ones. And it was a pleasure to meet you, Finlay. Do come again." With that, Finn and Abbie set off for home, their story well-rehearsed, two souls bound by a terrible secret.

THIRTY-NINE

A gentle, steady rain fell from the pewter heavens, leaving the world looking dreary and wet. Everything was dripping moisture, drops of rain sliding off the leaves like tears. Louisa Whitfield gazed out of the window, tears siding down her face like raindrops. She'd never been so miserable and confused. All her life she'd been cherished and protected, always surrounded by people who loved her. Suddenly, everyone was gone. No one could give her a clear answer as to where her parents and brother went, and now Aunt Louisa and Uncle Kit were gone with the baby and Bridget. It had been two weeks since they'd left, and officials from the town had come to the plantation to question Charles about their whereabouts. Louisa wasn't quite sure of what happened, but she heard that her aunt disgraced herself in public, forcing Uncle Kit to help her escape prison, knocking out a guard in the process. They would never be able to come back now without facing severe punishment.

Charles and Annabel had taken over Louisa and Kit's room, settling in for the long winter to come. Louisa knew of the rift between her father and Charles, but she wasn't sure what caused it. It had something to do with Cora's death two years ago, but no one spoke of it in front of her, treating her like a little girl as usual. Ever since Cora was killed in the spring house and Amelia hanged herself in the attic, Charles was less than a frequent visitor to Rosewood Manor. Now, he was suddenly in charge, telling everyone what to do and lording it over the field workers. He'd reduced rations for everyone in preparation for the winter, cutting back on food for the workers by half. Mrs. Dolly now had to dole out the portions herself rather than just let the workers serve themselves. Louisa hadn't been to the barracks, but according to Minnie, the men were underfed and growing angrier by the minute. She said her father had noticeably lost weight, and she was saving some of her own food to share with him during her visits.

Louisa worried about the lack of supplies in the colony, but her more immediate concern was her upcoming wedding. Charles agreed to wait for her parents to return, but after Aunt Louisa's offense, he couldn't allow for any more scandal in the family, so the banns had been read a few days ago announcing the marriage of Louisa Whitfield and Thomas Gaines.

Louisa hadn't been allowed any contact with Tom since Charles brought her home and her anxiety increased daily, worrying about Tom's reaction to this forced union. She tried writing to him, but he didn't respond. What if he hated her? She couldn't bear it. She simply couldn't. Louisa tried talking to Annabel, but her future sister-in-law wasn't receptive. She was still angry with Louisa for trying to play her for a fool while sneaking off to seduce her brother. Louisa sighed. She would have given anything at this moment to have Annabel on her side. She missed her parents and aunt and uncle terribly, but she also sorely felt the absence of Bridget. Bridget had been her nurse since the day she was born, always there to soothe, comfort, and give unconditional love. Louisa wished that she could just sneak up to her room at night and climb into bed with her like she did when she was upset about something, having Bridget sing to her in her lovely Irish lilt until the world just fell away, leaving only a haunting Celtic tune and the night outside.

FORTY

The room was lost in shadow, the pitter-patter of rain beating a steady tattoo on the window as Alec woke up from his nap. Valerie had been right. He did feel better. Breathing was easier, and the area where he'd been clubbed wasn't as tender to the touch. Alec looked around. Where was Valerie? She must have come back while he was sleeping and gone downstairs to get them something to eat. He was starving. He hadn't eaten at all, and his stomach was growling in protest. Alec reached over for the bread Valerie left for him in the morning. It was a bit stale, but it would tide him over until he got a proper meal. He would get dressed and go downstairs.

Shirt and breeches were easy enough but pulling on his boots was a challenge that left him breathless, with stars exploding in front of his eyes when he bent down, putting pressure on his ribs. Alec exhaled deeply; giving his boots a good yank before sitting still to catch his breath. It would take at least another week until he healed properly, possibly even more. He locked the door and headed to the taproom.

The hum of conversation greeted him as he entered the bar. Most of the benches were already filled with patrons, the air smoky and reeking of spilled beer. The proprietor's daughter was skillfully maneuvering between the tables, bringing fresh tankards of beer and removing the empty ones, while avoiding the admiring looks of the men and the straying hands of some of the bolder patrons. Mr. Clements was behind the bar, filling tankards and setting them on the counter in readiness.

"Ah, Mr. Whitfield. I trust you're feeling better. Your wife said you'd been ailing." The publican pushed a tankard toward Alec, giving him a friendly smile.

"Thank you, Mr. Clements. Is my wife in the dining room?" Alec took a long sip of beer waiting for the barkeep's reply.

"Not that I know of. I haven't seen her since this afternoon. She had some of those leaflets with her and a pot of glue." Alec set the tankard down, his insides suddenly twisting with worry.

"I'll just check the dining room. Maybe you haven't noticed her coming back," he said.

The innkeeper shrugged his shoulders as he turned to serve someone else, laughing loudly at a crude joke the patron had told him.

Alec stepped into the other room. This room was much quieter with several tables set up for guests wishing to dine in peace. A few tables were occupied, diners enjoying something that smelled good, but Alec wasn't interested in the food. He looked around. There was no sign of Valerie.

"Mrs. Clements, have you seen my wife? She might have come in to get some supper," Alec asked the woman as she erupted from the kitchen, carrying several bowls of stew. She looked at him in surprise, thinking for a second before shaking her head.

"I'm sorry Mr. Whitfield. I haven't seen her since this morning when she came down for some breakfast. She said she was going out to put up broadsheets. I'd think she'd be back by now, it being dark and raining and all." She shrugged her ample shoulders as she set the steaming bowls in front of waiting customers, who tucked into them with relish.

Alec felt terrible apprehension as he left the room and stepped outside. Where was she at this hour? It was already dark, a miserable drizzle falling steadily, turning the dirt road into mud. Alec looked to the left, then to the right. Which way would she have gone? He settled on right and began walking, peering into the darkness for any sign of his wife.

Nearly an hour later Alec had to admit that Valerie hadn't come that way. She wouldn't have gone this far. He was now at least two miles from the inn, and he hadn't seen a single broadsheet with Finn's likeness. Alec turned around and headed in the other direction. It would take him an hour just to get back to the inn. Maybe she returned by now, wondering where he'd gone. Alec began walking faster. He was wet and cold, his stomach growling from lack of food.

At last, he was back at the inn. He trotted upstairs to their room, but there was no sign of Valerie. According to Mr. Clements, she hadn't come back, and he saw everyone who came and went from his vantage point behind the bar. Alec went back out into the dreary evening, heading in the opposite direction.

The night was getting darker, the moon obscured by thick clouds. Falling leaves fluttered past his face, landing on the wet street in front of his feet. The street was virtually deserted. An occasional light from a window lit a small square of sidewalk, but for the most part, it was silent and black. By this time, most people would be at home in front of a warm fire, spending time with their family after a long day of work.

Alec continued to push forward. The buildings grew sparse as he walked in the direction of the college. He was about to turn back when he saw a glimmer of something white further up and went to investigate. The image on the broadsheets was nearly disintegrated from the rain, but he could still make out the smudged features of his son. The broadsheets were scattered in the road, some torn to shreds by wheels of passing vehicles, some clinging to the wall of a nearby building where the wind must have blown them before they got wet. Valerie's pot of glue lay shattered nearby, the contents still clinging to the shards.

Alec looked around bewildered. There was nothing there save a few houses, their shutters closed firmly against the dreary night. Alec's heart pounded in his chest as the realization that something terrible must have happened to Valerie flooded his soul. He had no idea what to do.

FORTY-ONE

The place had no windows, but a feeble light from the moon shone through the cracks between the planks. The rain must have stopped, the sky finally clearing up. Valerie turned her head to the side, trying to determine where she was. It took a few moments, but her eyes finally adjusted to the darkness allowing her to make out some shapes. She was in some kind of tool shed, rakes and spades fighting for space with broken bits of furniture and bags of something. She was tied to a chair, her hands and feet bound securely to the wood. Thank God they hadn't gagged her. She supposed there was no point in screaming for help. No one would hear. Would they come back or just leave her here? Valerie looked around again. The vision in her left eye was blurred since it was tearing and swelling from the blow she'd received. Her head throbbed, and her bladder begged for relief. She had to find a way to get free before her attackers came back. It was her only chance.

Oh, Alec, how will you ever find me? she thought, knowing that Alec must be out searching for her by that time. *Okay, calm down and think rationally. There must be a way to get free.*

Valerie looked around again. She needed something sharp to cut through the ropes binding her wrists. Then she would be able to untie her feet and look for a way out of the shed. She'd just spotted something that looked like a broken scythe when the door to the shed opened up with a creak of protest from the rusted hinges. Valerie froze in helpless terror. The man was alone, and he'd obviously been drinking heavily. He limped into the shed, peering into the darkness. Valerie had no trouble recognizing him. His features were etched into her brain. He stopped directly in front of her, filling the shed with the reek of stale sweat, strong drink, and tobacco. His words were slurred, but Valerie had no trouble understanding him.

"Are ye enjoying yer new accommodations, ducks? Ye best get used to it. Ye'll be here for a while, I reckon. I 'ave not quite decided what to do with ye yet, but till I do, ye'll just stay as ye are. 'Twill give ye some time to think of what yer man must be going through. I'd be frantic if someone took my woman, if I 'ad one, that is," he said with mock sorrow, laughing at his own wit. "Shame 'e'll never find out what 'appened to ye. I plan to use ye well, ducks. Show ye what a real man can do." He came closer, grabbing her breast and squeezing it painfully. "And after I'm done, I'll decide 'ow to best get rid of ye." The man grinned at her, obviously enjoying himself.

"I need to pee," Valerie announced. She'd noticed Percival Gale limping noticeably when he entered the shed. If he would just untie her, she might have a chance. She could outrun him if she managed to get past him. The man was built like a brick house, but if she squatted, pretending to pee, maybe she'd gain some element of surprise if she charged him, possibly knocking him over. Valerie's hopes of escape were quickly dashed as Percival smiled at her, revealing rotten teeth. The slap came as a surprise, leaving her ear ringing and her lip bleeding again.

"Now, what kind of talk is that for a lady of yer station, I ask ye? No breeding. What would that pompous British 'usband of yers say if 'e heard ye talking like a common fishwife? Shame on ye. I reckon ye'll just 'ave to piss on yerself. That'll give ye something to think about as ye sit 'ere all night, wet and stinking. I'll be back in the morning to check on ye, ducky. 'Ave a lovely evening."

With that, he left the shed, locking the door after him. Valerie could hear a key turning in the lock as a heavy chain clattered against the wooden door. Untying herself would not be the only problem.

Valerie waited until all was quiet again before turning her attention back to the floor. The only way to reach the broken piece of scythe would be to turn over the chair, falling on her side. It would hurt, especially since she had to fall on the side that had already been battered. Valerie took a deep breath and began rocking from side to side. She'd seen people do that in movies, but it wasn't as easy in real life. The chair was low and sturdy; the legs firmly planted in the dirt floor of the shed, pinned down by her weight. She counted to ten to calm herself and started again. It took her some time to budge even a little, but she kept trying until the chair began to tilt. *A few more times*, she thought as she leaned to the left with all her weight.

Valerie hit the earth hard as the chair finally toppled. The wooden back crashed down on her upper arm, smashing the bone. The pain that radiated through her arm left her breathless and gasping. To move her arm even a fraction was absolute agony, but Valerie couldn't afford to waste time. She had to get close enough to reach the scythe, which was somewhere behind her head. If she failed, she would be at the mercy of her captor once the drink wore off, and he was ready to deal with her. The thought of him touching her, galvanized her into action.

Valerie used her bound feet to try to rotate herself to bring her hands closer to the scythe. She bit her lip to keep from crying out as every movement put pressure on her injured arm, grinding it into the dirt floor. She had to stop every few minutes to catch her breath while stretching her fingers in an effort to reach the scythe. Her head was pressed to the floor, so she couldn't see where the metal was, having to grope blindly. It must have taken her nearly an hour to finally position herself in such a way that her fingers could grasp the piece of metal. It felt cold and hard in her hand as she carefully wrapped her fingers around it, feeling for the sharp edge. She had to position the sharp part against the rope and cut through it without cutting her wrists. If she cut herself, she could bleed to death.

Valerie moved the scythe experimentally, sliding it against the rope binding her wrists. She scratched herself painfully, stopping to readjust her grip on the metal. Valerie tried again, more carefully this time. She felt the resistance of the hemp against the blade, but at least she had it at the right angle. She moved the scythe very slowly, moving the blade only a few millimeters at a time. Her left side was growing numb from lying on the ground with the chair pressed against her, and she was shivering with cold and the need to go to the bathroom, but she forced everything out of her mind, focusing only on the broken piece of metal in her hand.

The light in the shed grew dimmer as the moon rose higher in the sky, no longer shining through the cracks. The light was so feeble that Valerie could barely see the door. She closed her eyes in concentration, continuing to saw at the thick rope. She had no idea how long had passed before she finally felt the rope loosening around her wrists. She had to be even more careful now, not to cut herself as the blade came closer to her skin. She moved it carefully back and forth, back and forth, until the last of the fibers finally gave, allowing her to free her hands. Her fingers were bleeding from slipping on the sharp blade, but it was nothing—just scratches.

Now she had to free her feet. That was quicker, since at

least the binding was in front of her rather than behind, but she could only use her right hand since her left arm was still pinned under the chair, and she couldn't manage to push herself back up. Valerie must have been on the floor for several hours before she finally managed to saw through the rope and free herself. Her legs shook so badly she could barely stand, but she pulled herself up, walking around the shed to get the circulation back into her numb legs and feet. She held her left arm against her side, unable to move it even a little without extreme pain. She stepped into the corner and peed, sighing with relief as her aching bladder finally emptied itself. Now, she had to get the door open before they came back for her. If she couldn't do that, she had to be prepared, striking her captors as they entered the shed.

Valerie looked around again. There wasn't too much she could do with a broken rake or bits of furniture, but the spade could be useful. She tried inserting it between the planks and applying all her strength, but the wood wouldn't splinter. It was too thick and might break the spade. She needed a new plan, and she didn't have too much time. Valerie began to dig frantically, trying to make a hole large enough to crawl through to the other side. She had to get away from this place well before dawn, or all her efforts would have been for naught. Every time she lifted a spade full of dirt, she thought she would pass out from the pain in her left arm, but she had to keep going.

Valerie was shaking with strain as she emptied one shovelful after another onto the shed floor, digging with all her might. She was drenched in sweat, her dress covered with dirt, but she didn't care. There was no chance of rescue, so she had to rescue herself. It couldn't be more than a few hours till dawn, so she didn't have much time.

Valerie froze as she saw a dark shadow just outside the shed. It stood silently, listening, barely breathing. She had no idea what to do, so she huddled in the corner, holding her breath.

Was she safer in or out of the shed? The shadow shifted, moving away from the door.

Valerie leaned against the wall, panting. Whoever it was seemed to have gone and she needed to keep digging. She was just about to drive the spade into the dirt when the sound of wrenching metal stopped her in her tracks.

FORTY-TWO

Valerie positioned herself in the darkest corner, spade raised above her head. Her heart was pounding, her knees buckling with fear, and her arm was on fire, shaking with the strain of holding up the spade. The door of the shed vibrated with every blow, the sound of screeching metal thunderous in the quiet of the night. Valerie slid to the ground with relief as Alec burst into the shed, catching her just before she hit the ground.

"Valerie, are you hurt? Val, look at me." Alec grabbed her by the arms, gazing into her face. She could barely see him in the darkness, but she didn't need to. He'd found her. She opened her mouth to answer him, but a terrible blackness seemed to swallow her up as her body gave up after hours of fighting against the fear and excruciating pain.

Valerie heard Alec's voice coming from somewhere very far away. He was calling her name, begging her to wake up, but she simply couldn't. She was floating peacefully up above, no longer scared or hurting. He'd come for her, and now she could just rest for a while, safe in the knowledge that Alec would take care of her.

"Valerie, please wake up." Alec was gently slapping her

cheeks in an effort to get her to come around. He sounded frantic. Valerie felt a jolt as her soul rejoined her body on the cold, damp floor of the shed. She forced herself to open her eyes, gazing up at Alec.

"Alec, how on earth did you find me?" Valerie was shaking now, the shock wearing off and the pain setting in again. Her arm felt as if an elephant had stepped on it. Valerie made an effort to sit up but fell right back with a moan of pain. Her teeth were chattering, her body convulsing uncontrollably. Alec held her up as he wrapped his coat snugly around her, holding her close. He took in the overturned chair, rope, and the hole she'd been digging, gaping like a freshly dug grave.

"They left you here tied up overnight?" he asked, his voice low with fury. Valerie just nodded.

"Alec, let's go before they discover I'm gone. How far are we from Williamsburg?" Valerie nearly fainted again as Alec took hold of her arm, helping her to her feet. "My arm..." she gasped.

"Is it broken?" Alec was gently feeling her upper arm, looking for broken bones.

"I don't know, but it hurts like hell." She held her arm by the elbow with her right hand as they walked toward the woods. It hurt less that way.

"I want you to wait for me in the woods, Valerie. I have some business to take care of before we leave, and I need to know that you're safe." Valerie saw the gleam in his eyes and shook her head.

"What are you planning to do? There are two of them, and they're armed, Alec. Please, let's just go," she pleaded. All she wanted was to get away from this horrible place and lie down for a while. Her head was spinning, and her legs were wobbly from strain and fatigue, but Alec had his own ideas.

"Valerie, I can forgive a few bruised ribs, but I can't forgive the kidnapping and beating of my wife. God only knows what they were planning to do to you. I can't walk away from this—

not now." Alec's face was set in a look of grim determination, leaving Valerie in no doubt that he would see this through.

"I'm coming with you, and nothing you say will change my mind."

"All right," he answered with a sigh. "Let's go then. I have a plan."

The sky was just beginning to lighten in the east, going from an inky black to a muted gray, as they slipped into the woods at the edge of the clearing. It was still dark in the woods, the milky light of early morning unable to permeate the thick foliage nearly blocking out the sky. The house was clearly visible from their vantage point, a thin spiral of smoke curling lazily from the chimney. It was a one-story structure with a sloped roof and two small windows at the front, the shutters open and hanging at an odd angle. The whole place looked derelict and unkempt. Percival Gale was obviously not especially handy. There were only two outbuildings on the property. A barn and a privy. Alec primed his gun and pushed it into the waistband of his breeches. He wasn't wearing a sword, but a dagger was sticking out of his boot, just barely visible above the shaft.

"What if there are women and children in there?" Valerie whispered, grabbing his arm.

"There aren't."

"How do you know? Alec, I don't want you to have the death of these men on your conscience. Let's just go. We can report them to the authorities once we get back to Williamsburg."

"Valerie, let me handle this my way. I walked away once and look what happened. I nearly lost you. I didn't aim to kill Percival Gale when he attacked me, but I should have. They were going to hurt you and possibly kill you. I would kill a hundred men to protect you and keep you safe. Now, let me do what I came here to do. Please wait for me here."

Alec didn't wait for her to answer, walking stealthily toward the house. He was just a few feet away from the door when it began to open, revealing the squat figure of Percival Gale. He looked sleepy and disheveled as he stumbled from the house, unsteady on his feet and probably hung-over from a long night of drinking. His face was covered with dark stubble, his unbound hair in disarray. Alec had just enough time to step behind a pile of chopped wood before Gale passed him on the way to the privy. He was scratching his balls as he entered the outhouse, closing the door behind him with a bang. Valerie watched as Alec calmly emerged from behind the stack of firewood and yanked open the door to the privy. Percival Gale sat there, his breeches around his ankles, his face slack as he did his business. His eyes flew open in shock as he realized he was no longer alone.

"Ah, I see you remember me," Alec said conversationally, leaning on the door jamb, his gun pointed at Gale's chest.

"Please, it was just a prank. We weren't going to 'urt her or nothing, I swear. Just let me get dressed, and we can discuss this like men." He began to rise from the wooden seat, but Alec pushed him back down.

"There's nothing to discuss. You sealed your fate the minute you laid a hand on my wife." Percival Gale seemed inclined to say something else, but Alec didn't wait to hear what it was. The shot sounded surprisingly feeble in the quiet of the early morning. Alec stood still for a moment as a trickle of blood ran from the man's forehead down his face. His eyes were still open, staring in horror as his body slumped on the privy. Alec kicked the door shut and turned toward the house. Bobby Mann was already running out the door, a rifle in his hands.

"I'll kill ye, ye bastard," Bobby yelled as he raised the gun to fire. He never stood a chance. He fell face down, sprawled in the mud of the yard, the musket trapped beneath his body.

Alec made sure Bobby was dead before turning his back on the corpse. His eyes met Valerie's across the yard as she came toward him, eager to get away from this gruesome scene. She made sure not to look at the privy. The door was half open, the body of Percival visible within.

"Alec, please, let's go," she begged. Her head was pounding, and her stomach did a somersault as she was sick against the wall of the house. Alec was at her side in a moment, grabbing her before she collapsed again.

"Let's go," she whispered.

"We can't leave them this way. I don't want to be accused of murder, justified though it may be." Alec led her to a chopping block and sat her down, cupping her cheek tenderly. "Just sit down for a moment. I won't be long."

Valerie was too sick to argue. She sank onto the chopping block, grateful to be off her feet. Alec handed her his gun before setting to work. He pulled Bobby's body back into the house and went back for Percival. Valerie looked away as he dragged the corpse past her, Percival's eyes staring accusingly at his killer. Her head was spinning, and all she wanted to do was lie down somewhere and never get up. Alec reappeared a few moments later, closing the door of the house behind him. Valerie was about to ask if he was going to just leave the two men inside when she saw the orange glow of flame through the window.

"Come, love. It's time we were going." Alec put his arm around her waist, leading her away from the house. Valerie could hear the crackling of flames behind her, the smell of burning wood strong in her nose. Her attackers would never have a Christian burial, but they would be cremated.

The horse was grazing about half a mile away from the farm, oblivious to what just happened. It looked at them indifferently as Alec gave Valerie a leg-up, getting on behind her. Valerie made sure not to lean against him, knowing it would hurt him, but he pulled her close, inhaling her scent and kissing her temple. "All the way here I kept thinking that had I been man enough to kill Gale the day he attacked me, none of this would have happened. Men like him don't accept defeat easily. I should have known. I nearly lost you because I failed to recognize the danger."

"Alec, it's over. Don't blame yourself. Just tell me how you found me." Valerie snuggled against him, needing to feel his solid form behind her. She was still wearing his coat, but she was shivering as much from the shock of what happened as from the cold.

"It was by sheer luck," Alec answered cryptically, refusing to tell her any more. Valerie's eyes began to close as the motion of the horse lulled her to sleep. She drifted off, surrendering to the oblivion of sleep after the trauma she'd been through. She'd get the story out of Alec later.

FORTY-THREE

Alec felt Valerie grow heavier against him as she finally fell asleep. They still had a while to go until they reached Williamsburg, and she needed to rest after her ordeal. His ribs burned every time the horse moved beneath him, making it almost impossible to draw a deep breath, especially with Valerie slumped against him. He tried to examine his conscience and pray for the souls of the men he'd killed, but he just couldn't. He simply didn't feel any remorse.

Alec had told Valerie the truth when he said he'd found her by sheer luck. After finding the broadsheets scattered in the street, he had no idea what to do. The street was dark and deserted, the windows shuttered against the cold, rainy night. He stood there for a little while, trying to imagine who might have wanted to harm her or where they could have taken her, but his mind was blank. No one except the proprietors of Shield's Tavern knew them, so he couldn't imagine what could have happened. Alec felt helpless just standing there, so he decided to walk back to the inn and get his gun. He'd walk around all night if he had to, searching for Valerie then, come morning, start asking if anyone had seen her.

He was just passing Whetherburn's Tavern when two men came stumbling out, drunk and unsteady on their feet. One of them nearly fell in front of Alec, as the other caught him and pushed him up against the trunk of a tree. They were laughing and cussing as they trod behind Alec, obviously bound for home.

"I'd love to see the prick's face when 'e found out 'is wife was gone," one of them blurted out, laughing hoarsely. "I 'ear she's comely. Percival and Bobby will use her well before they're through with 'er. I 'ear Percy likes to rough 'em up a bit; 'elps him get it up, if ye know what I mean." The man was still chuckling as he shuffled behind Alec.

"Gale is a coward," the other man answered. "If 'e wants revenge for getting stabbed, than 'e should take it out on 'er husband, not on the poor woman. She'd nothing to do with it. Percival's just afraid to be outsmarted again. That British sod might not be as strong as Percy, but 'e's definitely smarter."

"I'd say Percy is the smart one, Joe," the first man argued, slurring his words. "The man will never know what 'appened to his wife, and blame 'imself all the while. 'Tis much better revenge than just sticking a knife between 'is shoulder blades when 'e's not looking. It lasts longer."

"A little humiliation and blood doesn't warrant killing an innocent woman, 'specially since we both know Gale attacked the man and not the other way around," Joe said, suddenly sounding sober. "No one deserves that. What if it 'ad been yer wife?"

"I'd thank the man who did it," hiccupped his friend. "'E'd be doing me a great favor, ridding me of that dumb cow."

Alec couldn't bear to hear any more. He quickened his stride, nearly running back to the inn. He had to find out where Percival Gale might have taken Valerie without arousing suspicion and get there as soon as possible. He prayed that he would find Valerie alive when he got there. He didn't want to ask Mr.

Clements since the man was sober and would remember come morning, so Alec asked a man taking a piss behind the inn. He never even bothered to glance at Alec as he answered.

"Oh, aye. Percy's place is about eight miles north of Williamsburg. Right past the fork in the road, and to the left. Can't miss it. Why are ye looking for him?" The man laced his flies, ready to go back inside.

"I owe him some money," Alec answered evasively.

"Oh, he'll be glad to see ye then," the man was already halfway back inside. Alec went around back and entered through the back door. He didn't want Mr. Clements to see him walking in and walking out with his gun. Alec grabbed his gun and a pouch of powder and stuck a dagger in his boot. He considered taking his sword but changed his mind. It was too cumbersome.

Alec slipped out the back door without being seen by anyone. Mr. Clements had several horses in the barn behind the inn that he used as a livery. Alec would just "borrow" one. It would take him too long to walk eight miles, and Valerie might not be in any condition to walk by the time he found her.

Alec could barely remember the ride to Gale's farm. He'd whipped the poor horse into a lather, galloping down the dark road at breakneck speed. If his ribs had been cracked, they were surely broken by now, the pain a constant agony. Alec had come upon a farm after the fork in the road, but it turned out to be the wrong place. It took him nearly an hour to figure that out and then another hour to find the next farm. He hobbled the horse at a safe distance and crept to the house, peeking inside. The fire had nearly died down, but he could see the silhouette of Percival Gale in the feeble light from the dying flames. He was slumped in his chair, his head resting on folded arms as he slept at the table. Bobby Mann was sprawled on the floor in front of the hearth, snoring loudly. There was no sign of Valerie. Alec checked the back of the house and then the barn before finally noticing the shed some distance away. All was quiet as he approached the shed, but he heard someone inside and prayed it was Valerie.

The outline of Williamsburg finally came into view. It was fully light now, but few people were about since it was Sunday. They'd have their breakfast and then get ready for church, grateful not to have to work for one day. Alec gently woke Valerie as they neared the inn. He returned the horse to the stable and gave it some water and hay. The poor girl deserved it. He tried the back door. Thankfully, it was unlocked, so he helped Valerie up the stairs and to their room.

FORTY-FOUR

The Mallory family was just finishing breakfast on Sunday morning, when they were startled by a knock on the door. Mr. Mallory reached for the gun mounted above the mantel, loading it quickly before instructing Jonah to open the door. An early morning call on a Sunday didn't warrant good news. Most people were getting ready for church, not traipsing around the countryside, bothering their neighbors. The gun was instantly lowered as Mr. Fletcher came in, hat in hand, apologizing for the early house call. He was the exact opposite of his plump, smiling wife. He was tall and thin, with a dour expression that could sour milk.

"Bill, won't you have some porridge?" Mrs. Mallory asked, already reaching for a clean bowl.

"Thank you kindly, Hannah, but I've breakfasted already. Actually, I'd like a word with John, if you don't mind. I think it might be wise to send the children out of the room," he mumbled apologetically.

"Of course. Girls, fetch your cloaks and come with me. We'll take a walk to the chicken coup and collect some eggs. Martha, you can start on the washing. The men need to speak privately." Mrs. Mallory replaced the bowl on the shelf, threw her own cloak over her shoulders and slung a basket over her arm.

Finn was surprised that he and Jonah weren't asked to leave as well but was glad to be allowed to stay. This sounded interesting. Sarah and Annie ran from the room, eager to go collecting eggs, but Martha and Abbie threw resentful looks at their mother before finally filing out of the house. They were certainly old enough to hear whatever Mr. Fletcher had to say, so Finn thought this might be something serious. He would have liked to take his customary seat in the corner to be able to listen and observe without being in the center, but the men remained seated at the table, and he had no good reason to change seats.

Mr. Fletcher accepted a cup of beer while waiting for the women to leave the room, draining it in one gulp. He was noticeably upset and eager to tell his story.

"What's happened, Bill?" John Mallory asked once the door finally closed behind Mrs. Mallory and the girls.

"There's been a murder, John. Two British soldiers have been discovered three miles from my farm. There were remains of a fire and the horses were hobbled nearby, so they think the soldiers might have camped there overnight. There's no sign of a struggle, and nothing's been taken. One of the men was found in a state of undress. He must have gone to relieve himself when he'd been set upon. The truly disturbing thing is that the second soldier had been scalped, but the scalp was still there, next to his body. The British are up in arms. There might be reprisals against civilians if they think the soldiers were killed in cold blood by the Militia."

Bill Fletcher looked around the table, eager to gauge the reaction to his story. Finn tried to look impassive while Mr. Mallory just looked thoughtful.

"They got what was coming to them. Doesn't matter who

did it. Maybe they'll take a hint and go back home," Jonah declared, a smile on his face. He was too young and naïve to understand the repercussions of such an attack.

"There's a difference between being killed in battle and being murdered in cold blood while taking a piss, son," Mr. Mallory said, his gray eyes thoughtful.

"Nothing's been taken, you say?" he asked Bill Fletcher.

"No. According to the officers who found them, they still had coin in their purses, and the weapons were left by the bodies. One of the men had a miniature framed in gold that was still in his pocket. Definitely not a robbery, John."

"A curious business. How did you come to learn of this?" Mr. Mallory leaned forward, pouring himself another cup of beer. His reaction was surprising, Finn thought.

"The British came to my house last night to question us. We are the closest homestead to the scene of the crime, and they thought we might have heard or seen something. They were very hostile indeed. I fear for what they might do, especially since my boys are in the Continental Army."

"I have to admit that I'm puzzled by these events, Bill. Must have been the Indians. Maybe the soldiers came across them in the woods and threatened them." Mr. Mallory was watching his neighbor intently. "Have you seen any Indians around these parts recently?"

"Not in a long while. They don't normally come so close. They keep to their own territories these days." Mr. Fletcher scratched his jaw in puzzlement, the stubble making a raspy sound against his nails.

"Yes, that has been the case for the most part. Well, please keep me informed, Bill. I'll be seeing you at church today, I trust?" Mr. Mallory rose from the table, reaching for his hat. He had chores to see to, and Bill Fletcher would no doubt go to the surrounding farms to spread his story.

"Yes. Stay safe, John." With that, Bill Fletcher left, as anxious as he was when he came.

Jonah was saying something about how the Indians were preferable to the British, but Mr. Mallory didn't seem to be paying any attention. He was lost in thought, looking past the boys' heads, his hat still in his hands.

"Finn, walk with me a moment." Mr. Mallory took his pipe off the mantel and lit it before heading for the door. Jonah threw Finn a curious look as Finn followed the older man out the door. What did Mr. Mallory want to talk to him about that he didn't want Jonah to overhear? Finn tried to look as bland as possible, walking next to Mr. Mallory without speaking.

John Mallory leaned against the stile, sucking deeply on his pipe as sweet smoke wafted away in the fragrant autumn air.

"Curious business, that," Mr. Mallory said, watching Finn. "Mrs. Mallory mentioned that you escorted Abbie to the Fletchers not two days ago when she went to fetch a cut of lace. Is that so?"

"Yes, sir. I did. What of it?" Finn leaned against the stile, curious as to where the man was going with this.

"Did you think Abbie might be in danger?" asked Mr. Mallory, his eyes never leaving Finn's face.

"No, sir. I simply wanted to take a walk with her, it being such a glorious afternoon and all," Finn said innocently, averting his eyes in mock embarrassment. He hoped Mr. Mallory wouldn't take offense to him walking Abbie.

"Hmm, I see. You like her, don't you, son?" asked Mr. Mallory gently.

"She is a fine young lady, sir," Finn answered, hoping he sounded sufficiently proper.

"That she is." John Mallory remained silent for a few moments, sucking on his pipe and gazing off into the distance.

"What I find puzzling, is that nothing was taken during the attack. You see, neither the Indians nor local men would have walked away without spoils. To leave weapons and horses after going to the trouble of killing the soldiers simply doesn't make sense. What do you think, Finn?" Mr. Mallory was studying him, head cocked to the side, as Finn considered the question.

"You are right, Mr. Mallory. It seems wasteful not to at least take the muskets and horses. Both the Indians and the revolutionaries could certainly use both, I'm sure." That was a noncommittal enough answer, thought Finn as he looked up innocently at Mr. Mallory.

"Yes, I'm sure they could. That's why I don't think it was an attack by either Indians or Militiamen. There hasn't been an Indian attack in these parts in some time, and the Militia would have nothing to gain by killing two soldiers in the woods. I have a different theory."

John Mallory suddenly reached out, pulling Finn's Indian amulet from under his shirt. "Start talking, boy."

"I'm sure I don't know what you mean, Mr. Mallory. What possible connection could I have to the murder of two British soldiers?" Finn's stomach clench with fear. What would Mr. Mallory do if he connected him to the murder? At best, he would ask him to leave and never come back. He would have no place to go and no means of supporting himself until he found some kind of employment. He would also never see Abbie again, which worried him more. At worst, he would report him to the British, and he would face a death sentence for the murder. Finn faced John Mallory squarely, refusing to look guilty.

"Finn, have I ever told you about my father?" Mr. Mallory asked suddenly. Finn shook his head, surprised by the abrupt change of topic.

"My father was in the British Army for many years before marrying my mother and settling down in Virginia. He was a very clever man, who was much more than a mere foot soldier. My father was a spy. He gathered intelligence and analyzed it for his superiors, which often led to an otherwise uncertain victory for the British. My father died when I was a boy, but he taught me many things, and I listened." Mr. Mallory looked off into the distance, probably remembering the father he lost so long ago.

"You see, Finlay, one event is just an occurrence. Two related events might be a coincidence, but three events are as telling as a smoking gun. There are no farms between us and the Fletchers, so the path is not exactly teeming with travelers. Two days after you and Abbie walked to the Fletchers, two soldiers were found dead in the woods, just barely off the path. That's an occurrence." Mr. Mallory folded down one finger to mark the event.

"It seems that someone wanted this to look like an Indian attack, but I don't believe it for a minute. Even if it were the handiwork of the Indians, they would never have left horses or weapons behind. Those are prized possessions, too useful to waste, especially after going to the trouble of killing their owners. Indians like souvenirs, so I can't imagine that they would leave behind a gold watch or coin either. Coincidence? I think not." Mr. Mallory folded down another finger, his eyes never leaving Finn's.

"Lastly, you wear an Indian amulet beneath your shirt, and I saw the tomahawk at your belt the day Jonah found you in the barn. Is it under your bed, Finn? Clearly, you know something of Indian ways." Mr. Mallory triumphantly folded down the third finger, holding up his hand in front of Finn's face.

"Now, I've known you for several weeks now and I believe that you are a decent lad. I think I'm a fairly good judge of character, so, if you killed those soldiers, you must have had a damn good reason. You can trust me, Finn. I won't turn you over to the authorities, but I need to know what happened. Would you care to enlighten me?"

Finn looked away for a moment considering his options. Mr.

Mallory was certainly more observant than he gave him credit for. Most men would never have made the connection, but Mr. Mallory must have listened to his father very carefully when he taught him about espionage. Finn's best bet was to throw himself on Mr. Mallory's mercy and hope for the best. He faced the older man and started talking. Mr. Mallory listened carefully to Finn's account, interrupting him only once to clarify a point.

"Finn, was it your intention to make it look like an Indian attack?" he asked thoughtfully.

"No. I didn't have time to think it through or come up with a plan. I was outnumbered, so I had only one chance to take them by surprise." Mr. Mallory put his hand on Finn's shoulder.

"Finn, I owe you a debt of gratitude for saving my daughter. You did what any honorable man would do. I know you must feel some remorse for taking human life but seems to me as if you didn't have much choice unless you chose to sacrifice Abbie. She is a lucky girl to have your friendship." Mr. Mallory momentarily looked away, overcome by emotion and the thought of what his daughter would have endured had Finn not chosen to come to her aid.

"Now, there's more than one reason why I brought you out here. You are brave, cunning, and you know how to keep a secret. We need men like you working for us. Have you heard of the Committee of Secret Correspondence?"

Finn nodded, unsure of how to respond. He'd heard something about the Committee's activities but wasn't sure exactly what they did or how. He had a feeling that John Mallory was about to tell him.

FORTY-FIVE

"How long will you be gone?" Abbie asked, sitting on the stile next to Finn. She snuggled closer to him as much for affection as for warmth. "I'll miss you."

Ever since the incident in the woods, Abbie had become more open in her affection for Finn, not caring if her parents noticed. Nothing had been said, but there was an understanding between them, that their lives were now bound together, and they were both happy with that. Mr. Mallory hadn't said anything to anyone about his conversation with Finn, but the look of approval in his eyes was unmistakable. Finn had proven himself to be a worthy candidate for his daughter's hand, despite his lack of family and means.

"I'll be back as soon as I can, Abbie, and I'll be thinking of you the whole time I'm gone. Your father has entrusted me with an important task, and I can't let him down. I thought he would send me packing for sure, and instead I've been recruited to help the Revolution." Finn pulled Abbie closer to him, warming her against the cold night air.

"I thought you didn't believe in the Revolution," she said

quietly, but Finn could hear the hope in her voice. "Have you changed your mind?"

"I'm beginning to. What will the Fletchers do now that their farm has been torched by the British? They didn't even have anything to do with the murders. It's so unjust." He still burned with guilt every time he thought of it. He was the one they were looking for, yet an innocent family paid the price simply for being closest to the scene of the slaughter.

News of the burning came on Sunday evening, shortly after the Mallorys had finished their Sunday dinner. The British had set fire to the farm while the family was at church, therefore effectively preventing them from salvaging anything of value. The Fletchers returned to find their home burned to the ground, black smoke rising into the sky as flames still licked the charred beams sticking out of the ground. The only thing that remained of their home was the stone hearth, which was now a soot-covered monument to the life they'd known. Even the apple orchard was put to the torch. It was a forest of black stumps, smoking in the wind.

Thankfully, the animals hadn't burned with the barn. Mr. Fletcher had left them grazing in the field, unwittingly saving something of their possessions.

"Pa said they're going to go live with Mrs. Fletcher's brother in North Carolina. The British couldn't accuse Mr. Fletcher of the murder outright since there was no evidence, but they needed to make an example of someone, and the Fletchers happened to be the only people in the area. Thank God Pa is on good terms with the British. He walks a fine line. He doesn't tell us his business, but we all know what he does. He must remain above suspicion to carry on with his activities." Abbie leaned against Finn, taking his hand in hers. He chose not to remind her that the two British soldiers had made a remark about her father's patriotism. Maybe they just assumed that all the locals were rebels.

"It seems to be a family business. I've met your uncle Alfred in Williamsburg."

"Yes, Uncle Alfred is the one who brought my father into it. There's a whole network in place, but no one knows who the members are. It's safer that way."

"Did Sam not want to be a part of it?" Finn asked. He was curious about Sam, especially since he would be meeting him soon.

"Sam is young and idealistic. He thinks fighting muzzle to muzzle in an open field is the honorable way to win a war. My Pa knows better than that. He believes that wars are won by cunning and strategy. He learned that from his father."

"I'm surprised you know all this, Abbie. Your father doesn't seem like the type to give away information easily." Finn had never actually heard Mr. Mallory talking politics in front of his children. The odd remark was made here and there, especially by Jonah, but for the most part, the talk in the house was very neutral.

"He doesn't. My bed is just on the other side of their wall, so I hear him talking to Ma when he thinks we're all asleep. I don't mean to eavesdrop, but I like to know what goes on. I haven't told anyone, not even Martha. She might tell Gil, and who knows whom he might share the information with. People's lives depend on secrecy. Speaking of lives, Finn, you will be careful, won't you?" She was looking up at him in the darkness with those beautiful dark eyes, her face full of concern for him. He would be careful, if only to come back to her.

"I promise to be very careful, Abbie. Will you give me a parting gift?" He lifted her chin with his finger, kissing her tenderly. She returned his kiss, wrapping her arms around his neck, her heart beating fast.

"Let's go into the barn, Finn," she whispered, taking him by the hand. Finn just nodded, unsure of what her intentions were. Abbie climbed the ladder to the loft, beckoning for him to follow. Finn's heart was beating so wildly he could barely breathe. What did she have in mind?

Abbie was already lying on the straw, waiting for him. Silvery beams of moonlight shone between the slats of the loft, illuminating parts of Abbie's face. She looked nervous and shy, but her intentions were clear.

"Abbie, are you sure this is what you want? I will wait for you as long as it takes. We don't need to rush." Finn had dreamed of being with Abbie but was suddenly nervous and unsure. Waiting for their wedding night would be the honorable thing, and he wanted to do right by her more than anything.

"I want to, Finn. I've given it a lot of thought, and it feels right. I want it to be you, and I want it to be now, before you go. Now, stop talking and come here." Her voice was shaking a little, but she sounded determined, her eyes never leaving his, begging him not to refuse.

Finn lay down next to Abbie, pulling her to him and kissing her hard. He could sense her nervousness, but she kissed him back, guiding his hand to her breast. It was so soft and round in his hand. He'd never done more than hold her and kiss her, so this was new territory for both of them. Finn caressed her breast through the fabric, watching her face. She seemed to be enjoying it. Her eyes were closed, mouth slightly open, her breath ragged in the silence of the barn.

Finn closed his eyes, trying to remember what Charles had told him about pleasing a woman. Finn hadn't really been listening, embarrassed by the images Charlie was bringing to mind, but he'd need to remember now. He wanted to do it right, and make sure that Abbie liked it. Abbie suddenly opened her eyes, looking at Finn. Her pupils were dilated in the darkness, but the expression on her face made Finn want to devour her. Abbie unlaced her bodice with trembling fingers and pulled down her chemise. Her white breasts were glowing in the moonlight, just begging to be kissed.

Finn bent his head, kissing the velvety skin and running his tongue over her nipple. She moaned with pleasure, exciting him. His cock was straining against his breeches, pushing against Abbie's belly. He gasped in shock as Abbie pressed her palm against it, rubbing slowly. No one had ever touched him before, and the sensation was unbelievable. Finn took Abbie's hand and moved it away. If she continued, he wouldn't be able to hold back. Instead, he slid his hand under her skirt. She was wearing hose today, but the flesh above them was bare and warm. Finn's heart raced as he pushed his hand between her legs, exploring her. Abbie seemed to hold her breath, her back arching as he probed her. He wasn't sure if this was the right thing to do, but she seemed to like it, so he continued, enjoying the sounds she made. She gasped in shock as he slid his finger inside her.

"I'm sorry. I'll stop," he said quickly, pulling out his hand.

"Don't," Abbie breathed. "I don't want you to stop." She reached down and began to unlace his breeches, her hands brushing against his cock. Finn felt like he was going to explode. His mind was screaming for him to stop and take Abbie back home, but his body wasn't listening. Finn positioned himself between Abbie's legs and followed his instincts. It took a few tries to finally penetrate her, but he felt her maidenhead tear as Abbie cried out in pain.

"I'm sorry. I didn't mean to hurt you." He wasn't sure what to do, but his body was already moving, instinct taking over as he began to move his hips, sliding in and out of her resistant body. Abbie looked tense and uncomfortable, but began to relax after a few moments, sighing as he spilled himself inside her.

"Was that all right, then?" he asked, terrified she'd tell him he'd done it all wrong, and she never wanted him to touch her again. She nodded, looking up at him, her eyes full of wonder.

"So, that's what all the fuss is about," she said smiling. Her breasts were still exposed, her nipples taut and dark in the dim light of the barn. Finn looked at her bare legs and the dark triangle barely hidden by her bunched-up skirt. His cock grew hard again, throbbing and wanting. Abbie saw his predicament and smiled at him, spreading her legs in silent invitation.

The second time was better. He lasted longer, finding a natural rhythm as he made love to her. Abbie was more relaxed this time. She just lay there at first, but then began to move her hips with him, drawing him in deeper, heightening his pleasure. He cried out as he collapsed on top of her, satisfied. God, he'd never expected it to be like this. No words could describe what he was feeling, their bodies still joined. Was it like this for everyone, or just for them?

"I love you, Abbie," he breathed into her hair. "I love you so much."

"I know, Finn. I love you too, and now I know that we'll never be parted." Abbie got to her feet, looking around for her cap. It had come off and her hair tumbled around her shoulders, released from its pins. Finn had never seen her with her hair down. It was so beautiful, cascading down her back and framing her face. He wished he could see it in the daylight, lit up by the bright rays of the sun. It must look like spun gold.

"We best go back now before we're missed," said Abbie, as she felt in the straw for her pins. She found a few and quickly put her hair up again before replacing the cap on her head. Finn couldn't see her face clearly in the darkness, but he thought she was smiling. He smiled back. Now he was truly a man. He'd bedded a woman and was going on a secret assignment come morning. How things had changed in only a couple of weeks.

FORTY-SIX

After nearly a week, Louisa was totally frantic. There was less milk with each day, Evie cried pitifully, kicking her legs and flailing her arms in frustration. Louisa was drinking a cup of ale per hour, but it wasn't helping. If anything, her stress only made things worse. She alternated between bouts of crippling depression and anger. She raged at Kit for having sex with her, at herself for causing them to leave Virginia, and at Bridget for failing to do something to help. Her baby was going hungry, and there was nothing she could do.

By the seventh day, Evie stopped crying. She just lay there, lethargic and limp, her skin almost translucent. Louisa cried silently as she put the baby to her breast, praying that something would come out. Her heart was hammering with fear, her womb contracting painfully as Evie sucked desperately, starving for nourishment.

"We're going to lose her, aren't we?" Kit whispered, watching the baby's struggle. He was deathly pale, his eyes full of fear. "There must be something we can do. We can't just let her die, Louisa."

Louisa felt something snap within her. She glared at Kit, her face hot with fury. "We are in the middle of the bloody ocean, in case you haven't noticed. What am I supposed to do? There isn't a lactating woman in sight. If it weren't for you, this wouldn't be happening." She froze at the sight of his face. She hadn't meant to lash out at him, especially since he didn't know about the possible pregnancy. Kit rose slowly, his face a mask of disbelief as he stared at her.

"What do you mean, if it weren't for me?" he asked quietly.

"I'm sorry. I didn't mean it, Kit. I'm just so scared." Louisa looked away from his expression of pure shock. He looked as if he was about to burst into tears, making her feel awful. It was all her fault. If she hadn't had that little outburst in Jamestown, they would be at home right now, possibly with Valerie, Alec, and Finn.

"What did you mean when you said it was all because of me?" he asked again. Louisa could see the tension coursing through his body, his fists clenched at his side. There was no way he would just let this go. She sighed and faced him.

"Bridget thinks that the milk is drying up because I'm pregnant." There, she said it. It was out there, although there was no way to verify if it was true. She hadn't had her period and with no pregnancy test, only time would confirm Bridget's suspicions.

Kit sank back onto the berth, the agony in his eyes painful to behold. She shouldn't have said anything, but now he would blame himself for the situation. Kit looked away, unable to face her.

"Kit," Louisa called out to him. "Kit, look at me." He just shook his head, lost in his misery. Then he rose and walked out of the cabin, the door slamming behind him. If there was ever a moment when Louisa wanted to die, this was it. Her baby was starving, her husband was heartbroken, and she was possibly carrying a baby that was pickled in ale thanks to her attempts to get the milk to come back. Louisa's face contorted in agony as she began to wail, rocking back and forth with the silent baby in her arms.

Louisa cried until there were no tears left in her. Evie fell asleep lulled by the rocking, but her little face was pale and sickly looking. How much longer would she last?

FORTY-SEVEN

Kit leaned against the wooden railing, staring into the choppy waters of the Atlantic. The day was overcast, and the water was a murky gray that reflected the quickly darkening sky. He hoped there wouldn't be a storm. The air was so saturated with moisture that his face and hair became instantly damp, making him shiver in the cold wind. Kit wrapped his coat tighter around himself, his eyes never leaving the horizon. What he wouldn't give to see land. Of course, there was no land to be seen. They were in the middle of the ocean, weeks away from any port.

Kit looked around. He could have sworn he heard Evie crying. The sound of her desperate screams followed him day and night, tearing through his brain and leaving him numb with fear. It was bad enough to think that his daughter might die of starvation, but to know that he'd caused it was pure torment. How could this have happened? First Finn vanished, and then they had to flee in the middle of the night to avoid Louisa's sentence. At the time, leaving had seemed like the only possible solution, but now Kit tortured himself day and night, thinking of what he could have done differently. Leaving Louisa to her fate simply wasn't an option. No matter the outcome of the trial, her punishment would be fearsome. The thought of Louisa being publicly branded with a hot iron or flogged left Kit in no doubt that he'd done the right thing. How could anyone do that to a woman, even if she had sinned? All she did was utter a few wrong words in an unguarded moment. Did that really warrant such cruelty?

But now, her punishment would be far worse. Louisa would have recovered from the pain and humiliation of her sentence, but she wouldn't recover from Evie's death. Kit's mother had lost a baby when he was five, and he'd never forgotten the heart wrenching sound of her weeping, or the weekly trips to the cemetery to visit the tiny grave. His mother had learned to live again, but she was never truly joyful, the death of his little brother always there, making her feel guilty for being the one who lived.

He'd seen that same sadness in Valerie when they first came to Virginia. She'd recently lost a baby, and the pain of that loss was right there in her eyes every minute of the day. Finding her sister after all that time distracted her from her suffering, but she would never fully recover from the loss of her son. At least Valerie and Alec had never gotten to know the child they lost. He'd been a stillborn, but Evie had been alive and well, and would certainly grow up if not for the dastardly chain of events set off by Frederick Taylor's arrival.

And now Louisa was pregnant. Kit couldn't even spare a thought for the new baby. He had no right to another child, when it had been his anger that brought that child into being and caused Louisa's milk to dry up. Kit had never felt so utterly powerless in his whole life. He had no way to save Evie, and no way to spare his wife the agony that would follow. Kit sank to his knees on deck and began to pray like he'd never prayed in his life. He would gladly die in exchange for Evie's life if that's what the Lord wanted. If only he would spare her.

FORTY-EIGHT

Louisa looked up as she heard footsteps outside the door. Maybe Kit had come back. She had to apologize, make him see that she wasn't blaming him. How could he have known that this would happen?

"May I come in, yer ladyship?" Bridget asked. She was carrying a cup of something, which she set on the small table under the porthole.

"Have you seen Kit, Bridget?" Louisa asked miserably. "He is very upset." That was an understatement, but Louisa didn't really want to go into it. She was sure Bridget had noted her red-rimmed eyes and blotchy skin. Bridget missed very little.

"No, I haven't seen his lordship. I've been in the hold, milking Lizzie."

Louisa just looked up at Bridget, awaiting an explanation. No one was allowed in the cargo hold except the sailors, so why would Bridget go down there, and who was Lizzie? There was no cow on board.

"There are two goats in the hold, as well as several chickens. The captain suffers from a stomach ailment and only eats biscuit soaked in goat milk and the occasional egg. No one is allowed to go near the goats except Will Lawson, who milks them every day. I asked Will to let me milk Lizzie. This is our only hope of saving Evie." Bridget pulled a thimble out of her pocket, setting it next to the cup. She took the sleeping baby from Louisa, unwrapping her blanket. Nothing woke Evie faster than a blast of cold air.

"Wake up, my pet. I have something for ye." Bridget dipped the thimble into the cup, filling it halfway with milk and holding it to Evie's lips, gently pouring the milk into her mouth so she wouldn't gag. Evie made a face and tried to turn her head away, but Bridget held her firmly, periodically dripping some milk into her mouth.

Louisa just sat there, unsure of what to say. Evie's stomach wasn't ready for animal milk, but there was no other choice. They had to try. Bridget patiently refilled the thimble, working her way through half the milk in the cup.

"There now, doesn't that feel better, my sweet?" she cooed to Evie. "Is yer belly full at last?"

In response to that, Evie threw up everything she had eaten, milk running from her mouth onto her blanket and gown. She was crying, her legs kicking madly as she unwrapped herself. An acrid smell filled the cabin, alerting them to the fact that the goat's milk went right through her. Louisa began to cry again, but Bridget just busied herself with cleaning the baby.

"'Tis normal, that is. Her belly is not used to the goat milk. 'Twill take time. We have to keep trying. There's milk left in the cup. We'll try again in an hour. Just let her rest for now. Her belly must be aching something awful." Bridget washed Evie's butt in the basin, putting on a clean clout and gown and wrapping her in the spare blanket.

"Just hold her. Yer warmth will soothe her bellyache. I'll just go wash these things up on deck. They should dry quickly in the wind. We'll be needing them again soon." She let herself out of the cabin, leaving Louisa cocooned in her misery.

* * *

It took Evie several days to get used to the goat's milk. She cried nonstop for the first twenty-four hours; her belly aching as her system rejected the milk. Louisa was terrified that she would become dehydrated, using the thimble to pour some water into her mouth. Evie had noticeably lost weight over the past week, going from a lovely, plump infant to a scrawny writhing banshee. Kit rarely came back to the cabin, unable to bear his daughter's crying. He slept with the sailors in the hold, huddled into a hammock. Louisa tried talking to him, but he just walked away, his eyes never meeting hers.

Every time Evie fell asleep, Louisa curled around her, begging the baby to absorb her energy, to take whatever she needed to survive. She held her close, hoping that the little girl would feel her love and the desperate desire to keep her alive. They were still weeks away from England.

Bridget went down to the hold every day to get a cup of fresh milk. Captain Reeves was exceedingly sympathetic when he found out about the problem, urging Bridget to take as much milk as necessary. He even offered to boil one of the hens to make chicken broth to feed Evie. Bridget thought they might have to try that if the milk failed.

By the third day, Evie seemed to feel better. She managed to keep down the milk without spitting it up. Bridget and Louisa waited with bated breath to see whether her belly would ache, but she seemed content as she fell asleep in Louisa's arms. For the first time in days, Louisa felt a surge of hope. They continued to feed Evie every few hours. It was a slow process since they could only dribble a few drops of milk into her mouth at a time, but they took turns, making sure she got at least a quarter of the cup into her before falling asleep. Evie still spit up a little, but not like before, keeping down most of the food.

"I think she's gotten used to it, yer ladyship. She's a survivor, that one. Just wait and see." Bridget showed Louisa the empty cup. "We've gotten nearly a whole cup of milk into her since this morning."

Louisa cried with relief as the next feeding went equally well. Her breasts were nearly dry now, only a few drops coming out when she squeezed her nipples. The goat milk had to work. Evie began to regain some of her color, getting visibly excited when she saw the thimble coming toward her. Every drop that made it into her mouth was the elixir of life. Louisa began to breathe a little easier, seeing Evie's recovery. As long as the goats had milk, she would have food. Now it was time to patch things up with Kit.

FORTY-NINE

Louisa found Kit on deck, looking out over the ocean. His face looked blank as he watched the gathering storm, the black clouds rolling in from the north, bringing with them a driving rain and gusts of wind that nearly tore off her mob cap. It was just past noon, but it was getting darker by the moment, flashes of lightning illuminating the pewter sky with frightening frequency. Louisa pulled her cloak tighter around herself to keep out the chill and the rain and walked over to Kit. He didn't turn his head as she stood next to him, just continued to look out over the churning water. They hadn't spoken in days other than to discuss their daughter. Kit came to the cabin to check on Evie but left as soon as he could. He couldn't bear to look at Louisa, his face betraying his hurt every time their eyes met.

"Kit, please, talk to me. I'm so sorry about what I said." Louisa put her hand over his, grateful that he didn't yank it away.

"How's Evie?" he asked. He'd inquired about Evie several times a day, anxiety darkening his eyes.

"She just went to sleep. She seems much better. Her belly is not aching like before."

"Thank God." He continued to stare out over the water, his hair blowing in the wind, freed of its customary tie.

"Kit, it's not your fault. It never was. I was just hysterical and mad with fear. Please forgive me," she pleaded. Kit turned around slowly, looking at her as if seeing her for the first time.

"Forgive you?" he asked, confused. Louisa just nodded, suddenly afraid. Would he never forgive her for her outburst? How could he not understand how terrified she'd been? He'd forgiven her for not telling him about her past. Surely, that had been worse than an accusation blurted out in a moment of panic.

"Louisa, there's nothing to forgive. It's myself I can't forgive. You're right. It's all my fault. My behavior was unforgivable the night you told me about the time travel. I was so angry; I didn't give any thought to you or your health. I only wanted to hold you and lay my claim on you. Well, I've done that, haven't I? I nearly killed our child. I don't deserve either of you." He looked so miserable that Louisa just wanted to hold him like a child and rock him until he felt better.

"Kit, plenty of women nurse their babies while pregnant. The milk doesn't normally dry up. It wasn't anything you did. I was just scared and needed someone to blame. Everything will be all right once we get to England and can find a wet nurse for Evie. She is strong, like her father. She will survive. Now, Kit, please hold me. I feel utterly lost when you're not there to support me. Your love means everything to me. You know that, don't you?"

Kit wrapped his arms around Louisa, holding her tight. His heartbeat was steady and strong against her chest, making her feel secure. "Kit, let's go back to the cabin," Louisa said, lifting her face to receive his kiss.

Evie slept peacefully in her hammock, rocking gently from side to side as they walked in. She was tightly swaddled in her blanket to keep out the cold of the cabin, but her cheeks were a lovely pink, not the bluish white they'd been only two days ago. Bridget was curled up on Louisa's berth, looking exhausted. She immediately excused herself, having assessed the situation correctly. Louisa barely waited for the door to close behind Bridget before throwing off her wet cloak and pulling off her mob cap. Her golden hair cascaded down her back, framing her face. Kit had already pulled off his doublet and was fumbling with the laces of his breeches, his eyes never leaving her face. They were burning with desire, making Louisa feel feverish with need. She pushed aside his hands, untying the laces of his breeches. She couldn't get them undone fast enough, needing to feel him inside her.

There was no way to lie down together on the narrow berth, so Kit lifted her up, pushing her up against the door of the cabin. Louisa wrapped her legs around him as he took her, crying out with exquisite pain as his cock pounded her womb with every thrust. She slumped against him as her body finally reached its climax, their bodies still joined. She never wanted to let him go, not ever.

"You *are* with child," he whispered, kissing her face. "It might be too soon to tell, but I just know it."

FIFTY

Finn threw another log on the fire, settling in for the night. The sounds of the forest were all around him, reminding him of the times he went hunting with his father and they spent the night sleeping rough. He complained then, but he would have given anything to have his father here now. Being alone was the next best thing. He had to admit that after sharing a room with Jonah for the past few weeks, it was nice to have a bit of quiet for a few nights. Jonah talked until he literally fell asleep mid-sentence, finally leaving Finn alone with his own thoughts.

Finn untied his bedroll, spreading it as close to the fire as he could without setting himself aflame. The crackling of the twigs was soothing, the leaping flames casting eerie shadows on the world around him. Finn closed his eyes and inhaled deeply. The night smelled of rotting leaves, pine, and wood smoke. He loved that smell. It reminded him of home and the woods by the house, but he wouldn't think of home tonight. Finn linked his fingers behind his head, staring at the stars. It was a beautiful clear night; the countless stars scattered around the half-moon like shards of diamonds. It was cold, but the warmth of the fire was enough to make him comfortable and drowsy.

Finn closed his eyes, thinking of Abbie. Leaving her after what happened had been hard, but he had no choice. His breath caught in his throat as he remembered her willing body under his, warm and inviting. He thought he'd wanted her before, but now that he knew exactly what he was missing, the hunger he felt was overwhelming, gnawing at him every hour of the day. He had to admit that it would have been wonderful to have her there with him, but he was on a mission, and Abbie was safer at home.

Once Finn agreed to undertake the assignment, Mr. Mallory explained to him what the Committee did and what part he would play. They needed someone inconspicuous to deliver a few coded messages and then pick up a message from Sam. It seemed that Sam was supplying his father with information about troop movements and battle plans. Most of the men and boys living close to Williamsburg could be easily identified since they'd lived there all their lives, but Finn was new to the area, with no family and no special ties to anyone but the Mallorys. It reminded him just how alone he was when presented with that fact.

Finn huddled deeper into his blanket, knowing that he would get cold once the fire burned out. He had to get some sleep. He would be meeting his first contact tomorrow morning and he was a little nervous. But he was also excited. The notion that he was doing something to help the Revolution made his heart swell with pride. He'd heard enough talk over the past few weeks about the injustice of the British and he had to admit that he was definitely on the side of the rebels. The look of admiration on Abbie's face was an added bonus. She was proud of him, thinking him courageous and loyal. Finn was still smiling as he finally fell asleep.

FIFTY-ONE

"Martha, are you asleep?" Abbie whispered, fearful of waking her parents. "Martha?" She nudged Martha in the ribs, hoping to wake her. They'd shared a bed since they were little, always talking and giggling until they fell asleep, but lately Abbie found herself wanting to lie quietly, and think her own thoughts rather than whispering with Martha. Martha would be gone soon anyway. She'd be a married woman and Sarah would most likely take her place. She was getting too old to sleep in the same room as their parents and Annie.

"I was until you started hissing at me. What's the matter?" Martha was always grumpy when woken up. She turned on her side, eying her little sister from under the flounces of her night-cap, which was the only thing visible in the darkness.

"Martha, do you love Gil?" Abbie asked quietly.

"I'm marrying him, aren't I?"

"That's not the same thing as loving him. Do you love him, Martha?" Abbie asked again, sounding more urgent this time.

"What's this all about, Abbie?" Martha was wide-awake now, obviously curious.

"I just wanted to know what it feels like to be in love," Abbie replied dreamily.

"I wouldn't know," answered Martha gruffly. "Gil is a good man. He is loyal, hardworking, and more importantly, he loves me. I don't believe in these romantic notions. What's the point? There aren't that many young men for me to choose from, so I chose Gil."

"Do you think you'll be happy?" asked Abbie wistfully.

"You are relentless, Abbie. Of course, we'll be happy, especially if this war ever ends, and we can build a home of our own. Living with his family until then will have its difficulties to be sure." Martha sat up in bed, propping her pillows. "Are you finished interviewing me, sis?"

"Not yet. I was wondering, have you and Gil ever, you know?" Abbie whispered urgently, afraid to be overheard.

"Of course not. What kind of trollop do you take me for? He'd never even dare try it. That's what wedding nights are for. To tell you the truth, I can't say I'm looking forward to that part. It sounds rather appalling." Martha rolled her eyes, making Abbie giggle.

"I think it's probably very nice," said Abbie, smiling.

"And how would you know? You've never even been kissed." Martha suddenly gave her a suspicious look. "Abbie, who are we talking about, me or you? Come now, we've never had secrets from each other." Martha's eyes bore into Abbie, waiting for an answer.

"I think I'm in love with Finn." Abbie's voice shook with emotion as she said it. This was the first time she'd articulated her feelings, other than telling Finn that night in the barn. It felt strange sharing her precious love with her sister, despite their close bond. Abbie felt as if she were betraying Finn somehow by confiding in Martha.

"Well, you better get over it, and soon. Finn's just a temporary worker. He doesn't have a pot to piss in. Pa would never let you marry him. Besides, his origins are questionable. No one seems to know anything about him. The sooner he goes the better, I say. Now, stop mooning over hired help and go to sleep." With that, Martha turned away from Abbie, ending the conversation.

Abbie stuck her tongue out at Martha's back, then turned toward the wall herself. She didn't care if Finn had nothing. He had her. For the first time in her life, she felt sorry for Martha. She'd always admired her big sister and had to admit that she was a little scared and jealous when Martha accepted Gil's proposal. She would be a married woman, and worst of all, she would leave. They would no longer share their tiny room, or gossip late into the night, sharing their dreams with each other, not that Martha was sharing much lately. She'd changed since her betrothal, becoming more distant with each passing day. Abbie thought that if she were engaged, she would be over the moon with joy, wanting everyone to share in her happiness, unlike Martha, who only seemed concerned with what she would bring to her new family.

Abbie said a heartfelt prayer, asking God to protect Finn on his mission and bring him back safely. She knew that Martha was right about Finn's prospects, but she didn't care. Finn wasn't afraid of hard work, and more importantly, he was cunning and smart. He wouldn't be penniless for long.

FIFTY-TWO

Valerie gasped as she looked at her reflection in the small mirror above the washstand. If she didn't know with one hundred percent certainty that she was looking at herself, she might have thought some other woman was gazing back. Her eye was a purplish blue, swollen almost completely shut, and the left side of her face was scraped raw and covered with dirt from her efforts in the shed. Her bottom lip was puffy and covered with dried blood where it had been split. Clumps of dirt and bits of wood were trapped in her wild hair, and her left sleeve was completely torn, which was a good thing since her arm was swollen to nearly double its normal size. And to make matters worse, she'd just gotten her period.

"Let's get you to bed," Alec said, holding his hand to his middle. He was visibly in pain, barely able to straighten up.

"God, we look like we've been in a war," Valerie said. "I can't go to bed like this. I'm filthy."

"I would gladly help you bathe if I could." Alec sat down heavily on a chair, attempting to pull off his boots, but giving up as soon as he bent down, his face turning a sickly shade of green. "I think we need help. I'll go down and ask Bessie to come up."

"Ask her to bring up some hot water." Valerie gingerly pulled the torn fabric away from her arm in an effort to remove her filthy gown. Her arm was turning the same color as her eye and was hot to the touch. Valerie waited until Alec left the room before sinking onto the bed, hot tears running down her face. How did this happen to them? All they wanted to do was find Finn, and instead they ended up fighting for their lives.

Valerie wiped her face with Alec's handkerchief as Bessie knocked on the door and entered the room carrying a pitcher of hot water and two clean towels.

"Oh, my. What happened to you, Mrs. Whitfield? You look an absolute fright," the girl gushed as she set down the pitcher, eyeing Valerie with undisguised curiosity. Bessie wasn't one for subtlety.

"You just let me help you. Now, let's get that gown off and I'll help you wash your hair." Valerie sat still as Bessie unlaced the gown and peeled it off carefully, removing the left sleeve last, so as not to move Valerie's arm. The chemise under the gown wasn't as dirty or torn, so Valerie kept it on as she bent her head over a basin, holding her arm against her side. Bessie poured warm water over her head before soaping her hair thoroughly and washing it out. She was gentle and efficient, her hands soothing on Valerie's scalp. She carefully washed Valerie's face, wiping away the blood and dirt with a clean rag. Her face was terribly sore, but it was nice to be clean.

Valerie didn't protest as Bessie picked up the brush and began to brush out her wet hair, humming a tune under her breath. The girl would have made an excellent nurse, had she grown up in another time. Valerie began to relax, exhaustion overtaking her. She hardly noticed as Bessie pulled off her chemise and helped her into a clean nightdress before tucking her into bed.

"You just rest, Mrs. Whitfield. I'll take your gown downstairs and mend it, shall I? My Ma says I'm good with a needle.

It'll be as good as new, just you wait and see." Bessie scooped up the torn gown off the floor and picked up the empty pitcher. Valerie was asleep by the time the door closed behind the girl.

* * *

Valerie forced herself to open her eyes as someone touched her arm, sending waves of pain crashing over her. She thought it was Alec, but the man bent over her wasn't her husband. He was elderly, with a bald pate surrounded by long, shaggy gray hair, which matched his bushy eyebrows. He wore a pair of half-moon spectacles and looked remarkably like Benjamin Franklin. Valerie suddenly realized that Benjamin Franklin was actually alive in 1775 and wondered if he had somehow wound up in her room, or if she was suffering from delirium.

"Valerie, this is Dr. Ferris." Alec appeared behind the man, looking at Valerie with concern. "I thought your arm needed seeing to. Is it broken, doctor?"

The doctor didn't answer right away. He probed every inch of Valerie's arm, then tried to move it, before listening to her chest with a wooden tube and taking her pulse. *Modern medicine at its best*, Valerie thought as she watched the doctor's face. He didn't bother to speak to her but addressed his comments to Alec as if she were a child.

"Your wife's arm doesn't appear to be broken, but the wrist is fractured, and the upper arm is very badly bruised indeed. The best I can do is bind the wrist and advise strict bed rest for at least a week. Now, let's have a look at you, young man. You seem in need of medical attention just as much as your wife." The doctor turned to Alec, giving him a quizzical stare. "What happened to you, if I might ask?" He motioned for Alec to lie down next to Valerie, coming around the bed to examine him.

"Ah, our coach overturned and rolled into a ravine. Seems

the axle broke clean in half, isn't that right, my dear?" Alec squeezed Valerie's hand, urging her to back up his story.

"Yes. It was dreadful, doctor," Valerie piped in. "I was thrown clear across the ravine. Thank God I landed on a grassy bank."

"That is dreadful, indeed. One sees these kinds of accidents all the time. I blame poor craftsmanship. No one takes pride in their work anymore." The doctor appeared to be warming up to this theme when he became distracted by Alec's injuries. He looked awfully serious as he ran his fingers over Alec's bruised middle.

"You have two broken ribs, Mr. Whitfield. You are very fortunate that they haven't pierced your lung, or you would be in very bad shape indeed. Now, I'll bind your ribs for you, and you must be on bed rest along with your wife. I will inform Mr. Clements that meals should be sent up for the next week. You are not to go up and down the stairs. Is that clear? I'll also fashion a sling for Mrs. Whitfield. It should take some of the discomfort away while her arm heals. Would you like some laudanum for the pain?" He looked from Alec to Valerie, his glasses sliding down his nose. Valerie was sorely tempted to ask for the laudanum but shook her head. It was too easy to get addicted or overdose altogether since there was no way to measure out the dosage. She wouldn't have said no to some Aspirin though.

"No thank you, doctor. I think I can do without," she answered, watching his bushy eyebrows rise in astonishment. She gathered people didn't often say no to laudanum these days.

"What about you, Mr. Whitfield?" Alec was focusing on the ceiling as the doctor went about binding his ribs. He was obviously in considerable pain, his face pale and covered in cold sweat.

"No," he grunted. "I'll forgo as well."

"Suit yourself. I will check on you in a week's time. If you need anything, ask Mr. Clements to send one of his stable boys to fetch me. Good day to you both." The doctor gave them a curt bow before putting on his hat and departing.

"Next time we buy a coach, we should look for better crafts-manship, dear," Valerie intoned, giving Alec an impish smile.

Alec started to chuckle, but his laugh quickly turned into a grimace of pain. His ribs had gotten noticeably worse over the past twenty-four hours, most likely breaking under the strain of galloping for hours in search of the farm. Dr. Ferris had been right in his suggestion that they might have pierced Alec's lungs, and with no way to re-inflate the lung, Alec might have died. Valerie felt a wave of panic as the realization of what might have happened washed over her.

If Alec hadn't found her, she would most likely have been raped and beaten to death, ending up in some unmarked grave, or dumped in the woods to be eaten by animals until there was nothing left but shards of bone gleaming among the colorful fall leaves. Alec might have died as well, but his death would have been slower and more agonizing as he suffocated from lack of oxygen somewhere on the side of the road, hurt and alone. Valerie began to shake, the shock finally wearing off and leaving her open to the emotions that devoured her from the inside. She turned away from Alec, not wanting him to see her grief.

"I don't know about you, but I'm not getting up from this bed for at least three days," Alec said, grunting with pain as he tried to move, "and neither are you."

"Alec, we need to have more broadsheets printed," Valerie protested. She needed to focus on finding their son in order to keep herself together. "Finn is out there somewhere, and every day that we are laid up, he could be getting further away."

"Valerie, we need to recover before we can continue searching for Finn. Besides, I heard talk of a fire at Percival Gale's farm while I was downstairs asking Mr. Clements about a doctor. The best thing we can do for ourselves and Finn is to stay out of sight for a while, especially since Mr. Clements knows full well that we don't own a carriage and that you'd been missing. I told him that you lost your way and fell into a ravine in the darkness, but he's no fool. Let's not make it easier for him to figure things out. No one needs to know that we were anywhere near that farm when the fire started."

"What do they think happened?" Valerie asked, suddenly afraid.

"They think that Percival and Bobby argued over some stolen goods and got into a fight, shooting each other and knocking over a candle in the process. I, for one, really like that theory. Now, stop talking and get some sleep. You look dreadful."

"Yes, so I've been told," Valerie answered tartly before closing her eyes. Suddenly, she wished she would have accepted the laudanum.

FIFTY-THREE

Louisa looked out over the swelling waves. The ocean was the color of graphite today, a dark gray that looked almost impenetrable from her vantage point. The moon was just beginning to rise, the only source of light in a sky devoid of stars. It was a strange orange color, almost red, reminiscent of warrior Mars rather than the benevolent muse of poets. Louisa huddled into her cloak, reluctant to go below again. She felt cooped up in her cabin, forced to deal with a restless Kit, who was tired of enforced idleness after weeks at sea. He took long walks on deck, thankfully taking Evie with him between feedings. The baby liked the fresh air and slept peacefully rocked by the motion of her pacing father.

Bridget spent a lot of time in her cabin, having never recovered from the seasickness. She was nauseated and weak most of the time, and barely managed to keep any food down. She also seemed awfully sad. Louisa wondered if she had been distressed by having to leave Virginia at such short notice. She had to admit that she knew very little of Bridget's life. Valerie had mentioned that her husband drowned many years ago, and Bridget left her young daughters behind to find work in

England, but Bridget hardly ever spoke of her children, and Louisa didn't want to pry. She had her reasons for coming to the New World with the Whitfields, no doubt.

Louisa was surprised to see Bridget emerge from below and head toward the prow of the ship. Her cap was whipped off by the wind, releasing strands of her long, red hair. Bridget didn't bother to put it back on. She simply stood, staring at the frightening moon, her cheeks ruddy from the brisk wind and the hair whipping in her face.

"You look as if you've seen a ghost, Bridget," Louisa observed, leaning on the rail beside her.

"'Tis I who's the ghost, yer ladyship," answered Bridget quietly.

"What do you mean? And please, Bridget, stop calling me "your ladyship". Just Louisa will do." They'd this conversation many times, but Bridget wasn't able to get past the title and treat Louisa as just another woman. To her, they were servant and mistress.

"I must admit that I was scared to go back to England, but as the days passed, I thought it was the good Lord's wish that I see my girls again. It's been seventeen years. I wouldn't know them if I passed them in the street, would I? They are married with their own children now. But it seems that it's not to pass." Bridget never turned to look at Louisa. She just stared out over the shimmering crimson path the moon drew on the black waters of the ocean.

"I'm sorry, Bridget, but I don't understand what you mean. Don't you want to see them?" Louisa was puzzled by the expression on Bridget's face.

"Ye see, yer ladyship, I never told the mistress and master the truth of what happened when my husband died. He didn't just fall off the boat insensible with drink — I pushed him. He was a terrible man, my husband. I would have never married him, had I not been pregnant. He raped me when I was just fourteen. I used to work at the tavern to help my mam. We were struggling for money after my father died."

Bridget's voice was flat, as if recounting the story of someone else's life, but then again, at this point, that life probably seemed as distant as the moon.

"Paddy was always a big one for the drink. He followed me outside one night when I went to the necessary and forced himself on me. I was still a maid, and he hurt me, but he didn't care. He was drunk. I didn't tell no one, hoping to keep it a secret, but I never went out by myself anymore when he was there. But the Lord had other ideas, and I found myself with child. My mam helped women get rid of unwanted babies, but she wouldn't do it for me. Said it was a mortal sin, and she wouldn't condemn me to hell for eternity. So, Paddy and I were married.

He was a mean drunk. He beat me so bad I thought I'd lose the baby, but she was born healthy and strong, as was my second daughter. He took no interest in them, and barely had a kind word for me, even when he wasn't drinking. As they got older, he started to beat them too. He could beat me black and blue, but I had to protect my girls."

"Was there nothing you could do? No one you could turn to?" Louisa asked, although she knew that even in modern times cases of domestic abuse often went unreported and unresolved. Bridget simply shrugged her shoulders.

"Everyone knew, but no one would dare interfere. He wasn't the only one, ye know. It was a hard life, with few comforts and joys, so the women found solace in their children and the men took comfort in drink, only most of them weren't as vicious as Paddy."

Bridget wiped a tear as she stared straight ahead at the endless ocean without really seeing it. She was lost in memories which she'd obviously kept locked up in her heart for many years and couldn't contain any longer. Louisa didn't press her to continue, giving her time to compose herself. Bridget sighed and began speaking again, her voice barely audible over the crashing of the waves against the hull.

"I looked at him one day and just knew that I couldn't take it anymore. We'd been married for nearly ten years, and they'd been ten years of pure misery. I prayed day and night that something would change, but nothing ever did. So, I decided that if God wouldn't help me, I would just have to help myself.

Paddy went out in his fishing boat every day 'cept Sunday, usually well before dawn. He was still drunk from the night before, so he hardly caught anything; just slept off the drink and came home empty-handed. We barely had enough to eat at the best of times. Well, one morning I went out with him. He barely even noticed I was there. He let me row while he fell asleep in the bottom of the boat, happy to be left alone. I rowed out to where I knew the water got deeper and pushed him overboard. He just went straight down like a stone. Never even tried to save himself. He was so far gone; he didn't notice he was drowning. I waited a few minutes, then jumped in myself and swam back to shore. I was at home with my girls before the sun even came up that morning. They found his boat later that day, and the body washed up a few days after." Bridget finally tore her eyes away from the horizon and looked at Louisa. There was apprehension in her eyes, but also relief. That was probably the first time she'd ever spoken of her crime to anyone, and her confession must have brought her some peace.

"Bridget, you did what you had to do to protect your children. Do you still blame yourself?" Louisa was shocked to see that this sweet, kind woman was capable of such courage. She didn't approve of murder, but in an age when there was no law to protect women, sometimes they had to take matters into their own hands.

"I left shortly after the funeral. I'd committed murder, and I wasn't fit to raise my girls anymore. Exile was to be my punishment. My mother raised my children while I went to England in search of work. I didn't deserve to be their mother, but I could try to give them a better life by working hard and sending everything home. I thought for a moment that maybe I might see them one last time, but that's not to be." Bridget wrapped her cloak tighter around her thin form. She looked so forlorn just standing there, her hair flapping in the wind.

"Bridget, we'll gladly give you time to go see your children. My husband will arrange for a carriage to take you home. You can take presents for your grandchildren and spend some time getting to know them. You've earned forgiveness for your sins. It's been so long. You've paid for your crime."

Bridget just smiled sadly and shook her head. "'Twould seem I haven't, yer ladyship. I'll never live long enough to see the shores of Ireland. I'm dying, you see."

"I know you've been unwell, but you'll get better. We'll find a good physician once we're back in England." Louisa studied Bridget's face. It glowed white in the moonlight, her eyes tinged by dark circles, and her frame almost skeletal beneath her cloak. She'd been rosy-cheeked and plump when Louisa first came to know her, but now she looked like a corpse.

Bridget shook her head, finally looking at Louisa. "I don't think I'll last until we reach England. I've been ill for some time, but I'm in the final stages now. I've seen this before. My gran had the same symptoms. I was just a girl then, but I remember. I found a tumor in my breast nearly eight months ago. I hoped it might just go away, but these things never do, do they? It's gotten bigger over time, and now the cancer has spread. I stopped getting my menses some time ago, but now I bleed all the time and there's pain in my lower belly and back. That's how it was for my gran. The cancer moved through her female parts, devouring her from the inside. It won't be long now, yer ladyship. I'm only sorry to burden ye with my problems. My only regret is that there's no Catholic priest on board to give me last rites. That would bring me comfort." Bridget sighed, suddenly smiling up at Louisa.

"Thank you for letting me talk. I must admit that I feel better having unburdened myself. At least I confessed before dying. Good night, yer ladyship. Don't fret on my behalf. Sometimes death is a blessing." With that, Bridget left the deck, leaving Louisa even sadder than she already was.

FIFTY-FOUR

The coat hung well past Frederick Taylor's knees and the
sleeves needed to be rolled up, but at least it provided some
much-needed warmth. Good thing Christopher had left it
behind when he made off for England with Louisa. He was
much taller than Fred; wider in the shoulders and narrower in
the waist, but beggars couldn't be choosers, could they?

Fred Taylor slung a basket over his arm and headed for the
woods. He'd been in the seventeenth century for nearly six
weeks now, and the experience had been truly eye-opening.
He'd been in the past many times since he'd invented the time-
travel device, but he'd never stayed longer than a few days. The
forays into the past had been exciting and educational, the times
and locales chosen with precision and the benefit of hindsight.

Fred could adjust to the primitive conditions and the
general ignorance of the population in colonial Virginia, but
what he couldn't deal with was the mind-numbing boredom
that he had to endure. The idleness was torture. In his twenty-
first century life, he filled his days with work, research, his
beloved chess club, and the numerous football and rugby
matches that were the closest thing he had to a religion. Here,

there was absolutely nothing to fill the days with. He'd found some books in the house, but they weren't enough to keep him occupied. Since he wasn't a part of the family or one of the servants, no one knew exactly how to treat him, so they were civil and pleasant, but distant and guarded. The only people who took the time to really talk to him were Mrs. Dolly and Minnie. Minnie was a sweet girl of fifteen, who reminded him of the girls of his youth. Her ruddy complexion and good-natured disposition were a welcome break from little Louisa's sullen moodiness and Annabel's chilly aloofness.

Mrs. Dolly—or Barbara, as Fred thought of her—had been a surprise. She was somewhat shocked when he showed up in the kitchen offering to help, but came around quickly, always eager for a nice chat. She was the kind of woman with whom Fred Taylor always felt comfortable—down to earth and uncompli-cated. She'd come to the colony with her husband early on but was widowed within the year and had found employment with the Whitfields. She never complained about her lot in life and accepted things with stoic reserve so lacking in the women of the future. Fred looked forward to their talks and insisted on taking his meals in the kitchen with Barbara and Minnie.

The lack of supplies in the colony, although potentially catastrophic, provided him with something to do. Fred Taylor took it upon himself to help as much as he could. After all, the whole situation with Finn had been entirely his fault. You'd think he would have learned by now not to leave dangerous items lying about, but alas, he'd bungled things up yet again. Fred desperately hoped that Valerie and her husband would recover the lad, but in the meantime, he would do what he could to assist at home. He spent countless hours in the woods gathering mushrooms and berries. He wasn't much for hunting, but he was well-versed in the flora and fauna of North America and intended to make the most of the situation. Barbara had been worried about the possibility of eating something poisonous, but Fred assured her that he knew which varieties were safe.

He made it a point to go looking for peanut bushes as well. Virginia was one of the leading peanut suppliers of North America, so there had to be bushes in the area. It took several days, but Fred located several bushes not too far from the house. He went out with a spade and a basket every day; digging for hours until his basket was full. He would show Barbara how to roast the peanuts and use them in cooking. They would be an additional source of protein, along with the mushrooms, which could be added to soups and stews. Fred strung the mushrooms on lengths of thread, which he hung up to dry in the kitchen and shed.

Fred found a sturdy stick and began his gathering for the day. He'd spent the last two weeks collecting peanuts, so picking mushrooms was a welcome break. He used the stick to move aside fallen leaves and bracken, looking for hidden caches of mushrooms. Barbara had given him two oatcakes and some cider to have for lunch. It wasn't much, but everything was rationed these days, especially since Charles had taken over. The young man obviously had a knack for management and took his responsibilities very seriously. He treated Fred's activities with suspicion at first, but quickly came to realize that the old man was only trying to help and encouraged his efforts.

Once the basket was half-full, Fred found a tree stump to sit on and took out his meager meal. Barbara had been very kind to him. Fred had known many women in his seventy-two years, but not many of them had been kind. Some were needy, some demanding, and some very ambitious, but not many were kind. When he was a young man, he thought that in time he would meet the right girl and settle down, but it never happened for him. He'd had a brief romance at university and then a long, dry spell that lasted into his early thirties. There'd been a few women then, but Fred found that he was much happier after the relationships ended.

Things were always promising at the beginning, but eventually the lovely, sweet girls would turn into overly emotional monsters who tried to devour him with their needs and put limitations on everything he found pleasing in life. Their emotions were simply beyond his comprehension. Fred found that he liked peace and quiet, a well-ordered routine, and his own space. He wasn't much for sex either. He wasn't driven by lust like a lot of his university friends, and the act of love left him more repulsed than sated.

Now, at the twilight of his life, he was completely alone, with no wife to look after him, and no children or grandchildren to love. Looking back, he wished he had tried harder to find someone who suited his needs, but it was too late for all that. In truth, he wished he'd found someone like Barbara. She was a woman who was capable and practical; comfortable with her place in life, and not given to bursts of erratic emotion. She would have made him a fine wife, had he met her in a different life and a different place. He would miss her when he left.

FIFTY-FIVE

Louisa Whitfield opened her eyes but made no move to get out of bed. She had no reason to rush. It was still early, but the sounds of an awakening household were already audible outside her door. She heard Harry squeal as Charles carried him down the stairs, and the sound of footsteps coming from the floor above. Mr. Taylor was coming down for breakfast. He liked to eat in the kitchen with Mrs. Dolly and Minnie since he wasn't actually a part of the household. Charles and Annabel were confused by his presence but didn't ask him to leave. Whatever Kit and Louisa told them seemed to have convinced Charles to allow the strange old man to stay.

Louisa frequently found him in the kitchen slicing vegetables or kneading dough. He liked to cook and couldn't abide boredom. Charles said that Mr. Taylor was being quite helpful with preparations for the winter as well. He spent hours wandering around the woods, picking mushrooms and edible berries. He even found several peanut bushes. Louisa was a little suspicious of trying the little beige nuts but found them to be very tasty. Mr. Taylor showed Mrs. Dolly how to make something called peanut butter. Annabel thought it revolting, but

Louisa liked it smeared on bread. According to Mr. Taylor, it was highly nutritious. At this point she was happy to eat anything. The supply boats still hadn't arrived from England, and unless the ships were delayed by storms, there would be no relief for the colonists. Either the ships had never left England or were lost at sea, leaving them without food for the winter. Charles spent hours obsessing about rationing. With the field workers, there were nearly thirty-five people to feed, assuming her parents and Finn got back soon.

Louisa got out of bed and threw open the shutters to let in the golden light of the November morning. The colorful autumn leaves were twirling in the wind, settling on grass and the glassy surface of the lake, floating serenely on the still water. The trees would be completely bare within the next couple of weeks, the winter truly here.

Louisa chose her favorite gown and began to dress for the day. Normally, she would be rushing to get downstairs; ready to receive birthday wishes from her family, and enjoy a special breakfast prepared by Mrs. Dolly in her honor, but today would not be that kind of day. Her parents were still mysteriously absent, along with her brother. Her aunt and uncle were likely somewhere in the middle of the Atlantic with her beloved Bridget and baby Evie, and Charles was preoccupied with bigger issues than her fifteenth birthday. Mrs. Dolly would remember, but there would be no special breakfast today. Food was now rationed stringently for fear that they would run out soon. Charles told them that some of the colonists were trading with the Indians again, preferring to deal with the savages who killed their neighbors rather than go without. Annabel had been outraged, but Louisa could understand. People had children to feed, so they chose food over pride and fear of attack.

Mr. Taylor was in the kitchen as usual, sorting through a basket of mushrooms that he must have picked that morning. Already strings of mushrooms hung in the shed, drying in the open air. Mr. Taylor said that mushrooms had something called protein and could be used in soups and stews to boost nutritional content. None of them knew what he was talking about, but there was no harm in having edible things come winter.

"There she is," Mrs. Dolly beamed as Louisa walked into the kitchen. "Happy birthday, pet. Ye look so lovely. Mister Charles and Mrs. Annabel have already broken their fast. I do have something special for ye," she whispered. Mrs. Dolly took a little currant cake out of the oven. It was no bigger than Louisa's fist, but it smelled wonderful, the top browned to perfection and sprinkled with something.

"What is that, Mrs. Dolly?" Louisa asked, taking a bite of her cake.

"Why 'tis some of those peanuts. Mr. Taylor said they go well with a cake. Don't ye like it, pet?" Mrs. Dolly looked so horrified that Louisa set down her cake, hugging the older woman.

"Mrs. Dolly, it's simply divine. Thank you so much. I was expecting some day-old porridge, and now I have this lovely little cake."

"Oh, I saved the day-old porridge for Mister Charles," answered Mrs. Dolly with a wink. "No cakes for him. So, what shall ye do today?"

Louisa just shook her head. What was there to do? She had been under house arrest since the incident with Tom, watched by Charles and Annabel at all times, not that she had anywhere to go. She'd never been so lonely in her life. The only person left who was on her side was Minnie, and she was run off her feet doing the chores in the house, then going to feed the workers with Mrs. Dolly. The poor girl hardly even had time for a chat.

Louisa finished her birthday cake, savoring every bite, then went to fetch her cloak. She needed to get out of the house, even if it was to walk to the lake. She felt a terrible sadness, wishing her loved ones were there. Louisa stepped outside, taking a deep breath. The smell of winter was already in the air, bringing memories of Christmas and snowball fights with Finn. Some of the trees were already completely bare, crows dotting the branches like black stains against the pale sky.

Louisa began to walk toward the lake when she noticed movement on the other side, closer to the tree line. For one mad moment she thought it was Finn, but then realized that wasn't possible. He wouldn't be hiding in the trees. He'd come straight home with her parents after such a long absence. Louisa peered into the distance. Maybe it wasn't safe to go to the lake. Who would be hiding in the trees if not Indians? She paused, thinking whether she should turn back, when the person stepped into the light, giving her a shy wave. She looked back at the house to make sure no one was watching, then began to walk toward the woods with renewed purpose.

"What are you doing here?" she asked as she stepped behind a furry elm, out of sight of the house.

"I had to see you, Louisa. Charles forbade me to come to the house. I've come here for the past two days, but you never came out. I also wanted to give you this." Tom pulled something out of his pocket, handing it shyly to Louisa. It was a small brooch, worked in gold and pearls.

"Happy birthday, Louisa. It belonged to my mother. Annabel took most of her jewels, but I asked for this. She used to wear it often when I was a little boy, and I remember sitting in her lap, tracing the design with my finger. I wanted you to have it." Tom looked at her shyly as if expecting her to return the gift.

"You're not angry with me?" She hadn't seen Tom since Charles brought her home, thinking him angry and resentful at their forced betrothal.

"I was angry at first, but I have no one to blame but myself. I took advantage of your innocence, and for that I am truly sorry. I never meant to hurt you in any way. I hope you know that." He looked so contrite that Louisa would have said anything to make him feel better.

"I know you didn't intend to hurt me. I'm not angry with you. The thirty days since the banns were read are almost up, and then we can be married. I wish my parents were here, but Charles insists that we should be wed as soon as possible."

Louisa was breathless with happiness. He'd come, and that was proof that he loved her. She was taken aback by the change in Tom's expression. His eyes slid away from her, looking somewhere over her shoulder. She noticed that he looked drawn and tired, not the gilded young man of only a month ago.

"Louisa, I came to say goodbye. The last ship for England is leaving with the morning tide, and I intend to be on it. Now, you can march right back to the house and inform Charles of my intentions, but I implore you not to. I'll go, one way or another, but I didn't want to leave without speaking to you first and telling you how I feel."

"How do you feel?" asked Louisa utterly confused.

"I feel trapped. I've spent most of my life in Jamestown, and if I marry now, I'll spend the rest of my life here as well. There's a big world out there, and I want to see something of it before I settle down. I might be back by spring, or I might never come back at all. I want to have the freedom to decide. I didn't want you to think that I ran away in the middle of the night in an effort to shirk my commitment to you. You are a wonderful girl, and you'll make a fine wife to some man. It just won't be me. Please tell me you understand, Louisa."

Louisa nodded miserably. What was she supposed to say? She wanted him to tell her that she was reason enough to stay, but clearly that wasn't so. He wanted his freedom, and if she prevented him from leaving, he'd hate her forever. He'd taken a chance by coming to see her, and she wouldn't betray his trust.

"Godspeed to you, Tom, and may you find what you're searching for. I release you from the betrothal, and I promise not to say a word to Charles." She kissed his cold cheek, knowing this would be the last time they'd meet. Even if Tom came back some day, their association was over. Louisa smiled up at Tom, wanting to end things on a friendly note.

"And how are things in town?" She hadn't been to town in nearly a month, but she heard that things were going from bad to worse. Tom's face was thinner than before, his doublet hanging on his tall frame under the cloak. Was he getting enough to eat?

"Things aren't good. I don't know if Charles told you, but when the *Misty Dawn* came into port two weeks ago, the cargo was looted before it even left the docks. People are hungry and scared, and they will stop at nothing to get what they need. The people in the settlements are hunting, but the people who live in town are mostly merchants, not hunters. Are you getting enough food?" He was looking at her intently, searching for changes in her face and figure.

"Charles is making sure everyone has enough to eat. He's been taking the men hunting, since there's not much work in the fields till the spring. Some of them come from fishing villages and don't know much about tracking and hunting, but some are quite proficient. They always come back with something, although a deer doesn't go far when thirty people need to be fed.

Charles has been sending the fisher folk to fish. They know how to preserve the fish in salt, making it last longer. I hope we'll have enough to get through the winter. I only wish my parents would come home. I'm so worried, Tom. No one tells me anything. Every time I ask Charles, he tells me not to worry, and to be patient. Where are they?"

"I don't know. I hope they come back soon. I must be going now. Goodbye, Louisa. May God keep you and bless you."

Louisa waited until Tom was lost from view before turning back toward the house. She couldn't imagine how this birthday could get any worse. She turned the brooch over in her hands, watching the sun glint off the gold. It was a pretty piece, but she didn't want it. It wasn't given out of love, but out of guilt. In time, she'd give the brooch to Annabel since it had been her mother's. Louisa stuffed the brooch into her pocket and went in search of Minnie. She needed the company of someone her own age, if only for a few minutes.

* * *

The news of Tom's departure broke by the following afternoon. Mr. Gaines came in person to tell them that Tom had left before dawn, leaving nothing but a short note saying goodbye to his father. By this time, he was already somewhere in the Atlantic, well on his way to England.

Charles paced the parlor, his hands balled into fists. He was carrying on as if he'd been jilted at the altar. "That vile cur, if ever I get my hands on him..." He glared at Annabel. "Did you know about this?"

Annabel shook her head, refusing to be drawn into Charles' wrath. She was probably glad that Tom was gone. They'd always shared a close bond, and although Annabel wouldn't be averse to having Louisa as a sister-in-law, she wanted more for her brother, who obviously longed for adventure.

"Have you got nothing to say?" Charles snarled at Louisa, who sat demurely, her sewing on her lap.

"What would you have me say, Uncle Charles? He didn't want to marry me. That's the end of it." Louisa drew the needle through the fabric, refusing to meet Charles' gaze.

"And the fact that your reputation is ruined means nothing to you?" he roared.

Louisa finally lost her patience, putting her needlework

aside and rising from her seat to stand directly in front of Charles. He was much taller than her, but she squared her shoulders and looked him in the eye. "I'm almost certain that you are aware of the fact that the supply ships have not come from England. The colony is facing the kind of famine it hasn't seen since the Starving Winter of 1609. People will die by the dozens, maybe even by the hundreds, and you are blathering about my ruined reputation? For those people who actually survive till spring, my reputation will be the least of their concerns." With that, Louisa marched out of the parlor, but not before she heard Mr. Gaines say loud and clear, "Bravo, child!"

That was the last conversation they had about her betrothal to Tom.

FIFTY-SIX

Finn looked up at the peeling sign creaking above the door of the tavern. It showed a burly Scot playing the bagpipes; his bonnet perched on his wild red hair at a playful angle, and his cheeks puffed out and red like apples. Finn had never met a Scot or heard anyone playing the pipes, but Mr. Mallory had told him what to look out for, and this had to be it. The tavern was on the side of a road between two villages, serving both and belonging to neither.

Finn scanned the room before choosing a table in the corner. The taproom was filling up with customers as late afternoon turned into evening, and people came in for a pint after a hard day of work. The air was heavy with the smell of spilled spirits and the reek of unwashed bodies. Several patrons were smoking, a hazy cloud of smoke settling over the taproom and making it difficult to see across the room. Someone on the other side of the bar began to sing, other voices joining in, some of them terribly off-key. Finn didn't recognize the song, but he liked it all the same. There was always an air of camaraderie about men singing together.

Finn ordered a tankard of ale and fixed his eyes on the door.

He'd delivered the messages sent by Mr. Mallory to two other members of the Committee, but this assignment was the most important. This was a message he had to collect before he could return to the Mallory farm. Finn pulled out the book and laid it on the table next to his elbow. That was the signal. Not many people would be reading *Faust* in a roadside tavern, so Sam would be sure that he was the one before approaching.

The door opened, several men walking in as a gust of the cool November air dispelled some of the smoky atmosphere of the room. They were talking and laughing, calling out to the barmaid to bring them drinks. She dimpled at them. Obviously, they'd been there before. Finn wondered if Sam would come alone or with someone. He should be easy enough to spot in his uniform. Finn took another sip of his ale, hoping the tankard would last him a while longer. He didn't have enough money to keep ordering more pints. Mr. Mallory had given him some paper money for food and lodging, but Finn chose to sleep rough, saving the money for an emergency.

As time passed, the taproom grew even more crowded, bodies packed in like sardines. Many of the people seemed to know each other, calling out greetings and openly criticizing the King and his policies. Finn was pressed into a corner. He grabbed the book off the table as some burly farmer nearly spilled beer on it on his way to the privy out back. Finn was just about to put the book back when a young man squeezed in next to him on the bench.

"*Faust* is it? It's always been one of my favorites. What a concept, selling your soul to the devil," the young man said, grinning at Finn. He was obviously the contact Finn had been waiting for, but most importantly, he was the spitting image of Mr. Mallory. His gray eyes looked at Finn, twinkling with humor.

"And who might you be?" he asked, taking a gulp of his own beer.

"I'm Finlay Whitfield. I thought you were in the army," Finn said, taking in Sam's appearance. He was wearing civilian clothes that helped him blend in with the crowd of laborers.

"Coming here in uniform would be a bit daft, don't you think? I'd stand out like a sore thumb. My uniform is back at the camp. Don't fret; my commanding officer is aware of my activities. I didn't desert my post." Sam took a long pull of his drink, studying Finn. "You're younger than most. How do you know my father?"

"I'm staying with your family, helping out on the farm." Finn wondered if Sam would resent that he was wearing his clothes and using his bed.

"How is everyone? I miss them sorely. Is Martha driving everyone mad with her upcoming wedding? Poor Gil, he doesn't know what he's in for." Sam laughed, his good humor contagious. "Tell me about Jonah and the girls. Do they miss me?"

"They all do. They talk of you all the time, especially your mother. They worry about your safety."

"Just tell them I'm all right. I don't want them to worry. I've been promised leave for the wedding. I haven't seen them all in so long."

Sam was chatting and drinking, acting as if he'd known Finn all his life. Finn hardly noticed when he slipped a piece of paper into his hand under the table, folding Finn's fingers around it. That was the message he'd been waiting for.

"Tell Pa that things are happening fast now. A British ship ran aground near Hampton recently and was captured by the Whigs. Several more ships have been repelled by the army. Governor Dunmore was in such a panic, he declared Martial Law throughout the colony. Word is he's offering to emancipate any Whig-owned slave who's willing to serve in the British Army. I can't see that winning him many friends, even among the Tories. They fear armed slaves even more than they fear the rebels. Governor Dunmore is safe aboard a ship in Norfolk, so he doesn't care about the havoc he might wreak."

"Is that what's in the message you gave me?" Finn asked quietly.

"No. That's something else entirely, and it's in code, so don't bother trying to figure it out. Some things need to remain secret. We should have another drink. It's on me."

Sam signaled to the barmaid, blowing her a kiss across the crowded room. The girl lit up, blushing prettily. Finn got the impression they knew each other a lot better than anyone might suspect. She brought the drinks over, sliding onto Sam's lap and wrapping her arms around his neck.

"Have you met Cissy? She's the prettiest girl in these parts. If only she would allow me to show her my affection," Sam said dramatically, pulling Cissy closer, trying to plant a kiss on her pouty lips.

"Ye just mind yer manners, Patrick, or I'll tell me Da," she said giggling, arching her back to bring her large breasts closer to Sam's face. "He'll skin ye alive if ye lay a finger on me."

"It would be worth it, my darling," Sam replied, tracing a finger over the creamy flesh swelling over her bodice. Cissy wasn't wearing a modest tucker like most women. Her breasts were exposed above the fabric, just a few inches below Sam's face. Sam leaned down and kissed the top of each breast, looking up at Cissy with mischief. "Will you meet me in the barn later, or shall we play this game a little longer?" he whispered as she giggled and slid off his lap.

"Give me an hour," she mouthed as her father's stern gaze found her in the corner.

"Why did she call you Patrick?" Finn asked as Cissy finally departed.

"Cissy is not known for her discretion. It's best she knows me by another name. I'm not the only customer she meets in the barn, and Cissy likes to talk. There's only one way to shut that pretty mouth of hers," Sam said with a wink, making Finn blush. "Where are you staying tonight?"

"I don't know yet," answered Finn, tucking the book into his sack. He wanted to stay and talk to Sam for a while, but the crowd was beginning to thin as men went home to their families after having their well-deserved drink. It was time to go. Suddenly, Sam stilled, his eyes opening wide.

"What is it?" Finn had no idea what caused that reaction.

"British soldiers. Go quickly. Use the back door as if you're going for a piss. Go!"

"What about you? Come with me," Finn urged, but Sam shook his head.

"You need to deliver that message. I'll be fine."

Finn pushed his way through the crowd, making for the back door. No one would pay any attention to someone going out back to relieve themselves. Finn couldn't help wondering if Sam had been mistaken. Everyone was still talking and drinking happily.

He stepped into the night, taking a deep breath of fresh air. His clothes reeked of smoke and spilled drink, and his stomach growled with hunger. He should have gotten something to eat while waiting for Sam. Were there really British soldiers, or was Sam just trying to get rid of him so that he could go meet Cissy in the barn? She certainly looked willing.

Finn was just about to walk off into the trees when he noticed several British soldiers taking position behind the tavern and blocking the back door. There were soldiers at the front as well, preparing for whatever they were going to do. Finn melted into the shadows, watching. The soldiers entered the tavern, their muskets at the ready. All was quiet for a few moments until chaos erupted inside. Several men were forced outside and lined up in front of a wagon. Finn couldn't hear what was being said, but the captain was obviously questioning them, and none too gently. One of the men doubled over as he was punched in the stomach by one of the soldiers.

Finn was distracted from the scene by the wagon as several men tried to escape through the back door. The British soldiers ordered them back inside, threatening to shoot if they refused. All the men turned around, except for one. He looked straight ahead and walked out of the tavern, refusing to be intimidated. A single shot rang out, finding its mark. Finn watched as the man fell to his knees, his mouth open in shock, before keeling over into the dirt. He was obviously dead.

Finn sucked in his breath as he saw Sam dragged out of the tavern by two soldiers. He was resisting, twisting around to punch one of the soldiers in the face. Two more soldiers came to the rescue, holding Sam between them as a third drove the butt of his musket into Sam's stomach, bringing him to his knees. They yanked Sam back to his feet and pushed him toward the line of men by the wagon before going back inside.

Finn had to get closer, so he crept from the shadows, hiding behind the privy since it was the only structure behind the inn. He tried to ignore the stench as he craned his neck to see the front yard, but it was making his eyes water, and his nose burn. Sam was sitting on the ground, his back against the wheel of a cart, his arm pressed to his middle where the soldier hit him earlier. His nose and upper lip were smeared with blood, but he looked at the soldiers defiantly, unlike the others, who just looked scared. The captain questioned the other men before Cissy was brought out into the yard, looking frightened. She had a shawl wrapped around her shoulders, her cap demurely on her head to hide the abundant curls she was so happy to display earlier. The captain swept her a courteous bow and kissed her hand before speaking to her. He was smiling cordially, obviously trying to put her at ease. Cissy was paraded in front of the four men slowly as she made a pretense of concentrating. She finally pointed to Sam and another fellow, but the captain wasn't content. He seemed to be asking questions of her while pointing at the other two. Cissy finally nodded, pleasing the captain. She was permitted to leave and ran back into the tavern, clearly distressed. What could she know about them?

Finn watched as the soldiers tied the men's hands behind their backs and forced them into the wagon, prodding them with the butts of their muskets. Sam was the last to get in before the wagon rumbled out of the yard, followed by the foot soldiers, their white wigs glowing in the moonlight. The mounted captain led the procession, his back stiff as a rod. Where were they taking them? Men spilled out of the tavern as soon as the soldiers cleared the yard, eager to get away. The ones who came out the back door threw nervous glances at the fresh corpse in the back yard but didn't stop. Finn hoped someone would claim the body and at least give him a Christian burial.

Finn stepped out from behind the privy, gulping fresh air like a drowning man. He had two choices: either be on his way and deliver Sam's information, or follow the soldiers to see where they were taking the men. He knew that the logical thing to do would be to just go, but he couldn't leave Sam to his fate. Whatever was happening, it didn't bode well for the young soldier. It didn't take long to reach a decision. Finn kept his distance, staying close to the trees whenever possible as he followed the wagon. It wouldn't do to be noticed by the soldiers, but they never bothered to look back. All their attention was directed toward the men in the cart.

FIFTY-SEVEN

As Finn followed the cart, his mind raced with questions. Where were they taking Sam and the other men and why? What would they do to them? Was there anyone Finn could alert to what happened? He had no idea where Sam was stationed or if anyone knew of his activities. Finn would just have to improvise once he saw the lay of the land.

It took just over an hour for the procession to reach its destination, which was a compound of some sort, surrounded by a high wall made of sharpened wooden spikes. As the gates opened to admit the soldiers and cart, Finn spotted several wooden structures and a sea of canvas tents, aglow with candlelight from within. There was a lot of activity in the yard, given the lateness of the hour. Finn glimpsed dozens of soldiers before the gates were closed again by the sentries. If only he could get inside somehow. *Don't do anything rash*, he thought to himself, retreating into the woods.

The first thing he had to do was hide his sack. If caught nosing around, Sam's message could betray him as well as others. Finn found a hollow tree not too far away from the outer wall. The space inside was nice and dry, just large enough to hold his possessions. He pushed his sack into the tree, marking the spot with two crossed sticks at the base, just in case he lost his bearings, then went back toward the fort. The logs making up the outer wall were driven into the ground with such precision that there wasn't even a chink of light escaping between them. He couldn't see anything at all, but heard activity in the yard. Finn decided to walk around the wall. There had to be more than one way in. No one would limit themselves to one exit, especially in a time of war.

Finn followed the perimeter of the wall on silent feet, but there wasn't much chance of anyone hearing him. There was so much noise inside that no one would pay attention to a snapped twig or the sound of footsteps. The compound was much larger than he expected, probably housing an entire garrison. The front half of the fort jutted out into a clearing, but the back half was surrounded by woods and didn't seem to have any guard towers. Finn didn't know much about warfare, but he'd seen the Jamestown fort and was expecting this one to be similar.

He was just behind the compound when a small door leading into the woods opened up. Two uniformed soldiers walked out carrying torches and spades. Thankfully, their torches didn't give off more than meager pools of light, leaving Finn in the shadows. The soldiers didn't go too far into the forest before stopping and driving their torches into the ground. They removed their coats and hung them from a nearby branch before beginning to dig in their shirtsleeves. They didn't seem too enthusiastic about their task, grumbling as they worked.

"Why are they having us dig these now with night coming on?" one of them asked. He looked no older than Finn, with a shock of dark hair that was tied back with a ribbon.

"The Colonel wants these ready for tomorrow. It's for the men they arrested today at McVie's place," the other one answered.

"Were you there, Arnold? What happened?"

"I'm not at liberty to discuss it, Paul," Arnold answered, wiping his forehead with the sleeve of his shirt. He looked hot and tired, probably longing for his bed.

"Oh, come now. There's no one here to overhear us. Tell us what happened then," the dark one persisted. He leaned on his spade, his eyes aglow with curiosity.

"All right, but you didn't hear it from me. It seems that the rebels know too much of our plans. They attack convoys and strike at strategic points. The Colonel has been suspecting that someone has been passing them information."

"No! You mean there's a spy here among us?" Paul was so shocked, he let go of the spade and it fell into the gaping hole, making a thud as it hit the dirt. "I don't believe it."

"Well, believe it. The Colonel hatched a plan to smoke out the traitor," Arnold replied, leaning on his own spade and facing his friend.

"How do you know this?"

"My cousin is on the Colonel's staff. He tells me things. Anyhow, the Colonel sent an undercover man to drink and socialize at the tavern just to see if he could learn anything. He's a local man, so no one would suspect him of being a sympathizer. Seems the innkeeper's daughter is rather pretty and likes a bit of a roll in the hay. She's very talkative too. Said one of the lads told her that he was part of a spy ring that met at the tavern. He was trying to impress her, I wager."

"So, what happened?" Paul was hanging on Arnold's every word.

"They sent a patrol to the tavern and had the girl identify which men she met with, and who was seen with the one who claimed to be a spy. Seems they were in luck. They got several rebels. The best part was that the one who claimed to be a spy is one of our own. The Colonel is having them questioned now." Arnold drove the spade into the earth again, grunting with effort.

"What will happen to them?"

"They will offer them a pardon for any information, but it will be the gallows for them come morning. Why d'you think we're digging this hole?" Arnold gave Paul a pitying look. The lad was obviously fresh off the boat, innocent of the ways of warfare.

"That's not honorable." Paul's face was pale with shock. "They try to trick them into confessing, and then hang them based on the word of some girl who spreads her legs for just anyone? Doesn't seem right, that doesn't."

"Well, it's not for us to decide, is it? We are told to dig a hole, so we dig a hole. I'm sure our betters know what they are about." Arnold seemed to be getting annoyed with the younger soldier, eager to be finished with the task.

"But what if they are innocent?" Paul persisted.

"No one is innocent. They'd kill us all in our beds just to win this conflict. Even if they're innocent of this particular crime, they're sure to be guilty of something else. Anyhow, sends a message, doesn't it? Others will think twice before betraying the king."

"Will they not even get to see a minister before they die?" Paul asked, shocked.

"Someone will ride to the village in the morning to fetch the minister. They will be given absolution before they die, don't you worry. Now dig faster. I want my bed sooner rather than later."

Finn waited for a few more minutes, but the conversation moved on to other topics that had nothing to do with the condemned prisoners. Finn quietly melted into the shadows, going back to the hollow tree to retrieve his things. He had no idea what to do but getting inside the fort no longer seemed like a good idea. Come morning, Sam and the others would be executed. Even if he managed to get inside the fort, there was no way he could get Sam out. With dozens of soldiers milling around, and the gates locked, there wasn't much hope of escape. The minister would come tomorrow from the village, but what good would that do? Unless inspiration struck, Sam would die in a few hours.

Finn spread his bedroll without lighting a fire. It was cold, but he didn't want to attract attention. He was hungry and tired, but he couldn't sleep. There had to be something he could do to help Sam. Finn stared at the overcast sky. Tonight, there were no stars, just a wooly blanket of dark clouds obscuring the heavens. Suddenly, Finn sat up, an idea taking shape in his head.

FIFTY-EIGHT

Louisa grabbed on to the doorjamb, trying to keep her balance. The ship was rocking hard, riding the monstrous swells that battered the vessel with relentless frequency. She tried hard not to spill the soup she was bringing for Bridget. Only a week had passed since their conversation on deck, but Bridget had taken a dramatic turn for the worse. Her face was drenched in cold sweat and tense with pain. She hadn't eaten anything all day, refusing everything but a few sips of water.

Louisa perched on the edge of the berth, balancing the bowl of soup on her knees. "Bridget, you have to try and eat something. I brought you some soup, and believe me, it wasn't easy getting here from the galley without spilling any, so you owe me at least a few spoonfuls. Now try to sit up a little."

Louisa's tone was light, but it was all an act. She couldn't bear to see Bridget suffering this way. In the modern world, she might have had a chance of survival, but here there was nothing anyone could do. If only Louisa had some morphine or laudanum to give her. At least it would ease the pain of the disease that was obviously devouring her from the inside.

Bridget clutched her belly, moaning as another wave of pain left her breathless.

"I wish I wasn't Catholic," she suddenly whispered, her eyes glazed with misery.

"Why?"

"Because suicide is a mortal sin. I would give anything to put an end to this misery. I pray for death to come quickly, but it looks like this world isn't done with me yet."

Louisa wished she could say something, but there was nothing to say. She took Bridget's hand, squeezing it in a show of understanding and support. "Bridget, is there anything I can do for you? Just name it."

Bridget licked her dry lips, her voice barely audible above the roar of the ocean outside. "Yer ladyship, I've written a letter to my daughters. I don't know if they'll be able to read it, but I hope someone will read it to them. I was illiterate when I first came to yer sister. She taught me to read and write. I don't know if my girls have been as fortunate." Bridget closed her eyes as another wave of pain washed over her, silencing her.

"Bridget, I promise to deliver the letter to your daughters and to read it to them. Now, try to eat something, please." Bridget just shook her head.

"Get some rest, yer ladyship. There's nothing more ye can do here."

* * *

"How is she?" Kit was lying on the narrow berth, his long legs hanging off, Evie sound asleep on his chest. Her cheek was pressed to his doublet, rosebud mouth open in peaceful slumber. Louisa sat next to Kit, tracing her finger over the rounded cheek of the sleeping baby. She couldn't imagine giving up her baby, no matter what she'd done.

"She's in a lot of pain. I wish I had something to give her, but there's nothing. She won't eat anything either. She can't last much longer at the rate she's deteriorating." Louisa wiped away a tear, as Kit took her hand.

"Louisa, that's probably a blessing. The woman is suffering. Why prolong it?" His other hand held Evie firmly as the ship pitched under them.

"Kit, I'm scared. The ocean is so rough tonight," Louisa said, grabbing onto his hand to keep from falling off the berth.

"It's normal at this time of year. We will be all right. I promise you. Why don't you stay with Bridget tonight? I'll see to Evie. Just feed her before you go. She should be waking soon." Kit caressed Louisa's face, his eyes never leaving hers. "Lou, everything will be all right. We will cross the Atlantic safely and Valerie and Alec will be back home with Finn by the time ships start sailing again in the spring. We'll have news of home. You'll see."

"But we won't go home, is what you're saying?" Louisa asked, reading between the lines.

"We will see what the situation is. Right now, we're fugitives from the law of the colony. If we go back, you might have to face punishment, and I might be accused of assault on the guard. We'll be safer in England until we know differently, besides, if you are with child, you'll be in no condition to cross the Atlantic again so soon. We'll have to wait until the baby is old enough to travel." He wiped a tear from Louisa's cheek. "I know you're upset, but we didn't have much choice, did we?"

"Kit, Valerie and Alec entrusted us with the running of the estate and the welfare of little Louisa, and thanks to me, we now can't do either. I can't begin to imagine what Louisa is going through. Her parents are gone; we've disappeared in the middle of the night without even saying goodbye, and Charles can't marry her off to Thomas fast enough. She's only fifteen. She's not ready to be married, even if it's to avoid scandal. What if he gets her with child? She's still a child herself. I've failed both my sister and my niece, all because I couldn't keep my mouth shut. And now I'm failing Bridget." Louisa sighed, carefully rising to her feet to avoid falling. "Just bring Evie to me when she wakes up. I'll have the milk ready. I need to see to Bridget."

FIFTY-NINE

"Will ye sing to me? My mam always sang to me when I was ailing as a little girl," Bridget whispered. She'd been quiet for the past hour, lying still and silent. Her face was still sheened with sweat, but the pain seemed to have abated a little. Louisa held a cup of water to her mouth, letting her drink. Most of the water ran down her cheek, but some got in, bringing some relief. The night was dark around them, only the sounds of creaking wood and flapping sails heard above the crashing of the waves against the hull. The waves seemed to pummel the ship with less force than before, the rocking turning to rolling under Louisa's feet. She hoped tomorrow would be a calm day, the water placid as they sailed toward England.

Kit had come and gone, bringing Evie for her feeding. Louisa held her daughter close to her heart, praying that nothing would separate them the way Bridget had been separated from her children. Was there any worse punishment for a mother? The baby drank contentedly from the thimble of milk, oblivious to everything around her, her dark eyes closing in blissful slumber once she was full. Louisa couldn't wait to get to dry land. Every day aboard the ship felt like a week, with no news of anyone. She returned the baby to Kit, wiping Bridget's face with a cool cloth and making sure she was comfortable.

Louisa began to sing softly. She couldn't think of any songs, so she sang "My Favorite Things" from *The Sound of Music*. Bridget closed her eyes, her lips stretching into a serene smile. "Ye have a good voice, yer ladyship. Ye should sing more often." She seemed to enjoy the song, a hum coming from somewhere deep inside her chest.

As the night wore on, Bridget drifted in and out of consciousness, her mind reaching into the past whenever she was awake. Louisa just let her be. Bridget seemed to be talking to her girls, acting as if they were still children. If she couldn't see them before she died, this was probably the next best thing, since at least she believed that she was with them once again.

SIXTY

Louisa cried softly as two sailors sewed Bridget's body into some sacking. Bridget had managed to hang on for another week, but finally gave up the fight. Her last few days were filled with agony — physical and mental. Louisa knew she was tormented with guilt over what she had done all those years ago, desperate for a priest to give her absolution. She'd never seen anyone receive last rites, but she had to help. There was no minister on the ship, the captain holding Sunday services himself, so Louisa decided to ask him for help.

Captain Reeves was surprised to see Louisa as he opened the door to his cabin. He was an older man who'd been sailing since he was a boy. At first, Louisa found him slightly intimidating, but she quickly learned that he had a keen sense of humor as well as a kind heart. He'd been a lot more approachable since the situation with Evie, always asking after her and even making her a present of a little carved ship. She was too young to play with it, of course, but in time, she might enjoy it.

Louisa looked around the cabin, wishing she and Kit could have accommodations that size. The first mate's cabin wasn't nearly enough for the three of them.

"How may I be of service, Lady Sheridan?" the captain asked politely, ushering her inside. He immediately sensed her agitation and went to pour them both a drink, giving Louisa a moment to compose herself.

"Captain, may I borrow your Bible?" The captain looked at her in surprise, the bottle frozen in his hand.

"Certainly. I thought you might have had your own," he said smiling, as he poured two cups of brandy, offering her one.

"As you know, we left in somewhat of a hurry," Louisa murmured, embarrassed.

The captain just gave her a conspiratorial smile. He was fully aware of the reason for their departure. "What do you need the Bible for; if I may be so bold as to ask?"

"I need to perform last rites for Bridget O'Brien. She's Catholic, you know. I thought maybe I would find some appropriate passage and read it. I'm afraid it's the best I can do for her under the circumstances."

The captain took a sip of his brandy, considering her predicament. "Actually, I might be able to help. Three members of my crew are Papists, but they prefer to keep their faith a secret, for fear of being discriminated against. I believe one of them spent a year at a seminary in Italy. He wasn't able to complete his education, due to the fact that his family fell on hard times and could no longer afford to pay his way. Would you like me to have a word with him?"

"I would be most grateful, Captain. It would mean so much to Bridget. She's suffering terribly, and I'm not sure how much longer she will last."

"I see. I'll send for him right away. Why don't you return to your maid's cabin and I will send the man along if he is willing." Captain Reeves set his cup down on his desk and pulled the Bible out of the top drawer, handing it to Louisa. She left the captain's cabin, praying that the man would be willing to help. He might not feel comfortable to take the role of a priest upon himself, but at this point, that was her only hope. Louisa let herself into the cabin, sitting across from Bridget.

Bridget's breathing was hoarse, her thin chest rising and falling under the blanket; her skin stretched tightly over the bones. Her face was gray, her hair greasy from sweat and lack of washing. Louisa wet a clean rag in the basin of water and wiped Bridget's face. Her eyes fluttered open in gratitude before closing again.

"It won't be long now, yer ladyship. 'Twill be a relief to leave this world. I can't take much more of this pain," she breathed, her face contorted with suffering. Louisa smoothed a strand of hair off Bridget's face, wishing she could do something to help. "God bless ye, Louisa."

Louisa put aside the rag as a soft knock disturbed the quiet of the cabin. She was surprised to see Will Lawson, his face tense as his eyes met hers. "The captain sent me," he said quietly as Louisa motioned for him to enter.

"Thank you for coming, Mr. Lawson. Can you help?"

The young man looked at Louisa, his eyes agitated. He was tall and thin, with intelligent dark eyes and a warm smile. Louisa had noticed him before since he stood out from the rest of the crew, his speech educated and cultured, but they'd never really spoken. He usually brought up milk for Evie but preferred to give it to Bridget rather than to herself or Kit. Had he known that Bridget was a Papist and felt more comfortable with her?

"Your ladyship, I don't want the rest of the crew to know about my faith. There's a lot of ill feeling toward Catholics, so I'd rather keep my head down, if it's all the same to you. I can help you here, but please don't ask me to read the funeral service. The captain would be happy to do that for you."

"Thank you, Mr. Lawson. The captain mentioned that you spent some time at a seminary."

"Yes, it was my life's ambition to become a priest. I attended a seminary in Rome, but my father died during my second year, so I had to come home to take care of my mother and sisters. Now I will never go back," he said sadly. "I'm not an ordained priest, but I know how important it is to receive last rites, so I'm happy to help. Shall I do it now?"

Louisa nodded as Will took a small vial out of his pocket. "It's oil," he explained, sitting down next to Bridget on the narrow berth. Louisa remained quiet while the young man went through the steps, starting with Penance, Anointing, and then Viaticum. She wasn't sure if what he was doing was correct, but Bridget's face seemed to relax, a look of rapture on her face as Will made a sign of the cross on her forehead with the oil he brought. It seemed as if a heavy weight had been lifted off her chest, leaving her cleansed and free.

"Thank ye, Father," she whispered, her eyes closing in exhaustion.

"Rest in peace." The young man rose to his feet, ready to leave.

"You've done her a great kindness, Mr. Lawson. I wish I could repay you in some way," Louisa said.

"Repay me by keeping my secret, your ladyship." He bowed to her, taking his leave.

Louisa sat next to Bridget, taking her hand. It was hot and dry, the bones already brittle. Bridget opened her eyes with difficulty; her pupils dilated in the dim light of the cabin.

"Thank ye," she breathed and closed her eyes. Louisa didn't need to check her pulse to know she was gone.

SIXTY-ONE

Abbie leaned against the wall of the stall, thankful that no one was there to see her. The wave of dizziness had passed, replaced by nausea. She had been feeling unwell for a few days now, especially in the morning. Could she be with child? She wished she had someone to talk to, but she couldn't tell her mother, and Martha wouldn't know much. Did it truly happen that fast? She'd lain with Finn just that once. No wonder her mother had insisted on a bundling bag both times Gil stayed over. Abbie thought that sewing him into a sack for the night was a silly precaution, but apparently, her mother had the right of it.

The wave of nausea finally passed, leaving Abbie panting and sweating. She had to get on with her chores. The cow wouldn't milk itself, and the eggs wouldn't get collected. With Finn gone, she and Jonah were doing most of the chores since Martha was making final preparations for her wedding, sewing madly. The wedding was in less than two weeks. Abbie hoped that Finn would be back by that time. She couldn't wait to see him again. Sam had promised to come for the wedding as well, if he could get leave. It would be a merry occasion with music and dancing.

Abbie stopped pulling the udders momentarily, lost in a fantasy about her own wedding. She envisioned herself and Finn, standing in front of the minister as he read the wedding service, the church packed with family and friends. She would get a new frock for the wedding, and maybe even attach some fresh flowers to her bonnet. Her fantasy was interrupted by another wave of nausea. Abbie had just enough time to run outside before she was sick into a bush. Finn better hurry back or she might have a lot of explaining to do.

SIXTY-TWO

The tavern was silent and dark, locked up for the night; a feeble chink of light just visible between the shutters of a second-floor window. Finn picked up a few pebbles and threw them at the shutters one by one, hoping this wasn't Cissy's window. He didn't want to talk to her. The shutters finally flew open, the irate publican appearing in the window.

"What'd ye want? Get ye away from here, or I'll be coming down with me gun." He looked like he meant it, but Finn wasn't leaving.

"I must speak with you urgently. Please let me in. It's a matter of life and death."

The man squinted into the darkness, trying to make out Finn's features. He looked torn between closing the shutters and hearing Finn out.

"Please. It's very important," Finn said.

"Oh, all right. Meet me by the door," the man said with an exasperated sigh as he closed the shutters. Finn walked around to the door of the tavern, waiting for a few minutes until the publican finally came down. He'd put on an old dressing gown, his nightcap still on his bald head. "What'd ye want with me, boy?"

"My name is Finlay Whitfield. May I know your name, sir?" Finn asked.

"Colm McVie. Now, state yer business and leave."

"Mr. McVie, four men were taken into custody by British soldiers tonight, and they will be hanged come morning. I need to contact someone in the Militia, and I think you can help." Finn watched the man's face carefully, but the publican kept his features blank.

"And what makes ye think I can help ye? I'm neither a rebel nor a Royalist. I keep me nose clean of all that. I'm just trying to make a living, so I serve British and American alike."

"Mr. McVie, your tavern has been used by rebel agents as a meeting place. I think you know that, or at least your daughter does. I can't imagine that you are not sympathetic in some way. I've seen you with your customers. You know everyone who comes in the door, and I'm sure you know where their sympathies lie. I have no doubt that you know how to find the Militia. Please help me before those men die. One of them is my future brother-in-law." Finn was momentarily stunned by referring to Sam as his brother-in-law. It wasn't until that moment that he admitted out loud that he wanted to marry Abbie, but even if he didn't, the Mallory family meant a lot to him, and he would do everything in his power to save Sam.

"Ye're a smart lad, I'll give ye that. The Brady farm is a mile east of here. Ask for Noah and tell him Colm sent ye. He'll help ye. As for Cissy, she won't be sitting down comfortably for some days to come. I tanned her hide this evening for betraying those men. I ken how scared she was, but she should have kept her mouth shut all the same. Now, get on with ye."

"Thank you, Mr. McVie." The tavern-keeper didn't reply, just grunted before shutting the door behind Finn. He took off at a run. There was no time to lose.

SIXTY-THREE

It was well past midnight by the time Noah Brady finally managed to assemble a few men. There were five of them, including Finn, seated around the table in Mr. Brady's kitchen. Mrs. Brady put out some bread and butter, apples, and a pitcher of cider before going back to bed, annoyed at being disturbed in the middle of the night. Finn could hear a child's voice coming from the back bedroom, frightened by the sudden activity in the house.

"Right, lads. According to Finlay, the men will be hanged come morning. We don't have much time. We have one chance to get them out, and if we fail — they die. Any suggestions?" Noah Brady obviously held a position of leadership, although Finn had no idea what the hierarchy of the Militia was like.

"Here's what I think, Noah." The man who had spoken was introduced to Finn as Davey Peterson. He was thin and wiry, in his early thirties, with black eyes and thinning dark hair tied back with a ribbon. "The regiment has only been in the area for a month, so the fort was hastily constructed using planks, dirt, and sharpened logs for the outer wall. There are several crude wooden buildings for the officers, but the foot soldiers are still quartered in tents. Their main objective has been to confiscate any military supplies they can find in the area. As you know, patrols have been scouring the countryside, seizing anything they find from gunpowder to weapons."

Davey looked around the table to make sure that he had everyone's attention before continuing, "Now, the British usually choose strategic locations for their forts, allowing for good visibility on all sides and open ground that would make any approaching enemy visible. This fort hasn't been constructed with the same foresight. As Finlay has mentioned, the back of the fort faces a wooded area which leads to a swamp. I reckon whoever chose the location thought that the swamp would prevent an attack from that direction. A swamp might stop an army, but it won't stop a few local men who know it like the back of their hands. That's our only advantage. We must approach the fort from behind."

"All right. That sounds reasonable. What do you propose we do once we are behind the fort, Davey?" Noah asked, giving voice to the obvious question. Davey smiled, enjoying the tension in the room and his moment of glory.

"I say that we get our hands on anything flammable: whale oil, gunpowder, tar. We douse as much of the outer wall as we can without alerting the guards to our presence, then set the whole thing aflame. By the time they get their bearings, the fire would have taken hold. Now, as commanding officer, what would you do? You would evacuate the fort before the fire spread to the inner structures, but you have no idea what's awaiting you outside the walls. You're obviously under attack, and you have no inkling of how many armed men will be waiting for you once you open those gates. You are trapped inside the burning fort, which creates chaos and panic. You're damned if you do, and you're damned if you don't. Prisoners would be the least of their concerns." Davey smiled again, looking around the table at the men listening to him with rapt attention.

"That's a fine plan, Davey," Norman Mills said, stroking his beard, "but how do we get the men out?"

"We sit back and wait. Now, a regiment is usually a thousand men strong, but the 14th Foot has been spread over the area, leaving no more than two hundred men at this location. They won't have enough water inside the fort to put the fire out. Sooner or later they will have to open the gates, or the back door, giving us our chance."

"Chance to do what? There are five of us and two hundred of them," cut in Peter Whatley. He was a burly man in his forties, with a graying beard and shaggy hair.

"Davey is right, Peter. We can't get in, so we must get them out. That's the only choice we have. We have the advantage of surprise and the knowledge of the terrain. We'll have the cover of trees, while they will be out in the open." Noah looked around the room to see if anyone else disagreed.

"We don't stand a chance, Noah. No matter how panicked or exposed they are, that's still fifty men to each one of us. The odds are impossible," Peter sat back in his chair, challenging Noah.

"Peter, you are free to leave. No one will think any less of you. You have a large family to care for, and you don't need to risk your life in vain. Anyone else feel the same way?" Noah looked around the quiet kitchen, his eyes settling on each man in turn.

"We must try," Norman said, rising from his seat. "At the very least, we'll buy our men some time and give them a chance to escape during the chaos. Count me in. We have to do this before the sun comes up; catch them at a disadvantage while they're asleep."

"We best get going then." Peter rose from his seat, slinging his musket over his shoulder. "There's no time to lose. Noah, what have you got in the way of burning things? We'll have to stop by my place. I have several barrels of tar."

Finn stood up, ready to follow the men outside. "Hold on there, Finlay," Noah called out to him. "You'll need a gun. You can shoot, can't you?" He handed Finn a musket, which had obviously been taken from the British, and a bag of powder and shot.

"Yes, I can shoot." Finn knew he was a decent shot, but he'd never shot at a human being. He'd already killed two men. How many more deaths would he have to have on his conscience? But that didn't matter now. He had to help Sam. Finn followed Noah out into the night. The men were already assembled in the front yard, waiting for him and Noah. Finn looked around their eager faces, wondering how many would live to see the next day.

SIXTY-FOUR

"Stay close to me, Finn," Noah said softly, his boots making a sucking noise in the mud. The five of them were slowly making their way through the swamp, laden with barrels of tar and gunpowder. The moon was the only source of light, making the swamp look eerie in the darkness, the bare branches of trees resembling skeletal limbs reaching to claim their victims and take them to the watery underworld. Finn's feet were soaked through, cold and slimy. He lost his footing a few times and nearly fell into the swamp, rescued only by the strong arm of Peter, who yanked him out by sheer force. The dark outline of the fort wall was already visible through the trees, the sharpened spikes piercing the sky at equal intervals.

As Davey predicted, there were no guards on the side of the woods. Luckily for them, the British hadn't had time to construct any watchtowers, leaving themselves unprotected. Noah held up his hand, listening to the sounds of the nighttime forest. Frogs were croaking wildly in the swamp, crickets and other insects making an incessant hum, but all was relatively quiet inside the fort. There was the occasional sound of a snorting horse, or the flapping of canvas from a tent, but the majority of the camp seemed to be asleep.

The men fanned out along the perimeter of the wall, dousing the wood with tar and pouring some whale oil at the base. As Finn got closer to the front, he heard the murmur of conversation coming from the guards at the gate. They were stomping their feet to keep warm and smoking to pass the time. It was still several hours till dawn, the sky as black as the tar Finn was spreading. He hastily turned back, afraid of alerting the guards to his presence. Finally, the job was done. The men reconvened by the back door, which they left unmarred. It might be a way in, so best not to set it on fire. Noah motioned for the men to retreat into the forest as he struck the flint several times, lighting a taper. He held the taper to the oil, watching as the flame spread with a whoosh, lighting the tar. Hungry tongues of flame licked the dry wood of the wall, devouring everything in their path. Thankfully, it hadn't rained in the past few days, leaving the wood nice and dry. Noah joined them in the woods, watching and waiting. With any luck, it would take the British some time to realize their fort was burning. The guards at the front would not see the flames for some time, and the brisk wind helped fan the flames as well as mask the smell of burning. The men waited, silent and tense, to see what would happen. They had no idea where the prisoners were held, or if they were out in the open or locked up in some shack, possibly fettered. At this point, there was no telling which way the rescue mission would go.

As the minutes ticked by, Noah began to relax slightly, smiling at them in the darkness. Every passing minute gave them more chance of success as the fire spread, devouring the outer wall. It was nearly a quarter of an hour before they finally heard a cry of alarm within the fort. Within moments, the cry of one man became a din of noise as men hastily rose from their beds, dressing and grabbing for their weapons. The sound of hundreds of boots hitting the dirt was thunderous as orders were shouted inside the fort, but the words were impossible to hear, carried away by the wind. All they had to do now was wait and see what the British would do.

Several spyglasses appeared among the sharpened spikes, trying to peer into the darkness to determine what was happening, but all they would see would be the silent, dark forest. There were sounds of running and shouting within the fort, but the gates remained shut for the time being. Finn felt a terrible anxiety coursing through him. They'd done a fine job of firing the wall, but now what? The prisoners were still inside. He shifted from foot to foot trying to relieve the stress.

"Stay calm," Noah whispered to him. "It will take time. We must bide our time and be ready to strike when the moment is right."

"What if they just shoot them?" Finn asked, fearing for Sam. Noah just shrugged his shoulders. "I can't imagine that would be their priority at the moment, but anything is possible I suppose."

Finn just stared at him in shock. How could the man be so calm?

Several buckets of water were hurled over the top of the wall, but they did little to slow down the hungry flames. The whole wall was ablaze now, the satisfying crackling of wood audible over the wind. The flames rose higher and higher, almost reaching the spikes at the top. Cries were heard from within calling for water as the fire began to spread to the canvas tents closest to the wall, devouring the fabric like a hungry beast. Finn felt a pang of pity as he heard the desperate neighing of panicked horses as they sensed danger and looked for a way out of the stable. Dogs barked madly, adding to the chaos within. It couldn't be long before the Colonel gave the order to evacuate the fort. Whatever awaited the soldiers outside the walls was still better than being burned alive or dying of smoke inhalation. Finn only prayed that they wouldn't leave the prisoners fettered inside.

The men froze, their guns at the ready, as the back door opened, stealthily disgorging four soldiers, each holding a prisoner in front as a shield. They walked very slowly toward the gaping grave dug earlier. Obviously, they had orders to execute them.

"Well, I'll be damned," Peter whispered. "What manner of fool gave that order?"

"Quiet, Peter. Shoot on my order." The men aimed at the British soldiers waiting for Noah's command.

The soldiers looked around as they lined the four prisoners along the edge of the grave. They were young and scared, fully aware that they'd been sent on a suicide mission. Evidently silencing these prisoners was more important than saving the lives of four soldiers. They stepped back a few paces, aiming at the backs of their victims.

"Now!" Noah whispered as four shots rang out, mowing down three of the soldiers. The one that wasn't hit dropped his musket in panic, fleeing toward the wooden door. Noah got him between the shoulder blades, just as he was almost through. The soldier slumped against the wall, his tunic catching fire. The men watched in horrified fascination as the flames took hold, turning the soldier into a ball of fire. Finn was glad to see that the man wasn't moving. Hopefully, he was dead by the time he hit the ground, avoiding a horrible death.

The prisoners looked around, unsure of what to do. Sam and one of the men dropped to the ground, but the other two just stood there frozen with indecision. Their hands and feet were fettered, so they were unable to take more than shuffling steps away from the yawning grave. Noah and Davey slipped from the shadows, urging the men to make for the cover of the woods.

Finn looked back at the fort, but there was no sign of

pursuit. The back door was burning now, set aflame by the body of the dead solider blocking it. The nighttime sky was lit up by the flames, a shower of sparks shooting up like fireworks. Finn turned to the rescued men. Sam was sitting on the ground, his hands and feet in front of him as Noah used a crowbar to wrench open the links of the chain. They would get the cuffs off later, but for now, the men needed to be able to move. Sam smiled at Finn, his eyes full of gratitude. He didn't say anything, but Finn felt a glow in his belly. He didn't need thanks. Seeing Sam smiling was thanks enough.

The men were about half a mile from the fort when they heard it. The explosion was like a roar of the gods, booming through the night like thunder. The fire must have reached the powder stores, igniting the kegs. They went off in a series of explosions, flaming debris falling from the sky like rain. The rebels could still hear the sound of screaming men and dying horses as they reached the swamp.

SIXTY-FIVE

Finn gratefully munched on porridge as he kept watch over the horizon in case of pursuit. He sat on a fence, the musket propped against his thigh should he need it, but no one thought the British would come. They had bigger problems at the moment. Peter worked to get the fetters off the prisoners as at least seven children came and went, curious to see what was happening in the forge. Noah had already departed, taking one of the freed prisoners with him. It had been decided during the course of their escape that they would go to the Mills farm long enough to get the chains off and have some food before leaving. Each man would go off in a different direction, making pursuit more difficult. Noah thought it would be best for the men to lay low until they knew more of what happened at the fort, and if there were any survivors.

Sam emerged from the forge, rubbing his wrists. They were chafed by the fetters, as were his ankles. The British had taken his boots, so he was barefoot, his feet covered in dried mud from the swamp. He gratefully accepted a bowl of porridge from Mrs. Mills before making his way over to Finn.

"You saved my life, Finn. I don't know how to thank you."

Sam was watching him, his gray eyes smiling. "You're a brave lad."

"I couldn't just leave you to die," Finn mumbled, embarrassed by the praise.

"Of course, you could have. Most people would." Sam spooned the porridge into his mouth. He was obviously starving.

"Were you afraid?" Finn couldn't imagine what Sam and the other prisoners must have been feeling as they awaited the dawn, knowing they would face the gallows come morning.

"Yes, I was afraid, but not sorry. As I sat there, trying to make my peace with God, I realized that there are only two things in this world worth dying for: love and liberty. I would be dying in the cause of liberty for the people and country that I love, so at least my death would be worth something. That thought brought me peace." Sam finished his porridge, eyeing what was left of Finn's. "Are you going to eat that? I'm starving." Finn just handed over his bowl. His stomach was still doing somersaults after the events of last night. Was he now officially a rebel?

"What will you do now, Sam?"

"The Brits never learned my real name, so I think it's safe to go home for a bit. They won't come looking for me there, if they come looking for me at all. I'm ready to go whenever you are, Finn. I'd just like to wash up first." He slapped Finn on the shoulder, giving him a serious look.

"Thank you, Finn. I'm forever in your debt." Finn wanted to reply but had to look away to hide the tears that sprang to his eyes. Sam just smiled and walked away, taking the dirty bowls to return to Mrs. Mills and giving Finn a few moments to compose himself.

SIXTY-SIX

The journey back to the Mallory farm took over a week. Finn and Sam stayed off the roads, keeping mostly to the woods to avoid British patrols. They had no idea if Sam was being pursued, but it was safer to stay invisible. Mrs. Mills had given them a little food, but with seven children of varying ages, she didn't have much to spare. Finn set makeshift traps in the evening before they bedded down for the night, hoping to have something by morning. Noah Brady had given them a musket, but they saved the shot for an emergency, not wanting to waste it on hunting. Finn managed to catch at least one rabbit during the night, giving them something to eat for breakfast.

Finn didn't tell Sam, but he was enjoying the walk back to the farm. Sam was like the older brother he never had. They spent hours talking as they walked, covering everything from the Revolution to Sam's romances.

"I wager you'd like to wring Cissy's neck for betraying you," Finn said, broaching the subject that had been bothering him for days. Would Sam seek some kind of retribution? After all, it had been Cissy's father who helped Finn organize a rescue. Sam just shook his head, walking carefully on the forest floor.

He was still barefoot, and his feet were raw from stepping on broken twigs and pinecones. Finn would have offered him his own boots, but Sam's feet were larger.

"It wasn't her fault," Sam replied, yelping as he stepped on yet another sharp twig. "Some people talk too much, especially to a girl. They think it's safe. Cissy was scared out of her wits, so she blurted out everything she knew. I don't blame her. I'm sure her father saw to her punishment though," Sam grinned. "That lovely arse turning all shades of red must have been a sight to behold."

"Have you been with many girls, Sam?" Finn asked shyly. He didn't want to overstep the boundaries of their new friendship, but he was curious. Most young men of his own time had little experience of women by the time they married, finding out about their bride after the wedding. The morals of this time seemed a little less rigid, allowing young people to court and get to know each other before they wed. Premarital relations weren't encouraged, but clearly not totally uncommon.

"Just two. The first one was still a maid, but Cissy gave me an education. That lass spends a lot of time in the barn." Sam gave Finn a meaningful look, making him guffaw with laughter. "She's not shy about asking for what she wants either. If only her poor father knew what kind of daughter he'd raised. I tell you Finn, when I marry, I hope to have only sons. Girls are lovely when they're moaning beneath you, but not so much when they're your daughters. I don't envy Pa having four girls."

"Your Pa has nothing to worry about," replied Finn; Abbie's naked thighs springing unbidden to his mind as he fashioned a spit to cook their supper. He positioned the chicken they'd stolen from a farm over the flames of the campfire, hoping it would cook quickly. He was starving.

Sam sat down on the ground examining his sore feet. "What I wouldn't give for a pair of boots," he moaned. "Should have taken a pair from one of the soldiers, but I was too stunned to think of it at the moment. I must admit I felt sorry for those poor lads. They were no more than boys, dying for something they probably don't even care about. They joined the army hoping for adventure and glory, and all they got was a quick death in some backwoods." He looked up at Finn. "How's that chicken coming along? It smells good. Wish we had some ale to go with it, or at least a heel of bread."

"Stop whining like a girl," Finn replied, handing Sam a chicken leg.

"I'm not whining — just wishing," chuckled Sam through a mouthful of chicken, grease running down his chin.

* * *

"You're sweet on Abbie, aren't you Finn?" Finn stared at the stars twinkling through the intertwined branches of the trees above their head. There was nothing to do after eating but go to sleep, but neither one of them could fall asleep, despite being tired from walking all day.

"Come, you can tell me. No need to be so secretive." Sam jabbed Finn in the ribs, urging him to answer. "Now, if you said you were burning with love for Martha, I might have to slap you around a bit to bring you to your senses," he continued, "but Abbie is different. Any man would be lucky to earn her love. Does she feel the same?"

"I hope so," Finn mumbled. "I haven't got much to offer her."

Finn could hear Sam grinning in the darkness. "Finn, you are a very useful individual to have around. You burn British forts, shoot the enemy, and set clever traps to keep us from starving. Who could ask for a better man?" Sam replied, pleased with his assessment of Finn's charms.

"I'm not sure that burning forts is something that would induce your father to allow me to marry his daughter. Arson is not a desirable quality in a potential husband," Finn said, grinning back at Sam.

"It is if the said arson saves the life of the bride's charming older brother, who would be oh so happy to be best man at the wedding. Leave it to me, Finn. I'll speak to father. You just say the word."

Finn nodded happily. Having Sam on his side would be a huge help in convincing Mr. Mallory. Finn didn't think Abbie would want to be wed right away, but if they were promised to each other, they could work together toward their future. Finn's stomach twisted as he thought of his parents. The thought of them not knowing his bride or being at the wedding hurt more than he could have imagined. His mother would love Abbie, he was sure of that, and his father would have been so proud of him for helping Sam.

SIXTY-SEVEN

Charles poured himself a large brandy, nearly spilling it as he raised the glass to his lips. His hand was shaking, making it hard to hold the glass. The fire in the hearth had been put out for the night, leaving the room gloomy and cold, but Charles had no desire to try and coax the flame back to life. He had his fury to keep him warm. He pulled the dressing gown tighter around his waist and slumped into a chair, drink in hand. This was the second time he hadn't been able to make love to Annabel. Things started off well, but then his cock went limp. It was like trying to pick a lock with a wet herring. Annabel pretended it didn't matter, which made him feel even worse. Didn't it matter to her if her husband proved unable to satisfy her? For the prim and proper image Annabel presented to the world, she was quite a passionate woman behind closed doors, and Charles had given no thought to any other woman since their wedding night.

He took an angry sip of brandy, trying to understand what was happening to him. The answer wasn't very difficult to come by. He was worried and scared—two emotions that were normally foreign to him. It had been nearly eight weeks since Alec, Valerie and Finn had vanished so mysteriously. There

had been no word from them in all that time, making Charles
fear that something terrible had befallen them. He had to admit
that the thought of losing his brother, as well as the rest of the
family, was terrifying.

Despite their differences, he loved Alec with all his heart,
even if he was too proud to admit it. Alec had been his older
brother and mentor ever since he came to Virginia in 1606.
Charles no longer harbored any resentment regarding Finlay's
death, and wished he had the bollocks to tell Alec the truth and
beg for his forgiveness. He'd apologized to Alec after accusing
him of Cora's death two years ago, but they never actually
discussed Charles' feelings about Finlay's death. Charles wasn't
sure if Valerie ever told Alec that Charles blamed him for
killing Finn in order to get to his wife. All that was in the past
now. What mattered was rebuilding his relationship with Alec,
if Alec ever came back. Charles sighed, suddenly feeling cold.
Where are you, Alec? he thought. *Please come back in one piece.
I need you here.*

Things at the plantation were not going well. Little Louisa
barely spoke to Charles or looked him in the face, but that was
the least of his problems. Winter was fast approaching, and no
ships had come from England with supplies. The *Morning Star*
was moored in the harbor, waiting for spring to sail to England
again, and the *Misty Dawn* had come in from the West Indies
with supplies, only to be looted as soon as the crates and barrels
hit the dock. These were desperate times, and people who
would normally never consider theft were now more concerned
with survival.

Despite careful planning, their stores would not last
through the winter. The strange old man who was staying with
them until Alec's return had proven to be unexpectedly helpful,
but they would still not make it. With twenty grown men to
feed, besides the immediate family and servants, they would
need ten times more than what they had now. The hunting had

supplemented their provisions so far, but it would be harder once snow fell and the animals retreated deeper into the forest, forcing the hunters to go closer to Indian territory. It wasn't safe to go that far, not after what happened in March. Charles wished Finn were there. The boy was so clever with setting his traps. Charles had never been much of a hunter, but Finn turned tracking and trapping into an art. Any additional meat he could bring in would be very welcome. Charles wasn't a good enough shot to take down a rabbit, but Finn managed to catch them by the dozen, disguising his traps so cleverly that the animals didn't know what hit them until they were caught.

Charles finished his drink and set the glass down on the table. He was tired and needed to go to bed. He was sure his sexual prowess would return once Alec showed up and helped him shoulder some of the responsibility for the estate. Charles had always wanted to inherit the plantation, but he never realized quite what a burden it was until he was suddenly left in charge.

SIXTY-EIGHT

Abbie curled into a fetal position, her hands over her stomach. She hoped she wasn't going to be sick. Martha was fast asleep, snoring lightly, oblivious to Abbie's discomfort. The cramps were terrible, forcing her to pull her legs closer to her belly to try and ease the pain. She wished she could call her mother, but then she would have to explain about her and Finn, and she wasn't about to do that. Abbie wished that Finn would come back. He'd been gone for over two weeks now, and she was worried sick. They'd just heard about the sacking of the British fort a few days ago.

British patrols were all over the area, questioning folk and confiscating anything they labeled as "military supplies". Over one hundred soldiers had survived the explosion at the fort, but none of them could provide any information about the attack. No one had seen or heard anything. It's as if the fort had been attacked by ghosts. Abbie wasn't sure exactly where Finn was supposed to be, but she thought it might have been somewhere in the vicinity of the fort. What if he'd been hurt?

Another cramp twisted inside Abbie's stomach, a moan forcing itself past her lips. She didn't want anyone to hear. She had to bear this alone. Abbie sat up in bed, pulled her knees up to her chest and began to rock back and forth. The motion seemed to ease the pain, finally allowing her to catch her breath. She was so tired. She had to feel better by morning. Martha's wedding was three days away, and preparations had to be made. Dozens of people would be arriving for the celebration, so they would begin cooking tomorrow. Some things could be made in advance, while others would need to be prepared the day before. Their mother had prepared a list with tasks for each of them, even the younger children. They would be in charge of decorating the house with colorful leaves and ribbons.

Abbie's task was to help with the baking and the barbeque. A pit had been prepared at the back of the house where the pig would be roasted. Abbie's task was to baste it periodically with sauce and juice and turn the spit to make sure that the meat was cooked evenly. The pig would take about twelve hours to cook through, so her father would light the pit several hours before dawn to make sure it was ready in time for the feast. The pig would be left in the hot pit over glowing coals while the family went to church for the ceremony. While Abbie was minding the pig, she'd also be helping with making apple tarts and baking biscuits on the morning of the wedding.

Despite the chilly weather, trestle tables and benches would be set up outside for the guests, since there was no room in the house for so many people. Abbie, her mother, and Sarah would have to bring dishes from the house as soon as they were ready to be served.

Tomorrow they would be making a large vat of pumpkin soup and preparing cranberry sauce to go with the meat. Abbie didn't care much for the soup, but she'd always loved the tart cranberry sauce, and snuck a couple of spoonfuls into her mouth before covering the bowl with a cloth to keep the flies away. She had to admit that she was looking forward to the wedding. It'd been a long time since there'd been a party. She hoped Sam would come home, but things could change at a moment's notice, like the attack on the fort. Her mother didn't complain, but Abbie knew that having Sam back with them would make all the difference.

Abbie lay back down on the bed as the cramps finally eased. She closed her eyes, hoping tomorrow would be a better day.

SIXTY-NINE

The afternoon shadows were just beginning to lengthen as the sun began its slow descent toward the horizon. The gutters were choked with fallen leaves, and the smell of approaching winter and burning wood was in the air. Valerie shivered in her cloak, unable to close it all the way due to the sling for her arm. She wished she had brought a woolen gown and thicker stockings with her. She might have to buy some. Alec walked next to her, his face ruddy with the cold of the approaching evening. They'd spent another day walking around town in the hope of finding Finn, but their search proved fruitless. Valerie snuck a peak at Alec. He looked tired and worn. His bruises had faded, but his ribs were still sore, especially when he got out of bed or tried to pull on his boots. These things took a long time to heal. Alec seemed lost in thought as they bypassed a laughing couple walking with their children. Something about the boy reminded Valerie of Finn when he was small, and she noticed Alec following the boy with his eyes. He must have thought the same.

"Valerie, I think it's time we went home," he said suddenly.

"I'm not leaving without Finn, Alec. We must find him."
Valerie stopped walking and turned to face Alec. "We will find
him. I know it." Her words sounded hollow even to herself. She
knew Alec was right. They'd plastered the town with broadsheets and walked around endlessly in the hope of running into
Finn, but it had all been in vain. No one had come forward
since Mr. Clements and Bessie. Valerie felt frustrated and helpless. Finn could literally be anywhere by now, perhaps even in a
different colony. Maybe whoever he'd been with was only
passing through. Alec's eyes slid away from her face as he tried
to argue his case. He couldn't bear to see her pain.

"Sweetheart, we've been here for nearly two months. The
trail has gone cold weeks ago."

"Alec, we can't leave. You can go back if you wish, but I'm
staying. Besides, people had seen him," Valerie retorted stub-
bornly. She began walking again, needing to do something in
her agitation.

"Valerie, those people must have been mistaken. No one has
seen him since, and it's been weeks. Clearly, he's not here. And
I won't leave you here alone, you know that." He began to walk
faster to keep pace with her, but Valerie suddenly stopped,
grabbing Alec by the arm.

"Alec, this is all my fault. I can't go back and live with this
guilt for the rest of my life." Valerie looked up at him, willing
him to understand.

"It's not your fault. How could you have known that Finn
would go into Mr. Taylor's room and start pressing numbers on
the watch? He hardly ever went up to the attic. It just
happened. It wasn't something you had done." Alec was trying
to reason with her, but Valerie was adamant.

"Yes, it is my fault. I should have listened to my instinct and
sent Mr. Taylor away. The man has a history of negligence.
Thanks to him, your grandmother and I wound up in the past. I

should have known better than to let him stay. If not for me, Finn would be with us at home and everything would be all right." Valerie walked faster, forcing Alec to lengthen his stride to walk with her, his hand to his tender ribs. She slowed down, feeling guilty.

"Valerie, blaming yourself will not get him back. Louisa and Kit must be sick with worry, and God only knows what they told the others. We missed our daughter's birthday with no explanation, and winter is only weeks away. Unless the supply ships came in while we've been gone, there's a lack of food in the colony that might lead to starvation. I'm responsible for the well-being of my workers, as well as for the family. I hope that Charles has stepped in to help Kit, but considering our relationship over the past two years, I'm not so sure. We must return, love."

Valerie looked up at the twilit sky. The first stars were just appearing as wispy clouds scuttled across the moon already visible in the darkening heavens. She knew Alec was right but couldn't bring herself to admit it. Admitting it would mean that there was nothing more they could do, and it was time to go back. The thought of a life without her son was unbearable. How could she go on knowing that she would never see him, never find out what happened to him? It was a fate worse than death. She had already lost one son, how could she bear to lose another? She knew Alec felt the same sense of bereavement, but he was able to be more practical, as he had been when it came to his brother's imprisonment and death all those years ago, whereas she was more emotional, incapable of admitting defeat.

"Alec, please, one more week. If we haven't had any leads by December 1st, we'll go home. I promise. I just need a few days to come to terms with the inevitable." She slid her arm through his, leaning against him for warmth and support.

"All right, love, one more week. Shall we have some

supper?" They were almost at the inn, the windows of the taproom glowing amber in the gathering darkness, the sounds of laughter spilling through the door as it opened and closed with coming and going patrons.

"I'm not very hungry. Why don't you eat in the dining room while I go upstairs? I just need a little time on my own."

"Shall I bring something up for you? You must eat Valerie. You hardly touched your dinner earlier." Valerie kissed Alec's cheek, grateful for his concern.

"I'm all right, just not very hungry today. I have a bit of a headache and want to lie down. Go enjoy your supper." Valerie let go of Alec's arm, walking through the door of the inn and trotting up the stairs, unable to watch people talking and laughing in the taproom when her heart was in pieces. She just wanted to be alone for a while, in the dark solitude of their room.

Alec went up to the bar to get a tankard of ale. He was tired, achy, and heartsick. He'd wanted to broach the topic of departure for some days now but was afraid of Valerie's reaction. Even if she agreed to go home, she would blame herself for the rest of her days, mourning Finn as if he died. Alec couldn't bear the thought of Finn being dead. He wanted to believe that his son was out there somewhere, making a life for himself in this remarkable new world. If he had been younger, he would have been excited to find himself in the future, part of events that would change the country forever.

"Mr. Whitfield, isn't it?"

Alec turned to find two men approaching him through the crowded room. One of the men looked vaguely familiar, but the other one was a stranger for sure. Alec hoped this had nothing to do with the events of the night of Valerie's kidnapping. People had speculated about the fire at the Gale farm for some weeks, but eventually the curiosity died down. Neither Bobby

Mann nor Percival Gale had been well-liked, and many secretly thought they'd gotten what was coming to them.

"Yes, how may I be of help?" Alec asked warily, not sure he wanted to talk to these men.

"Mr. Whitfield, I'm Alfred Hewitt. We met some weeks ago in this very room. This is Noah Brady. May we have a word?"

SEVENTY

Finn perched on the stile, watching wistfully as Sam practically ran toward the farmhouse. He told Sam he needed a few minutes, but in truth, he couldn't stand watching the family reunion. It was too painful. Sam disappeared inside the door as cries of joy erupted from the house. Finn could see through the window the rapture on Mrs. Mallory's face as Sam wrapped his arms around her, holding her in a bear-like embrace, his younger sisters wrapping their arms around his legs. Martha was standing off to the side, smiling, while Mr. Mallory set aside his pipe in order to give his son a warm hug. Finn couldn't see Abbie, but she had to be there somewhere, happy to welcome her brother home. Finn turned his back to the house, unable to watch any longer. He would never have a homecoming like this one. He would never see his family again. He'd never hug his parents, or watch his sister get married, or see Evie grow up. He would be forever alone unless Abbie agreed to become his wife and become his family. Finn looked up at the sky, trying not to cry. He was a man, and men didn't cry when they missed their mothers.

He hadn't heard Abbie come up behind him until she took

his hand, lifting it to her face. She was warm and soft, looking up at him with worried eyes. "Are you all right, Finn? I've missed you so."

Finn pulled Abbie closer, kissing her upturned face. "I missed you too. I was just missing my parents," he admitted. He hadn't been planning to tell her, but he had to share with somebody. "I can't bear knowing that I'll never see them again. I miss my family."

"We'll be your family now. Sam just told us what you did for him, Finn. You saved his life. You're a hero." Abbie was looking up at him, her eyes full of love.

"I'm no hero, Abbie. I was scared to death."

"You could have just walked away and left Sam to die, but you didn't. Of course, you were scared, but you still did it. My parents will never forget what you've done for us. I will never forget. I hope you never leave us, Finn."

"I'll never leave you, Abbie. I want to marry you and be with you forever. I can't offer you anything right now, but if you're willing to wait a few years, I promise I'll find a way to support us. May I ask your father for your hand?" Finn watched her face, terrified of seeing rejection. If Abbie said no, there would be no reason for him to remain with the Mallorys. He would have to go somewhere, anywhere.

Abbie walked into his arms, her cheek against his thundering heart. "I would be proud to be your wife Finn, but we might not be able to wait a few years." Finn looked down at her in confusion until her meaning finally sank in.

"Oh, God, Abbie, are you sure?"

"No, but I'm two weeks late, so it's a definite possibility. I haven't said anything to my parents yet. It wouldn't be right to ruin Martha's wedding, besides, I wanted to wait for you to get back. I'll have to tell them sooner or later."

"Why don't you wait until I've spoken to your father? I'd

much prefer to do it without a gun being pointed at my heart," Finn said, kissing the top of Abbie's head.

"I was afraid you might be angry."

"Why would I be angry?" Finn asked, confused. "I love you, Abbie, and I'll take care of you, no matter what."

"I don't want you to marry me just because I might be with child," she retorted, suddenly worried that Finn would feel obligated to marry her. She wanted him to marry her for love. Finn jumped off the stile and took her in his arms, kissing the tip of her nose.

"You are completely daft, Abigail Mallory, but I love you anyway. Now let's go inside. I'm starving."

Abbie didn't protest as Finn took her hand and walked toward the house. He might never see his family again, but Abbie and her family were the next best thing. He'd gotten lucky indeed.

SEVENTY-ONE

Finn offered to help Abbie with the pig, giving her an opportunity to sleep a little later. She looked exhausted the night before, worn out by worry over her possible pregnancy. Finn was only too happy to do something useful. He sat by the glowing pit in the darkness of the early morning, enjoying the smell of roasting meat. The house was already abuzz with activity. Mrs. Mallory had risen at 3 a.m. to begin the last of the cooking. She wanted to be done by noon when the family would leave for the church, returning after the ceremony with all their guests.

Gil's parents would stop by before the wedding to drop off their contribution to the feast. His mother had been cooking for days as well. Finn looked forward to the party. It would be nice to eat well after weeks of subsisting on rabbit and fish. The smell of the apple tarts had been heavenly as he walked into the house last night. Mrs. Mallory cut one up to celebrate Sam and Finn's return. Finn could have happily eaten the whole tart on his own, but the rest were for the wedding. He'd have his fill today. Finn dipped a ladle into the bucket of sauce and carefully poured it over the roasting carcass. The smell made his mouth water. He'd go in for breakfast once the sun came up.

The morning went by very quickly. Everyone was busy with last-minute preparations, putting the finishing touches on the decorations and the food. Finn volunteered to stay by the pit through the church service. Mr. Mallory was afraid that animals would get to the pig, devouring it before they came back. Finn didn't mind if it gave Abbie the opportunity to go to church and see her sister wed. He helped Abbie into the wagon, giving her hand a reassuring squeeze.

"You look beautiful," he whispered into her ear. "Much more beautiful than the bride. I can't wait until it's our turn." Abbie giggled, blushing prettily. She had a new frock for the occasion and a lace tucker covering her swelling breasts. "I'll see you soon."

Finn watched as the family drove away. Martha was lovely in her wedding dress and bonnet. She was a bundle of nerves, eager to be wed at last. She and Gil would be spending their wedding night at a nearby inn, a present from Gil's parents. Finn was curious to meet the elusive Gil. He would finally see him once the bridal party returned from church. Gil spent the night at his parents' house, forbidden to see his bride before the big day. Finn smiled thinking of where he and Abbie would be spending the night. He couldn't wait to hold her.

* * *

The guests began to arrive shortly after the church service. Martha was glowing as Gil helped her down from the trap. He was a tall, dark-haired youth, no older than nineteen. Finn didn't think he was particularly handsome, but his eyes lit up as he smiled at Martha, and she blushed crimson at something he whispered in her ear. Maybe Abbie was wrong, and she loved him after all. The tables were already set up outside. There would be dancing after everyone had eaten.

"How was it?" Finn asked Abbie as she joined him by the pit. She looked dreamy, her cheeks pink from the cold.

"Oh, it was lovely," she gushed, kissing Finn. "I have to help Ma bring the food out. I hope you're hungry."

"Oh, I am. I've been smelling this pig for the past ten hours." Finn's stomach growled with confirmation. He was glad to see Mr. Mallory coming to start cutting the meat. He was ready to give up his post.

"Go sit down. I'll see you later." Abbie ran off to help her mother while Finn walked over to congratulate the bridal couple. Dozens of people were already in the yard, talking, laughing and taking their seats at the tables as dishes were brought out from the house. Finn had never seen so much food. He tucked into the pork, enjoying the fruit of his labors. His plate was loaded with meat, biscuits, boiled potatoes and cranberry sauce. He'd never had it before, but he liked it. Sam slid into the seat next to him, his plate laden with food.

"I keep eating, but I'm still hungry," he said, stuffing his mouth with pork. "This is so good, Finn."

"When are you going back to camp?"

"In a few days. I was due leave for Martha's wedding anyway, but it's time I went back. Seems that no one has any idea who sacked the fort, so I think it will be safe for me to return. But first, I'm going to eat until I burst," he laughed, reaching for another biscuit.

Mr. Mallory lit a bonfire in the yard as the sky began to turn violet with the approach of evening. Everyone had eaten their fill, ready for a bit of entertainment. Several barrels of beer had been emptied, leaving the guests in good spirits. Finn was surprised to see a trap appear on the horizon. If these were guests, they certainly left it late. Mrs. Mallory had been concerned that her brother hadn't shown up at the church.

Maybe that was him. Finn grabbed Abbie around the waist as the first strains of music floated over the crowd. His belly was full, he'd had several cups of beer, and now he was ready to dance with his girl. They twirled around the bonfire, breathless with happiness, their cheeks flushed.

Finn was annoyed when someone tapped him on the shoulder. "Finlay, there's someone here to see you," Mr. Mallory said. "They're waiting by the stile. You'd better hurry, son." He had an odd expression on his face, one that Finn hadn't seen before. He felt his stomach twist with fear. What if this was about the fort? He doubted that a British patrol would politely wait by the stile while he finished dancing, but the anxiety wouldn't go away.

"I'll be back shortly, Abbie," he promised as he turned to walk away.

Finn left the sounds of merriment behind him as he walked into the gathering night. It was already dark where the light of the fire didn't reach. He could see the silhouette of two people standing by the stile, one of them clearly a woman, judging by the skirts. Suddenly, his heart began to pound, his breath coming fast as he broke into a run. They opened their arms to him as he hurled himself into their embrace, laughing and crying.

Finn just clung to his parents for a long time before finally finding his voice. "I thought I'd never see you again. I had no idea what happened to me. How long have you been here?" He was searching their faces, mad with joy at seeing them.

"Oh, Finn. We thought we'd lost you," his mother said, kissing him again and again. "We've been searching since the night you vanished." She was crying softly, her head on his father's shoulder. His father looked like he wanted to say something, but he was overcome with emotion, unable to find the words.

Finn looked at his mother. She looked older than when he

last saw her and her arm was in a sling, but the joy in her eyes was unmistakable. His father winced when Finn hugged him again. "Dad, are you all right?"

"I'll be fine, son. It's a long story. We're just so glad to find you well and happy. Mr. Brady told us what happened at the fort. We're so proud, Finn. Your real father would have been proud too," Alec said.

"Dad, you are my real father. You always have been. I'm just thankful that I got the chance to tell you that. It's you I wanted to make proud."

"You have. I've always been proud of you, and I always will be, as will your mother."

"Speaking of mother," Finn said, smiling at his mother who was wiping tears away, her face alight with joy. "So, what year did you come from, Mama? It's you and Aunt Louisa that are the time-travelers in this family, isn't it? I've had lots of time to think about things." Finn searched his mother's face, her look of shock confirming his suspicions.

Valerie smiled at her son. "You always were a clever boy. Yes, it's Louisa and I, and we came from the twenty-first century, but now is not the time to have that conversation." Valerie laughed as Finn's mouth opened in shock. "Now, why don't you introduce us to the Mallorys? We'd like to thank them for taking you in." Finn just shook his head in amazement. He couldn't even imagine what the twenty-first century must be like. They had a lot of talking to do, but it wouldn't be tonight.

"Come, I want you to meet Abbie." Valerie felt her heart squeeze as she saw the look in her son's eyes. This wasn't going to be as simple as she thought.

SEVENTY-TWO

Valerie watched as gentle fingers of light began to caress Finn's face. She'd stayed up all night watching him sleep, trying to memorize every inch of his face, unsure of whether she would ever get to see it again. The Mallorys had been very welcoming, offering them the use of the loft and sending Jonah to sleep on a bench downstairs. They seemed like good people; the type of people you could trust with your son. Valerie had watched Finn dancing with Abbie last night and chatting with Sam and Gil. Her son was not the same boy who left them two months ago.

She'd been delirious with joy as they drove from Williamsburg last night. Her efforts and patience had paid off, and someone had recognized Finn from the broadsheet. Alfred Hewitt not only identified Finn but knew exactly where to find him. Alec and Valerie listened with rapt attention as Mr. Hewitt and Mr. Brady had filled them in on the last two weeks. Alec was so proud; he couldn't wait to tell Kit how his son helped to fire a British fort to save the condemned prisoners. Valerie was just happy their ordeal was over. They would get Finn and finally go home.

Now she wasn't so sure. Finn had found something here

that he lacked at home — purpose, love, and friendship. He had come to believe in the cause of freedom, fallen in love with Abbie, and made friends with young men his own age who shared his ideals. Finn might not have realized it himself yet, but he wasn't coming home with them. He was home already.

Valerie smiled sadly at Alec as he opened his eyes, looking at her from Jonah's bed. He looked healthy and rested, which was a welcome change from the drawn look he'd been sporting over the past few weeks. Valerie thought that he hadn't realized the implications yet, but she was wrong.

"We must let him make his own choice. It won't be easy for him, especially if we put pressure on him," Alec whispered.

"I know, but how can we leave him?" Valerie sat down next to Alec, taking his warm hand in hers. "How do we live without him?"

"How do we live with him knowing we've taken away his chance of happiness? If we force him to come home, he'll never be whole again. It has to be his decision, Val, and we have to abide by it." Alec pulled Valerie down, holding her close as tears ran down her cheeks. There was no decision. She knew it last night as she saw her son smile at the pretty blond girl who looked at him with such devotion. They would spend a few days with Finn, but then they would have to return, whether he came with them or not. Valerie wiped away the tears as Finn began to stir.

"Good morning," he said, looking solemnly at his parents.

SEVENTY-THREE

A chill wind blew off the York River, permeating the air with the tang of fish and wet mud, murky sludge lapping at the banks choked with fallen leaves. Once beautiful, they were now an indistinct shade of decaying brown. Several boats could be seen in the distance, gliding peacefully along the sparkling ribbon of the rippling water, their purpose unknown. Valerie looked toward Yorktown. In six years, Lieutenant General Lord Cornwallis would surrender to General Washington only a few miles from where they stood, leading to the end of the Revolutionary War and the beginning of the nation known as the United States of America, but for now, the war was still raging, and many lives would be lost.

It had taken them some time to drive from the Mallory farm to the banks of the river, but she wanted a private place to talk, away from the overcrowded house or the noisy inn. This place provided the privacy, as well as a sense of continuity. This landscape would still be here in the twenty-first century; silent witness to all that took place. Valerie glanced over at Finn. He was waiting patiently for her to begin. There was so much to say, but the words wouldn't come. Valerie had kept her secret for so long from everyone but Alec, and now she had to tell her son the truth.

Finn walked over and put his arm around Valerie, kissing her temple. He'd changed so much in the two months since he vanished from the plantation. The boy who left was now a man. His eyes had lost the innocence of youth, and his stubbly cheek was no longer the soft skin of a boy. Valerie wiped away a tear, forcing herself to concentrate. She knew what would come at the end of her story, had known it from the moment she'd seen her son yesterday. Finn was lost to them forever, just as she had been lost to her parents the moment she moved the hands on the clock. They died without knowing what happened to her, believing her to be dead, and never getting the closure they so desperately needed. Now Valerie would be faced with the same fate. Once they left, they would never know what happened to their son, or how his life turned out. Would he live a long and happy life with Abbie, or would he perish in the flames of the American Revolution along with thousands?

"Mama, I know it's hard for you to tell me, but I must know. I deserve to know." Finn was looking down at her, his eyes tender and full of love. At least he didn't resent her.

"You are right, darling, and I will tell you everything. It happened when I went to England with your Aunt Louisa in the year 2010." Valerie heard Finn's intake of breath at the year, but continued, looking out over the timeless flow of the river. "There was this antique shop…"

* * *

The wind died down, leaving in its wake a lung-seizing freshness that left Valerie breathless. Or maybe it had been the story. Yellow and red leaves circled overhead, settling quietly onto the carpet of grass at their feet. Alec came up behind his wife, pulling her into his arms, more for support than for warmth. Valerie felt strangely empty now that she'd told Finn the story, and she told him everything, including the details of his father's death in the Tower. Finn had a right to know what Alec had done for his brother, even if he might not understand it just yet. He stood looking silently over the river, no doubt still processing what he'd just heard. Valerie could feel Alec's tension through his embrace. He was afraid of Finn's reaction, his rejection.

Finn finally turned, looking at both of them with something they'd never seen before — admiration. He seemed to be searching for the right words. He'd need time to fully understand everything that he'd been told.

"All this time I never knew you at all. I thought that you were like other parents — old-fashioned and set in your ways. If only you'd told me." Finn didn't look accusing, just amazed. "Things could have been so different."

"Finn, I didn't think it was wise to tell you about the time-travel," Valerie said carefully, not wanting to upset him.

"I'm not talking about the time-travel. I'm talking about my father. I always thought that he was heroic and brave, but you were the brave one, Dad." He turned to Alec, his eyes full of affection. "You risked your life to spare him a horrible death, and you loved me as your own son, and I repaid you with ingratitude and insolence."

"Finn, I loved my brother, and I love you. I've never thought of you as anything but my son. I butted heads with my father too, as did Finlay. That's what children do. It's all part of growing up and finding your own way in the world, but I never doubted your love for me."

Finn turned to Valerie, his face a shifting mask of emotions. "Mama, I can't even begin to imagine what you must have felt when you found yourself in the sixteenth century, but knowing what I felt, it must have been terrifying. I'm so glad that you wandered into Yealm Castle, or you would have never met my fathers," he said with a smile. "Would you have gone back, had you had the chance?" Finn was watching her intently, needing to hear that she would have stayed.

"For the first few days that's all I thought about. I looked for that clock high and low, knowing that I wouldn't find it. It wouldn't have been made yet. I was lonely, and desperately afraid. I never expected to fall in love, or to make a life for myself in the past, but it's been a wonderful life, and I wouldn't have it any other way. Finding my sister again made it complete." Valerie smiled at Finn, seeing his relief.

"So, you don't have any regrets?" Finn asked, searching her face.

"My only regret is that I never saw my parents again, and that they died without knowing what happened to me. They would have been so happy to know that I found happiness and had you and your sister. They never knew they were grandparents." Valerie sighed. That was all in the past now, and they had to move on.

"So, what about you, Finn?" She hated asking the question, but the anticipation was always worse than the reality. Valerie watched the conflict play out over her son's face. "Finn, you must do what you want. We'll understand."

"I want to stay here, but the thought of never seeing you again..." Finn looked away, torn in half by the choice.

"Is it Abbie, son?" Alec asked.

"Yes, and no. I love Abbie, and I want a life with her, but it's also the Revolution. I've never cared about anything before, not like this. I've never given any thought to the way things are. I just accepted that there is a king in England who rules us all. The idea of people ruling themselves is so radical, but yet, so right. Why should one person have all that power? This time is so exciting and full of promise. I can't bear the thought of going back to the life I knew." Finn's eyes were begging them for understanding, for their blessing.

"Finn, if I were a young man with no commitments, I would have stayed here too. This country is on the verge of something truly amazing, and you want to be a part of that. It's understandable. And there's Abbie. Is she with child, Finn?" Alec asked carefully.

"She might be, but I want to stay with her because I can't imagine a life without her, as I can't imagine a life without you." His eyes filled with tears as he walked into Valerie's arms, burying his face in her shoulder. "How am I supposed to say goodbye to you?"

"So, don't. Let's say au revoir, like the French," Valerie whispered into his hair, holding him tight.

"Till we meet again," said Finn, nodding into her shoulder.

SEVENTY-FOUR

DECEMBER 1622

Louisa pulled aside the curtain of the carriage to gaze at the city that she'd only seen in the twenty-first century. She knew of the poverty and unsanitary conditions, but at the moment, London looked like a Christmas postcard. Fresh snow covered every surface, glittering like diamonds in the mauve rays of the setting sun; windows beginning to glow with the warm light of the candles being lit against the impending darkness. Their progress was slow due to congestion and slush, but Louisa didn't mind. She was just happy to be off the ship. They'd docked that morning, and Captain Reeves had offered them his carriage to get to Lady Carew's house. Louisa was a bit apprehensive about meeting Kit's sister, but her more immediate concern was finding a wet nurse for Evie. She hoped Caroline would be able to help. At the moment, Evie was peacefully asleep in Kit's arms as he leaned against the back of the swaying carriage, watching Louisa with a small smile on his face.

"What do you think of London?"

"I think it's beautiful," Louisa replied, craning her neck to get a better view of the Tower of London, its outline nearly black against the setting sun. "Where's the palace?"

"Just there along the river," Kit gestured to the left of the Tower as the buildings of Whitehall Palace came into view. Louisa sucked in her breath in awe. She'd seen most of the attractions of London when visiting with Valerie, but the Palace of Whitehall had been consumed by a fire in the late seventeenth century, leaving behind only paintings of its splendor. The place was huge — a city unto itself. At the moment, the countless windows glowed with the rays of the setting sun as the rooftops glistened with fresh snow.

Louisa barely noticed as the carriage came to a stop in front of an imposing stone façade. This was obviously a street occupied by the titled and wealthy, with servants coming and going in the gathering dusk. They were ushered into a vaulted foyer, their footsteps loud on the flagstone tiles. Louisa felt dwarfed by the cavernous space and dark paneling, suddenly longing for a breath of fresh air. A servant appeared to escort them to a cozy parlor, aglow with the light of the fire blazing in the hearth.

"Kit! What a glorious surprise. And this must be your wife." Lady Carew was seated in front of the fireplace, a walking stick leaning against her high-backed chair. She was magnificently attired, but no amount of silk and lace could distract from her haggard face and jet-black hair liberally streaked with gray. She was probably in her late forties, but time had not been kind to her.

"Please, sit down. You must be tired from your journey. When did you dock?" She looked at Kit as he took a seat across from her, studying her face for signs of illness. "Kit, why didn't you tell me you were coming? It would have given me such pleasure to know I would be seeing you again soon. And is this Evangeline?" Caroline held out her arms as she smiled warmly at Louisa.

"May I hold her?" Louisa placed Evie into her aunt's arms watching the emotions playing over Caroline's face. Two pairs of black eyes stared at each other, taking measure.

"She looks just like Kit did when he was an infant," Caroline said softly. "I felt so alone and isolated after my mother's death, living with my father's new wife while he was at sea — until Kitty was born. He was so lovely with those black eyes and curls. I used to sit with him for hours, pretending he was my baby, and that he would love no one but me."

Louisa glanced at Kit, who looked wistfully at his sister. They obviously shared a very strong bond, unweakened by time and distance.

"I can't wait to spoil her. I only have sons, you know, and they haven't seen fit to bless me with any grandchildren," she said to Louisa, smiling at the little girl. "I've always longed for a daughter."

"Lady Carew," Louisa began, unsure of how to address her sister-in-law.

"Please, call me Caro. Kit always did. And may I call you Louisa?"

"Of course. Caro, we are in dire need of a wet nurse. I've been unable to nurse Evangeline for some time. She barely survived the crossing."

Caroline's head snapped up, her eyes aglow with purpose. "I haven't had to hire a wet nurse since my youngest was born, but you need a healthy, strong country girl. London girls are unclean and undernourished. One of my kitchen maids has recently had a child — a bastard, I should say, but I didn't have the heart to throw her out with the winter coming. She's just a slip of a girl. She'll feed Evie until a proper nurse can be found. Summon Ruth!" she ordered the manservant by the door.

The girl who entered a few minutes later was no more than fourteen, thin and frightened. Louisa's heart went out to her, imagining what her life would be with a newborn and no husband to care for her.

"Ruth, Lady Evangeline will require feeding until a proper wet nurse can be found. I expect you to feed her before you feed your own child to ensure she has enough milk. You will be compensated," she added as she saw the shock on the girl's face. "Now, take the baby and feed her right away. You may stay in Lady Evangeline's room with your own child and feed her as needed. Lady Sheridan will supervise. Get to it, girl!" She snapped at the frightened girl, who gently took Evie from Caroline's arms and scampered out of sight. Louisa resolved to do something for the girl, making sure she had a little nest egg to fall back on in case of hard times.

* * *

Louisa sighed with pleasure as she sank deeper into the steaming water of the bath. She hadn't had a proper bath since before her arrest, and only able to wash parts of herself on the ship, mostly with nearly freezing water. The fire crackled in the massive fireplace, warming the room against the frigid temperatures of the December night. She'd left Kit to spend some time with Caroline, giving them some privacy. The huge four-poster bed beckoned to her with its clean linens and fluffy pillows, but she just wasn't ready to get out. The hot water was absolute bliss. Evie was sound asleep in the adjoining room, full to bursting and wearing a clean clout and gown. Louisa made sure that Ruth was comfortable on the narrow cot, her own little girl warm and fed. The baby was lovely, with blond hair and round blue eyes, no doubt a gift from her father since Ruth was dark-haired and dark-eyed.

For the moment, everything was well. If only she had some news of Valerie and Alec. Louisa had prayed every day that they would find Finn and come home. What she wouldn't give to be able to send a message. Living in the future, she had taken communication so for granted. Anyone could reach anyone they wanted at any time and any place. The notion of not being able to send or receive a message for months was still strange to her, even after living in the past for nearly three years. Even then, there was no guarantee that the letter had reached its destination. Only time would tell if Valerie got the letter. Louisa might not have any news until sometime in the summer. She would just have to be patient.

Kit said that they would stay in London through Christmas and New Year, and then retire to his country estate in Essex. He hoped to convince Caro to join them. She'd been unwell, coughing up blood and feeling weak and frail. Louisa thought that she might have consumption, but there was no cure for this disease in the seventeenth century. She would stay alive by sheer strength of will until her body failed her. Louisa was glad that Caro had gotten to see her beloved brother before she died, and to meet her niece. Maybe the joy of having them near would extend her life for a few extra months. Louisa had seen the look of shock on Kit's face when he first saw his sister. He understood the implications of her illness, grieving for her already. This would be her last Christmas, and he wanted to make it special for her, surrounded by family.

SEVENTY-FIVE

Alec took Valerie's hand as they stood in the woods outside their house. It was wonderful to see the house, bathed in the cold sunlight of early December. Everything looked exactly as they had left it, except for the dusting of snow on the grass and bare branches. Mrs. Dolly would be preparing supper, while little Louisa would be reading in her room or embroidering in the parlor; and Louisa would probably be feeding Evie as Kit finished up some last-minute chores before going in to wash before supper.

"Ready?" Alec asked, looking down at Valerie.

"Ready." They set off for the house, their boots crunching on the newly fallen snow. They were eager to see everyone, if not to explain why they'd come back without Finn. It would be extremely difficult to tell people that Finn was dead, but that was the only way they could explain why he was never coming back. They'd tell everyone that Finn had run off and had been killed by Indians in North Carolina. Only Louisa and Kit would hear the truth of what really happened.

"Mama!!!" Valerie looked up as her daughter came flying out of the house, running toward them as if the hounds of hell were on her heels. "Oh, Mama. Where have you been? So much has happened." Louisa was crying as she hugged first Valerie then Alec before giving them a gimlet stare. "Where have you been all this time, and where is Finn?" And so, it had begun.

* * *

Valerie slipped a nightdress over her head, climbing into bed next to Alec. It was nice to be home, despite everything. A merry fire crackled in the hearth, throwing shifting shadows onto the walls, and giving the room a cozy warm glow. Alec pulled Valerie closer, warming her cold feet with his.

"I just can't believe it, Alec. All this time we thought that everything was all right here, and so much was happening. The house seems so empty without Louisa, Kit and Evie. I pray they're all right. We won't have any word from them until next spring, when the ships start sailing again. I'll go mad not knowing if they are safe. It must have been difficult to make the crossing so late in the season with a newborn. And Bridget is gone." Valerie was still shocked by the events of the past several months. Little Louisa filled them in, tripping over her words as if she couldn't get them out quickly enough. Valerie supposed she wanted to tell them her version before Charles had his say, which he insisted on having in private with Alec.

"I'm sure they're well. They'll be safe in England until Louisa's crime has been forgotten. They're probably better off, considering the situation within the colony. At least they won't go hungry. Thank God Charlie was here to take over for Kit. He's done very well, considering." Alec and Charles had spent an hour in Alec's study discussing estate business and the upcoming winter, not to mention Louisa's near marriage to Tom.

"Oh, he's done well, has he? He nearly married Louisa off without even consulting us." Valerie was stunned to find out that Louisa had been engaged to Thomas Gaines. "She's only fifteen, for the love of God."

"Valerie, he did what he thought was best. He was only trying to protect her. No harm done. Tom is gone, and Louisa will get over it in time," Alec replied.

"You're right, of course. In time, there will be someone else, someone who'll appreciate her and love her." Valerie was secretly glad that Tom had chosen to run away. He was a handsome young man, but there was something about him that she found disturbing. He was selfish and self-absorbed, and no doubt had only been toying with Louisa all along. Valerie's thoughts were interrupted by Alec.

"Life in town is going to be very difficult this winter. It will be a fight for survival, and things will be dire here too. We must do all we can to prepare. I'm glad that Charles and Annabel will stay with us. They'll be safer here, and I need Charlie's help. Mr. Gaines should come too, but Charles says he refuses to leave his home. He's a stubborn old man."

Alec kissed the top of Valerie's head, sighing. "Charlie and I had wasted enough time resenting each other. We'll have bigger problems to deal with. We need each other."

"Well, he did accuse you of adultery and murder, but I'm glad you're ready to forgive him. He loves you more than you know, Alec, and you are alike in so many ways." Valerie snuggled closer to Alec, needing his warmth.

"I can't stop thinking about Finn," Alec sighed. "I never really noticed it before, but he's so much like his father, not just in looks but in temperament. He's passionate and headstrong just like Finlay, always following his unruly heart. I hope Finn keeps his promise not to join the Continental Army or the Militia. I just want him safe."

Valerie could almost see Finn's face as they said goodbye to him that afternoon. He'd promised not to do anything foolish, but he was a sixteen-year-old boy. Doing foolish things came with the territory. At least he promised not to get married until he turned eighteen. Finn confided to them that Abbie had begun to bleed that morning, a great relief to both of them, after which Alec took him aside for a private talk. If Finn and Abbie were lovers, he had to know how to protect her from unwanted pregnancy until they were ready to start a family. Finn would stay with the Mallorys and work for the Committee of Correspondence. He liked the intelligence work a lot more than actual combat. Valerie hoped he would just stay safe.

"What did Mr. Taylor speak to you about? I saw him going into your study. He seemed rather secretive." Valerie couldn't say she was overjoyed to see the old man, but Charles had mentioned that Mr. Taylor had made himself useful in every way he could think of.

"You're not going to believe it," said Alec with a huge grin on his face. "Mr. Taylor has asked my permission to marry Mrs. Dolly and stay with us. He'll be the oldest bridegroom in history. I gave my consent. I hope you don't mind."

"Why would I mind? If they're happy, who am I to object? Let's get some sleep. I'm absolutely exhausted." Valerie snuggled next to Alec as his hand cupped her breast, kissing her tenderly.

"Just as soon as we rechristen our bed, love." Valerie had no objections.

EPILOGUE
MAY 1623

Valerie folded the letter, stuffing it into her pocket. It was such a relief to hear from Louisa at last, even if the tidings weren't all good. She was devastated to hear about Bridget's death. To think that she had been hiding her illness from them for so long, not to mention the reason she'd left Ireland. Valerie always suspected that Bridget wasn't telling her the whole story, but she didn't want to press. Everyone was entitled to their secrets.

Valerie couldn't blame the woman for being driven to murder. No one dared to step in when a wife and children were abused, leaving them to either suffer in silence or take matters into their own hands. Bridget didn't have a father or brothers to whom she could turn to in time of need, so she did the only thing she could think of to protect her children. Her conscience wouldn't let her rest though, forcing her to live a life of self-inflicted exile. At least Louisa had been there with her at the end, bringing her some comfort, and making sure she was shriven before she died. Confessing her sin at last would have meant the world to Bridget. A sailor they'd met aboard the ship went to Ireland to see Bridget's girls and deliver her letter. They would have forgiven her, even if she couldn't forgive herself.

Valerie would ask Alec if they could put a cross for Bridget in their cemetery. Her body might have been buried at sea, but she deserved some marker to commemorate her life, and give them a place to remember her.

Louisa and Kit had stayed in London through the winter, looking after Caroline. She'd been jilted by her young lover and deserted by her friends once she became ill, leaving her melancholy and alone. Louisa and Caroline had formed a strong friendship, as two strong-willed women were bound to do. Caroline had died peacefully at Kit's country estate just before Easter. Kit had been happy to spend time with his sister since they hadn't parted on good terms before. Anyway, the reason no longer existed, since Caroline wholeheartedly approved of his choice of wife, even if her background was a bit murky.

Valerie was immensely grateful that her sister and family were well, even if they were halfway across the globe. The winter had been even worse than they'd anticipated. Over four hundred colonists died of starvation, Minnie's father and Mr. Gaines among them. Everyone else on the estate had pulled through, but they were all skeletally thin with loose teeth and bleeding gums. Supplies had finally come in; setting the colony on the path to recovery, but it would take time.

Alec came striding across the lawn to sit next to Valerie on the bench overlooking the lake. He was grayer and thinner than he used to be, but happy to have come through the winter with minimal loss of life.

"Are you finished reading the letter? Are they well?" Alec had watched Valerie run off, clutching the letter to her chest after Charles brought it from town that afternoon. She had to read it alone before she could share the news with everyone else.

"They are well. They had to get a wet nurse for Evie, but she's thriving, and Louisa is pregnant. She is due sometime in July or early August. The pregnancy is going well, and they're hoping for a boy to inherit the title and estates. There's some bad news as well. Bridget is dead, Alec. It turns out she had a tumor in her breast and hid it from everyone for months. She died during the crossing. Louisa was able to find someone to give her last rites, so at least she was shriven. That must have brought her some relief. Oh, I miss them so much, Alec."

Alec put his arm around Valerie, drawing her closer. "I'll tell you what. After we bring in the harvest in September, we can sail to England to visit Louisa and Kit. We can spend the winter with them, and maybe spend some time in London. I'm sure our darling hellion of a daughter would enjoy that, especially if we promise her a visit to the theater and maybe a ball or two. Would you like that?"

"Oh, I would. I'd like that very much." Valerie leaned against Alec, already thinking of seeing Louisa again.

"Actually, I have a little surprise for you. I gave Mr. Taylor and Cook a cottage on the estate as a wedding present, and Mr. Taylor has given me a present as well." Alec pulled out the time-travel watch out of his pocket holding it up in front of Valerie. "He won't be needing this anymore, so you know what this means? We can visit Finn any time we want."

"Oh my God, Alec. When can we go? I know you're busy with the estate now, but maybe we can go in the summer."

"If we set the device a few years ahead, we might be grandparents by then," said Alec smiling.

"Don't put the cart before the horse, grandpa. I'm not ready for that yet."

"Actually, there is somewhere else I'd like to go after we visit Finn and return from England. I still want to drive a car and see an airplane," Alec said, grinning.

"You're on!"

A LETTER FROM THE AUTHOR

Huge thanks for reading *A World Apart*, I hope you were hooked on Valerie and Alec's epic journey. It continues in book four, *A Game of Shadows*. If you want to join other readers in hearing all about my new releases and bonus content, you can sign up for my newsletter.

www.stormpublishing.co/irina-shapiro

If you enjoyed this book and could spare a few moments to leave a review that would be hugely appreciated. Even a short review can make all the difference in encouraging a reader to discover my books for the first time. Thank you so much.

Although I write several different genres, time travel was my first love. As a student of history, I often wonder if I have what it takes to survive in the past in the dangerous, life-altering situations my characters have to deal with.

Thanks again for being part of this amazing journey with me and I hope you'll stay in touch – I have so many more stories and ideas to entertain you with!

Irina

KEEP IN TOUCH WITH THE AUTHOR

facebook.com/IrinaShapiro2

x.com/IrinaShapiro2

instagram.com/irina_shapiro_author